BRUTAL PLANET

NORTHEAST COAST, UNITED STATES OF AMERICA

A ZOMBIE NOVEL

BY

SEAN P MURPHY

Copyright © 2014 by Sean P Murphy
Copyright © 2014 by Severed Press
www.severedpress.com
All rights reserved. No part of this book may be reproduced or transmitted in any form or by any electronic or mechanical means, including photocopying, recording or by any information and retrieval system, without the written permission of the publisher and author, except where permitted by law.
This novel is a work of fiction. Names, characters, places and incidents are the product of the author's imagination, or are used fictitiously. Any resemblance to actual events, locales or persons, living or dead, is purely coincidental.
ISBN: 978-1-925047-57-8
All rights reserved

Table of Contents

The Island	1
Chapter 1 ~ Dry Places	11
Chapter 2 ~ On the Boat	14
Chapter 3 ~ Plague	21
Chapter 4 ~ Refuge	33
Chapter 5 ~ Guests	55
Chapter 6 ~ Leaving Bangor	78
Chapter 7 ~ Shopping	83
Chapter 8 ~ A Bigger Boat	92
Chapter 9 ~ New Friends	109
Chapter 10 ~ Lost Souls	120
Chapter 11 ~ Murder by Numbers	144
Chapter 12 ~ Blood and Oil	160
Chapter 13 ~ Run	179
Chapter 14 ~ In the Navy	211
Chapter 15 ~ A Bright Light	235
Chapter 16 ~ The Battle for Long Island	242
Chapter 17 ~ Cassandra	265
Chapter 18 ~ The Tone of the Thunder	276
Martha's Vineyard	303
Definitions/Abbreviations	306

Are the Green fields gone?
Herman Melville, *Moby Dick*

The Island

A poet from the 'Show-Me' state once declared that the end of the world will come with a 'whimper'. I now know he is wrong. It will come with a roar.

May 30th

The *Providence* is a 35-foot Beneteau First 35s5 sailboat, beautiful, sleek, sleeps eight and was considered somewhat of a status symbol in the old days; this was not the old days and there were thirteen of us on board.

It has been almost forty-eight hours since we made it to the boat. At first, it was a relief at last to achieve the goal for which we had sacrificed so much. A chance to distance ourselves from the horrors of the past week when we fought our way through the hordes of the undead and watched as friend after friend died. We deserve a time out. We are exhausted, out of food, almost out of water, and each desperately in need of some space and time to come to terms with what the hell had happened. What happened, for humans, at least, were the closing stages of the end of the world.

It was hot and humid with almost no breeze, so coming upon the island was seen as nothing short of a Godsend. We were absolutely going nowhere near the mainland; didn't know our exact location since all the nautical charts were on Robert's old boat, but Robert could guess. Cell phones worked sporadically, but whom would you call? We all knew what had happened. It should be the start of tourist season here in Maine. I used to love summer, looked forward to the warmth. Now I pray for winter.

The island was essentially just a big flat rock, maybe two acres in size and about two hundred yards from shore, a decent safe distance. It had a small, one boat dock with a set of weathered wooden stairs leading steeply up to a massive two-story house. I'm thinking mid-nineteenth century; grey shingled, gabled roofs, lots of oversized windows with big shutters to keep out winter storms and a wrap-around porch. The building just oozed New England.

Everyone crowded the deck as we looked for signs of movement, and maybe, just maybe, some signs of real life. All of us wanted a break, and I needed to get the fuck away from some of these people. Cautiously, we motored in and scanned with our binoculars. After growling something about not capsizing the boat, Robert used a sharp blast and whoop-whoops from the siren on the bullhorn to see if he could attract anyone, or anything's attention. I searched the island and house using binoculars with a magnification of 7 X 50 with no real clue as to what that means, but I could clearly read the writing on a calendar through the kitchen window. Looks like Neil was supposed to be making a shipment of lobsters and quahogs this week. Well, if this works out, we should be able to find our own. Most of the curtains were drawn back and when the light was right, I had a decent view of some of the houses first floor interior. Nothing was moving. Maybe that break was finally coming our way.

As the boat came round to the dockside of the island, I inspected the shore and could see a collection of houses maybe half a mile down the beach south of us. It really didn't matter. I could see Them and They clearly saw us. They were running up the shoreline in our direction, not as a cohesive group, but more like a spastic mob. Robert slowly edged the boat closer to the dock. We weren't under sail, so how the hell did they see us so quickly? Yeah, Robert fired the siren, but these guys did the distance like a bat out of hell. There were four in front and three behind, already almost even with the island. Damn, they're fast, we're talking Olympic fast. They were all in good shape and had all their limbs attached. As I watched them get closer and closer, and more dots coming from the south, I thought, could we really be safe here? We believe, so far, they can't swim and... I put my binoculars down and glanced backwards. Everyone was armed and staring at the top of the stairs, ready and waiting... for me.

In case a quick retreat was needed, we didn't tie off. Robert stayed at the helm with the motor idling. You could sense he did not like being left out, but it was his boat. He knew her best and the rest of the passengers were his responsibility. So I armed myself. The Mossberg felt right but I instinctively checked. The Ruger was ready to go. I took the number two position and stepped onto the dock. There were five of us, our own little Special Forces team. I have no clue, but since the start of our little endeavor, I always seem to end up near the front. I was definitely not macho or brave; maybe just impatient. Okay, I am a bit of a pain in the ass, and by now, a little crazy. No. I mean really crazy.

We were a bunch of scared civilians playing a very serious and deadly game of S.W.A.T.; you know, like that old 70's TV show with the cool opening theme that I used to watch as a kid. We had no real clue what we were doing, but at least we could make it look good.

Silently, we crept up, using hand signals and alternating right and left with several steps between us. Doc, a tall lanky guy with an odd sounding southern drawl, was first with his M-16A2, never did find out where he got it. One day, it was just, 'Hey, Docs got an M-16.' I didn't know if he knew how to use it or even if the safety is off. I was second with my shotgun, which I knew how to use and had already switched the safety. Zack was third with his AK-47, then Mary and Matt. If we were attacked now on these steep stairs, in these tight quarters, I would definitely get shot in the ass. This sucks.

From below, I could hear some commotion and realized the rest of the boat must have noticed our welcoming party on the beach. I didn't look over. My heart was racing. Sweat was just pouring off me in sheets and screwing up my glasses, but I kept my mind on the moment. My whole world was the top of the stairs. We inched our way closer. Doc quickly glanced over the lip, looked back to me, and nodded. I shook my head, gave him a thumbs-up, and sent the word down the line. He held up his right hand and started the countdown by dropping his fingers, and at zero, we acted aggressive and stormed the top. I followed his lead, ready for war, looking everywhere at once. He fanned left, and I went right, leaving just enough room for the other three. We all know from experience just how fast these things are, and that distance and a whole lot of firepower was our best chance at staying alive. Then… nothing! No movement and no crazed berserkers, just some seagulls sitting on the porch railing casually looking at us.

Good, looks like no one is outside. We hadn't done that much house clearing. In fact, we had never done this before. Someone thought it would be a good idea to put the shotgun in front. Thanks! The few people I have done the wild-west tango with, and would love to have at my side right now, are either dead or not here. I had the most experience, so it kind of made sense, but I have never played indoors. Just when I had started to relax, and think it was okay to forget, I was back in an absolute state of terror.

We stayed as a group with Mary and Matt covering our backside. Matt was a hyper quiet middle-aged guy with a Glock and a general 'can do' attitude. He seemed like a nice person, but he was in the other Winnebago and in the week or so we have been together, we have never talked. Mary was in her early seventies; razor-sharp, and full of energy. Hammer introduced her to me as a 'pistol of a gal', which is funny, since her weapon of choice was the largest handgun I have ever seen. Think, Dirty Harry meets the grandma from *Beverly Hillbillies*. Although I had already been convinced you don't screw with Mary, her performance back at the dock with the cartoonish cannon made me a true believer. That means that should I get shot on this endeavor, it will, more than likely, be from Zack or Doc. Doc was an unknown but he was always cool and collected, about my age and one of the founders of this whole adventure. Zack, in his early thirties, smart, friendly, 6-2, thin, jet black hair, with a two week old, 'I don't give a shit' beard, chiseled chin, and piercing blue eyes. Zack had the complete 'guy I wished I looked like' package. All males secretly wished he would die in a grease fire. He was okay in a fight, but his weapon was an insane AK-47 with no butt or whatever it's called to aim from your shoulder. He would quite literally be shooting from his hip. I don't think I have seen him fire this weapon or anything from his hip. Damn, I am going to get shot. But we had become friends and in the middle of a very close trivia game, so I guess that would be okay, but might constitute cheating.

So away we went, door by door, room by room, and closet by closet. First floor was all clear with large open rooms, rooms we had a good view of from the boat, and a small apartment for the innkeepers. The second and attic were all guest rooms. The basement was large and like the first floor, mostly an open area that once housed a bowling alley. The zombie's aggressiveness would work to our advantage, since once, they saw or heard us, it was off to the races. I have never seen a zombie target something that did not absolutely dominate its attention. Our activities in the house were not subtle. When finished, we were confident it was empty, and a very nice house it was. At last, we had caught a break.

It took over an hour to clear the place and when done, I ran to the top of the dock stairs and signaled all clear. Yes, time to breathe. It was then that I looked over to the shore. The original half a dozen or so from earlier, had now turned into at least thirty. Most of them just stood there staring at us, many with their arms folded and leaning from one side to the other. Some sat, and a few paced back and forth, but none went into the water any further than maybe knee-deep. There were men, women, and children, but no hierarchy or any obvious organization. They just waited. Either we would come to them or they would get to us. If I had my binoculars, I might be able to identify the wounds I knew they all had. Each injury told the individual's story of how they died. How they became part of the undead. A torn throat here, a lost limb there, or some large unspecific blood stained piece of clothing covering who knows what. I knew that a scratch breaking the skin would rapidly turn into a horrendous fatal infection, but sometimes not. Bites, well, bites are another story and always fatal.

The house had been a bed and breakfast called Molly's Rock, and the small town a summer beach community, South Kingston. The beach was one of those rare exceptions on the Maine coast, where you actually have sand, and not rocks. Although the water is so cold, I wondered if anyone actually got in. From the reservation book, it looked like things were going well, being full for the entire summer. The good news was that the B&B had plenty of food, fully stocked bar, bottled water, a walk-in refrigerator, and lots of space to spread out. The bad news was that the generator had run out of fuel a couple of days ago. There were a dozen bedrooms, all decorated in a quaint old nautical New England theme. You know, part of me actually thought that I would bring Liz here when I am done with this shit. We could walk up and down the beach, holding hands, and I could tell her about the time when…

We ate as a group, scattered around a large sunny parlor with paintings of old boats and sea captains, dominated by a beautiful river-stone fireplace. Even though it was ninety-plus outside, I still wanted a fire. I wanted the comfort of a fire. No one said that much, just some small talk about making this our home base for a few weeks, gathering supplies, getting another boat and heading south before winter set in. No serious planning, just something to get our minds working, give us some new direction, and something to focus on. Poor Madeline is deaf and none of us knows sign language, so she just curled up on a couch in an isolated corner. Up until two days ago, it was just, get to the boats and head south. Even with all that happened and everything we left behind, we could now really start thinking about the Caribbean. We still had hope.

After eating and more casual talk, people drifted off to one of the rooms or a corner of the house, some to sleep, most just to be alone. Robert and I moved out to the seaside portion of the porch, since a cool ocean breeze had started to come in. We plopped down in a couple of Adirondack chairs. From above, I heard someone crying and felt jealous. My time will come. The two of us didn't talk. We just stared out into the vast expanse of the indomitable Atlantic Ocean. The sea was a blank, no ships in sight, and the immensity was both disturbing and comforting. In front of me was normality. The Atlantic was the same and always will be, but behind me on shore, everything had changed. Since making it to the *Providence,* I haven't spent much time looking at the shore.

Robert and I had grown close since this whole thing started. He was part of the Roy's original group and I was an outsider. I don't know why we gravitated to each other, maybe since we both had taught at the University of Maine, Orono. This link gave us that icebreaker and soon we knew more and more about each other, and that friend thing happened. He was a professor in mechanical engineering, retired, and I was in anthropology. He got most of my jokes and didn't seem to mind my quirky sense of humor. We didn't talk that much, just seemed to think in tandem. Whenever there was a plan of action or crisis during our struggle to get from Bangor to the coast, we were always on the same page. If not, he quickly put me on his. It was no surprise that after about two hours of reflection, we got up, went inside, grabbed a large jug of water each, and started to head down to the dock. Zack and Matt were sitting in the kitchen smoking, talking in low voices and it looked like Matt had been crying. I told them we were going to make sure the sailboat was ready, work on the desalinization system and maybe tool over to some boats that were moored near South Kingston, siphon gas, get some charts and anything else we might need.

"We'll radio if there is going to be some shooting."

They just stared at me for a couple of seconds and Zack said, "John, why the hell would we care if you started shooting? You have the boat. Are we going to swim to your rescue?"

You could tell that both of us were physically and mentally trashed, but that was a legitimate question. I was also a mess, but needed something to do, to keep moving. If I stopped now, I don't think I could start again, I'm not sure I'd want to. Looking at them, it dawned on me how beat up we all were, I was. Spending more than a week impossibly stressed with no chance to bathe, no real sleep, no time alone, crappy food, oh yes, and just waiting for that second when you knew your life would end. I was surprised no one had taken it upon themselves to stop their suffering.

After tidying up the boat and storing the water, I went back up to get my shotgun while Robert started a checklist of essentials. I always had a sidearm, but the feel of my now trusty Mossberg 500 gave me that extra confidence and was indispensable for the boat clearings we had ahead. The 500 is a tactical shotgun often used in law enforcement and was given to me by Roy at an overrun National Guard roadblock we passed on the day we left Bangor. Someone had tricked it out and although it was not good for distance fighting, it would clean house at anything under 100 feet. I was now more than competent with its use and limitations.

The house was quiet and smelled of summer at the beach. Man, it would be nice to lie down for a couple of hours and just absorb the coolness and comfort of a freshly made bed and clean sheets. I knew that Robert was also beat but wanted to get everything in a rapid go mode. There would be time to crash out tonight. A damn real thing to look forward to, things were looking up. I did see Zack again on my way out. As he went up the stairs, all he did was look at me, groan, pull out his little black book and give it a tap. I just nodded my head, Yes, Zack, I know you are going to win this one and I trudged down to the boat.

As we untied, I looked at the dock and my brain was telling me, 'What is wrong with this picture?' We were ready to motor off when Leslie called down from the top of the stairs, asking if I could bring up one of her cameras. She was a cute twenty-something pain-in-the-ass grad student in film studies at the U of Maine, who had contributed exactly zero to our survival over the last few days. She had brought along two nifty handheld Sony Camcorders, the kind you use to preserve your kids first soccer game, Christmas, Halloween, or any of the thousands of things that are never going to happen again. All of us had taken turns at filming our brutal trip to the coast and the aftermath. I think we did it to prove to ourselves that this was really happening. We were recording our own Odyssey, but this time, you didn't need a Cyclops or Sirens to perk up the story. I don't think anyone has had the fortitude to review what we had recorded, maybe someday, but for me, I doubt it.

I had just started looking through her duffel bag when I heard the first gunshot. At the time, I thought it was some idiot taking target practice at the zombies onshore and was pissed about the wasting of ammunition and the additional attention it might generate. As I reached topside, I heard a lot more gunfire, shouts, the sound of breaking glass and that now familiar dull moaning roar. Robert and I looked at each other, his face awash in disbelief. I glanced up and Leslie was gone. I had my shotgun at the ready and was just about to step off the boat when I saw the first one peer down from the top railing.

The boat's engine revved and I turned toward Robert. He had his pistol in one hand, furiously working the controls with the other. About the same time, I heard the sound of bare feet coming down the stairs, fast. I turned and saw the zombie. He was once in his late teens or early twenties, thin, blond hair, dirty jeans worn through at the knees, and a soiled t-shirt that read UConn. The right side of his face and ear were gone and you could actually see teeth where his cheek should have been. The zombie got about a third of the way down when he slipped and tumbled to the dock. He laid there for about a second before jumping up to face me, growling. I was still in firing position, fewer than seven feet away, and pulled the trigger. Don't know if it was me or the rocking of the boat, but I missed the head and hit him in the neck, just above the sternum. The shot left a hole the size of a grapefruit with very little tissue connecting skull to torso, and the force of the blast spun the body in such a way that the creature ended up falling on its chest, with the head looking up to the sky. Its eyes darted back and forth and I could hear the teeth click, as the jaw frantically moved up and down. It sounded a bit like someone hastily stacking porcelain plates. After a few seconds, it slowed and stopped. I was fascinated and tried to remember all my cranial nerves, what had I severed?

Somewhere in the distance, Robert was yelling and I felt the boat lurch forward. My mind screamed that more were coming, but I just kept staring at this head. Out of the corner of my eye, I saw movement, and instinctively turned and fired. The shot caught the zombie in the shoulder. She spun like a top with arms flailing about and dropped at the bottom of the stairs. This caused the one immediately behind her to trip and fall face first onto the dock. I fired again as the closest zombie was rising to her feet, the force of the blast literally blew her into the water as if somebody had wrapped a rope around her waist and quickly jerked her backwards. Robert gunned the motor and it took only seconds to gain safety.

I know we heard additional sporadic gunfire, but not much. By now, there were at least half dozen on the dock and stairs. We assumed they couldn't swim, so how the hell did they get on the island? In my mind's eye, I was cool and composed, talking to Robert in a rational, controlled voice about what we should do. Later, he told me that all I could say, "Was a literary cornucopia of swear words over and over again, in at least three languages." I have never asked but always wanted to know what the hell a literary cornucopia was?

Robert took the *Providence* about a hundred yards away from Molly's Rock and anchored. We grabbed the binoculars and searched the water, hoping that someone had made it in, but I knew the truth. It just happened way too fast. Scanning the house, I saw some movement inside, just flashes of things passing in front of windows. By now, the island seemed to be crawling with the undead. I could see them running in and out of the B&B frantically searching for something to attack. Soon there were no more gunshots and I knew my friends were gone.

In a top floor window, I spotted Mary standing, her arms above her, palms flat against the glass panes. The quality of light made her look decades younger than her seventy-two years. She was not shouting or crying, just staring at me with wide shock-filled eyes. I turned away to yell to Robert, and when I looked back Mary was gone. There was some commotion in the room and it seemed like someone had splattered dark paint across the window. It was over.

From the place we anchored, I had a clear view of the land, leeward, side of the island. We had all seen and talked about the channel. Everyone just assumed it gave us a nice safety buffer. As I now studied it, I could just make out the white of continuous small waves breaking over something. This break seemed to extend all the way from the beach to the island. The break was not there when we cased the place. It was probably only a second but it seems a lot longer now before my brain worked it out and connected the dots. Then it hit me hard. Oh my God, a sandbar!

How could we have missed it? We were patient. We were organized. We had gone through so much; so much pain, so much fear, so much sacrifice. How could we have not thought it through? We were survivors. We were good, fast, efficient, and smart. Hell, half of us grew up on the water! How could we have missed... Low tide?

Chapter 1 ~ Dry Places

My name is John Ross Patrick. I am 46 years old, 5-10, 185 lbs., brown hair, short beard, average build, and unremarkable in many ways, I guess the only item of note is that I am still alive. The world I once knew is gone. There are no more tests to grade, no more bills to pay, no more papers to present, and no more dreaming of finding true love.

I was in the Atacama Desert in the north of Chile when things really started to heat up, i.e., I was in the middle of nowhere. I had heard about something going on in central Asia before I left, but my focus was on three weeks of reconnecting with old friends, excavation, and adventure in the driest place on earth, a place I had lived off and on for more than five years. I didn't have much grant money, so this trip was solo and on the cheap, we're talking street vendor cheap. When I got there, the shortwave I had left at the museum during my last sojourn was gone, but that was okay. I had lots of books to read, and some time away from it all seemed like a good idea. I quickly touched base with some friends in town, sent out mail, and took off in my rented jeep, which accounted for exactly sixty-two percent of the trip budget (including gas). I spent most of the time alone, mapping Incan roadway in the high Cordillera Occidental, home to the highest permanent human structures on earth. I did make a few side trips to tiny mountain towns when I needed supplies or just wanted to check them out. These were the type of places where you would be lucky if they spoke Spanish, most only spoke Quechua. I had a great time and spent most of it in this daydream of what I would say when I returned to Liz.

When I did venture back, I found it odd that there were no tourists in San Pedro de Atacama, the small town I was working out of and popular with backpackers doing the South American circuit. A traditional quiet pueblo with a great museum, ruins, hot springs, volcanoes, good food, and flamingos, an ideal side trip. Yeah, it's the start of winter, but still, there should be somebody coming through. I didn't dwell on it but the mystery lingered in the back of my mind, for about … that long. I was also kind of bothered that the museum was closed and all of the non-town staff gone. No chance to say goodbye. The one museum guy I did find, Hector, a local who has worked there since he was a kid, told me they had been called away. To be honest, I was relieved because I didn't want to stay any longer than necessary and there was a distinct possibility I would be asked to give a review of what I had accomplished, not to mention the various dinners and lunches I would have to attend. All I could really think about was Elizabeth, and where our relationship would go once I got back, so I just shrugged it off, maybe there was a holiday or a meeting in Santiago.

    I was only in San Pedro for two days and spent that in isolation, reviewing my notes, deciding what I was going to store, and the best angle to get more grant money so I could return. When I did leave, I was in a rush to catch my plane in Arica, an eight hour bus ride north. Leaving San Pedro, the bus passed the town's only church, built in 1641. It was packed to overflowing. What the hell? It's nine-thirty in the morning and a Tuesday, a holy day? Funeral? And that was about as much as I thought about it. I stayed to myself on the long bus ride up the coast, working on my notes while everything was still fresh in my head. It had been a productive trip, but I was now more than ready to get home. It took me some time, but I slowly noticed there was something in the air, the speaking in hushed tones, the way people moved and stole glances at you out of the corner of their eyes. I assumed that this was just because I was the only gringo on the cheapest bus to Arica. Now I know it was fear. If I was not so absorbed with the work at hand and dreams of a happy homecoming, I might have paid more attention, not that it really would have mattered.

    Arica is on the Pacific coast and known as the city of the eternal spring, since it is always around seventy degrees and it almost never rains there. It's a nice port town and only a dozen or so miles from the Peruvian border, also one of the cheapest ways of getting to Bolivia. There's always something going on. I was only staying for a few hours and then off to Miami, but still something was odd, fewer people on the streets, none of the 'buzz' the town normally has, and where the hell were all the tourists?

The taxi to the airport should have been the wake-up call. I get in, the driver never looks at me, keeps all the windows down, and just waits.

"Airport please." I could have said this in Spanish, but the guy was kind of an ass. He didn't look me in the eye or try to help with my luggage. As soon as we pull away, he starts to talk to himself in a low voice. I could see him through his rear-view mirror, and he never looked back. It took me awhile and a few stoplights before I could start to hear what he was saying,

"Áve María, grátia pléna, Dóminus técum. Benedícta ...." It's the Hail Mary in Latin! After he finished the prayer, he would kiss a gold medallion he had on a heavy gold necklace and start the prayer all over again, never looking back.

I got to the airport in time for a two-hour delay in which no one said anything, and I mean nobody, nothing. We just sat there in our cheap plastic seats and stared at the dirty linoleum. It reminded me of the grade school dances in the basement of St. Benedicts School back in Rhode Island. Nobody wanted to be there, but there was this strange something going on that made the uncomfortable situation somewhat interesting. I was still not putting one and one together, totally absorbed in 'John-World'. I boarded the plane, got to my seat, took a couple diazepams, and was just ready to crash out when I glanced at a guy reading a newspaper across the aisle from me. My Spanish is not great, even with all the time spent in Latin America, but I could easily translate the bold oversize headline, '¡La Caminata Muerta!' The Dead Walk! I chuckled to myself, thinking that this must be some Chilean version of the *National Enquirer* and drifted off to sleep. When we landed in Miami and stood to leave, I looked again at the newspaper now left on the empty seat, and the hairs on the back of my neck stood up. It was not some Latin tabloid but *El Mercurio*, Chiles' top newspaper.

Chapter 2 ~ On the Boat

May 30th (Continued)

"Something is off our stern! Shit! Sorry, John, I wasn't paying attention to the radar." This jolted me back to reality. I was on *Providence* with Robert and all my other friends were just slaughtered by zombies. Robert and I had not said a single word to each other since the incident on Molly's Rock. I think we are both in denial, and definitely in shock. He did all the sailing and I was supposed to be a general lookout. I glanced back. "Let me get the binoculars and give it a look." The white dot was clearly a sailboat, a large one.

"Okay, Robert, um, I don't see anyone yet, but somebody had to set those sails."

"I am going to move us to intercept. Let's get ready." This was an order, not a suggestion.

I knew what Robert meant and armed myself. We had just fucked up big time and the cool, pragmatic Robert, was being hyper cautious, although I had no clue what he intended since the boat was too big and moving way too fast.

"I want you on the bow. I'll take care of port and don't assume anything!" We were not going to screw up again.

"Roger that, Robert!" I took my position, ensured my shotgun was fully loaded and scanned the boat again. We were coming up on her port bow and as we got closer, more detail came into focus.

"Robert, I got someone on the bow!" I could see one individual, standing with its side to me, staring out at the open ocean.

"Let's see... It looks to be an adult male and ..." I paused as the figure turned in my direction. "Ah shit! It's a zombie!" I could now make out that the left arm was gone below the elbow, the skin had that shiny gray look, and the clothes, shorts, and a white short-sleeve shirt, was covered in what was almost certainly dried blood.

We passed within twenty-five yards of the ship, a magnificent schooner, two masts under full sail, all white and dazzling in the summer sun. She made me think of *The Great Gatsby*, and that long, lost, gilded time of almost innocent indulgence.

The zombie didn't move. I half expected him to be holding a martini glass, but he just stood there, silently looking at us. His expression was eerily one of sorrow and pity.

"Do you see any more?" yelled Robert.

"No." As the ship passed, I caught a glimpse of her name, *Comfort*.

And so we continued to cruise down the coast.

It had now been over a week since the shit hit the fan in this area and it was beginning to show. As we sailed on, we ran into more and more deserted vessels, mostly sailboats. Some had zombies but we left them alone. They would just end up eventually sinking in a storm or drifting ashore. It wasn't until later that I realized this was not such a good idea, since there were a lot of islands in the immediate area that may have survivors and this would be an excellent way of infecting them. Then again, it wasn't my damn job to kill every fucking zombie we happen to run into. We did pass one boat where someone had hung themselves from the mast, he (or she), just dangled in the wind like some macabre wind charm. I did notice something that I thought was particularly odd. Every now and then, we would go by a collection of abandoned boats all crammed into one little area of the shore. Not being a seaman, I could only guess that it had something to do with the tide and currents. It just looked so surreal as if some giant child had gathered his toys in one area and would be right back. We never saw anyone living and would have certainly picked them up. Maybe we should have made more of an effort, you know made some sound and see who came running, but we didn't. A number of fires were burning close to shore and once, I saw a gigantic explosion far inland, I have no idea what it was, maybe one of those large oil storage tanks or something. Whatever it was, I heard the rolling thunder of the blast maybe half a minute after the flash.

We did 'explore/liberate' two boats that afternoon. The first was a motorboat that looked like a grown up version of the one from *Gilligan's Island*, a sports fisherman as Robert called it. It was just drifting a couple of hundred yards from shore and seagulls covered it. We pulled up within twenty yards, made lots of noise, and waited for a response. Without asking, Robert started to give me a rundown.

"My guess is early eighties, sleeps ten, we're looking at a V-birth, a few guestrooms, master, engine, salons, dining...this is not going to be easy. You game?"

"Why not?" Distraction is a good thing. I had been eyeing boats all morning, wondering what little treasure-chest they might have and looking for any excuse not to think of yesterday, or the day before, or last week.

As usual, Robert was right. It was no walk in the park. The birds were there for the two corpses in the back of the boat. It looked to be what was left of an adult man and woman. I based this on clothing, since the bodies were pretty chewed up by the gulls, wind, and sun. The male was definitely in a black tux, but I had no clue what she was in. Whatever it was, the fabric must have been very light. It looked like they had a party before checking out. several bottles of Stolichnaya Elite were next to them, rotted food and trash were scattered about and a large mirror (now covered in seagull guano) lay on the center table. Outside, the scene was not that bad, except for all the guano, this boat-robbing thing could work out. Once we went inside, everything changed for the claustrophobic. The corridors were too narrow, the doors were all funky sizes, and the boat creaked and rocked. My fun index was exceedingly low and I was just plain nervous. Overall, it kind of sucked. Once the boat was clear, we just went around and collected stuff. Whoever owned the boat was wealthy, but didn't know shit at all when it came to basic survival gear, but hey, we scored some canned oysters. The next was an abandoned sailboat where we spent the next three hours planning, measuring, screwing around, and planning some more in a vain attempt to retrofit Robert's boat with this vessel's reverse osmosis water-filtration system. Oh, well, we did score several cases of Monadnock bottled water and some nautical charts. Funny, I never looked at the names of the two boats.

That night, we anchored in a small cove well away from shore. We had visible light till almost ten, and, so far, no visitors. As the day cooled down, our spirits rose ever so slightly. We didn't talk much, just spent a lot of time staring off into the distance. For some reason, I started spending more and more time looking at the shore. Even if I live to be a hundred, which is highly unlikely, I will never truly be able to absorb the past week.

Dinner was Campbell's Chunky New England clam chowder, Saltines, and a warm Dr. Pepper. Not the greatest, but it would have to do, and I wasn't hungry anyway.

Robert is a big guy, 6-3, maybe 220, mid sixties, short grey hair, grey beard, and in great shape. The tattoo on his arm told me that he had once been a Marine, something he never talked about. A short conversation with him and you could easily tell that he was totally laid back, well read, and very smart. He always wanted to be a pilot but ended up teaching engineering. He loved sailing. Retirement was supposed to be this boat and the rest of the world. Robert had another passion, competitive pistol shooting. Yeah, I know. What are the odds of ending up with Dirk Pitt for a partner during a zombie apocalypse? One of the guys told me he had achieved a Masters rating with the International Defensive Pistol Association, regularly competed in NRA competitions, and was somewhat of a legend at the Capital City Gun and Pistol Club. This was obvious when you saw him in action. He was calm, almost Buddha-like, and seemed never to miss. Whereas, I counted down each shot as my shotgun only held seven, Robert always knew exactly where he was with his clip and when to reload. I think he tolerated me because I had tried to wrap my mind around what had happened, and like it or not, had somewhat come to terms with this new paradigm, and so had Robert.

I just sat at the galley table, nibbled on a cracker, and stared at my now cold clam chowder. Out of the corner of my eye, I could see him studying me.

"You know we all made the decision. It was unanimous. We needed food and water. We needed rest."

"Yeah, but at least we should have sailed around the rock. Maybe then, we would have seen it. I noticed the tide change when we went down to the boat, it just, it just never crossed my mind that..."

"Too tired! Too thirsty! We had just spent the good part of a week getting our asses kicked! Hell, we were worn thin and barely keeping it together. We can go round and round over this, John, if I had my charts, if we had more water, if my fucking tablet worked, if this whole shit storm had never happened! We all screwed the pooch and you and I are just plain fucking lucky to be alive. End of story." I had never heard him raise his voice and I did not want to see him really pissed off.

"Right, Robert, end of story," I said, in a voice that sounded like complete defeat. Of course, I knew he was right. We had made stupid mistakes before, at the barn, getting out of Bangor, when we changed the tire... Shit, I didn't want to think about that one, not yet, maybe not ever.

Robert mumbled something to himself and went aft to get his bottle of Dewars. I grabbed a blanket and sleeping pad, and went up top to lie down. The night was warm, the water calm, sky clear, and the stars were magnificent. Most people in the US never get a chance really to see the stars. With the electricity out, it was like being in the backcountry, the night sky is a physical presence and you can understand why ancient people venerated it. I found some comfort with the stars. They were forever. Beyond the obvious, what bothered me the most right then was that I knew there were probably not many people around to appreciate or contemplate them, and our numbers were dwindling every day.

I watched Scorpio rise, my birth sign, and tried to identify other constellations. There was Orion and I think Leo, lots of satellites (as if we need them now) and ... oh fuck! It made an arc from east to west, starting out dim, but moving fast and becoming the brightest object in the sky for about two minutes. How could I have forgotten, it was the International Space Station. What the hell were those poor bastards going to do? How many are on board? What did they see when they passed over the night side of our planet? Could they all leave? Where would they land? I've only heard of Kazakhstan as the landing site. I guess because it's big and flat and hard to miss. I tried to imagine what I would do. I think in the end, I would stay, I mean, what a view!

I closed my eyes and tried to shut the same old questions out. With all our science and technology, were we that easily defeated? How long is this going to last? What is the decomposition rate? How much time? How the hell can we get through this? My mind raced, yet I still came back to Zombies! The world is going to end because of zombies! You have got to forgive me but, Fucking Zombies?

I now had accumulated enough time in the 'What outer ring of hell is this and can I get off now?' zone, and had thought through all the various scenarios. Unfortunately, every way I looked at it, humanity was in very deep kimchi. Fantastic, I get to personally experience the greatest genetic bottleneck in human history, while never playing for our team (read, I don't have any children). There are over one hundred billion galaxies in the known universe. That means there has to be a hell of a lot of intelligent life out there. Maybe it's just one of those things, statistically speaking, that every now and then, a sentient species gets taken out by its own zombies.

I knew Robert was right and I damn well understood that the two of us had dodged a bullet from hell, but all our friends were gone. All that effort was gone. All that trying to be human was gone. It just didn't seem right to have endured so much, just to end up as one of them, slowly rotting away in eternal rage. I had thought of going back and retaking the island to ensure everyone was really dead, but with only Robert and me, it was just too impractical. I never even mentioned it to him. Times like this, I wished I had smoked. At least it would give me something to do. With the gentle rocking of the boat and the soft sound of waves lapping against the hull, I calmed down and slowly drifted off to sleep. Eventually, I dreamed of better times, I dreamt of Elizabeth.

Elizabeth was a student in my paleoanthropology course, The Evolution of Ancient Hominids. She was about the same age as me, slightly taller, with long brown hair and average features, but the kind that made you look twice. She was going to school finally to get her B.A., one that she had given up decades ago to get married and to raise a family. Now with her children grown, and a divorce, she was free to do the things she thought had passed her by. She loved to travel and wanted to live life for life. She told me once that all this freedom was like learning to breathe again. I was in a funk, not having dated in a while and not really looking. I had resigned myself to a life of bachelorhood, too old to have children and only now regretting it. After the fourth class, she stayed late to ask me some questions on the similarities between *Afropithecus* and *Sivapithecus* and the conversation drifted, we hit it off right away. After several long coffee talks at the Store Ampersand, we found out that we liked to do similar things, we read the same books, watched the same movies, and wanted more adventure. Dating someone taking your class is strictly forbidden, but she was a biology major and this was her last anthropology course. As the semester wore down, we saw more and more of each other. When the class ended in December, she went to New York to spend the holidays with her mother and I went to visit my family in Rhode Island. We talked every day and made plans for a backpacking trip in Utah next spring. I knew I was a goner, she was just too nice and after everything I had been through, my life was finally getting itself turned around, the timing was impeccable. Just after Christmas, her mother died suddenly. I wanted to go see her and help in any way I could, but she said no and would give no real explanation. Later, she told me that her ex had come out and she wanted to avoid the inevitable awkward situation. I was hurt and confused, but when she ended the call with "I love you", I was rocketed to the stars. I was not teaching next semester, just working on some papers and leaving for South America in March, hoping that after I returned, things would really take off. Life is good.

Chapter 3 ~ Plague

May 31st

The suns hot rays brought me back to the real world. I will never get over that unique disappointment you feel when waking up and knowing it was all just a dream. My watch read 5:41 am. The crystal clear sky gave every indication of yet another broiling day, but man, what a sunrise. I rolled over and studied the shore. The small cove we had anchored in was densely forested with pine and deciduous trees, and the shoreline was covered in smooth blackish-grey rocks. It was a serene place and would be absolutely sublime when the fall foliage peaked. I was pleased to see that there was no one waiting for us. I knew our plan was to head south and hit moored boats for essentials, the last thing we wanted to do right now, was to set foot on the mainland. Too early to wake Robert, I put am arm across my eyes to block out the light and dozed.

~

By the time I got back to Bangor from South America, it was obvious that things were rapidly spiraling out of control and I was lucky not to be in some quarantine hellhole in Florida. The only thing saving my ass in Miami was: A. South America had yet to report an infection, B. I was a U.S. citizen in good standing and C. I was just one plain lucky SOB. Everyone at the airport seemed stunned, like they just woke up.

I quickly found out that this illness or whatever it was, had been going on only for a couple of weeks, in small isolated places no one had heard of. Nothing big in the mainstream news, just strange reports here and there, I think we may have been desensitized by all the hoopla surrounding the H1N1 pandemic and the threat of bioterrorism. Then some video leaked from a UN medical team on the Ukok Plateau in the middle of fucking nowhere Russia. Online so rapidly that you might think you were seeing it all live. It was like John Carpenter decided to do a remake of a remake of The Thing. Most of what was posted was really shaky, often slightly out of focus, hard to make out exactly what was going on, but one thing was clear, something really bad happened, was happening. Nevertheless, it was okay. I mean the Ukok Plateau? Give me a break. A day or two after that, and over eight million views on YouTube, it just took off. The press put the Ukok incident and isolated news reports/stories together and came up with the obvious conclusion, 'We Are All Going To Die A Horrible Plague Death!' Odd considering this speculation was correct. The news got worse by the hour. Soon, reports were coming in from relatively large cities in China: Turpan, Qumul and Ürümqi of 'strange demonstrations' and a disruption of internet and phone. CNN reported that the Chinese and Russian military had been placed on high alert.

When I walked into my condo, something switched inside me and I was home, I was comfortable, and everything was going to be alright. The guy next to me on the flight to Boston was a doomsday asshole, it's not that bad. I pulled blinds and opened windows; the fresh air and sunlight, yes, everything will be okay. I didn't feel like playing with the computer or the idiot box, so I turned on the radio. NPR was reporting that Ulaanbaatar, the capital of Mongolia, was infected, although I could have sworn the British reporter on the ground said 'infested'. The U.S. was responding to the growing crisis with the activation of something called a National Strategy for Homeland Security (read Marshal Law), along with a flood of travel restrictions. The Armageddon dude might be right. The switch inside me was now turned off and things and were not going to be alright. I was absolutely stunned and went for the full sensory override, TV. I decided to forgo reason and head straight for hysteria, so I turned to Fox News. It took only a few minutes of watching to begin to realize that humans might lose this one. The blowhards were going off on the government restricting our rights and our need to fight and restore America. The little time the network allotted to the real problem had a distinctly religious bend when it came to the ambiguous wherefore and the why. I shouldn't pick on a specific network, since all they were, was ahead of the curve.

For maybe the sixth time in the last couple of hours, I tried to get Liz or anybody from my family, but couldn't get through. I ran into one of my older building mates picking up the mail, an actual retired Maine lobsterman. Danny was a widower and loved to gossip. He told me to ignore everything.

"Listen, Professor, it's all the Liberal Media's doing. We're like sheep to them. Turn left, we turn left. Okay, a couple of Chinamen get the flu, God rest their souls but let them figure it out. We got enough problems." He put a heavily weathered hand on my shoulder. "Listen to me, Mongolia? Are you kidding me? Professor, you and me know that Mongolia ain't been around since the time of Genghis Khan. Who do these Harvard ass wipes think they're dealing with?"

The next day, the shit hit the fan. Our military, hell the world's military, was placed on the highest level of alert. The UN was called into a special session. I ran into a fireman who lived a few floors below me on his way to work, but with a backpack and duffel bag. Everybody who had anything to do with local law enforcement, fire, EMS, the whole works, was called in. "Circling the wagons," he said. I can't explain it but the total vibe was one of muted fear.

"Plan on staying for a while?" I asked casually, as we stepped off the elevator.

"Yeah." He walked a couple of steps, stopped, and without turning, asked, "Have you ever heard of the national response framework?"

"No."

"Good." And he just walked away. I forgot his name, but, unsolicited, Danny had filled me in on all the pertinent stuff: his messy divorce, that he doesn't watch television or keep up with sports, had been decorated by the department for something-or-other and is a nationally ranked chess player. Now I was officially fucking scared.

In Central Asia, things were moving fast. All of China was under martial law with vast areas in complete blackout and almost no news coming from Beijing, Shanghai, or Hong Kong. What little did get through was obviously heavily censored and with each passing broadcast, became more and more surreal. All signs indicated that something beyond belief was happening. China is the most populous nation on Earth, world-class scientists and a totalitarian government that can deal with this kind of situation, but she's dying.

By the end of the week, China was gone and Taiwan was about done – just a few reports from bloggers describing massive death and destruction, real Hell on Earth stuff. South Korea had outbreaks in every major city and there were rumors of the U.S. Military pulling out. North Korea was massing its armies on the border, but we knew they had it. Japan had outbreaks. The government just kept insisting the disease was under control. Later that day, India started issuing an eerily similar notice.

Within the next few days, Nepal, Vietnam, Laos, Thailand, Indonesia, Philippines and Malaysia, all had officially declared outbreaks and plenty of rumors said that it was in western Russia, parts of the Middle East, and Africa. Crazy news reports suggested it might have even originated in Central Africa, where humans became Human, but why the hell did China get whacked so quickly? Nothing was making sense. We just were not getting enough information. Everything was confused with reports constantly contradicting themselves. The one thing that was clear was that humans were the same old asshats they have always been. Looting and riots seemed to be the SOP for every city infected. With civilization crashing around you, why the hell would you want to steal a wide screen LCD HD 3D TV? All the chaos did, was to hasten the destruction. We all held our breaths and prayed. I simply started at my computer screen for hours on end with my brain screaming, No this cannot happen! Every Western country, or for that matter, every country, had now imposed some form of quarantine, with Great Britain being the strictest. There were videos of the British Navy shooting sailboats trying to cross the channel. They would all fail, miserably.

The press simply called it The Plague, invoking the spectra of the Dark Ages. We had been told it was something like Bird Flu; a new virus that would require close contact with the infected, only then could you be contaminated. If this was true, why was it spreading so damn fast? Why was it hitting all age groups? If it is the Bird flu or some new strain of influenza, then a vaccine might be found. Something in the back of my head was telling me this was not an influenza virus. The government was quickly getting more and more involved with information dissemination, and by the hour, the bullshit started to pile up. The (official) incubation time between initial infection and the first clinical signs was unknown. This could potentially mean that an infected individual might be spreading the disease for days or weeks before they knew they were sick. Most news reports agreed that the virus brought high fever, incontinence, nausea, delirium, and wide spread hemorrhaging, and eventually death. I knew damn well that influenza, as primarily a pulmonary disease, does not cause hemorrhaging, so what the hell was going on? It had a very high mortality rate, (some on the internet reported 95 - 100%), with most victims dead in three to four days (although bloggers on the internet claimed it was only hours?). We were not officially informed about what happened after death, but with all the videos, eyewitness accounts, rumors, and unofficial reports, everyone either knew or put their heads in the sand and prayed. Doesn't matter, all the airways with were filled with fear, redemption, and the 'End of Days.' I was beginning to think they might be right.

After almost a week of isolation, and another frustrating day at home, trying to make phone calls, eating microwavable food, staring out over the city, and pretending this was not happening, I called a good friend at the Center for Disease Control. Dr. David Clark was not in infectious disease, but is unbelievably smart and high enough on the org chart to get at least a dim view of what was going on. I got through on my third try at his office number. Maybe calls to the CDC were somehow prioritized. We exchanged some tense small talk and he had me switch from my cell to a pay phone and a different number. Luckily, Bangor is a bit behind the times and still has pay phones. Aren't payphones just pay cell phones?. Anyway it was good to get out of the condo and as I wandered to find a phone, I realized there were few cars, hardly anyone on the street, and it was strangely quiet.

"Damn, David, what the hell is happening and what's with this espionage shit?"

"Fuck if I really know, John, everything is in chaos." David was not a small guy and he was already breathing heavily. You could almost feel him shaking. "Okay, this is what I do know. It's in the *filoviridae* family, very Ebola-like right down to the Sheppard's crook, but a big one, okay? This isn't like eighteen or nineteen K long, we're talking well over twenty K nucleotides! Way too fucking big. Something is peculiar about the composition and obviously, one we have never seen. John, there's some kind of Prion shit going on that has nothing to filoviruses! This is bad. Okay, no one knows for sure, but it looks too familiar to be extra-terrestrial or some deep ocean vent stuff, there is talk, very credible talk that it could be human made." Dave's voice was now shaking with fear.

"What? Man made! Oh No, No, No! This fucking blows! You have got to be fucking kidding me!"

"You got it, brother. You think you are ready for something like this. You train, you plan a million scenarios on a thousand computers, and then we get zombies! John, some guys in Canada actually worked out a real mathematical model for an outbreak of a zombie infection? You know what they came up with? A rapid aggressive response! A bunch of dorks in Ottawa tell us we should fight back, shit man, their zombies were the slow type and even then, the odds were strongly against us." Dave wanted to rant and the sound of his voice told me all I needed to know. "You know what R- zero is, right?"

"Sure, disease multiplier, right?"

"Well hold on to your britches, because this one's coming in between thirty and sixty! It's impossible to get credible data…this is so fucked up man! Hold on." Dave covered his mouth piece, but I could still hear him talking with somebody. Between thirty and sixty! This means that each infected individual might be expected to infect up to sixty individuals. This is incredible, the R – zero for smallpox is something like between three and twenty! David came back on.

"Sorry about that. I don't know, John. Maybe you should have stayed isolated in your Chilean desert, I can think of lots of worse places to be. Every day, more and more don't show up for work, or just fail to return from lunch, I don't know why I'm still here. You ask for a report and you're told it might take a week, the network crashes and another day is gone while IT tries to fix it, if they can fix it. No one is fucking talking to each other! We're all sitting in a big pile of shit and everyone is still playing spy vs. spy. Who the fuck thinks they are going to get a promotion out of this? We are not even close to understanding this thing, let alone find a cure. Even if we did have our shit together, my best guess would be two to three years. The government has already gone COG on us and we are essentially under military control. As far as research is concerned, it's all bullshit. It's a damn Chinese Fire Drill. The bastards in the military will not talk to us. It's take, take, take. I try to call friends in Russia and I am told to submit an official request! The U.S. is copying the stuff the British have done, the British copying the Russians, the Russians doing the same with the Chinese. The Chinese, well who knows, they're gone. Right now, the best guess for Asia is already over two billion infected."

"What?" Two billion! People don't normally think about numbers this large and I couldn't comprehend something like that. I didn't know how to respond.

"John, that's a low-ball guess. That number is tossed around to make people feel good. There is a lot I don't know and every day, I am locked out of more and more. This might be it."

"It? David, what's IT?"

"Armageddon. We could all very well be toast. China, Nepal, Bhutan, Taiwan, and a great part of India are just gone, and from the looks of it, I mean everyone. Wildfires of this shit are now worldwide, two billion ain't nothing, and John, this doesn't take into account the fucking nuke games India and Pakistan are playing. If I were you, I would head north, go where it gets really cold and stay there. My best guess is that's already been happening around here. I just know I won't be invited on the ark when the rain showers start. Man, I hope you are flexible enough to kiss your ass, because I think the last waltz is playing buddy. I'm sending Jenny and the kids to a friend in Idaho, can't get them into Canada." Dave seemed on the verge of tears, and so was I.

"We're all very scared here in Atlanta. Nobody seems to know what to do. Oh man, I'm from California, you know a 'sun and surf' guy, and I'm going to die in Georgia! Yep, somebody somewhere is having a cosmic belly laugh over this one. I wish all of us the best of luck. I have to go my friend. I don't think we will talk again, so you take care."

"God speed, David."

I held on to the phone for a long time and stared at the number buttons. My mind kept reading them backwards from nine to one. I didn't expect the call to be uplifting, but I also didn't imagine it would hit me as hard as it did. At times of real crisis, the US is often very good, even brilliant, and the little child in me was almost sure we would pull a rabbit out of our ass on this one. But if David is right... A man made filovirus? Who? Why? What for? Why the fuck would you do that? What, nukes are too twentieth century? Two billion is a low estimate? What the hell was going on with India and Pakistan? Some guy was yelling at me to get off the phone and when I turned to look at him, he just stepped backwards and ran away. I hung up, walked over to a store window, and looked at my reflection. I now knew why he ran. Sweat was running off me and I was shaking. I looked at my hands and they were white.

The *filoviridae* family is a class of single stranded negative sense RNA. It has several genera with *ebolavirus* and *marbergvirus* the best known. Both are some extremely deadly shit. As a grad student, I almost switched to microbiology to study this type of virus. Ebola is fascinating because it runs the mortality gambit from zero percent, as in Ebola Reston, to over eighty percent in Ebola Zaire, one of the most lethal pathogens known. It causes a hemorrhagic fever and a just plain nasty way to die: massive organ failure and bleeding through every orifice, the whole nine yards. Filoviruses, unlike influenza type viruses, are not airborne. They require direct contact with infected material: blood, tissue, vomit. So when you do get an outbreak, usually in some bum fuck isolated backwater (Sorry Reston, VA), it quickly burns itself out. Well, this one is not going to burn out, since we have this dire new twist to the whole epidemiology tango; fucking zombies.

I got home and tried Liz again, but with no luck. It seemed like the system was still up and running, but this time, I did not get some pre-recorded circuits are busy message. It just did not go through. In a sense, the end of the world kept me distracted and I tried not to think about Liz and my family, or whether I would ever see them again.

Each day, it got worse and worse. Egypt, Kazakhstan, Turkey, Romania, Brazil, Germany, Argentina, Israel, France, Australia, and the list went on and on. It was just a classic example of a novel lethal virus in a virgin mobile population. I was bothered that both South America and Australia now had it. I half hoped that they might be able to isolate and weather this storm.

By the start of my second week back, everyone knew that it was in the US, it had to be. I placed a call to my brother in Montana and almost got past the first ring when it cut off. As the world went to shit, the news media fed us the same crap. Nobody could cross our borders, the quarantine restrictions in US were the best in the world, we will have a vaccine soon, everything will be under control in a couple of weeks, and the dead do not rise. We were now all treading water in the deep end of the pool.

I thought about heading south and getting back to my mother in Rhode Island, but it was too late, the major highways were now restricted for military and official use. From Internet, TV and radio reports, it looked as if most of the secondary roads were a mess. I95, Route 1 and the 202 were nothing but a linear parking lot. Short of a helicopter, if you had clearance to fly, or a boat, there was no way to get south.

Like everyone else, I had made several runs to the grocery and hardware stores to stock up on essentials, hoping that I could hang out in my condo and let this thing slide by. To be honest with you, I didn't know what essentials really meant. I was lucky since I could walk to both stores and use one of my large expedition backpacks to haul stuff back. As expected, the stores were packed. It wasn't like waiting for a hurricane or big winter storm to hit. No one looked at each other, and no gossip about projected landfall or wind speeds or storm surge. Everyone was on a mission to get what they needed and get back to their families. We were all wracked with fear but trying really hard to act normal. In the supermarket, I passed one woman who was holding two cans of baked beans, different kinds of my favorite brand, B&M, original and maple. It was as if she was trying to decide which one to buy. She must have been there for some time since the entire aisle was wiped out, nothing left. Her shopping cart was empty. I walked over to see if she needed help and overheard her talking to herself about the caloric difference between the two. I just stood there and it dawned on me that I cannot help this woman. By my second grocery run, the woman was gone, and there was almost nothing to get and no one paying. I ended up with cans of anything I could find, mushrooms! I absolutely fucking hate mushrooms!

Miami was the first U.S. city to be "officially" infected, but hey, the states a big peninsular and sections could be quarantined. I heard an 'expert' telling us that we could build a fence across Florida, like the Mexican border fence, in a few days. Problem solved! Then: LA, New York, Philadelphia, Atlanta, St. Louis, Omaha, Denver, Houston, and on and on. I don't know the exact order because the dominoes fell so quickly. In the U.S., like everywhere else on the planet, the human response was to riot, loot and burn. In essentially forty-eight hours it was over. When Boston was declared an infected city, I filled my bathtub, sinks, and any container I had with water. I was on the top, fourth floor, and the only way in was my front door. I decided then and there to isolate and wait. Shoot it out if I had to and save the last bullet for me. Yeah, right. If I rationed, three weeks was no problem, but what then? My neighbor Burt was out of town and I guessed he would not be coming back anytime soon, so I let myself in (we didn't really hang out together but had exchanged keys years ago) and raided his place. I first went for water. Burt is a bachelor like me, in finance, and a bit of a health nut. While the bathtub filled, I checked his cupboards. Unlike me, he apparently does not eat anything out of a can, with one exception…mushrooms. I knew the power would eventually go and I'd have to eat all the veggies first, not that there were many of them. Carrots, green beans, tomatoes, broccoli, some bagged salad mixtures and kale. Kale? Who eats Kale? From my quick look around, nothing in the apartment stood out. I felt like an intruder so I didn't open drawers and closets, yet. My other two neighbors didn't answer their doors. I gave myself a day to decide if they were home before I broke their doors down.

Two years earlier, I had bought a Ruger SR9 and a bunch of ammo. It was a semiautomatic with seventeen round clips and once you put the holster on, you really felt like a badass. I took a class in gun safety and actually motivated myself a total of two times to a firing range to play with it. I have absolutely no clue why I bought the thing. I was not in danger, nor in love with guns, just your classic American consumer. It looked cool, I had cash, had no record, now I had a gun. As with most of my impulsive purchases, I soon lost interest and to the back of the closet, it went. Now it seems like one of my better life choices.

    I sat down on my balcony, turned on the radio, and opened a Royal Crown Cola. I kept trying to call Liz, but the lines were jammed and all I got was a beeping tone. Lines, there are no lines anymore, so maybe the system will last for a bit. I looked out over the Penobscot River and downtown Bangor. Things were starting to change, some smoke in the distance, car horns honking, sirens, and no reported riots. Yet, if you could tune this out, you might be able to convince yourself that it was just a beautiful day in May with a great summer ahead. I just sat there in a daze. My mind was racing. It was easier to comprehend when hell was breaking loose elsewhere but the pigeons were finally home and the end of the world had reached my doorstep. The human mind is a crazy thing, because my train of thought quickly transitioned from the end of the world to a lament that I would not be able to make it to the Orono Farmers Market this year. Part of my 'eating better/living better' strategy, that usually lasts a month or two, and I started thinking that this could be my last address. After about an hour, I kind of came out of it and my brain started to register that there were more fires on the horizon, a whole lot more sirens and my soda was flat. I got to thinking that the city has a population of around 31 thousand, immediate surrounding area about 150 thousand. I had fifty-two rounds for the Ruger.

    While the government could control the print and mainstream media, it could not easily shut down the internet and the truth poured in. The actual Plague was not the main problem. The real issue was with the rising dead and the vicious nature of their being. It was now widely known that a bite quickly led to infection, death, and reanimation. We were hearing that the undead ate only part of the newly dead, at least till reanimation. One report talked about zombies being easily distracted by the living. Well, thank God, I am good for something. The average victim would take less than an hour to reanimate, everyone who died of a bite reanimated and you needed to disrupt the brain in order to "kill" the undead. The anatomist in me was a bit bothered by the whole shoot them in the head thing. Some inner part of my scientific brain was telling me that this did not make complete sense, as if the world being destroyed by zombies was part of your daily dose of rational thinking.

My cell phone rang! It was Elizabeth; pure luck she got through. I was relieved, overjoyed, and I wanted to wax romantic, but she essentially told me to shut up and listen. Her ex, Roy, had a plan and she wanted to invite me along. He knew about our friendship and was surprisingly supportive. They had parted friends and after six years and his remarriage, he wanted the best for her. As it turns out, Roy was a bit of a survivalist, something Elizabeth had never mentioned. He liked guns and large motorized things. Yes, this goes hand in hand with the whole survivalist motif, but yet again, something she never mentioned. He had two friends with big campers and a couple of others with sailboats. Roy had a Hummer, which was tricked out, and according to Liz, he was almost giddy at the apocalypse that lay ahead. The idea was to get together ASAP, make our way to the coast, get to the boats, head south, find an island, and wait for this to blow over. I would have to meet her on the other side of town. In was clearly time to go, so I did.

Chapter 4 ~ Refuge

May 31st (continued)

"Tan is looking good!" I had heard him messing around below deck and was waiting for Robert to come up.

"Well, you know my motto, 'it's not how you feel, it's how you look'."

"I guess skin cancer is not a big concern these days."

"Melanoma is on the list, just not as high as it used to be. Make any coffee?"

"In the galley, it's instant. I have been looking at the charts we got off those boats yesterday and thought we might try for Monhegan Island, see what's up. Ever been there?"

"Would it help if I have been there?"

"No."

"I've never been there."

I heard the rustling of paper and opened my eyes. Robert was sitting next to me, laying out a nautical chart on the deck.

"It's about forty miles from here. National Weather Service is off the air but the barometer and weather look favorable. With a little luck, we should make it today."

"Well, my dance card seems to be empty this morning, so why not. How many do you think?" I pulled myself into a seating position with my back telling me clearly that: A. You are forty-six years old. B. Even with a ridge rest, the deck is hard. C. There is a damn empty bed down below!

"Well, as our good friend Bill Shakespeare would say, 'now there's the rub!' Everyone and their brother might have sought refuge there, but worst comes to worst, should be plenty of boats to raid and a place to anchor if the weather turns." He looked off into the distance and for the first time, I could visibly see the enormity of our situation on his face. No fear or real sense of sadness, just a deep understanding of it all.

"What about Mantinicus? I heard it's a nice place. Might have fewer people, less of them?"

"Well, you might be right on that point, but those folks like to keep to themselves. Don't think we would find open arms waiting for us. Too bad, has some great lobster fishing. Well, anywhere we choose is going to be a crapshoot. We just roll the dice and see what lady luck brings us."

"Yeah, that bitch has been a real pal lately."

Robert stood, slapped me on the back, "Serenity now, my Boy! Serenity now," he yelled and went below laughing.

It took me a minute...oh yeah, Seinfeld. Thanks for reminding me about TV, asshole.

I followed him down.

"So, why the hell are you in such a good mood? I thought between the scotch and all the other shit, grouchy would be the theme for today."

"You know, John, you're right. I should be pissed off, life sucks, but we should be dead and we are clearly not. Everything we knew and loved is gone. Pain rules! I think it's about time the two of us grew up. It's not a sin that we did not die with the rest of them. We have to forgive ourselves, you in particular. John, what you did on the mainland was one of the greatest acts of pure love I have ever seen. Remember that, and remember we have to survive." He turned around and handed me a large cup of coffee.

"And you will have to forgive me. This stuff, as my grandson would say, sucks ass." He half caught himself and I saw pain in his eyes. I took a sip. Yes, it indeed sucked ass, but with a box of Thin Mints Girl Scout cookies added, breakfast wasn't half bad.

Robert quickly composed himself.

"Okay, so we set sail and check out this island. Generally, there are fewer than one hundred people, but with tourist, I mean refugees, I expect a great deal more. If they got themselves organized, who knows? What do you think?"

"Well, we're going to need some supplies before venturing out. We're short on batteries."

"And on Dewars. Let's make Tenants Harbor our next stop." He caught me thinking and gave me a stern look. "You know we are not thieves and there ain't no way we are pirates." He gave a short laugh and I gave him a no-shit look.

"We are survivors," I said, "Our moral obligation is to the living, to real people. The rest are just...very dangerous animals."

I busied myself with preparation to get under sail, but in the back of my mind, I kept thinking of Robert's concept of forgiveness. Hell, I was raised Catholic, 'guilt, yeah, give the gift that keeps on giving.' Can I really forgive myself? To live, I knew I had to. I had to keep saying that it was not my fault, but fate, whatever that means. I also knew that I had to calm down, rationalize and no matter how tired or how damaged I was, I need to think through everything carefully. I need to let go of ego and take to heart that I was not that smart, fast, or careful. I think what Robert was hinting at was to stay in the moment and live one day at a time, one hour at a time. I tried not to spend that much energy on my future and contemplating what was becoming more and more obvious. I just focused on that one word which adorns the Rhode Island state flag, Hope.

Once we got underway, I started to settle down and got into a routine. Robert spent some time going over the basics of sailing, again. I also practiced knots and kept an eye out for other boats.

Tenants Harbor is a typical New England seaside town and a great place to spend your summer vacation, go sailing, play golf, check out some galleries, and eat lots of seafood. Now it was teaming with the undead. Under full sail, our entrance did not go unnoticed. They quickly rushed to the shore and crowded the docks, climbing over each other and pushing those in front into the water just to get a good look at us. They reached their arms and fingertips as far as possible, eyes almost pleading. There were hundreds of them with more coming. The crowd let out a collective muted roar, as we got closer. I had never seen so many in one place and shuddered at the thought of what Portsmouth or Boston would look like. The wind shifted and the stench was unbelievable. Out of the crowd, I noticed one in particular. She was tall, blonde and would have been SI swimsuit beautiful in real life. She wore the remnants of what looked like a wedding gown, soiled and torn. One breast exposed and stumbling on high heels was both an erotic and depressing sight. It jolted my brain and I realized that I would probably never make love again. I tried to think back to the last time, a couple of years ago, for the life of me, I just can't remember her face.

We had agreed upon a carefully planned routine for a boat we wanted to board. First Robert would sound the bullhorn siren to announce our presence. We then hailed the vessel to see if any of the living was on board. Armed and ready to go, we would circle the vessel checking out all angles. Once it looked like the coast was clear, we would approach along side, I leap on, shotgun at the ready, and Robert would pull away. The plan is that if I ran into anything I thought I couldn't handle, I would jump into the water and swim for him. Once things looked safe, I would signal him to come along side and tie off. Both of us, would them go below and check things out. We would initially make a lot of noise to get any creatures inside excited, then wait, and listen. Closed locked doors were always the worst and I fired a few rounds opening them. You just didn't know what would come charging out or just be sitting in there waiting. Once the boat was cleared, we went shopping.

The raids were a great success. We got plenty of gas, batteries, food, water, and Dewars. We also stocked up on non-essentials like flares, clothing, books, toiletries, and just about anything else we thought we needed. With only the two of us, space was not an issue. We only encountered two zombies, both quickly dispatched. They were aboard a large yacht where we enjoyed a late breakfast, showered, and scored an additional shotgun and ammo. There was still more boats to raid, but we had plenty and were ready to move on. Robert thought it was a good idea that once we found a semi-permanent 'home', a database should be compiled of all boats and locations that we had visited, what we took and what was left behind. Great idea, but with the lack of electricity and the scarcity of batteries, we would have to do it by hand. So much for the Excel refresher course I took at night last semester.

As we made our way out of the harbor, another sailboat appeared in the distance heading north. Robert fired a flare but she tacked away. Since heading north was not in our game plan, we did not pursue, but headed south to Monhegan Island.

When not listening to Robert or playing with string (it's a knot thing), I monitored the radio and scanned various frequencies. There was, surprisingly, a lot of activity. We got a few French speaking groups out of Nova Scotia, a bunch of rural Maine, and a few New Hampshire communities were still with us and EAS was running, although it was the same crap from last week about staying indoors and obeying state and federal authorities. We also connected with a few other boats. The general gist was that if you were rural and alert, you might have a chance, anywhere near a population center and you were SOL. No one really had much current information and everyone told the same story about how this all happened faster than expected. A few were actually waiting for rescue believing that there was still a government, that somebody out there cared and was going to save them. Some of the groups we talked with were in short wave contact with Europe and the Caribbean, but they were in the same situation as the U.S., fucked. We also caught some rumors about naval activity south of us and about something that was happening on Martha's Vineyard and Nantucket. Each group had its own idea of how to save themselves. Like us, some were heading south, some north; 'embrace the cold and freeze the fuckers', others staying quiet and staying put. Two of the communities in southern Maine were going nowhere. They were under siege.

We made contact with a fishing boat, the *Queequeg*, about ten miles, and her captain, Josh, who informed us that Monhegan was a complete loss.

"It looks like most of the village has burned. Some small fires were still going and lots of smoke inland. From the amount of boats, my guess is a whole bunch of people had the same idea we had. The harbor was packed and there are wrecks all around the island. Over."

"What about shore activity? Over."

"Plenty of them on shore. Seeing is believing. We counted over two hundred in the village area. Couldn't get anywhere near land without attracting their attention, under power we are anything but stealthy. We're not well armed and made no attempt to land. It's that bad everywhere? Over."

"It's worse on the mainland, Josh, a real shit storm. What about the moored boats? Is there anything to interest us?"

"Sorry, Robert, but between the *Queequeg* and some others, we seemed to have picked the harbor clean. Might be worth a visit, your needs are different from ours. Did see a couple of sailboats in the distance but they wanted nothing to do with us. We are a bit screwed when it comes to fuel. Plenty of food, but hell, man, we're a fishing boat!" I was relieved the 'over' game had stopped.

"I guess we're back to putting our thinking caps on. So, where to now, Josh?"

"Well, we were in the George's Banks when things really took off, sat tight for a while and followed the news over the satellite and radio. We all thought maybe it would blow over like the yearly flu or that the US would figure out how to deal with it. Monhegan woke us up and well...the crew took a vote. It was unanimous. We are going home."

"Where's home?"

"New Bedford," Joshua said quietly in that classic Massachusetts accent.

We looked at each other in disbelief, are they insane? New Bedford is a famous old whaling town tucked between Providence and Boston. New Bedford is suicide.

"You sure? It's going to make the island look mild. There's nothing left there for you and your crew, Josh. Do you really want to see what happened to everyone you loved?"

"Yeah, well, we talked it over and over. We have to go back...it's our home." You could tell from his voice that we could say nothing, because they had made up their minds and I hoped, found some peace in the decision. Like the woman in the grocery store, I could not help them.

"How about you, Robert?"

"We're heading south, maybe find a small Caribbean island, and try to wait this thing out."

Josh laughed, "Sounds a hell of a lot more comfortable than North! Good luck."

"God speed, *Queequeg*."

"And to you, *Providence*. Over and out."

"Damn," Robert stared at the radio. He shut it off and we stood there in silence for a minute.

He cocked his head and looked at me. "Queequeg?"

"Moby Dick," I answered.

"Never read it."

"Don't worry, most people haven't, unless forced too."

"Were you forced?"

"No."

"I could have guessed that one."

Why would you go into a certain death trap? I know we all have to handle what had happened in our own way, but they hadn't seen the complete devastation and horror. I prayed that as they got closer, the shit would really sink in and they would change their minds.

"So, what's next on the agenda? We've still got lots of…"

"Hold on a second, John, I got something on radar! It's big, not industrial."

"How far?"

"About twenty-five miles east, they might be heading for the island. Looks like we both had the same brain fart."

"Well, misery loves company."

"Let's check her out!"

Our spirits were up after Tenants Harbor and the prospect of actually meeting people made everything all that much better. The wind picked up and the day cooled down. We yakked away the next couple of hours telling stories and lies. I fed Robert cold beers and me cold Cokes. A gull overhead, the smell of the sea and the sound of the boat ripping through the water are nothing short of magical. It is hard not to imagine that this was just a normal great day, two friends, a wonderful boat, and a whole ocean in front of us. You could almost relax.

As we got closer, we could see that the boat was a nice motor yacht, and by nice, I mean 'frigin' big. Robert said it was custom built and could easily hold twenty in style, not including staff. It was the kind of thing the villain usually has in James Bond films. As we got closer, the tension mounted. She had not responded to any of our hails and never attempted to change course or speed. We saw movement on board and it definitely looked like the living. We were not expecting a big welcome, but a hello would go a long way to making us feel less nervous. She could clearly see us and we stayed a very healthy distance off her stern. Eventually, I could see at least two on deck, scanning at us through large binoculars. It looked like they were wearing some kind of uniform. After ten minutes, still nothing! I mean if they were concerned, they could take their helicopter and check us out.

"What the hell? I don't think they are infected and they can clearly see that we aren't. You would think they would at least want to talk and see what's up, trade info."

"John, you don't watch that much television, do you? My guess is that anyone who can afford something like that, does not wish to slum with our likes. Why take the risk? We have nothing they want." He took one long look at the behemoth.

"Let's get the hell out of here."

We tacked away from her and headed west, back for the coast.

"Call me naïve, but THAT is fucked up!" I looked up at Robert, "The world has gone to hell in a hand basket and we are still dealing with this shit!"

Robert gave me that fatherly stare, "Why take the risk? And yes, you're naïve."

We anchored at sundown in some nondescript cove and crashed.

June 1st

I woke up with a massive dehydration headache and feeling shitty. The days in the sun were taking their toll. After passing several harbors and lots of boats, we came upon a very interesting prospect. It was a lighthouse sitting on a small island about maybe fifty yards from shore. It was larger than Molly's Rock, and even had a few small trees and in patches, a real lawn. The whole island was surrounded by fifteen to twenty foot cliffs, but on the lee side, the cliffs dipped to maybe five feet, and there was a small dock. The only real issue was that almost directly across from this dock, was the small village of God's Haven. It's a place you go in the summer to experience the "real" old New England and take lots of photos of this lighthouse. A small cove for sailboats with a traditional old school Maine town built on a hill that winds down to a long wooden wharf lined with restaurants and souvenir shops. It was also a jumping off point for whale watching tours. And yes, there were zombies. They saw us and flooded down to the dock. In five minutes, we had forty with more coming from deeper in the village.

We were coming up on low tide and we decided to see if the channel offered any real protection, and we would sail through. Time for us not to repeat our last fuck-up. Sure enough, it was plenty deep with a fast current that even at low tide, and would offer us a decent barrier. As we passed the wharf, the undead were whipped into a frenzy. They made a collective roar and reached out almost pleading for us to come closer. As the crowd followed the boats progress, two fell into the water and just disappeared, we never saw them surface.

Robert had a big smile on his face. "This could be a real winner!"

We were tired, Robert more so since he had done all the sailing and planning. We dropped sail and decided to motor around it one more time, nice and slow. We gave several bullhorn blasts and hails, but nothing answered from the lighthouse. The building itself looked to have been made sometime in the nineteenth century and was in very good shape. The tower was about seventy-five feet high with a twenty-five yard covered pathway leading to a beautiful two-story house. All the buildings were painted in white with red roofs, with the exception of the tower whose top was black with a large metal walkway encircling the light itself. Everything was freshly painted and the dock and stairs well maintained. I had seen an automated light on the way in and assumed this place was preserved for either historic reasons or a private residence. Either way, we were going in.

This was a gamble, as there could be a dozen zombies inside the house and tower, although this seemed unlikely. If we were going to investigate, we had to go one hundred percent. Still, far too little time had passed not to have that déjà vu feeling. We quickly tied off and went up the stairs and still no sign of trouble. At the far side of the house was a small modern windmill, something I hadn't noticed during our circumnavigation, things were looking better and better. Nice day. The tower had only one door and it was closed. Better day.

"Ever seen one open a door?" Robert asked.

"No. You?"

"Not yet. John, let's hold up here for a second." We were midway between the tower and house. I went to one knee and just assumed nothing was coming up my backside, Robert pulled out his binoculars.

"Okay… Lots of the blinds have been pulled upstairs. Morning sun is giving me excellent light." Robert continued his scan for at least another minute, while I tried to relax and control my breathing. Please let this fucker work out.

"Looks good, front door is closed. Okay, nice and easy."

The house was made of wood with glistening white clapboard. Two stories, a small porch and a well manicured yard. Very tasteful, very nice, very expensive. This place did not give the 'historical society' vibe. Part of the yard was segregated by a white picket fence and had a small flagpole still flying the stars and stripes. Jackpot!

There was a large window to the right of the windowless main door. Reflection from the sun made it difficult to see inside. Feeling a bit giddy and positive that we have this in the bag, I moved on to the porch and listened. After about a minute of silence and without really thinking it through, I cupped my hands and put my face to the glass.

Okay, stairway, no movement, a couple of doors, no movement, and… "Shit!" I screamed and fell back, dropping the shotgun and popping my glasses off. Within an inch of the glass was the face of a large obese woman. She had that grey waxy look, long stringy greasy hair, bulging blank bloodshot eyes, and bloody drool oozing from her nose and the corner of her mouth. It fucking freaked me out. Our face had to have been no more than three inches apart.

"Oh fuck, there's one in there!" I was shaking and hyperventilating.

Robert, from a more reasonable distance, looked in.

"I don't see anything."

"Oh, she's there!"

"Could she be alive? It didn't attack."

"Nooo, I don't think so." I had recovered my stuff and trained the Mossberg on the window.

He took a long look at me. "How are you doing?"

"Great, you know without a couple of millimeters of silica, I would have been locking lips with one of the undead, and not one of the better looking ones." I was still breathing heavily and more than a little embarrassed by my reaction. But hey, give me a break, that was close.

"Okay, you know the routine. I'll get the door and you get the zombie." My heart still raced.

"How about I get the door and you get the zombie? Spice things up a bit."

"Sorry, son, but you're the one carrying the big stick. Be careful," he laughed.

Robert went up to the door. The hinges indicated that the screen door would open outward and the main door inward. I stood about twenty feet away, shotgun at the ready. Robert pulled the screen door open and secured it with a convenient hook. It was well oiled and it did not make a sound. Robert glanced over to me and I gave him the thumbs up. As soon as he twisted the knob and pushed, he would quickly back off to avoid catching any of my blast. This all assumes the door is not locked and the zombie will come out.

"Okay, John, on three. Ready? One, two, three."

He slowly turned the knob and pushed.

The door soundlessly swung inward and nothing. Wow, twice in a row, what's going to happen this time? The inside is dark and from our angle all we could see is a small foyer with steps leading to the second floor. So we waited. After about a minute, the sun started to get really hot and the back of my neck was itchy.

I looked over to Robert and mouthed, "Where the hell is zom…"

With a gurgling roar, out charged two-hundred and fifty pounds of naked pissed off zombie. At about five-five she looked almost spherical. She charged at me with cartoon-like strides. The sight was surreal and I waited a second longer than I normally would, so she was really close to the barrel when I fired. The shot obliterated her head. I mean there was nothing left! Just like in the movies.

"Holy shit!" I yelled.

Robert was in his firing stance and edging to get a better shot should something else come through the open door. He glanced over at the corpse.

"Whoa! Holy Cow! That's a keeper. Hey, where the hell do you think Mister Orca is?" he yelled.

"I don't see any movement inside. Let's give it a second." I dropped to one knee to give me a better stance and regain my composure. I didn't look over at the human whale, but was sure there had to be more. It was just then that I realized I had almost never seen a zombie alone.

After a good minute and no sound or movement, I stood and went to the open door.

Robert was a few yards behind me scanning for threats other than from inside the house. The place gave off a slightly rotten smell. Not too powerful, but it definitely had a zombie funk.

I started to feel a tiny bit relaxed and glanced back at the woman I shot. "Damn. Maybe she ate everyone. I mean look at the size of her!"

"Thank God, there wasn't a pod. Okay, John let's get this done, but real careful like."

I moved in. Directly in front of the door were stairs leading up to the second floor. To the left, a large parlor, and to the right, something we used to call a mudroom, where you took off your wet boots and coat. That room had three doors which were all closed. In the center of the mudroom was a large pile of what looked like diarrhea or vomit, something yellowish mixed with blood.

I whispered to Robert, "So far, so good. Cover the stairs, I'm going left."

Slowly, I entered the parlor. A large, long, rectangular room, at the far end an open archway led to the dining room. Several large windows gave ample light, nothing moved. The parlor was very nicely decorated, a plush couch, sitting chairs, an extra large Oriental carpet and lots of nautical antiques. The place even smelled like money. On the fireplace mantle was various family photos, but the painting above it is what immediately got my attention.

"Man, did these people have money. Robert, that's a Winslow Homer above the fireplace!"

"No shit, John, they live in a place Yankee Magazine would pay you to put on their cover. Stay with it."

"Okay, let's hold for a second and listen."

Dead silence. I used the break to clean my glasses. Somewhere in the house, windows were open and I could feel a soft breeze. My neck and back were quickly soaked with sweat. Yeah, fear and humidity suck, but something just didn't feel right.

"Robert."

"What's wrong?"

"I'm not sure. Watch my ass."

I moved over to the fireplace and went forward. The dining room was surprisingly informal, with stuff of the day scattered everywhere. This was obviously a very popular room. I didn't take time to investigate, but the well-worn dinner table, that could easily sit ten, had to be from the Colonial Period. The archway into the room was partitioned on either side, so I couldn't get a clear view of the entire space. The rest of the house was off to my right, so the only other way out of the dining room had to be on the right.

As I slowly entered, I could just see the top of a wooden swinging door with a little round window that I assumed led to the kitchen. So far, the room looked deserted. The only problem was that when I looked at the door again, I realized it was stuck three quarters open. I froze. Robert froze. Time froze. Then, creeping forward, I just caught the top of what I assumed was Mister Orca's shiny grey baldhead, but from my angle, I could tell he wasn't lying on the floor. Maybe he was sitting down? All my Spider Man senses told me this was wrong. Then the head twitched. Oh, shit! I inched closer and peered around. For that split second, our eyes locked. He looked like some massive mastiff; at least three hundred pounds, naked, on his knees, head up and resting on the stumps of his elbows. Both of his lower arms were gone! It took only a second and in a bizarre crawling fashion, he charged. My first shot hit him in the back and destroyed his lower spine. With legs dead, he still came on fast using his stumps in an impossibly rapid peg leg fashion, roaring at the top of his lungs. I jumped out of the way and he smashed into the wall. The second shot did not miss.

"What the hell was that? Why did it wait? We've never seen them wait! Robert, what the fuck just happened? Was that was a fucking ambush?"

"That's three shots, John, reload, I'll cover you," Robert said calmly.

It took me maybe four seconds to grab three rounds from my bandoleer and chamber them. "Why eat only the forearms?"

"You eat chicken wings right?"

"Point made."

"I don't think this is over. Did you see the photos on the mantel, John?"

"Not in any detail. Why?"

"Well, there is a Pod. They got two kids, both teenage boys and schools out for the summer. You're right, that was some bizarre undead shit. Let's calm down and get this thing done."

"Bizarre? I tell you what, you take the big stick next time and get up a big load of bizarre. And why the hell were they both naked?"

We entered the kitchen. Large, modern, and all stainless steel, the best of everything. I think I would look like a member of the Pod if I had a place like this to cook. I was relieved that the room was empty and only a bloody trail on the floor from papa orca, if all goes well. We'll be using this space and it would suck to have zombie guts all over your kitchen. The cleanliness of the place strongly indicated a housekeeper was involved. The size of the two zombies strongly suggested that physical stress was not part of their normal day-to-day routine. We checked out the well-stocked pantry, and found the top end of everything you could eat. Who heard of kangaroo sausage? Did you really need to get your mustard from Germany? Vanilla from Mexico? Oh, well, it was all ours now and I am definitely going to make the best of it.

The kitchen had two additional doors; one led to a sitting room and bathroom and ended up back at the mudroom, and the other to a large room that had been added on to the original building. In here was a big tank connected to some boxes and something that looked like a pumping system.

"Oh man! That's a fucking desalinization system!" Robert yelled.

"You think that is cool, check out this." In the back was a series of long, black, plastic boxes with wires attached. I had never seen anything like it, but I knew what it was.

"Batteries?"

"Yup, these people spared no expense. Put all this a thousand miles south and we would be home."

"Hey, Robert, all those boxes are lit. Holy Crap, we have power!"

"That would explain why the refrigerator is working," Robert replied calmly. "Let's be careful."

"Okay," I said. "Further?" I emphasized the u and just knew that anti-hippie Robert would get the reference.

"Yeah, like on the bus, further."

"What would possess you to read a book with electric, Kool-Aid, and acid in the title?"

"Shut up, John."

The second floor was next. This area consisted of three large bedrooms all leading off from the landing. They shared two bathrooms and it was set up so you could make a big loop through all the rooms. Fortunately, for us, all the doors were open and we had clear views. As expected, everything was large and expensive looking. I know they have king sized beds, but this thing needed its own area code. One of the kid's room had a huge *Where The Wild Things Are* lithograph personally autographed to him by Sendak, and yes, it was number one in a limited series. I was really starting to dislike these people, or was it envy? Since the windows were closed, it was oppressively hot, but empty of zombies. They had tons of cash but no air conditioners, huh? We went back to the first floor.

The third door in the mudroom opened on to the covered walkway that led to the light tower, from studying the exterior we had guessed as much. Since the walkway had no walls, we could see all the way to the closed black tower door. It was then we heard this strange sound.

"Is that a cat?"

"No, John, that is not a cat."

We backed up into the yard and saw another zombie on the upper outer walkway of the tower, running about, occasionally looking over the railing, frantically waving his arms and screaming high-pitched gibberish at us. This guy was young and had to be one of the children. I turned to Robert.

"Going up there and getting him is not going to be fun. Any chance we can just leave him up there?"

"You got that right, and no. Hold on a second and let's just watch."

The creature continued his erratic movements around the walkway, but was always coming back to lean over and scream at us. Robert's eyes never left the thing and he took his firing stance, almost like a samurai getting ready to unsheathe his katana. He held his Glock with both hands in the down position.

"Just wait, he's going to show himself."

After about half a minute, the zombie stopped and again looked over the railing at us, panting. In one fluid motion, Robert raised his arms, aimed, and fired. From our distance, it looked like a puff of smoke exploded from the back of his head and he dropped to the deck.

"I've seen you shoot, but... damn Robert. That was one hell of an Olympic quality fucking shot!"

"Thanks, let's hope that leaves us with one more, but we must consider ground crew, servants,..."

"Housekeepers, yes I know. What do you think? Do the tower now?" I was getting excited.

"After the way papa orca acted, let's cover our backs and look around."

There were two relatively small outbuildings, also freshly painted white with red roofs. The first was about twenty-five yards from the house and stored what looked like various maintenance equipment. It didn't hurt that the building had windows on all sides, so we knew it was clear when we opened the door. As expected, lawnmowers, trimmers, hoses, rakes, the whole shebang. In one corner was a desk with a couple of photos and a large calendar, open to May. It can't be May. Is it June? What day is it? I guess all that doesn't matter anymore.

The other building was further away, maybe a hundred yards. A small side window seemed to indicate that it was also empty, but we had to go in and make sure.

"Yes, yes, Robert, I know...I get the zombie."

"If there is one."

So here we go, Robert as the door opener, and me the bait. This time, nothing charged out. After a minute, I moved closer. With just the little light from the window, it was like twilight inside. I edged to the open door. Some large objects obscured my view and I knew I would have to enter. I stepped inside the room and it immediately exploded with sound. I screamed and came within a nanosecond away from just letting loose with the Mossberg when a little voice in the back of my head said, "that's not a zombie you idiot!" It was a really good thing I listened to that little voice, since as soon as my eyes adjusted, I saw that the room contained a diesel engine and a very large fuel tank, which I later learned was three-quarters full.

Robert looked in, and then looked at me.

"You weren't thinking of shooting, were you?"

"Oh, God no, not without a verified target, I mean come on, Robert, I have done this before." What had happened to the calm, fearless zombie fighter I was last week? Or was all that two weeks ago?

He entered the building.

"Must be on some kind of timer," he yelled back at me. He found the light switch and after tinkering around for a bit, he came over.

"Oh shit this is great! We have hit the jackpot. Let's clear the tower and have a real meal. I'll cook!"

"What? I can't hear you! Outside!"

He repeated himself and filled me in on the details, including dinner.

"Oh, happy day," I muttered under my breath as I walked to the tower.

This time, the door opened out. Robert pulled down on the lever and pushed the door open. Nothing! Thank God. As usual, we both waited a minute, ready for anything that would emerge into the shaft of light made by the open door.

"Hey, we're out here! Come and get us!" I yelled.

Still nothing. I moved into the doorway but the room was too dark to see anything clearly. I risked it and started groping the inside wall with my right hand. My shotgun was rammed into my pelvis and if I had to fire, I would pay with one hell of a bruise. It had to be here. I inched in and kept sliding my hand up and down the wall. Finally, I found the switch and flicked it up. This turned on a series of lights scattered all around the room. It wasn't your standard incandescent light, but instead, it was a soft, white warm light.

The base of the tower had been turned into a tastefully done office with a monstrous mahogany desk and an equally over sized leather chair that might have been able to fit Mr. Orca. How the hell they ever got the furniture in here has to be one of Man's great mysteries. To the left, a set of steel stairs corkscrewed upwards.

"Shall we?" I said as I looked up trying to see where the stairs ended.

"Don't see why not."

As we made our way over, Robert noticed another light switch and flipped it. This one illuminated the stairs all the way to a hatch that must lead to the balcony. So, up we went. As with the exterior, everything inside was freshly painted and immaculate, no dust, rust or cobwebs. The hatch was unlocked and I used the barrel of my shotgun to push it up and over. It fell with a loud clang onto the metal walkway. We waited. We had only seen the one up here but you could never be sure and as with everything these days, just a tiny mistake could cost you your life.

I peeked over the lip and could just see the tips of a pair of sneakers sticking out from around the bend, not moving. The other direction was clear. Once on the balcony, I covered Robert and we then made our way around. The coast was clear. In the center of the tower was a glass room with a small entry door. Inside was a large reflecting mirror. I have never been on top of a lighthouse, but I knew this was no place to be with the light active.

The view was magnificent. Even with my preconceived notion that the town was a tourist trap, it actually looked quite quaint. From up here, you could see farms, rolling hills, and patches of forest, which started right at the outskirts of town, no suburbs, no strip malls. This would really be an okay place to live, even with the tourists. None of our activities went unnoticed. The zombies saw us and with the wind coming off the mainland, we could clearly hear the moaning and roaring as almost in unison. There were several hundred by now.

We threw the dead child, a young teenager, over the railing. Eventually, he would end up with his parents in the Atlantic. As we lifted him, I noticed the large hole in the back of his head, the exit wound, with brain tissue hanging out and looking fairly fresh. It still maintained that bluish-grey color and firmness that I had seen in the hundred or so autopsies I had participated in. Strange, the rest of the body showed obvious signs of decay, but the brain still looked good. It would be interesting to get one on the dissecting table.

"Let's head down and check out the office."

I was lost in thought, staring at the crowd on the wharf.

"Sure, I think I'll come back later. Spend some time getting to know our friends over there."

Beyond the desk and chair there was a well stocked bar and mini fridge, a large flat screen TV, oriental carpets that looked almost hallucinogenic and an overly comfortable well tooled leather couch. Now this is what I would call a home office. Roberts' interest lay with a series of grey metal boxes fixed to the wall just under the stairs.

"What's up, Robert?" I asked as my body oozed and became one with the leather. What a couch!

"Circuit breakers and some switches. I could be wrong, but I think these activate the tower light. Some of this wiring is brand new." You could hear the childlike excitement in his voice.

"Are you telling me we can fire up the light?" I am never moving from this chair.

"Yeah, I think so." He continued to examine the boxes and hummed to himself. It was nice to know that he was distracted and somewhat happy.

"Where do you think the other kid is?" My stomach grumbled and the comfort of the chair quickly faded from importance.

"Good question. Maybe he was with friends and got trapped on shore. I think we are clear, since we pretty much covered the place." He continued to hum.

"Yeah, well... let's be careful and check the house out one more time. Besides, I'm getting hungry!"

The mention of food was probably the only thing that would pry Robert away from his new toy.

"We can try to power her up after dinner. Who knows, we might be able to attract more survivors our way." I unglued myself, stretched, and headed for the door.

"John, you know how I promised to cook dinner?"

"Yes."

"Well, I lied."

"Oh, thank God," I muttered under my breath as I stepped into the blinding sunlight.

We went methodically through the house for a second time, but still no sign of the other kid. I started to pay more attention. The clothes in the closets told me that these people did not spend the winter, or maybe they had a new wardrobe sent in when it got cold. Mr. Orca, or should I say Mr. McKenna based on the open mail lying on an open antique roll top desk, was a partner in some New York law firm that doesn't exist anymore, and one of his kids just got accepted into Andover Academy, which also does not exist. After disposing of the Orca family, I started to get dinner ready and Robert cleaned.

Dinner was grilled rib eye steaks, baked potatoes, frozen veggies and biscuits. Robert washed it down with a fine, well he actually called it fucking outrageously expensive, merlot, and me a Coke. We didn't talk, just ate.

"Oh, God, stick a fork in me, I'm done!" I leaned back and actually risked feeling a bit normal. With all this food in me and the excitement of the day, I knew I would crash out tonight.

"We should take a week here. It will be nice to get the old batteries recharged." He poured the last of the wine and rocked back in his chair.

"Don't suppose there is any chance we could ride out winter here? Snag fuel and stockpile food," I suggested.

"Maybe, but if the generator goes down, we would be in for a rough time. They don't have any wood, so do you want to go collect a few cords? My guess is this place was just used during summertime. Anyway, we need a change of environment. Let's get the hell outa Maine."

"Yeah... I guess you're right, but I will enjoy this while we have it." I stood up and started to collect the plates. I can use the dishwasher; a luxury I had assumed was a thing of the past.

Robert stood and let out an enormous belch.

"Let's see if we can attract some boats our way." He went to the window and scanned the yard, unholstered his weapon and made his way to the mudroom.

"Hold on a sec, we need to stick together. You know the whole firepower thing." I quickly loaded the dishwasher and looked out the kitchen and dining room windows. So far, the coast was clear.

"Okay, let's see if she works." I grabbed my shotgun and bandoleer.

The sun had not yet set and we had plenty of light to ensure the coast was indeed clear. Back in the light tower, Robert went right to work on one of the boxes.

"Well, it looks like this is pretty straight forward." He threw some switches and the building shook, a loud humming was heard from the top of the stairs.

"Okay, let there be light!" and he pulled a large lever upward. The humming was now accompanied by a creaking sound and light flooded the top of the tower.

"Hey, it worked. Shit, I'd half expected everything to blow up."

"Ah, thanks, Robert. How about next time you fill me in on these little details."

We went outside. The light made a rotation about every ten seconds. Now, all we could do is wait and hope.

"Let's lock the house down, take turns keeping watch, three hour shifts, and I'll take the first one."

"Works for me, I'm beat. Hey, Robert, ah...no really, please let me in on the small details."

We went back to the house, ensured all windows and doors were secured and I went upstairs to crash. I thought sleep would come easily, but as usual, it didn't. I had earlier opened all the upstairs windows to create a cross breeze, but it still had not cooled the place down.

He woke me around two, and in a fog, I went downstairs. We had a three quarter moon and combined with clear skies and the functioning lighthouse, the outside visibility was pretty good. Anybody moving would certainly make shadows. I sat in a big overstuffed chair and examined the painting over the fireplace. It was classic Homer, a grey brooding sky and stormy sea with huge waves crashing over a dark, jagged, rocky shore. I knew Homer had painted a great deal in Maine. Is this what I am leaving? The hours dragged by. What the hell are we going to do? How many people were still alive on the planet? The last I can recall is that there were about seven billion. Could there be ten million still left? Isolated groups scattered around the globe with the number dropping every day. To continue this line of thinking was depressing, so I got up and made a check of all the windows. I decided to lie on the couch, knowing full well the probable outcome, and in about 30 seconds, I was fast asleep.

Chapter 5 ~ Guests

June 2nd

When I opened my eyes, the sun had clearly risen. Shit, what time is it? My watch read eight thirty. Oh well, we both need the sleep and nothing bad happened. I got up and quietly made my way to the nearest window. I stood in front of the curtains for a minute or two trying to break the kinks out of my back and listening. Okay, so far so good. I glanced out the window. Where the hell did all the seagulls come from? There were hundreds, just sitting there, not looking at anything in particular, and just hanging out. WTF? But no zombies! I went to a few more windows and it was the same, just lots of birds and no zombies. The birds were not just gulls, but also a variety of shorebirds and even some Mallard ducks. Robert's going to love this.

I went to the kitchen and rummaged around till I found some ground coffee (of course it was Jamaican Blue Mountain) and a French press, put some water on to boil and went up to roust Robert.

Going up the stairs, I looked out the porch window, and saw more seagulls, hundreds of them. Maybe this is where they hang out in the morning. Can't believe Mr. Orca would have liked dealing with all the bird shit.

"All right, time for some real breakfast. Bacon, scrambled eggs and real coffee!" I felt good, no guilt from sleeping late, we've lived to see another day.

"You let me sleep? It's a quarter to nine."

"Well, I thought you could use the rest after all the stuff we've been through, and well…"

He rolled over and gave me that look. "Fell asleep?"

"Of course." I turned and started to go down to make breakfast. "Hey, Robert, do you like birds?"

"They're okay, why?"

"Oh nothing, I'll see you downstairs."

So far, the lighthouse's electrical system was still working properly, but we wasted a lot of energy on the stupid light. There has to be more people around.

As expected, there were plenty of eggs and thick-cut maple bacon. Combined with canned chilies, a whole bunch of different cheeses (are you kidding me? Oregon Blue Vein? Hooligan from CT?), real coffee and toast, the meal should be transcendent. I sat in the living room waiting for Robert and basking in the aroma of caffeinated bliss.

"Hey, John!" It was Robert from upstairs. "Have you looked outside? Have you seen the birds?"

"What birds?"

He came thundering down the stairs and went to the porch window. "The yard is full of fucking birds."

"Yes, but there's no zombies."

It took him a second. He looked at me, looked outside and went to the kitchen via the mudroom muttering something under his breath.

Breakfast was great and once again, I had that full and safe feeling. We're going to find a way of surviving this.

"Well, let's go shut the light off and see what the day brings."

We checked to see if the coast was clear and made our way to the tower.

"Robert, what's up with the gulls?"

"No clue, I think they are afraid, like us." Robert went inside and I walked over to check out the birds and the scene on the wharf. Wow, I actually had a whole day to fuck off and a real lunch and real dinner to look forward to, so not bad John, not bad. Then I looked up.

"Oh shit No! Hey, Robert, the light worked! You have got to see this." Here we go again.

I heard him approach from behind.

"Oh fuck! You have got to be shitting me!"

While the light did not attract any boats, it had done wonders for the zombie population. The two hundred or so undead that was on the wharf at sundown had now multiplied into at least a few thousand. They were everywhere, on every side street with more coming in.

"Well, at least we had no plans on going to the mainland," he said half stunned.

"Robert, we should have known." Another mistake, our luck could not last forever. Just standing there was enough to excite the masses. The din of so many hoarse, dead voices, grew louder and louder. I could see others running to the wharf. The crowd grew so large that every half minute or so, one was pushed in and carried out to sea. Yes, we were definitely not going anywhere near land now. The wind suddenly shifted and we were again immersed in the putrid smell of decaying flesh. My work in forensic anthropology had put me around the not so recently dead before and it's kind of funny, but compared to animals, humans have this almost sweet undertone to their odor, I guess it must be what we eat. I intentionally took a big whiff; something was a bit odd. Yeah, there was the overwhelming flesh is starting to go south bouquet, but with a distinct industrial undertone, something almost metallic. Strange.

We went down to the boat, Robert to recheck things, and me to grab some binoculars, the video camera, and a notebook. By now, we were feeling more comfortable with our water buffer. None had come close, but I made a mental note to take a look in a few hours and see what changes the low tide brought. For now, I planned on making the most of our unique situation and spending as much time as possible observing what zombies do. Zombies! You have got to be kidding me! Why did I once think they were so cool? All the movies I watched. All the books I read. I fucking hate zombies.

When I got to the tower balcony, I made myself comfortable and scanned the mob onshore. They had calmed down a bit and were slightly dispersing, although more were stumbling into town every minute. I tried to make a count but ended up confused once I got to two hundred. Yes, once again, if only we had thought our actions through.

I gazed down on the mass of former humanity and thought that a well-educated man like me, with all I had been through, would have some quotable insight into my current situation, but all I could come up with was, Fuck Me.

After a couple of hours observing and note taking, I started to doze and daydream. During my early days of sobriety, I got lots of advice, but the one that stuck and eventually played a key role in my recovery was the concept of mindfulness, staying in the moment. It's a very Zen thing about walking that razor's edge, no past, no future, just the present. It was hard for me to do with school, research, and a lack of any real significant social life, but eventually, it started to stick. In the end, I thought, what if the whole world was practicing this 'mindfulness'? Well, I guess we all are mindful now and that razor is literally cutting us in half. By now, the sun was starting to bake and I decided that it was best to retreat and come back later in the day.

As I approached the house, I could hear music coming from the windows that Robert had opened to cool the place down, and help reduce the stench. I recognized it as one of the few operas I knew. It was Caruso singing the aria 'Che gelida manina' from Puccini's *La Boheme*. I sat down on the meticulously cut grass that's going to need mowing in a day or two and in about a minute, I was weeping uncontrollably. How can something so beautiful be so easily lost? Maybe it's not lost. It's just going to be misplaced for a long while.

I went inside and made a sandwich of sliced aged wild boar and some cheeses like, *Constant Bliss* from Vermont, *Vermont Shepherd* from, well Vermont. Yes, of course the mustard was Grey Poupon.

"Hey, we got at least a thousand, more coming in. Think we should turn the light back on tonight? Kind of like fishing for zombies," I yelled.

"NO!" Robert was lost in the music.

Ah, screw it, and I went back to the tower office. I half-heartedly turned the TV on. He had a dish on the back of the house and probably got a billion channels. After scanning several dozen with nothing but snow, I was shocked to get a picture. It was WNBC out of New York City. It didn't show a picture, just a blue screen with the words, Please Stand By, and the station's logo. I started to think about The City. I haven't been there in a couple of years. There still had to be thousands and thousands of people there, holding up in some high-rise apartments, waiting to dehydrate or starve to death. They are stuck with no hope of ever being able to leave their fortress alive. God, was I lucky? Just chance? Was all this really just chance? Sure, I had done what was needed to stay alive, but without a lucky break or two, I would be trapped sitting in my condo in Bangor waiting to die.

I went back up top, once some clouds moved in and the temp and humidity started to drop. This time, I brought along a folding beach chair from the mudroom. The video camera was still up there, and without thinking, I just picked it up and began to shoot. Just a general overview of the town and our little wafer thin slice of paradise. After some inane commentary, I heard a beep and I saw I had reached the end of the cassette. For maybe five minutes, I just looked at it, and the tiny blank screen that stared back at me. I was tempted to rewind, but was not sure of what I would find and where I would be. The more I thought about it, the more the whole concept scared the shit out of me. I broke out of my brain-fart and rummaged through the camera bag, eventually finding another cassette and I ventured into one more episode of how the hell do you unwrap these things? Why does everything seem hermetically sealed these days and made to last a hundred years. Oh well, maybe considering, never mind, popped in another tape. Scanning back and forth, I kept noticing some flashes. I assumed one of the zombies was playing with something that reflected, so I had to see this. I grabbed my binoculars and started searching, and I quickly found the source.

Oh, fuck me! My God, it's people! It looked like two, a man and maybe a woman on the roof of a three story red brick building that looked to be an old warehouse. I waved and they signaled back. Yep, the undead generally don't wave back. Holy Crap, real people! Once I was pretty sure they knew I had seen them, I raced down to get Robert. How had someone held out surrounded by Hell for over a week? At least, I almost always had a change of scenery.

Puccini had ended and he was in the living room looking through a large rack of CD's.

"You are not going to believe this, but we got survivors in town!"

"What," he stood and looked at me as if I was stoned, "are you sure?"

"They're on the roof of some building and definitely not the undead."

"Then come on!" and we raced for the tower. As we entered, it dawned on me how careless I had been in leaving my shotgun up on the railing. Yes, I had the Ruger, but I made that mistake before and it almost killed me.

When we got to the top, I handed him my binoculars. "Just to left of the main road about four blocks up, red brick, on the roof."

"Okay, got them...Holy cow! Hey, he's holding up something...looks like a walkie-talkie. It's got be a radio. And he's holding up fingers. You look, you've got better eyesight."

He handed me the binoculars. "Okay, it looks to be a one three, yeah a one three, I think."

"Let's get to the boat."

As I raced down the stairs, I was overcome with this giddy feeling of anticipation, kind of like you get as a kid on Christmas morning.

As we got to the boat, I could tell that the zombies were sensing something was up, as they became louder and more active than usual. We went below deck and Robert got the radio going.

"This is *Providence*, do you read me? Lighthouse to you guys on the roof, do you read me?"

"Thank God! We read you, *Providence*, Bill and Barbara here, over."

"Well, you got Robert and John here."

"We were beginning to lose hope, nice to hear your voice. So, you guys are the Einstein brothers that thought to turn the lighthouse on!"

"I'm afraid so. Sorry. What's your status?"

"The building we're on top of is my Army Navy store. We got plenty of freeze-dried and survival shit, but running low on water. Our purification system hasn't worked from the very start. We had planned to make a run for it to the lighthouse. I guess that's now all changed."

"Yeah, Bill. Let's put our heads together. You armed?"

"Shit, we got more weapons than God, a bit of an obsession of mine. At first, I thought we might be able to take out the locals, and make a run for it, but your arrival changed all that. Not your fault really, we have had several boats stop by, but no one stayed. Turning on the light sealed the deal."

While Robert traded info and continued to brainstorm with Bill, I went up top and scanned the shore. They would have a four block run to make it to the water. It was a straight shot, straight run, maybe two hundred yards and all. Everything's downhill. I mean you could fall and roll to the water. It should be no problem, except for the zombies wandering about. Just don't trip. I'm sure it's just paranoia but it seems they are real fast at picking up when something is going on, and that's not good.

I left the boat and went to the southernmost part of the island, still within sight of our onshore friends. The zombies followed me, a massive mess jostling for position to be the first to greet me in case I decided to swim over and pay a visit. Their obsessive one mindedness is fascinating. I bet if I ran from one side to the other that I could get them moving in unison, kind of like dancing in a chorus line. This all-consuming constant drive to obtain living flesh had to be a key to their defeat. I continued to study the town as I reviewed our options. Maybe they could move from building to building, do it at night and get closer, or even make the whole run at night. We might be able to join forces and thin the crowd a bit. We could shoot from the boat, and Barbara and Bill from the roof. Robert and I could hoist the sails and distract them, draw a majority of the undead away from the wharf. We had many shitty options to choose from.

Wait a minute. A short distance down the beach, the town became less Bar Harbor and more like a real working fishing village. You know, fishing boats, cluttered docks and a seventies era rusted Buick. Surrounded by a high chain link fence was a large industrial sized propane tank, one of those big guys that everyone draws off of. Boy, if we could blow it up and shock wave the town that would qualify as one hell of a distraction. My assumption was that these things are designed not to explode, but it wouldn't hurt to run it up the flagpole and see who salutes.

Robert was on deck staring at the harbor with binoculars.

"You know, with enough of the right kind of distraction, we might thin them out, and give them a chance."

"Huh?" He was moving the glasses in such a way that I knew he was running their most probable route.

"Move our uninvited guests on the wharf away. Clear a lane. There's a large propane tank south of us. Pull them south with the boat, and blow up the tank. It might distract enough of the crowd and they might make it."

Robert looked over to where I was pointing, thought for a minute and scratched his head. "Yeah, it might work. It would be one hell of a bang. The only problem is that those tanks are not designed to go bang, and we don't have the firepower to puncture it. I do like the idea of trying to draw them off with the boat. I'll talk to Bill and see what he thinks."

Robert went below deck and I continued to study the village. The undead had become a writhing mass. I had no clue how anyone could make it through without being scratched or bitten. About ten minutes later, Robert returned topside, a big smile on his face.

"Well, Bill's got a big toy that he thinks will do, an M82A1. He has the right kind of rounds to do the job." His eyes were wide with excitement.

"An M what?" I asked.

"In layman's terms, a really big-ass gun. And he's got armor piercing bullets, phosphorous tracers." He was almost drooling. "The best part is, and this is GREAT, they are both going to do the run with BXPs akimbo, extended clips and modified rounds, shit, this just might work." Robert paced back and forth. He almost sounded jealous.

I just folded my arms. "I'm assuming a BXP is not a bike."

"South African version of a MAC-10, better than ours, whole apartheid arms embargo thing. He certainly didn't buy the cheap stuff." With the way Robert's voice sounded, Bill did not indeed buy the cheap stuff. I was just curious how people got a hold of the not so cheap stuff, because hell, I would be happy to get the cheap stuff.

"Okay, so what's our role?"

"A bit up in the air right now. He agrees the boat would be a mighty big help, give our friends something to focus on. My guess is we motor out, draw some off, and Bill blows the tank. This gets everyone's attention and they come running in our direction. All this distraction clears a lane for them, they storm the street, mayhem ensues, and they make for the water. Apparently, both are very good swimmers and hope to use the current to get to us."

We both stood in silence just staring at the village. All I could think was damn that's a lot of zombies! The wind died and the stench rose. Go decay go!

"So, Robert, even with their super cool toys, what do you think?"

"Well…we need to put on a good show and I mean a really good show. Okay, we get all the attention, herd the zombies, and the tank goes. If they keep their cool, they just might make it."

Robert was back on the radio and I was getting nervous. How can we screw up this time? Yes, Robert and I had our moment on the glory road and without the fancy armament, but not the massed horde these guys will have.

"This is it." I heard Robert say. Here we go. It would be a run in broad daylight and ASAP. Why wait for more to gather? They would like to see where they were running. Our job would be to do our best to distract our mainland friends, then a big ass boom and we meet somewhere in the middle. Great! We had a nice ambiguous plan with a couple of hundred zombies thrown in. Whoever Bill and Barbara were, they were right. Once I got on deck and scanned the town, it was go time. I could see most of their escape path and all these zombies running as if to block them. Huh?

My mood was not as enthusiastic as my Captain was. Too many unknown variables, but hell, best shot is best shot. So…we made a show of it. Robert wanted to have as much control of the boat as possible and opted for no sails. Sirens blowing and me shouting, waving, and dancing, probably over the top since a little wave would have gotten the same results. Getting closer than we ever have been before, they were whipped into a frenzy. If only the ladies had liked me like this when they weren't dead! They followed us en masse. Then another funny thing happened. We got very close, maybe ten feet and it was more than clear they desperately wanted us, but no one really tried. Not one of the hundreds of undead made a concerted effort to jump to us. A bunch were pushed in by the ever increasing crowd and it would have to be a standing jump since the masses made a running start impossible, but no one really tried. It was as if they instinctively knew we were just out of reach. We were the only show in town, but they loved us and followed. When we got about even with the tank, I began to think of more immediate concerns; like just how big a boom it would be, I mean there's boom and BOOM.

"Hey, Robert, about how big of an explosion are we considering here?" As if in answer, the radio crackled. "We are go. Firing at target."

We looked at each other and dove for the deck. Probably a good thing too, because I don't think Bill wanted to hurt us, but he had his shot and that was the time. It was lightning fast. The heat and pressure ripped over us and I instantly smelled something like burnt hair. The boat dangerously listed to the opposite side. Thank God, we didn't have the sails up. From my angle face down on the deck, I could see zombies on fire; just roasted in half, still running towards the flame. As I watched in amazement at the self-immolations, this little annoying voice in the back of my mind was saying, 'I always thought you counted to three or something.'

The boat was a mess. The rigging had taken a serious hit. Once again, great judgment about the sails, Robert. Without saying a word, he jumped up and turned the boat around, kicked her in high gear and cruised back up the channel. I stood on the bow. It didn't take long to see Bill and Barbara running down the road. They were a killing machine. By akimbo, weapons in both arms, I mean fucking AKIMBO! Blazing away, short controlled bursts, one goal, intense focus and they made it with ease. Not a single zombie got even close. Both entered the water with large black duffels that looked really heavy when they were running and I was surprised when they floated.

We pulled them on board.

"I'm thinking...Three. Could be wrong, but doesn't someone go one, two, three before you ignite the world?" I think Robert was pissed!

Hoping to diffuse the situation, I said, "Hi, I'm John, and not only did you almost kill us, but you really fucked up Robert's boat, a boat he happened to appreciate a great deal!"

The guy gave me a sullen look, "Hi, I'm Bill, this is Barbara. Pleased to meet you." He extended his hand.

I took it. "Thanks, okay. Formalities aside. Bites? Cuts? Scratches? You know we will find out sooner or later." Wow, that actually sounded like I have done this before.

She was quickly examining herself with much interest and excitement. "I'm good, I think, and you, Bill?"

He just looked out toward the village with its teaming undead, eyes not really focusing on anything. "Holy shit! We did it! Barbara, your calm, controlled bursts. You were magnificent. You never skipped a beat." Pride just welled up in his voice.

Robert and I stared at each other. These guys are really clueless. Don't they know they just nuked us and are happy as clams?

Nonplussed, I looked at Robert, and then to Bill and Barbara. "Okay, you guys up for a real Maine lobster dinner?"

B&B, as we started to call them, were both in their late fifties or early sixties. Bill was about my height, medium build with a narrow face that reminded me of Vincent Price. Barbara was short, maybe five-two, thin with long blonde hair. Turns out, friends had hooked them up and their first date was a moose-hunting trip. They would celebrate their fortieth wedding anniversary on the fourth of July.

That was that, really nothing more to be said. Yes, we had work to do on the boat, but we had a safe place to do it and we helped save two lives, not a bad day overall. When they opened the duffel bags, out popped two machine guns, Bill later mentioned something about them being German made. All right, more machine guns! First, with Roy and Hammer, now these guys. How does every other person in Maine seem to have automatic weapons? How come I didn't get mine? Yes, I was not born here, but I had been in state for seventeen years. Surely, I qualify.

So as it turned out, they saw the storm clouds coming, put the obvious one and one together and knew what was going down. Like with us, it just went to pot too fast. B&B had it going good.

They were refinishing the upper two floors of their store, a nineteenth century warehouse, when everything ended. They were going to rent out the third floor and take the top for themselves. Hang out, party on the roof, with incredible views, and sell all kinds of stuff to the tourists, whom they genuinely liked, and live the highlife.

"When it came, it was like a tidal wave, calm one minute, then everything is just gone," Barbara described the zombie overthrow of God's Haven, Maine. One second, it was okay to be on the street, the next no, never.

They had seen the downfall from a deeply personal level. Twenty-three years in the same small town. Same people in the same coffee shop, same fishmonger, butcher, dentist, best friends... gone. Bye, Bye. Now it was all Brutal Planet. Robert and I were kept in transition, and shed our losses. The hurt and the pain were not going away, but we weren't dwelling on it. We had to keep moving, no time to think or reflect. Maybe we had it easier. On to the next adventure. I hope I make it to the next round. It was around now that I think I started to like fucking up zombies. My body count was getting acceptable.

Yes, I guess I could be hard-core. It still just bugged me that we were going out like this. It did not seem fair or just. Maybe if an alien species with advanced technology invaded, it would be okay, but not like this?

June 3rd – 4th

I decided to keep my word and spend what time I had observing them. Besides, the scientist in me was dying to see how zombies behave when not agitated. I mostly did this from the top of the tower, but occasionally I crept to the boat for a closer look. I tried to stay out of sight since I wanted to see them au naturel. Once spotted, it generally took around an hour for them to calm down, but some never did. They just stood there, glaring or pacing back and forth, always looking to the particular place they had last seen me.

I set up a small tarp I found in the tool shed for shade and sat for hours with my binoculars, video camera and notebook. Just observing and letting my mind wander down certain paths, other areas were off limits for now. The balcony became my semi-private sanctuary. Sometimes, I would stare out to sea, listen to the surf and pretend I was on vacation and Elizabeth was taking a nap back at our hotel room. Once she woke, we would go for a nice seafood dinner and maybe take a sunset stroll along the beach. The future would be bright; I was losing weight, I had tenure, grant money and at least two articles ready to go. If I stayed with this fantasy long enough, it became real to me. The people I loved were alive. I would get together with my family for the fourth of July and introduce them to Liz. Everything was okay. It felt good to relax, breathe, and dream. The world was normal again. Then something would distract me and I would turn around.

The Buddhist have a discourse called the Upajjhatthana Sutta. In it are, *The Five Remembrances:* I will lose my youth, my health, everything I hold dear and beloved and then life itself, by the very nature of being human. But there is a fifth: I am the owner of my actions and good or bad I shall become their heir. What a lineage I have sired over the last eleven days and I am no longer afraid. I'm going to make it through this.

Eventually, I started to give some of the more distinctive zombies' names. There was the School kid zombie, holding one of those thick candy canes that places like Ye Old Candy Shoppe sells and dressed in what appeared to be an authentic British school uniform, similar to the guy from AC/DC. He had most of his right face gone and just walked from one end of the wharf to another holding on to the candy cane which was now cemented to this hand. There was Spinner, a young topless woman with one breast missing who only moved in a spinning fashion, almost as if she was dancing. There was Meatloaf, missing his left arm but looking exactly like the rocker, I mean the young Meatloaf not the *Fight Club* Meatloaf. Lurch, nuff said. One of my favorites was this dude in a business suit who still had his thick black framed glasses on. He would do the same circuit around town, only stopping when he got to the edge of the wharf, then stand there for a few minutes looking around with this kind of 'What the fuck' look and then off again. Perhaps the strangest was this one dude who looked like an old homeless guy and didn't quite act like a zombie. He would come and go and moved around more than the others did. His skin didn't seem gray, had no visible wounds and a homeless guy in this part of Maine? I pointed him out to the others when they came to visit. We were evenly split over whether he was actually one of the undead or not. Really weird. At dinner, we made up stories as to how they got here and who they really were, but never once did we imagine that given the opportunity, they would not tear us to pieces.

We didn't shoot them, just be a waste of ammunition, although I really wanted to play around with the machine guns just for shits and grins. There was only one exception, some poor schmuck stuck in a small Plexiglas booth that sold tickets for Cptn' Ahab's Whale Watching Cruses. We figure he was in there when the shit hit the fan and had to watch the world come to an end with nothing to do but sit, stare at a bunch of stupid brochures and wait for death. We couldn't see how he became infected. I figured we owed it to him, and for Bill, it was an easy shot. What really bothered me was that we all knew what was happening and yes, it went way faster than anticipated, but whale watching? WTF?

The longer that I watched and learned, the more grave our situation was becoming. It's not that the crowd on shore was growing to dangerous proportions, if there was a such a thing, or they were going to find a way to get to us. We had all assumed decay would rapidly take its course and we could reclaim the mainland. Just give it a little time, maybe six months and they will be taken care of was the general idea. The big money question was, how much time? Everything I now saw suggested that the time was going to be longer than expected, maybe a lot longer.

I had always thought they went around looking for prey or generally screwing off like a zombie, but no, not these guys. During the day, the only time I could see them, they just kind of hung out. They didn't move, explore or wander off to find the local mall. Most laid around or sat down. Maybe because we were so close, we kept them transfixed. Maybe they were kind of lazy, their bodies not wanting to expend energy needlessly. I mean it's not like they stood there staring at us. They just didn't cover a lot of territory. They definitely got excited when we were out in the open and moving around. Occasionally, you would see one or two move off, like to chase a bird or something, but for the most part, every morning it seemed to be the same old gang, plus maybe another forty or so. You could attract more, such as when we blew up the propane tank, and some would drift off but the majority would just hang out until something else distracted them.

I also noted that they tended to stay in the shade. At first, I thought it was just a coincidence, but the more I watched, the more I realized this was part of their nature. An attribute pronounced during the hottest part of the day, like some part of their reptile brain was reacting to the heat. The bigger more intact zombies tended to get the best spots, just pushed the smaller out into the sun. This whole conservation of energy thing was bugging me. The more I watched the more I was concerned. I was really starting not to like the trend.

On the second day, I noticed something else. When we exploded the propane tank, because of its proximity to the water, we killed a lot of fish. These fish were now washing up on shore and the zombies had found some and were eating them. It never occurred to me that they ate anything but people. If they ate fish, what else are they eating?

Later that day, I got part of my answer. The big guy I called Lurch always hung out near this tourist trap crystal shop. It had a nice big awning which gave lots of shade and he was usually sitting on the corner which I imagined had more air circulation, i.e., cooler. I decided to play with him and see if I could get his attention. I took a compact from one of the upstairs bathrooms, and using the mirror, tried to get a reflection off the shop window or some of the crystals inside. Kind of like the game, I used to play in grade school with my watch face and the blackboard. I thought the distance was too far but I was bored so what the hell. It took me about thirty minutes to get it right but eventually I did get some of the crystals in the store window to reflect. Lurch didn't notice but another zombie did, this one a young girl. She ran toward the window and collided with Lurch. I don't know if this startled him, maybe he was deep in thought, but he suddenly became animated, gave a huge roar and attacked the girl. I couldn't believe his speed and ferocity. He simply grabbed her by the shoulders, lifted her up and tore a monstrous chunk out of her neck.

Okay, about Lurch. He is big, white, maybe twenty-five to thirty, well over six-five, short blond hair, total muscle and, with the tattoos, has a very Aryan thing going on. One thing that bothered me was that Lurch had, at all times, this huge erection. You see most of his khakis were in shreds and well, there he was. The piercings actually went with the overall look quite well. Was the Limbic System still working?

Squirming in his arms, she looked like an extra large doll. He then threw her to the ground, grabbed one of her arms and tore it from her body in a mighty twisting motion. He stared at the arm for a couple of seconds and then started to eat it. What the hell? The girl remained motionless for maybe a minute. When she started to crawl, he threw her arm away and pounced on her. I heard him roar again as he started gnawing at her hip. He kept this up till he could pop the femoral head and twist and tear the leg away. Satisfied, he staggered off, eating the leg. Several others noticed this and attacked what remained of the girl. Fuck, they eat each other. In my time at the lighthouse, I never saw this happen again. If they could use each other as a food source, this shit is going to last a lot longer than anyone has suspected. Then things got worse.

In the late afternoon, a storm rolled in off the ocean. The temperature cooled down and in fifteen minutes, it started to rain, big heavy squalls of the stuff. I was just about to seek shelter in the downstairs office when I decided to check out how zombies like rain. Zombies like rain. Almost all of them were now standing, heads tilted up to the rain, mouths wide open. Lurch had actually gone under a waterspout, just letting the stream flow into his mouth. Could he drown like that? Zombies hydrate! We are in deep shit.

At dinner that night, I talked about Lurch and what had happened. I didn't go into the other stuff until I had more data. Bill and Barbara hadn't seen them attack each other but admitted never really watching the creatures. While they were trapped in their store, they thought it was best to stay out of sight, probably a very good idea. Robert and I hadn't had the opportunity to observe them in any detail and at the time, I really didn't care how zombies interacted. Bill did tell us about one woman whose head was nearly torn off and she flopped in such a way that she was always looking up.

"She must have caught a glimpse of us or something because all she did was to circle our building and paw at the walls. Others would come over and see what's up but they soon lost interest. She did this for days and days and days. There were a couple of times I was up on the roof at night and I could still hear her." He leaned back, put his hands behind his head and stared at the ceiling. I thought he was going to say something else, but Bill just seemed to drift off into thought.

"Yeah, we noticed that. They just lock on to something till distracted. It's almost like a child fixated on some flashy toy till mommy gives him something else to look at." Robert reached out and poured himself another glass of wine, looked at me and winked.

"Some of them lock on and never get distracted." We hadn't talked about why I did not drink, but he knew and now he was just busting my balls. After all we had been through, he was my closest living friend and earned the right, oh, but I will retaliate.

In order not to press our luck and to keep the town relatively quiet, all of us decided to be as inconspicuous as possible, difficult considering the size of the island and its proximity to shore. To get to my spot on the balcony without one seeing me was almost impossible.

"Are they thinking?" Barbara asked as she finished her fourth glass of Bordeaux.

"I don't know, it more than likely is just an involuntary reaction, a simple neural response to stimuli," I replied as I looked at her glass and seriously considered my almost six years of sobriety.

"Well, they are well coordinated physically but I have yet to see any evidence of organization," Bill chimed in, still staring at the ceiling. "A real organized group effort and they could easily have gotten to us."

"I don't know, Bill, our doors are awfully strong."

"If they collectively knew we were there, they would have found a way. Organized or not, they would never stop trying." Bill took a gulp of wine and seemed to study a painting on the wall behind me intently. "They'll never leave as long as we're here," he said to no one in particular.

"I wonder what they would be like in numbers against a fixed target? You know, like being behind a good fence," I said as I looked around the room for more soda.

"Well, John, you'd better have a damn strong fence...and a high one, electric wouldn't hurt. They would just keep gathering, more and more." He took another gulp. "Around sunrise three days ago, a truck came through Main Street. Big tires, all souped-up, ready to rumble. They went by so fast I didn't have time to get a good look. About twenty minutes later, they hit. There was thousands, maybe tens of thousands. Like water, they just flowed around any obstacle, buildings, light poles, cars…all heading south, in the trucks direction. The horde almost swept us clean of zombies! Maybe only a hundred or so left, scattered." Once again, Bill sort of drifted off.

"They were relatively docile now because some part of them instinctively knows they cannot get to us, but remove the barrier and all bets are off."

"Does anyone think there is someplace on the mainland safe? Protected?" Barbara's face was flushed from the wine and she sounded very tired.

Robert chimed in, "Well, there's Cheyenne Mountain in Colorado Springs; Raven Rock, Mount Weather, missile silos, various military bases. I bet Offutt is still with us, Hell, I bet they even used The Greenbriar although that is one party I would not want to be invited to. Islands, both natural and manmade, I mean cruise ships." He paused for a second, before continuing, "A lot of guns in this country, and a lot of people who know how to use them. I do believe America is going to show a different response than the infected has yet seen."

"So, Robert, are you saying Area 51 is more than likely still with us?"

"Yes, John."

"Ha, I knew it! They called us crazy, but now who's crazy?"

He ignored me. "We talked briefly with some small middle of nowhere communities, and all but two were doing well." Robert scratched his stubble. "There has to be plenty of remote places in the mountains or the backwoods, and I would imagine there are survivalists who are happy as a pig in shit that this went down. I just wouldn't want to be near any city trying to weather this storm."

"Well, I guess that just about eliminates the whole East Coast. You know, it only took a modicum of attention to see what was happening. I'm sure some people got ready. Hell, we did." I stopped for a second. "Although I don't know how many of us are still around?" Of course, I was not about to mention that I had originally planned to see this through with a pistol, a bathtub full of water and some fucking canned mushrooms.

"What's really bothering me is that we all believe they attack for food and food only, I don't think that's the case. I mean, Robert and I have seen them attack one person, take a bite and immediately set off for another human, another target. Kind of like they are aware that one bite gives them yet another recruit. They seem to have so much anger and rage. Yeah, it sucks being a zombie, but where does that come from?"

"Some aspect of the virus?" Answered Bill.

"Obviously," I answered in a voice that seemed distant and detached.

"Do you think they still have a soul?" Barbara's voice slurred a little.

"No!" Her question jolted me back to reality and my reply was harsh and had required no thinking, but her question was a valid one.

"I'm sorry. I don't think they are who they used to be. Maybe their fury comes from the knowledge that they have no soul. They had some part of humanity that the living still poses. Maybe by attacking us they can regain something of their former lives."

Robert stood. "Okay, enough of this philosophical masturbation, I'm going to bed."

The perverted back of my mind wondered if he had just made a Freudian slip.

"Yeah, me too." If anyone wants to join me tomorrow on the lighthouse and add their two cents to my notes, you are more than welcome. Good night."

June 5th -6th

During this time, Robert made triple sure that the boat was as ready as possible and then hung out and read. Weather held and life was good. We knew that a new radar was top priority and would probably get one from the boats moored near us, but that was all Robert's domain. Bill and Barbara spent most of their time wandering around the small island, sometimes just standing there, arm in arm, looking back at the town. I thought they acted a bit strange, as if there is such a thing as normal these days, and they were pissing me off for not staying out of the undead's view, but… I still did not know them, so I gave them some slack. Something was going on. I just couldn't put my finger on it.

I spent most of my time on top of the lighthouse daydreaming, watching, videoing, and taking notes. More than once, my mind wandered back to Barbara's comment about the soul. There they were by the thousands, as if forced by some invisible hand to crowd the docks and shoreline. Had they been in a zoo, I would have had nothing but pity for them; not being allowed to wander free in their own environment, to do what nature intended them to do. So many. They were the majority now. I thought back to the Matheson classic *I Am Legend* and the protagonist, Robert, sitting in his cell, looking at the masses of vampires and awaiting his death. Maybe everything has switched and I am the one who belongs in the zoo. Were these really sentient beings? Could there be some way we could connect with each other? Was destroying them a moral issue that needed to be considered? NO! Funny I should think that way, since all they had done is rain pain and sorrow on the world and me. I guess that's what made me human, and maybe why I found such satisfaction in destroying them.

I quickly inventoried our storeroom and as expected, supplies were going fast. I guess the unrelenting fear/tension/confusion/despair had made us hungry and we gorged. I was also amazed it only took a few stress-free days for me to revert to the old ways and I was once again throwing away good food. I had a mantra a few years back that I now needed to lean on. It's from the poet David Whyte, *'Alertness is the hidden discipline of familiarity.'* We are still, and may always be, walking that razor's edge.

For the last couple of days, Robert and I had manually run the generator to keep the desalinization unit active and the food cold. This was cool as it gave us something to do and made time relevant. It also saved considerably on diesel which should easily last a month or three, but we only had enough food for about two weeks. The harbor had a few moored boats, too small to be of any real value. There were a couple of bigger ones, but they were docked and our friends on shore ensured we weren't going there. The crowd was not getting larger, but also not getting smaller. Both Robert and I were rested and wanted to move on, not get caught by comfort and routine. We knew what we were running from, but not where we were running to. I, for one, felt a growing tension between R&J and B&B, and needed to leave. Yes, we had a good deal going on here, but I need something permanent.

Dinner was a pleasant surprise. Bill had caught stripers that afternoon and did a magnificent job cooking them. Once finished, we fell into a bull session about our situation. I let Robert lead off.

"Well, we all knew staying here was not an option. This is our fifth night here, John and my sixth. I think we should get ready to head south. We can resupply as we go. Our raid of Tenants Harbor and running into this place proved that food and fuel should not be a problem, if we are cautious. We have the weapons, and best of all, we have some knowledge about what is what. Boat's in okay shape with plenty of room. We should go while the weather is good, while we are all in good health. Get down and settled in before storm season starts."

"I don't know, Robert, we got a real nice stable set-up here, which is a very rare thing in these times. Very rare. Who knows what lies to the south? How bad is it? Not many people lived near the harbor and look how many we got! There're going to be in the millions. I agree we are lucky and should eventually leave, but not right now. Let's see what we can find around here, use this as our headquarters and really think this through. Maybe there are more people, more survivors. Winters are not that bad, I live here." Bill spoke rapidly and had an undertone of desperation in his voice. Where did this come from?

"We need a solid plan. We Need Information!" He pounded his fist into his palm. "We can't just go running off and hope for the best. Hell, look at our dinner from the sea. We can last here a lot longer than you think. I mean what do you guys really know? Ever lived off the land? Both of you are just academics!"

Yes, and you are a shopkeeper, albeit one with a ton of guns. Robert was quiet. You could tell he also noticed something.

"Well, there are some towns we could check out that are just a day or two away. You know, see what's moored. Do some fine tuning on *Providence*." I was trying to appease and calm Bill. I had no clue what had set him off, but seeing that we were all armed and both he and Barbara had had plenty of wine and who knows what else, this seemed like a good option.

"Yes, yes you two could reconnoiter, get some supplies, and see what's up out there. Barbara lived and sailed around the Portland area and knows it like the back of her hand. We'll put our heads together and find us a solid, safe destination."

"Okay," said Robert calmly and a bit slowly, "but hurricane season starts in a few weeks and we no longer have a weather service to tell us how big, when and where. I think we all agree that staying this far north for the winter is problematic at best. The boat isn't designed for that and we don't have enough fuel and food. One little thing goes wrong in the middle of January and we're screwed."

"Yes, we know, just a little more time, a chance to rest." Bill's eyes darted back and forth and it looked to me that he was at the point of sweating. We both knew that Barbara would do anything Bill suggested. I had never seen them apart. She just sat there, passively nodding.

After a tense dessert of canned fruit and lime Jell-O, Robert and I went down to the boat on the pretext of getting her ready to leave early tomorrow morning for a raid south.

"What the hell was that all about?" growled Robert.

"No idea. It might be the wine going to his head." We headed below deck.

"I call bullshit. They have been squirrely since we met them. Barbara has got to be on some pharmaceutical and Bill's rubber band might have broken a while back." Robert opened the cabinet and took out his handle of Dewars.

"Well, that might be true, but I don't think they are any kind of threat. Think about it, they are tired, their brains are fried and they have seen enough." I spied Robert's scotch. It's the fucking end of the world John, so I made a silent vow to take the next pot stash I found.

"We will be fine. We've got the team thing down and when we come back, I'm sure they will want to leave. I know I am looking forward to someplace with a little more room."

"You said it, brother. I'm thinking something a little more tropical too!"

"I know you think it's stupid, but I would like to see how the cold weather affects them. What does freezing do?"

"You are right as usual, it's stupid."

"I think I'll crash on the boat tonight, give them some time alone."

Robert took a big shot of scotch and headed to his cabin. "Let's leave at dawn, lot of ground to cover, good night."

"Sounds good, let me get some of my stuff and let them know what's up. Good night, Robert, sweet dreams!"

I exchanged some small talk with B&B and went over our plans as detailed as I could. They were going to stay up a bit and play some cards. I noticed that someone had opened another bottle of wine. Ah, well, why should I care? I took my time heading back to the boat, moving cautiously, letting my eyes adjust to the night. Before boarding, I sat on the dock stairs. The night was warm with stars, a nice breeze and very Norman Rockwell. I could smell smoke. Somewhere north of us the horizon was interrupted by a huge blister of dull orange. No idea what's burning but it's big. I couldn't hear anything from the mainland, just the lapping of the water on the dock and boat. I wondered what they do at night. Do they sleep? If so, do they dream? So much, we don't know, I don't know. Somebody somewhere had to be paying attention, taking notes. Well, Robert, here we go again, another adventure waits. Trying not to wake him, I tiptoed to my bunk. I was tired and it didn't take me long to dream. I dreamt of Bangor.

Chapter 6 ~ Leaving Bangor

May 24rd

It took eighteen minutes for me to pack. I grabbed all I could in two of my largest backpacks and one of my expedition bags. In my stash was all my freeze-dried food, easily a month for one person, headlamp, and two sets of extra pain in the ass to get 4.5V batteries, and a sleeping bag. Of the three sleeping bags, I took the mid-weight. I included clothes made for rain, wind, and tropical stuff, camping stove, two fuel tanks, almost three liters, jump bag, and big first aid kit. I also packed books, mostly first aid and some plant guide books, and a whole variety of other crap I knew I would probably not need. It was eerily like going on a backpacking trip, the only difference being, I was not coming back. Outside, I could hear car horns, sirens and an occasional pop, usually more than one. I didn't lock the door, figured if some of my neighbors were going to stay, they would appreciate the water, and of course, they could have the mushrooms. I also left Burt's door unlocked, said a silent prayer and left.

I quadruple checked the Ruger and placed it on the passenger seat, and locked the doors. I have a 06 Subaru outback that I love and keep in good shape, a good thing too, since it looked like I was going to push it to its limit. Thank God, I had the foresight to keep the tank full. From the parking garage, it looked like most of my condo-mates had split. Just as I was to fire up the ignition and looked around for one last time, damn, that's the Washburn's car.

They were a nice elderly couple that lived on the third floor. I had watched their Corgi, Conrad, on a few occasions and we got to be friends. At least once a month, I would go over on a Sunday morning for fresh baked, whatever fruit is in season, scones, coffee and a discussion of the news of the past couple of weeks. They had lived in Maine their whole lives with tons of odd facts and interesting places to go in the area. They also kept me updated on the latest Unitarian Fellowship news. I attended the Fellowship once every couple of months. It turns out Mr. Washburn or Chip, was a Korean War hero, one of the 'Frozen Chosin'; Purple Heart, Silver Star and something else. His wife, Francis, told me, not him. Ah hell, I had to go check up on them. I saw them, what? Two days ago? Like everyone else, they were just scared and confused. It will just take a minute.

Somebody on the first floor was cranking the title track of Metallica's *Master of Puppets*. I could definitely smell pot and something else, kind of like plastic burning. By the time I arrived on the third floor, I was getting antsy and a hidden part of my brain was telling me some important information. One, that I had to go, two, don't be stupid, you don't owe these people anything, and three, the Ruger is in the car on the passenger seat. Did you lock the car? Just as I started to listen to my brain, I found myself in front of their door, so I knocked.

Nothing. Thank you, God.

Okay, I tried. Time to go. Shit.

This time, I pounded.

"Guys, it's John! It's Dr. Patrick!" I pounded again and waited. They had to be home unless they left with friends. I put my ear to the door. There was music, something classical. Conrad was not barking. In an instant, I just knew. I leaned against the door for a bit and closed my eyes. Holy Cow, I did not see that one coming. I always joked about life being cruel. Well now, I get to live the joke.

When I got outside things were changing fast. The roads were jammed with panicked people and yes, I had left the car unlocked. As the chaos mounted, you could smell the fear. Yeah, it was fear of the zombies, but I think even more, it was fear of the chaos, the unknown. Everybody was in the process of seriously losing their shit. I fired up the Subaru, went out the rear entrance, and across some neighbor's backyard to reach a side street I hoped would be less crowded. I had to get to the other side of town to meet the group and this was not going to be easy. I had never been there, but my GPS apparently had, almost. I was not receiving any audible commands and the connection was less than perfect, but I knew the general location. I slalomed around several abandoned cars and tried to tunnel vision just the road and direction. Right now, my goal was not to stop.

I came to a sudden stop. In front of me was an ambulance that looked like it had plowed into several cars, one of which was on fire. People were everywhere; some from the accident, some trying to help, but most were just confused. This was the first time I noticed what I was passing. I was in an average middle class neighborhood full of raised ranches and adequate lawns. There was a family a house ahead of me with what looked like a mother and two children just standing still, all in a row staring intently at something I couldn't see. On the other side of the street was an elderly woman on her back, just lying there with no one around. Was she from the accident? Was she dead? Several front doors were wide open. Everything felt strange, even time seemed different. I needed to focus and get moving, but I used the delay and called Elizabeth. Holy Shit, I got through, another miracle. The connection was crappy, but I told her I was on my way and how crazy things are. She said that there were some others also bogged down and that police scanners were already talking about infected within the city limits. She started giving me additional directions when the connection died. It's okay, I am kind of sure I know the way and besides, Liz knows I am coming. I just have to keep moving.

Okay, so I made a hard right, jumped the curb, and moved through the less crowded section of the roadblock. At maybe five miles per hour, I gave the crowd plenty of time to get out of my way. People started banging on the car and yell at me. I began to hyperventilate and the already copious sweating went into overdrive. I needed to stop and help. Should I stop and help? By now, I could see what the family was looking at; some kind of sedan with a camper trailer attached and lying unmoving next to it was a man. His body faced the underside of the trailer with some tools next to him. There appeared to be a large wet stain coming from the body down the short driveway, not blood. He did not move, and the family did not move. They seemed to be studying the body. A body. It really was a body and I can do nothing. How?

Heart attack? Stroke? The vehicle behind me was not so interested, and with horns blaring, hit me from behind. Yesterday this was a fender bender, but today it is a wakeup call, telling me that it is time to get my ass moving.

I decided to swing out and around Bangor rather than going straight through. I did everything I could to keep moving; avoid the main roads, screw stop signs, ignore red lights, curbs, small hedges, lawns, accidents, pedestrians, and anything else that would slow me down. If the other lane or sidewalk was open, I took it. Just keep moving. There was one slight deviation. In front of some nondescript house, by the walkway that led from the driveway to the front door was one of those jockey statues holding a ring. I hate those damn things. By now, my mind was having some issues with reality and it seemed like running this over was a good thing to do. Besides, it probably came with a black face and nobody is coming to your fucking suburban house on a fucking horse! This will at least be some stress relief. It was just then that my GPS found its voice, reminding me to make a left turn. This was just enough to bring me out of my brain fog and realize that most of these statues are made out of concrete, and who knows how serious the owners were when they planted the thing. Screw slavery and the equine class, keep focused. By now, my Tom Tom was helping me along, not just with direction, but giving me the false impression I was not alone. Man, I don't know who pressed the panic button, but it seems like everyone got the message at the same time.

It was during a shortcut, in some new suburb full of McMansions and immaculate emerald green lawns that I saw my first one. There was smoke from a side street and I glanced over. Nobody was behind me so I slowed down. About three houses up, a car had hit a utility pole, smoke and fire rising from under the crumpled hood. A woman was lying in the middle of the road with a small figure on top of her. Oh good. At first, I thought he was giving her CPR and I should stop and help. Suddenly, the child, probably around ten, looked up at me. Even from fifty yards or so, I could see blood running down his face and covering a grey New England Patriots t-shirt. In his hand was some grayish pinkish ropy material that I instantly knew was intestine. He jumped up and started running at me. Time to leave, so I hit the gas and in my rear view mirror, I saw him round the curve. Seeing them on the computer or TV is one thing, but in real life, wow! The kid ran like a sped up version of Forrest Gump with his head straight ahead and arms pumping away at his side. All that I could think of was how determined he is. A large black SUV bolted by me in the opposite direction doing at least sixty. The kid ran right into it. He disappeared from my rear view mirror for a second and then, thud! It was as if someone had dropped him from the sky. The force must have propelled him right over the SUV. As I pulled away, I caught a brief glimpse of the kid standing up.

Chapter 7 ~ Shopping

June 7th

I opened my eyes and tried to focus at the wood above me. No way can I make out the grain. Note to self, glasses are a major pain in the ass during an apocalypse. My eyesight has been going south since my mid thirties, without them I can't read. It was a major relief to score a pair in Tenents Harbor, an almost identical prescription. It was nice just to lie there, the gentle rocking of the boat, comfortable, safe, still sated from the night before. I began to see Bill's point of view. Why don't we hang out for another week or so and rest some more? I wasn't certain when hurricane season began, but we surely had time to get some place south for winter. I mean, shit, it's only June, or is it? What day was it? Thursday? It felt like a Thursday. If I got a calendar, I was fairly certain I could reconstruct the past couple of weeks. I wondered how long I could do this. Do I really care? Eventually, I heard Robert grunt, move around, and fart.

I stood, stretched (God that feels good), looked out a small side window (I guess you don't call them windows on boats) and glanced at my watch; six, and yet another clear 'hey gang let's broil on the boat' day. Robert entered from his cabin, yawned, scratched himself, and looked at me.

"God, John, you are some ugly in the morning."

"Well, with at least a little cleaning, my ugly goes away. Hung over?"

"A bit. I need a shower."

We started up to the house to get some real coffee, clean up and say goodbye. As soon as we got topside, the roar from the town began. The undead were generally quiet during the night, but upon seeing us, they got about as excited as I did slow dancing with

Mary McCarthy in the eighth grade. It was kind of like they remembered, 'Oh yeah, that's why I am hanging around.' We entered the kitchen and surveyed the damage from the night before.

"Did they go through another bottle of wine?"

"Who cares, we didn't buy it. What do you want for breakfast?" I was motivated to cook, and eat.

"Coffee, black."

"Omelet it is! Who knows when eggs are going to come our way, let alone cheese I can't pronounce."

So Robert went to shower and I cooked. This all seemed so normal; a frying pan, butter, toast, a spatula, a metal bowl, eggs, the smell of frying bacon. Halfway through, I just stopped and stared at all this crap spread out in front of me. Would I ever cook like this again? But just like thinking about today's date, why should I care? Once we had finished eating, it was my turn to bathe. For a second, I actually think Robert considered cleaning up the kitchen, but only for a second. I yelled up goodbye when I left and closed the door. I think I heard someone holler something.

We cruised along the coast, hitting up a couple of moored boats. Most of them had already been worked over. Occasionally, we did see some other boats in the distance, but only half-heartedly tried to make contact. We originally planned a nice easy score in Casco Bay, Ha! Fat chance. The bay is famous for its variety of small islands; unfortunately all inhabited and by now chock full of the undead. We talked about clearing one and moving down here. At least we would be going in the right direction. It took all of two minutes to realize that this would be a waste of time and seeing the behavior of Bill and Barbara, maybe not a viable option. After checking out a couple of locations, we came upon a restaurant on Seal Point. A descent size dock was next to it, the kind of place you could cruise in, eat, and cruise out. We were shocked to find no zombies around. The last place we looked, we had picked up three fans that were desperate to meet us. We inexplicably lost them a couple of minutes ago. Gated community? Staying as quiet as possible, Robert came around and dropped sail.

"Let's give it ten." So we drifted around for a few. There were some decent looking condos further inland and a path along the shoreline with nice wooden benches every dozen yards. No zombies. Things were looking better and better. I might be able to do some shore time.

"Any guess?"

"I don't know, John, maybe a gated community?" The minutes crawl by and still no zombies.

"Okay," Robert whispered. We docked and waited.

"Well, what do you think?"

"The quiet part bothers me, but this could be the goose that laid the golden egg. I don't see any signs of looting."

We continued to scan and assess the situation. The dock was empty so we had a clear view and a nice kill zone should we get attacked. The front of the restaurant was all glass and looked to be the main dining area. Between the building and the water was a small service road that led to the back. I could just make out a set of concrete stairs and a yellow pylon with black bumpers attached.

"Robert, that's got to be the loading dock over there, far end of the building, maybe a hundred yards one-way."

"That's a hell of a commitment. We cut ourselves off from the boat."

"Yes, but the water is right there if things get out of hand, and we can swim for those guys." There were two small sailboats about twenty yards from shore. By small, I mean nothing but a glorified Sunfish. It would be one boat each and we would lose *Providence*.

"Good point. I take the green one, let's go!"

I put my string skills to use and tied off of the boat while Robert stood watch. I made sure my knots would hold, because coming back to find it had drifted away would suck.

We crept up the dock. God, I was scared. It had been a while since I spent time on the mainland and I felt naked not having some tangible barrier between the undead and me. Every fifteen seconds or so, we would stop and listen. The wind, water, and some papers blowing about just increased the tension. Upon making it to the corner of the building, I peeked around. It was the loading dock. The stairs led to a metal door, and next to it was a large garage style door that the trucks would back up to unload. The layout of the stairs meant that we could not use our old routine, so it was up to me. I slowly went up and tried the knob. Oh, thank you, God, it was unlocked. It opened outward with a nice long squeal.

Unfortunately, just inside the door was a series of long plastic strips. I guess this was intended to keep flies out, and I couldn't see in. I had the big stick, so I went first.

"Fuck it," I whispered, and rushed in. Fortunately, no one was home because one of the plastic strips knocked off my glasses, and I was suddenly thrust between the conundrum of not stepping on them, or saving my life. I had to think about this one, but as I said, the place was deserted.

Inside, was a large storeroom flanked on one side by a continuous row of windows. They were high enough so you couldn't see in from the road. The various windows gave us plenty of light and a great view of the bay. It looked like the set from some sitcom; very clean, orderly, and a million-dollar view. Robert entered and we stuck together while we checked the place out. We knew right away that this was the golden egg. There were cases everywhere and a series of shelves, all well stocked and orderly. Knowing that the power had been out for a couple of weeks made not opening the couple of walk-in coolers a no brainer. I found a handcart we could use to transport our booty. There was a larger one, but this meant opening the main doors; they were automatic. We knew they would make too much noise, so we didn't even try.

On our first trip, we loaded up on pasta and sauce, probably enough for a solid month of the stuff. I worked the cart and Robert carried two cases of pasta. Every minute seemed like hours. Where are they?

After storing the goods, we just looked around. It was eerily silent. The second trip went well and I relaxed just a bit. It was a nice haul of canned vegetables and soups. On the boat, we looked around.

"This is just too weird."

"Yeah, John, I'm with you on that one. Where the hell are they? I don't want to make ourselves noticeable, but this is just too good to be true."

I started to think that maybe there was a gate and we really did have this place to ourselves.

"You know, if we are alone, this is some sweet ace in the hole, as long as no one else finds it."

"Don't count your chickens just yet. Let's hang for five or so and see what is what."

We both had binoculars and so far, our immediate vicinity stayed free of the undead. Further up the harbor, I could see a few scattered about but no one paid attention to us. On our third trip, we loaded up on a variety of foodstuffs of everything from green beans to peaches. It was time to get fat, again. Hell, another raid here, a few cords of wood, and we could survive the winter at the lighthouse. During the fourth trip, I started getting nervous, so was Robert.

"Okay, let's not push our luck. I really don't like being on the mainland and this place just seems wrong." You could easily hear the concern in his voice.

"Just thinking the same thing. I am with you on the creep factor, way too silent. Alright, let's make this the last load."

I started to wheel the handcart to the open dock door when I saw movement. She was young, maybe early to mid teens coming along the side of the building. Greasy blonde hair, shiny gray skin, and the tilt of her head were clear indicators that she did not bat for our team. The zombie hadn't seen us yet, but must have heard something, as she was moving in our direction.

"Shit," I whispered and froze. Robert instantly had his Glock out and a bead on the plastic strips, why they ever had these things is a mystery to me, but at least it would give us precious seconds before we were discovered. Then, there she was; a dark form in front of the dull opaque plastic. His shot would make the least noise, so it was his game. She stopped and her figure teetered back and forth. Although I couldn't be sure of it, I knew she was staring at the plastic. I also knew that there was no way she could see us. This gave me a second to lean back and peer out the window. When it rains it pours, because now, at least three more were coming our way. I guess the cans of chocolate pudding and tomato soup were not going to make it on this run. Damn, I like tomato bisque.

"More on the way!" I said loudly.

Robert almost looked over, but maintained his composure. Good thing too, since at the sound of my voice, she came rushing in. As the strips parted, I could see she was wearing a summer dress, once white and cut low, now soiled and falling apart. Robert waited until she just cleared the plastic and fired a single shot. An arc of red mist sprayed over the strips. He had time to line up the shot and as usual, it was right on target, almost directly between the eyes. She dropped to her knees and looked at us. I mean she was still really looking at us. I thought for a second that this might be a new type of undead, and she was going to get up. It took another second before she fell on her face.

"Robert, we got at least three coming up the lane."

"Okay, we go through together. You look right, and I'll cover the rear," then we charged the door.

Going through those strips, you lose your vision for a second or two, but with homicidal maniacs waiting outside, those seconds seemed an eternity. I jumped the stairs and rounded the corner. There they were. The width between the building and the water was like that of a wide driveway or narrow road, and it made a nice killing lane. I charged forward to shorten the distance and fired. I don't know if it was a man or a woman, the body was so badly mangled and bloated. My shot hit it in the chest and lifted it into the air, arms and legs still moving as if running through space. I now realized that I had loaded slugs and not my usual shot. These suckers don't spread pellets, so it is essential your aim is accurate, but when you do hit, the results are nothing short of spectacular. I had to be closer to be accurate. A chest shot would sever the spinal cord, not dead, but not moving very far or very fast.

I could hear Robert firing and not in my direction. I had no time to look and see what was behind me, so I charged forward, fired, and missed. The next two were about thirty yards away, even with the dock. I fired again and caught one in the hip. It went down with a cartoon-like tumble. The next had once been a cop, its right arm hanging uselessly by its side. Then my pump jammed, so I did what every red-blooded American would do and started banging my loaded shotgun on the asphalt. I got it working and looked up for the second zombie. I did not have to look far. Running at me from about ten feet away was the cop. I went to the one knee stance a little too fast, lost my balance and tipped over on my butt. The aim was good and the monster very close, so as I fell backwards, I fired. The slug hit the upper chest with devastating results, but the zombie never slowed. He continued his forward momentum, passing directly over me, drenching me in decayed flesh and blood.

I was now on autopilot, jumped up, and sprinted for the boat. Ahead, I saw more coming, a lot more.

"Robert, get to the boat, NOW!" I screamed at the top of my lungs and shot at the group.

As I approached the bow, I just blasted the line.

I untied the port line and pushed off, giving the boat some slight momentum. By this time, the next zombie was in range. I went to one knee, took careful aim and fired. He was a portly fellow and I hit him where his once generous beer belly had been. Although it spun him and knocked him down, he was up again quickly. The next round seemed to clip his head and he went down and stayed there. I could feel the boat moving away from the dock, inch by inch.

I saw another near me drop, so I knew Robert was on his way.

Next in line was a small girl with long red hair and a leg brace. Having never had children, I was clueless of her age, so let's just say six. She was ahead of the others and I could just make out what she was trying to vocalize. It was high pitched and melodic, almost like she was singing. She had a limp, but this didn't seem to have any real effect on her speed. She was a smaller target and by now, I should have known she was too far away, but I fired anyway and of course missed. I have to calm down and let her get closer. Having never had children meant I had no sentimentality when it came to shooting them. Watch my breathing. Come on baby, come to oblivion. At about ten yards, I pulled the trigger.

Click. Oh, shit!

This sucks! I was about to be sent into the ranks of the undead by a six year old. You know the human brain is a funny thing, because my next thought was, with all I had been through, I deserved to be killed by some badass zombie, like the guy at the airport in Dawn of the Dead. Then again, he didn't do anything. She was in midair and I was still thinking about how unfair this was when the side of her head exploded. She hit the boat's rail and flopped into the water.

"Use your fucking sidearm, asshole, nothing fancy, just hit the chest!"

This brought me back to reality in a big way. I pulled the Ruger and fired. My clip had seventeen rounds and I burned through them in less than a minute. I fired with a calm calculated aim, and I think I hit almost every other time. Robert had modified my ammo into something he called 'Dum-dum' bullets. At first, I thought it was in honor of me. They were vicious things that tore great gaping holes with each impact. I fired as fast as I could, not going for the head, just center mass to knock them down. Somewhere in the back of my mind, I heard the motor start. I lost count when I fired, and probably changed clips with rounds still in it. The narrow dock limited their access. I only had to deal with six or seven. We made a safe distance just as my third, and last clip ran dry. Only one had actually made it on the boat and Robert just turned and shot her.

In the middle of the harbor, he killed the engine. The whole two-minute trip, I stood there frozen trying to catch my breath. I had dropped the Ruger to the deck.

"Are you okay? Bite, scratch, anything? Anything?" He seemed genuinely concerned and moved closer. I was a little apprehensive since he still held his Glock in his hand.

"No. Close, very close, but I'm okay."

"Good. Well, you look like shit! Time to clean-up." With that, he pushed me overboard.

The water was cold but felt great. I grew up around the ocean and have always been a good swimmer, so I let myself drift a bit downward, surrounded by a cloud of red as the blood and gore washed off me. WOW, we made it through another one. I could actually start to begin to think that there really might be a God on our side.

I surfaced.

"Thanks, I needed that! What about you, you okay?"

Robert was dropping the anchor. "Yeah, but I think we have just used up our nine lives."

He took his boat shoes and shirt off and jumped in.

As he surfaced, I asked, "So, what happened on your side. I didn't have a chance to look around."

"Half a dozen within twenty feet, more behind them. I was running for the boat when I saw the cop go over you. Damn, that was close."

I took a big mouthful of seawater, gargled, and spit it out. "You're telling me." I floated on my back and just drifted for a while.

"Hey, Robert, I don't think any shit got in my mouth, but if I'm sick in the next hour...well, I will end this song myself." I looked over at him.

He gave a nod but we had always understood.

We lazed in the water in silence for a few minutes. I stared at the clouds and let my mind go blank. Maybe not entirely blank, we just dodged another one. How many more did we have in us? Probability, Chaos Theory, coincidence, chance; odds are this venture was going to end badly.

Once back on the boat, I took stock of what we had scored. I should have paid more attention to our food selection.

"Well, we can probably eat pasta for the next few months, I hope you like green beans and corn. Too bad about the pudding, but overall, not bad." I started to get the stuff organized. "Hey, what were you carrying back on all those trips?"

"Pasta."

"Of course."

"Overall? John, that was an unnecessary outing; one that could easily have cost us our lives. Bill better appreciate our effort. I think we'll give them another week tops, and then we are going to leave, with or without them!"

"Roger that!" I went forward to make sure I didn't put a hole in the boat when I shot the bowline. There was a bit of a scratch but nothing I couldn't buff out when he wasn't looking. We started to motor out of the harbor when Robert suddenly grabbed the binoculars and killed the engine. He stood there for a while. I tried to see what he was looking at but the glare was too much.

"Oh...My...God," he whispered.

"What's up, Robert?" I instantly got nervous.

"It's a navy frigate."

Chapter 8 ~ A Bigger Boat

June, 7th (continued)

Holy Cow! The United States Navy! I guess America still exists. What is holding us together? I hadn't been monitoring the radio with any regularity since we got to the lighthouse. I just assumed the worst and figured anyone still alive was holding on the same way we were, staying low, and taking it one day at a time. It was hard to believe that in front of me was a navy ship flying the stars and stripes, looking clean, looking ready, looking fierce, looking normal.

Robert gunned the boat right at them. As the ship got closer, I realized this was going to be the biggest thing I have ever encountered on the sea. Considering I didn't spend much time actually on the water, that was not saying a great deal, but the frigate was huge, sleek, grey and sharp. She had that 'don't fuck with me' look. I was very impressed. I don't know why, but the navy had not crossed my mind. They were in the perfect position to ride this storm out. I had considered cruise ships, large cargo and oil, but not the navy.

"Well, I will be damned!" Hey, I sounded happy. "Robert, how big?"

"Four hundred plus feet."

"That's big."

"It's bigger than us." The sense of relief was profound. Oh man, maybe things were not that bad. Do we still have a President? A Congress? Laws?

"What the hell are you so cheery about?"

"Robert, come on. That's the US Navy. It's over. We're saved!"

"Saved? John, you really are naive. Jesus Christ, have you not been paying attention?"

The radio crackled.

"Sloop, this is the U.S. Navy frigate *USS Kauffman*, please identify, over."

Robert picked up the receiver and dangled it in his hands for a few seconds while he looked at me. He gave me this weird stare; you know like in *Jaws*, Quint on the bow of the Orca, with the sun setting after they just had their first battle with the shark? He has this damn odd grin. You don't know if it's a crazy grin or a sage-like grin.

"This is *Providence* with two souls aboard, both male, and both human, over."

"It's good to see any humans these days, *Providence*. We will be boarding and check you out. Over."

"Thank you, Kauffman, we look forward to seeing you."

"I guess, when your boat is so big, you don't have to ask for permission. Do we have any issues here, Robert?"

"No, these guys are legit, and what could we do?" Then he keyed the mike, "Roger that, Kauffman, we look forward to the company."

"Okay, John. Just remember these are the good guys, but serious as a heart attack, no fucking around."

"No problem, they have a bigger boat and larger guns, so they win."

Ten minutes later, a zodiac came alongside with some trepidation. Robert killed the engine and we stood on deck, hands in the air.

"What do you want to us to do?" I yelled.

"Just stay where you are."

"Just the two of us on board, but there are two more, male and female, at the lighthouse in God's Haven."

"Don't worry, we'll get them."

"God, is it good to see you guys?" Robert seemed genially friendly, maybe my giddiness was catching, but then again, he is an ex-marine. We helped secure the zodiac and they stepped on board, all armed with M16s and dressed in battle gear. For a couple of seconds, everyone sort of stood around and acted like they were trying not to be nervous, then I realized Robert and I were still armed.

"I assume you want us to disarm, sorry."

"That would be a good idea. Where are you guys from?"

"Bangor," Robert replied, as we both undid our holsters and carefully placed them on the deck.

"Bangor!" I could almost see him drawing a map in his head trying to find Bangor.

"Maine's always been a bit isolated." I tried to help. Nobody did anything with our weapons but push them to one side. Our new friends visibly relaxed.

"Man, you guys were lucky to be on the coast and with a boat."

"No such luck, took us five days and there were originally twenty-two of us."

He got the point. We stayed on deck with the ensign while the two seamen went below.

"It's that bad? We've been at sea through all this, seven weeks and counting. You're the first people we've rescued in last five days."

"You don't want to be anywhere close to the mainland, It's literally a hell on Earth." We've been rescued?

He registered my remark with a blank look, I don't think this guy has a fucking clue what was happening, what has happened.

"Well, you guys got the navy to protect you now. I am ensign first class Spencer. I have some good news. We have retaken Nantucket and are working on the Vineyard, maybe a day or two."

"We?" Robert asked.

"We, as in a Carrier Group and a whole lot more. The navy sent everything they could to sea, isolate us, and ride it out."

"You have cleared Nantucket?" I chipped in.

We chatted for a few minutes until the other two joined us on deck. He turned to the two seamen and nodded. "Let's get you guys onboard and give you something decent to eat. We can do a proper debriefing when the captain is ready. These gentlemen will take good care of your vessel." Everything about Spencer suddenly changed and it was obvious that we were no longer talking to each other as survivors, as equals.

"Guys, I want you to put on these life jackets. Okay, quick overview. You may or may not be aware that we are under Martial Law. This means we have the right to register you, inventory your belongings, and assure your safety and well-being. It also means you have to listen to people like me, sorry, guys. We just want to know who you are and how you made it through. Everything will be okay." I guess 'rescued' is just a kinder gentler word for prisoner. I gave Robert a sideways glance. He seemed fairly calm, as if he was expecting this.

"Okay, fine by me," I said. You know when you eliminate, choice decisions become so much easier.

We climbed on board the zodiac where a third seaman, equally armed was at the helm. I didn't have the heart to tell Spencer that for the last week we have been dining on lobster, rib eyes, and fillets.

Once we got on board, we were escorted to the ship's doctor and given a quick exam. She remarked that all things considered, we were in great shape. I was psyched. My blood pressure was great and I had lost fifteen pounds.

"Dehydration and slight malnutrition have been our biggest problems. I haven't seen a bite victim in over a month." I didn't ask what happened to the victim.

"Any other survivors on board?"

"Nope, you two are the first in quite a while. Once we get you checked out, we will move you to someplace more permanent and comfortable."

We were then led to a lounge area and asked to fill out some questionnaires, and by some, I mean a small forest must have been sacrificed to generate this much paperwork! The medical stuff makes sense, but my home address? Phone number? Emergency contact? You have to be fucking kidding me. So I decided just to get comfortable and settle in. I don't know if it was the day's events catching up, or my adrenalin crashing, but I was tired. I laid my head on the table and in a minute, I was gone.

When I did wake up, Robert was talking with Spencer and some other guys.

"It's alive! Welcome back and we have to go." He slapped me on the back.

It was hard to get straight and the tableside of my face was numb. God, did I need a bed, or couch, or the floor. In a total haze, I followed Robert and Spencer through a labyrinth of doors and corridors. Every time we went through a door, I tripped, since no one had bothered to make the door flush with the floor. Eventually, we arrived at a nice walnut paneled room with comfortable chairs surrounding a large well-polished table. The ensign left and we were alone. I went over to the far wall and examined an oversized map of the world. Little by little, I started to come around. Coffee would be good. To kill time, I started to tap at different countries. How many of us are left? How many did we lose each day? By now, the numbers had to be stabilizing in some areas. Places in China are a month ahead. I would love to know what is going on there. Would that amount of time make a difference? I felt Roberts's presence behind me.

"Yeah, it boggles the mind to think how much is gone, how enormous this all really is, and we get it on our watch." He walked over and sat down.

"I don't know, man. We've seen so much this last couple of weeks. Humans seem to be doing as much damage as the zombies." I joined him at the table.

"So, what happens next?"

"Well, my brother from another mother, I do believe we are going to get debriefed."

"Okay, Robert, what's with this whole debriefing thing?"

"Oh, it's standard. They just want to know our story. It's a way of gathering intelligence. These guys have been out almost two months. My guess is they have never seen a real zombie or watched people die in real life. When everything is on video, it can be truly difficult to comprehend what has happened."

"Intelligence gathering. All right, well, you'd better let me do the talking." I laughed but he just glared and quickly fired a plastic coaster, hitting me in the chest.

Just as I am struck, the door opens and in walks a man dressed in a light brown shirt and pants, with a crease that looked like it could cut you. Two other guys in uniform follow him. Robert immediately stands up, and not knowing protocol, I follow his lead.

"Good day, gentlemen. I'm sure you had quite the trip and I am sorry to detain you like this. I am Captain David Walker. Do you mind if we talk a bit and then get you settled in?"

"Of course, sir," replied Robert. "Robert Barr and this is John Patrick." I was silently pleased he didn't try to bust my balls and introduce us as doctor. What the hell did he mean 'settled in'?

"I don't know how much you know about what is going on, so I will give you a quick rundown of our situation. When the outcome of The Plague became obvious, the navy was quickly sent to sea, everywhere on earth, with everything she had and anything she could find, borrow, or steal. The Atlantic Fleet was then divided into two groups. One is in the Caribbean and we were sent north. Our task is to search for survivors and secure any safe zones. So far, we have found over forty-five thousand, mostly from situations like yours, although there have been some isolated shore cases and a few actual mainland rescues. I am sorry for being rude. Would either of you like something to drink or eat?"

"No, thank you. So we still have a government?" David ignored my question and continued.

"We have cleared Nantucket and operations on Martha's Vineyard are currently underway. We should be completed in a day or two. Once that's done, we will move on to Block Island. Our goal is to gain as much safe land and supplies that will allow us to see the Plague burn out and the zombies decompose."

Shit! My mind was reeling. How many people lived on the East Coast of the United States? It has to be over one hundred and fifty million. They have only forty-five thousand? Is that all? Yeah, it sounds like a big number until you consider what you started with. I thought there would be more, lots more. My attention started to wander and do some quick and dirty calculations. What's the age range? How many sub adults? How many males? More important, how many females? The Captain continued to talk, something about cruise ships and container vessels, but I was lost in thought.

"Mr. Patrick, you have something on your mind?"

"Sorry, just a bit distracted. Um, you don't happen to have any rough demographics on the survivors handy. It doesn't have to be too detailed, just age and sex will do for now."

"I can get you that information, why?"

"Well sir, combined with your fleets demographic profile, I think I can give us a rough clue if we can win. Mind you, this will be very rough, just a quick snap shot of where we stand."

"Win? Do you mean on the Vineyard?"

"Oh, no sir, I mean on the planet."

Captain Walker stared long and hard. "What line of work are you in, Mr. Patrick?"

"I teach Anthropology, Biological Anthropology at the University of Maine, sir. Well, I used to."

This time, the pause was about a minute and you could see the concern on his face.

"I will make sure you get that data, and Mr. Patrick, let's keep this between you and me."

"Yes sir." But I knew the answer already. Forty-five thousand! No! That can't be right! Please, God, No! But what the hell did I expect? 45 K plus the fleet might be enough and who knows what is going on south of us or in the Pacific? Thousands of islands, right? This all might work out.

"Okay, why is a captain of a navy vessel interviewing two survivors? Well, you two are late in the game and I would like to know how you made it. Alright, gentlemen, let's hear your story. How did the two of you survive all this, and if it is okay with you, I would like it taped."

We both said it would be fine to record the interview and spent the next two and a half hours telling our story. I let Robert do most of the talking and he deferred to me for the technical zombie stuff. The Captain seemed mostly interested in our zombie observations and was astounded we had collected so much insight, that both of us had actually spent time thinking about the zombies, studying them. It seems the military had very limited first hand intel on what they were up against. They had not yet come to understand just what a zombie was, what they did. What they did was just hang out, sit in the shade, drink water, linger, kill and eat anything that moved. When we had finished, he just stared at us for half a minute.

"That's quite a tale." Captain Walker took a second, "Thank you." He continued to look at us and you could tell more was coming. "There's going to be some people who will want to talk with you. Meanwhile, let's get you squared away and I will let you know what happens next." Another officer entered the room.

"Don't worry about your personal belongings. Dr. Barr, your vessel is being taken care of and you will both get receipts." Once again, the Captain paused. "I don't have to tell you that what you went through is remarkable. You two have had the most intimate contact with the infected I have yet encountered, and your observations are very important. I don't know of any survivors actually spending time studying them. Almost everyone we have rescued have basically hidden themselves, either on a boat or in an isolated area. Are you gentleman hungry? Care to shower?"

"No sir," we said in unison.

"You mentioned some video tapes. May we have a look at them?"

"Sir, I don't think either one of us will ever watch them." Robert was right, so I just nodded.

"Okay, get some rest and let us know if you need anything. I'm sure I will see you before you go."

"Go, sir?" I was a bit confused

"Yes, we are moving rescued civilians to secure areas. I believe our report on your activities will get some attention and more than likely, you will be transferred to the *Truman*, our base of operations."

Robert looked at me and made a big grin, "Oh, John, you're going to like this. It's an aircraft carrier."

We all stood and started to leave.

"Dr. Patrick, a second please." Robert was led away.

Once again, Captain Walker took a moment to compose his thoughts. "Dr. Patrick, you already know the answer, don't you?" So much for beating around the bush.

"Well, I have a sneaking suspicion, sir."

"On a scale of zero to ten, what are our chances?"

"Well, Captain, humans are spread out rather thin. There's so much we don't know about this disease and then there is the question of fertile women, and…"

"Dr. Patrick, just a rough guess please." We looked each other in the eyes. I don't know what mine were saying, but his was anything but confident.

"Three. Maybe."

Robert and I shared a nice little (e.g., claustrophobic) room, from which he commandeered the bottom bunk immediately.

"Sorry, John, but I'm at the age where it's convenience over status."

"So you're the military, guy, what happens next? And what the hell is with the receipt thing?" Holy crap, this bunk is a pain in the ass to get into.

"They will figure out something for us to do to earn our keep. Right now, I think everything is still in a cluster fuck."

"Two months? Where are they getting the food and the fuel? Who's in charge?"

"Get some rest, buddy. We're safe." Robert killed the light.

With no window and very little light creeping in from under the door, it was easy to shift about, get comfortable, and drift. The boat was not as noisy as I would have thought, just a nice steady hum. My mind went blank.

The auditorium was packed and I could sense something important was about to happen. Suddenly, there was some kind of load banging going on just off to my left and the whole audience turned to look. Oh, thank God. As if by divine providence, I was going to be saved from delivering the accumulation of my life's work to a distinguished gathering of colleagues while naked.

It's that weird interval between being awake and being asleep, you know you are in a dream and there is nothing you can do about it, but if you concentrate, you can have some fun, you can manipulate things. It's okay, I can talk naked. Then the light, which I did not realize was approximately three feet from my face, went on.

June, 8th

"Okay, guys, it's show time." The voice was way too chipper for whatever the hell time it was. I just grunted and rolled over to see who was at the door. Robert farted and a way too young and perky blonde in a white lab coat entered.

"Sorry to bother you, gentlemen, but you have a meeting scheduled in three hours. Here are some clothes and I will be back in fifteen to show you where to shower and get some lunch, start some ship orientation. Oh, my name is Lorie." So that was the end of my blue jean fashion period, which pretty much encompassed my entire adult life. We now had olive jump suits and cool all terrain sneakers.

"John. When you snore, you snore like a son of a bitch! God damn, son, if you pulled that shit back at the barn, we would have been toast. No, you would have been toast."

"Yeah, like the barn." Asshole.

Lorie came back after what I can only assume was fifteen minutes, since Robert and I and the room had no timepiece.

Showers were down the hall, but we both balked because of hunger. Lunch was Salisbury steak, frozen, and canned gravy. Sides were mashed potatoes, powdered, canned green beans, saltine crackers and a fresh salad. What? Lorie went over what we already knew, although she did add that orders were being sent to send some non-combat personnel to the Vineyard, so we may not be going to the *Truman* after all. I guess pacification operations were going better than anticipated.

Since there is no such thing as a free lunch or dinner, Lorie forced us sit and review some of the more important points of living under martial law. Just three simple rules: One, do as you are told and don't fuck with the military or anybody in authority. Two, always remember rule one. Three, don't fuck with the military. It turns out that all our personnel belongings were reviewed and items deemed necessary to the mission were confiscated. They get to take what they want with no questions asked. Robert got to keep his boat because he was still alive to say it's his, but he still didn't know what happened to her. After dinner, our photos were taken and we got ID badges; another rule, don't go anywhere without your badge being visible.

"I've never lived under a military system." I guess the closest would be with the Boy Scouts at Camp Yawgoog back in Rhode

Island. Considering what has gone down, it makes as much sense as anything. The jumpsuit was making me itch.

"You'll get used to the whole rank and orders thing. We're civilians, so they'll generally cut us some slack and leave us alone. Martha's Vineyard. I haven't been there in over thirty years. I was too stuck up to visit during tourist season."

"My last time was at least twenty years. Oh, and I am this huge *Jaws* fan. They filmed the movie there." I started to examine one of two little black bags left on our desk, toiletries, well all right! I know I stink.

"I will see you shortly, my good fellow." I stood up and went down the hall. The showers were empty and just standing under all that hot water, feeling it cascade over my naked body, was truly a transcendental moment. Wow, did it feel good to relax.

When I got back, Robert was asleep. Instead of waking him, I decided to sit down at the small desk. It took a full two minutes before my head was down on my arms. Sometime later, there was another knock and we were off to our next meet and greet.

"Nice hair, John."

Ah, crap! All attempts with the shitty little black comb the navy provided probably made things worse. On the way, we were informed that we would present our survival story and take some questions from the group.

What group?

It was a small auditorium with maybe thirty people: a mix of officers, navy, marines, doctors, army, and couple of civilians. From the number of cameras, I guessed this was also being taped and maybe teleconferenced to somewhere else. The two of us sat at a table up front with a couple of bottles of water.

"This is a standard debrief?"

"No."

It started with a short introduction by a female navy doctor with great legs. As expected, Robert and I would tell our heroic story of survival and answer any questions. So off we went and Robert gave them a five minute synopses of the last two weeks. So far so good, I think. Then the questions started.

The room had no clocks or windows and after a bit of time, I started to wonder how long this was going to last. We had to have been going at it for at least an hour and no one had mentioned zombies; just background stuff, work, education, research, travel, special interests, where I grew up. Who the fuck cares about how I grew up. Who are these people and why are we here? Eventually, it did roll around to our escape from Bangor and fighting the undead. It very quickly became clear that this was going to be a long afternoon.

The first time had been relatively easy, one on one and just the facts. Now it seemed like everyone, including people from who knows where, had to ask a question about everything we did, and sometimes, why we did it. It seemed, at times, like I was being cross examined. Not what I expected. We eventually started to stray into areas I was not comfortable talking about and decided on a mini conference with Robert. He was not happy about the tone of some of the questioning and deferred to my judgment. So we basically told everyone that some things were off limits. This went over like a fart in church, and a break was ordered.

The nice navy doctor came over.

"Guys, I know this has to be hard, but we need to know as much as possible." She leaned over to get her head at our level. This makes the patient feel more comfortable, and I was able see the open folder she was carrying. The top sheet, among Dr. Goodlegs scribbling, was a printed copy of our interview with Captain Walker. I was also able to glance at her watch. We have been here for over three hours.

"Hey, whoever you are, you have our story. You know some personal shit went down. Right here, right now, is just not the right time, okay?" I got up to try to find a bathroom.

When I got back, we were ready to go again. I have always had a short temper, particularly when being interrogated by the military, but I may have jumped the gun. Once we got into zombies, things settled down and we really got into zombies. All formality disappeared and it turned into a nice old bull session. It then occurred to me that all these people didn't come from the Kauffman, and may have never met each other. There were three distinct groups. The first one seem to have members from all the military branches and asked general questions like zombie activity, response to stimuli, possible thought process, tool use, horde formation, horde psychology, etc. The second, also all branches, stuck to physiology, anatomy and epidemiology. The third, all marines, was tactics. Their research extended only as far as a video screen. Robert and I had a more personal touch when it came to data collecting. Their biggest advantage was the bazillion hours of video to study and giant piles of reports to digest. The more we talked, the more it became apparent that these guys saw it all as something that happened in the theoretical. I'm not saying they didn't understand what was happening or try to empathize with Robert and me; they were all just a bit distant. I guess everyone thinks they are going to survive this. I did. Now, I didn't give a damn about the time. This was interesting and actually fun, for me at least. Everybody seemed to be on the same page as far as our general situation; we're screwed. The real differences came about when we got into specifics. Rickenbacker was right; the devil is in the details.

The first point of contention was the most important, decay rate. Essentially, how long is your average zombie's lifespan? Two sides quickly formed.

A. Standard decomposition. Summer heat and zombie activity should speed up the rate. Maybe two months.

B. Decomposition rate is unclear. Bodies do not appear to be undergoing normal post mortem changes. They consume food and drink water. Time is unknown.

Both sides did agree on the importance of ongoing research (ongoing?) and we slipped into a long back and forth over whether we could distinguish between a new zombie, say a one day old, and an old zombie, a week plus old. In the end, we had to say we could not.

This was the key issue, because it set the stage for what we do next, get busy or wait it out. I started to hear both sides mention some new insight presented on the video. What video? After another undetermined length of time, the meeting was adjourned and we went back to our cabin. Well, all right! Somebody put cool navy wristwatches on our bunks.

June 9 and 10th

The next two days were just R&R. Robert and I played a lot of chess, he won most. Lorie scrounged and found me Aleksandr Solzhenitsyn's *The Gulag Archipelago*, all three books. Captain Walker ate most of our meals with us and gave us more insight into our strange new world. Yes, there was a government on St. Croix in the Caribbean. Yes, the legislative, judicial and executive branches of the US were still working. Russia, Britain, via the Falkland Islands, Greece, Iceland, Greenland, Australia, and a number of other countries still had functioning governments who were trying to work with each other. The captain thought the Kaufmann would stay in this area, in US territorial waters, for at least the next couple of months, although he would have liked to go further north. David was a nice guy. Originally, from Indiana, he ended up at Annapolis through a hilarious series of unlikely twists of fate. He had a ring on his left hand, but we didn't talk about that.

At our third lunch together, we got the news.

"Guys, I got the report from the lighthouse rescue party this morning. The operation was delayed due to some unforeseen issues I will not discuss. The place was abandoned; doors left wide-open, rotting food, lots of empty wine bottles, and the lighthouse was turned on. They found what are apparently their shoes just above the lowest set of cliffs, sorry."

I had received some demographic information from the captain the night before, just a quick overview; age, sex, and a bunch of other metrics I didn't care about. I should have jumped right in, but I knew this data was incomplete, and biased or not, the results would have depressed me. I hoped he wouldn't bring it up. I also kept hope that a cruise ship full of sixteen to twenty year old healthy girls would be rescued. We did find out that there was thirty seven 'major' outposts scattered around the continental US. By major, he meant a population in excess of one thousand people and the military is giving what help it can. David would not get into a whole lot of details, but the general gist was that things were better than I had anticipated. What I didn't find out until later, was that originally, there were over three hundred outposts and that only the biggest and best organized were still with us. On average, we were losing contact with one every week.

"There is another thing you two should be aware of. Your video, your group's video, has been worked over by our AV/IT techs." He stopped. I think he was anticipating a dramatic response. "You guys have never reviewed it?"

"I have no interest. John." I didn't say anything and just waited for the other shoe to drop.

"The only reason I mention it is because there was quite a bit of video, different levels of quality but...guys, they have put the tapes together in chronological order and with some editing, it is a very sobering and powerful story. I have seen it only once, and I will tell you I came away moved. I don't know if I could have gone through it. I have no clue what command will want to do, but I just thought you should know."

We eventually got our marching orders and I was going to get to see a real functional nuclear powered aircraft carrier, and named after my favorite underappreciated president.

June 11th

Just before sunset, we were coppered over to the *Harry Truman* on a SH-60 Seahawk. Like the type of helicopter really mattered. This was only the second one I have been in and the first one never left the ground. This is what I call a boat. At over a thousand feet, it is absolutely fucking massive. Plus it has a bunch of other, smaller boats all around it, which just gives it an even more regal look. When we got closer, I could see sailors, who looked like ants, scrambling over the flight deck. There seemed to be lots of activity. We stayed well off her port bow while waiting for a jet to take off. It gave me time to study this behemoth; a nuclear powered ship, one of the pinnacles of human ingenuity. As a liberal pacifist, I never thought it would be so easy to become spellbound by an instrument of war.

"I think we're getting what we deserved."

I forgot the mike was on and Robert quickly turned and looked at me, our eyes made contact and he slowly nodded his head yes, but in that Robert way of telling me to shut the hell up. The jet looked like a small rocket as it as it streaked skyward, banked, and headed south. Where the hell was he going?

After landing, we were quickly led off the flight deck, and taken to individual staterooms to rest for a bit, while they organized a meeting for another debriefing. From the sound of it, the Admiral and some other big shots will be in attendance. Holy shit, I am going to meet an actual Admiral! This would not happen until the following day, so we had time to kill.

We handed in our flight stuff and were told to sit down in a lounge area and wait.

"Robert, how the hell are they keeping everything running? Feeding people? Energy? Yeah, the ships nuclear but…" I said this in almost a whisper, thinking that somebody might be listening in.

"John, no one is listing in. You don't have to whisper." He sat down on this blue generic government issue couch.

"I have no idea how they keep the show on the road. I have been thinking the same thing, so keep your eyes open." He cupped his hands behind his head, leaned back, and shut his eyes. Keep your eyes open. WTF Robert? Keep your eyes open was the phrase you used to let your partner know something was wrong. What the hell was wrong?

After hanging out for an hour, we went on a tour of the ship with three other civilians. No introductions were made, just a simple 'hi', 'how ya doing?' Robert and I had our jumpsuits on, but these guys were in shorts, polo shirts, and deck shoes, very Club Med. It seemed to be the standard PR tour. The *Harry S Truman* is a Nimitz Class carrier, commissioned in nineteen eighty-nine, her homeport is Norfolk, Virginia. The ship's company is normally around fifty-seven hundred, but we were now at seven thousand, and with nuclear reactors, her range is essentially unlimited. The carrier's last upgrade was in 2010, making her one of the most advanced in the fleet. These are cheat sheets on how to get to the cafeteria and the rec. rooms, observe all restricted signs, obey all rules and regulations, and have fun.

So that was our introduction to carrier life. Once the dog and pony show was over, the three dudes went their way and Robert and I went ours, and ours was a direct line to the cafeteria. We both had long hair and beards, and combined with our gray jumpsuits we definitely stuck out. I guessed most had seen their share of survivors and people kept glancing. Anyway, lunch was great: hamburgers and French fries. How damn American can you get?

I was led to a tiny but comfy stateroom. This one actually looked like it should be for one, but I was told that like everything else, it was made for two. Once again, the gods smiled on me and I had the mansion all to myself, at least for the time being. I spent the rest of the day going over the ship's basics, trying to make sense of the massive vessel. I was told to wait here for the IT guys to bring me my computer and get me hooked up. I had two DVDs full of rules, maps, and SOPs I was supposed to watch before dinner. I unsuccessfully attempted to get comfortable on something I presumed was the bed. All in all, life is good. I am safe, I am not hungry, and I am warm. I guess I can take that deep breath now.

I stared at the grey metal ceiling. The bed was actually tolerable and I began to realize how tired I was. In Tennessee, people used the phrase bone tired. I guess this is what they mean. I just wanted everything to stop for just a little while. There was no gentle rocking like on *Providence*, but the stillness was reassuring and helped me relax. Retelling our story had been hard, but there were two of us there. I just mentioned facts and did not get into any real detail. It was only now on the carrier that I was ready to crack the door and truly relive some of the events. So many good people, gone in so little time, and for what? Even if we had made it to the islands, what would we have done? Stupid and naive, probably end up kicking the bucket from dehydration or disease. I never thought it would go down the way it did.

Endeavor to Persevere
Winston Churchill, or
Abraham Lincoln, or
Guy playing the old Indian chief in *The Outlaw Josey Wales*

Chapter 9 ~ New Friends

May, 24th

I eventually met the crew at some kind of storage facility/workshop surrounded by a high chain link fence topped with razor wire. It was your generic industrial park with a vast asphalt desert that, fortunately, looked deserted. I hadn't seen any zombies for the last twenty minutes; at least since I left the more populated areas. Like all predators, they definitely congregate to where the action is, but how do they know where the action is?

It had been a surreal hell just getting here. Traffic everywhere, panicked people rushing pell-mell, no one knowing what to do, wrecks all over the place, abandoned cars lined the road. It seemed like everyone at once wanted out of Bangor, out of everywhere, but where would you go? We had all waited until the last minute thinking, it won't make it all the way to us. One station I passed was in full riot even though multiple signs read, EMPTY – NO GAS! I was reminded of that scene from the old George Pal's *War of the Worlds* movie, where the scientists are trying to leave LA in a school bus and run into a mob in complete panic. They attack and tear the bus apart. They throw out the very people who are their only hope, everyone's hope.

When I slowed down, people pounded on my car and tried the doors. Four times, I had to point my gun at some desperate man trying to open the passenger door. One time, I could clearly see the guy's family behind him, a couple of little children wrapped in a blanket. I was just as panicked and although I had plenty of room, didn't even think of letting them in. If I open the door, I would get overwhelmed. I just wanted to make it to Liz. I tried the radio for a distraction. All it did was dial-up my anxiety level to eleven. Just one long stream of terrified reporters giving constant updates of zombies in the city, fires, widespread looting and rioting, things that everyone already knew. No new details and nothing to do if you were given them. Reports from Boston told of total destruction. New York City was in a blackout. Hell, the whole country is in a blackout.

I passed a deuce and a half full of national guardsmen heading into Bangor. They were moving slowly and I got a good look at the guys sitting in back. They were all way too young and obviously terrified. You signed up to get some money for college, make your first resume look good, and instead you get a suicide mission. What were they going to do? No hole was in the dike that you could plug with your finger. How are you going stop the ocean when you only have one little finger?

I double-checked the address I was given, 1026 Isherwood. Okay, here we go! There was a guy at the gate sitting in a cheap folding beach chair under a huge umbrella advertising Corona. He was wearing snakeskin boots on the outside of his jeans, a faded Van Halen t-shirt, black leather vest, cowboy hat, mirrored sunglasses, and holding an automatic weapon. Man, I hoped the address was right. I pulled up to the gate slowly and rolled my window down.

"Dr. Patrick?" It was more of an order than a question.

"Yes, I have ID."

"Name's Tim, come on in, John, we've been expecting you." He was young, maybe thirty, thin, with a goatee, and a strong New England accent. He opened the gate, and like me, he was looking around. Are they already here?

I pulled in. "Thanks, Tim, where to now?"

"Go on up around the side. You'll see the garage doors open, so just pull on in."

"Any trouble?" We shook hands.

"Here? Not yet." As he closed the gate, Tim pointed to the southwest where columns of black smoke rose over the horizon.

"Shit."

I drove off and left him all alone, standing guard at a flimsy gate at the far end of an empty parking lot during the end of the world. Wow, this is really happening.

In a large warehouse that used to be some kind of machine shop, people were swarming over two Winnebagos and a big black shiny Hummer. A slim twenty something redhead in farmer Johns waved me to the final resting place of my beloved Subaru.

"Just leave the keys and make sure everything is unlocked. You can stash your personal stuff over by that table. Name's Jane, you must be Professor John."

"John works for me, Jane."

We shook hands. "Welcome on board. Liz is around somewhere." She gave me a wink and walked away.

I left all the doors open and even went so far as to unlatch the hood and unlock the gas cap. My personal stuff was mostly clothes stored in two backpacks and a large duffel bag. I probably wouldn't need all the clothes, particularly my winter stuff, but I don't give a damn. If I am going to the Caribbean, some of that shit was expensive.

Everyone seemed to be either working on a vehicle, or running around looking very much like they knew what they were doing. And what they were doing was getting the final touches on an armored convoy that would take us the forty or so miles to the harbor. The Winnebagos had been tricked out with mesh on the glassless windows and diamond plate shielding skirting the bottom, but leaving the tires exposed. Smart, we can change a tire. A hole was cut in the roof and with a series of straps and webbing, acted as a kind of turret. The roof could not easily support the weight of a normal adult, plus gun and ammo, so they used PVC tubes to give a flying chair some struts and a series of contours for a 360 degree effect. The first thought through my rapidly disassociating from reality brain was, damn, that is some pervert who put that thing together. There were also shooting slits cut in the side. I was impressed that they used the cross technique for the slits, like you see in the old westerns, because it gives you a better angle of fire.

The Hummer was an H3T. The Hummer that wanted to be a pick-up truck with four doors, mesh over glassless windows, removable hardtop, and a diamond plate skirt. The front of the black Hummer was retrofitted with something resembling a locomotive cowcatcher. It appeared angry. From the looks of it, I would guess this retrofit was not done yesterday. I stood back for a better view. All the vehicles had that Road Warrior look that said, 'DON'T FUCK WITH ME,' very moody, very effective.

Liz was on the far side with a clipboard, reading some kind of list. I went over, wrapped my arms around her and gave her a kiss.

"Oh, thank God, you made it. From the news reports, I was beginning to get really worried. Most of the gang has been camped here for the past few days. This will be my third night. I missed you."

"I missed you, too. I can't believe that you are right in front of me." All Liz could do was smile.

"I've seen the smoke. Is it as bad as everything we heard? All the radio spews is doom and gloom." All of this was said in exactly two seconds. We embraced and suddenly, I felt that things might not be that bad.

"It's really going down fast, Liz. Everything is just chaos. It's weird. I mean it happened so quickly. The roads will be a serious problem." Okay, next appropriate thing to say might sound like, 'I hope your ex has thought this through.' Probably a better thing to say would be, "Hey, we have each other." It doesn't really matter since I went ahead and said both, in that order.

I saw her eyes change. "You dickhead! We have been working our asses off! Where the hell have you been? I have been calling for days! John, I have been scared shitless and you better have a good answer."

"Before you get really mad, it was probably a ten thousand to one shot your call got through at all. Liz, we're some of the lucky ones." Oh, my God, we really were. How many hundreds of thousands, millions, whose last final excruciation, would be to absolutely know they would never be with their loved ones again, or have any idea what happened to them. I have a small reprieve. I knew my mother and sister were gone when Providence fell three days ago.

"Liz, why all this work? The zombies don't use guns, I think. Let's just go now!"

"John, this is Roy's operation. We are waiting on a couple he has known since childhood. We all know we are entering the refugee game a bit late and we're not taking any chances."

With the exception of Liz, I didn't know these people from Adam. They were isolated and may not be truly aware that everything was progressing from very bad to fucking terrible on the outside.

"I'm sorry. Can this really be happening?" I just held her and tried to hold back the tears. A tiny ray of light had broken through. I had found my Elizabeth.

She started to introduce me. It was name after name; I was given no last names. There were about twenty in total, most in their thirties and forties with no kids. Two of the more unusual people in our group were a pair of middle-aged twin sisters, deaf twin sisters. Madeline and Matilda were in their mid to late thirties, with short brown hair, thank God for different cuts, average height and build, and deep green eyes. Liz told me they stay to themselves and was related to Roy's wife.

"Liz, can you or anyone here sign?"

"No, but they can write." She poked me in the head and we moved on. I was nervous to meet Roy. Shit, let's find out on the eve of the End Times that your girlfriend's ex is some kind of survivalist nut with a havoc fetish. This would have any red-blooded anthropologist wondering why that free university gym pass was never applied for, but he asked me to come along.

Roy was a mountain of a man, easily 6-4, heavyset, beard, short hair, piercing hazel eyes, and very friendly. He resembled some crazed Al Borland from the TV show *Home Improvement*. He looked to be in his young fifties, fit, and clearly in control. This was Roy's Game and I was playing for Roy's Team. We exchanged some small talk about road conditions and Bangor. I didn't know how to interact; was anxious and all I wanted to say was, 'IT IS TIME TO GO!' Instead, I just cruised with some chit chat. He approved my choice of handgun. The Ruger had a reputation that I was clueless about. I was instructed to carry it at all times, and make sure it's loaded and safety off. His road partner was another huge guy (huge, like a dump-truck is both large and massive) called Hammer, and when Roy declared, "Hammer's in the Hummer," I almost burst out laughing, but Hammer turned out to be like Roy, another vet and a really good guy. I was glad he was with us. He was bald and actually looked like the semi-enemy Kingpin from the old Spider Man comics.

Everyone was busy and Roy put me to work helping with the supply inventory. I added my meager amount to the communal stock. I should have brought the mushrooms. Liz informed me we would leave the next morning. Well, at least I had Elizabeth and time to figure who the hell each person was and what they did. Everyone pitched in. I knew we were all scared, but trying really hard to hide it. Actually, I was in a pretty good mood

I hit it off with a retired engineer, Robert. He had one of the sailboats. He was an ex academic from Orono. I guess I was also an ex academic. We shared jokes and talked about the good times at U Maine, while I packed food and gear and checked them off, or added them to the list. He made it a point to brag about some of the classic Maine football victories over one of my Alma Maters, URI. Later, he pulled me aside and explained with fatherly patience and in agonizing detail what the hell was attached to my waist and how to use it. He also deactivated the magazine safety so I could fire the chambered round with the magazine removed.

Dinner that night was on the roof of the warehouse. Hammer had set some ladders and hauled up a bunch of lawn chairs and a propane grill. Hamburgers and hot dogs with all the fixings the Hannaford Market still had, at least three days ago. The sun didn't set till around nine and everyone was on the lookout to spot the first zombie. Roy put up a bottle of Jack Daniels to the person who did. I guess that meant I was the only one to have seen a real zombie. At least three major fires were burning to the south and there was the constant distant wail of sirens, combined with the occasional gunshot. I said a silent prayer for the brave rescue workers, who must know they are fighting a losing battle, but were staying and doing their duty. Big, big, balls. Every bone in my body was telling me to run! So I did and they stayed.

During dinner, we went around, introduced ourselves, and gave a quick synopsis of who we are, what we did, and how we got here. There were twenty of us. I have spent my life talking in front of people I don't know, but now, I am nervous. I was so concerned about what to say that when it came my time, I said something, but I have no clue as to what. I also don't remember anything anyone else said. We reviewed the plan that Roy, Robert, and a guy called, Doc, had devised. People were assigned to a Winnebago and given special duties. Although the industrial park gave a false impression of isolation, the biggest concern was traffic. Panicked animals want to move, and with the large RVs, we were limited in our choices of acceptable terrain. Why didn't we just put together some killer ATVs and get our asses out of here?

John, not your game.

Play for the team. You're lucky your ass is alive. All in all, we thought it might take us a day or two to reach the harbor. I was assigned to Winnie Two, as was Liz. My particular position was at the back. I was part of a team of three assigned to cover the ass end of our little caravan.

We had a couple of survival radios that not only were waterproof, but also ran on electricity, batteries, and hand crank. I don't know, but they ran on even sea water maybe. They were pretty cool. We listened to the reports from Bangor and the rest of the East Coast. Rescue Stations had been set up a week ago but who wants to leave their home when they don't have to? Who wants to go live in a government camp and let them protect your family? When you did realize you couldn't do it on your own, it was too late. New England fell just like the rest of the country, just like the rest of the world. Once a town or city reported infection, it was gone very quickly. Everything was in confusion. The plan to establish these rescue stations obviously did not take into account the seriousness of our current zombie issue. Some fell in hours, others, days. This was the first time I heard of swarms. Swarms, also called hordes, are a gathering of zombies in a particular location, sometimes in the thousands. There are so many and they are so close together that they almost seem to react as one, and once a prey has been identified, it is pursued to its end, the zombies just don't give up. It was the swarms that were taking out the rescue centers.

I pulled Liz aside and asked about Roy's wife. She said that Elaine was in New York on a business trip when the quarantine of the city went into effect.

"John, there is no hope for her. She was a real sweetheart. You would have liked her. I think Roy is keeping himself busy so he doesn't dwell on her." I knew about New York, I heard about it days ago. Images on YouTube. Once the tunnels and bridges were clogged, things went Medieval overnight. New York, one of the greatest cities man has ever known, was gone, God damn.

I spotted the zombie shuffling down the middle of the road. Why say anything, I was the newcomer and didn't drink. At least I did not drink now, but if this shit keeps up, who knows. The honor of first sighting went to Paul, our ace mechanic, who before dinner, was last seen shouting epithets in perhaps an Eastern European language and ripping something out of the bowels of my poor Subaru. The zombie had once been a postman in his summer uniform with those crazy postal shorts. His left leg was not the pasty white of his right and even though I did not have binoculars, I knew it was blood. He didn't seem to notice us and just shambled on, heading southeast, same direction we were to travel; huh, great muscle coordination, I wondered if we would see him again.

The group was quiet so I decided to break the ice a bit and wondered out loud, "How come we have to get Danny Boyle zombies and not George Romero zombies?" Everyone looked at me and then started to move a bit away. I was saved when a guy named Zack explained the difference between fast and slow zombies. Ah, a kindred soul! We started chatting and eventually digressed from movies to zombie literature (although we did have an extended conversation on the zombie versus shark scene from the Italian film, Zombi 2, brilliant). It seemed that Zack had also succumbed to the bug of the undead, from a Creature Feature *Night of the Living Dead* on WKBG channel fifty-six out of Boston when he was eleven. I became hooked when I was sixteen, sitting by myself , watching a midnight showing of *Dawn of the Dead* at the Meadowbrook Cinema in Warwick, Rhode Island. For the next hour, we proceed to have an almost scholarly discussion on the topic. We covered everything; from Brian Keen, through Stephen King and Max Brooks, from the *Autumn* series to the *Morning Star* series to the Monster series. I was able to catch him when it came to one of my favorites, *Day By Day Armageddon*, but then again, we were living in Armageddon. Well, this is going to be great fun, two zombie nerds get to experience the destruction of the human race by, of all things…wait for it…Zombies!

People actually took an interest in our geeked-out dialog.

"So, you guys know about zombies?" It was Tom, the lawyer, who looked eerily like a young Larry Bird.

I took a couple of seconds and said, "No, you can always put down the book or turn off the DVD. This is real and we are in deep shit." I paused, "Sorry man, that was rude of me. Like everyone else, I'm fried. I just don't know if we can translate the stuff from books and movies, the stuff of fiction, to the real world and be of any help in our situation. Zack?"

"So far, things are going the way of a typical fictional zombie apocalypse. Strange virus, check. Reanimation of dead, check. Undead exhibit cannibalistic tendencies, check. Rapid breakdown of civilization, check. Small band of determined survivors, check.

"Holy crap, Zack, we are a cliché!"

"Hey, John," it was Robert, "every little bit helps."

"Yeah, if you guys notice anything, and I mean anything, just yell out and we all will listen," added Roy.

We all just sat there a bit trying to absorb maybe just a tiny amount of what was going on. Around eight, we heard a loud explosion. The only thing that came to mind was that it had to be at, or very near the airport. Throughout the evening, a few light planes and some helicopters flew over, all heading in different directions. Where were they going? Did they know something we didn't? Later, we saw a couple of big contrails, very high up, and all heading north.

"Those are big bastards, maybe B-52s or C-5s!" said Derrick. Derrick was a young guy, maybe mid-twenties, dressed in kakis, with a mustache and a ponytail. He was silent, stayed to himself, and just seemed to take things in. You knew he was hurt, but I sensed Derrick was the kind of guy who stayed focused on the moment, and what was going on outside our little group was a priority for someone else; he had his own shit to take care of. I instantly trusted him.

"Where are they going?" I asked.

"North, somewhere safe." Roy came over and placed his patio chair next to me.

No shit. Yeah, we are all going someplace, but where is safe?

"Iceland, Greenland, Canada. You know we got bases up there. The Islands are our only choice, but I do like cold weather and I've dreamed of going to the North Pole since I was a kid."

"I'll take any place that's safe," I said in a half burp.

"Cincinnati!" It was Robert.

Okay, I'll take the bait. "Why?"

"I want to be in Cincinnati when the end of the world comes, because it's always twenty years behind...Mark Twain." For a second, everyone seemed to kind of pause as if to sense whether it was all right to laugh, but only a second, and then everyone who heard Robert, lost it all at once. I was laughing so hard tears were coming out my eyes and snot from my nose. Oh, man that felt good. As we slowly regained composure, the rest of the group, including Liz, wanted to know what was so funny. It sucked because the moment was gone and I wanted her to laugh like I just did, to have that release.

The roof was one of those industrial flat tops covered with small stones, with sleeping pads not that uncomfortable. At least I had Liz, except now, I was self-conscious about showing any affection. A couple of bottles were passed around and I was jealous. I couldn't chemically relax like the rest of them, but alcohol and I have had a parting of ways.

"John, Liz tells me you know a little something about what's causing this shit." The gang was getting a bit greased up with the ethanol and I wanted to keep my distance and see who's who. This was not what I wanted to hear. Nor was I pleased that everyone seemed to have pressed pause in their various conversations just as he was asking me.

"Well, I have been looking into things as I am sure all of you have. I've talked with friends who are better informed and better educated and it seems we are up against a virus that humans have never seen before, really far out stuff." I was trying to make it as general as possible and not break into professor mode.

"Everyone is looking for a way to cure it. I just don't know." What could I say? I am not a virologist. I had worked for the government playing with this kind of stuff, but that was decades ago!

"Can't we just come up with a vaccine? We have antibiotics, so why not develop antiviral drugs? It can't be that hard, it just can't be!" I had forgotten the name of the guy asking the question, I think it was Norm. He was older than I was, maybe in his seventies, but someone who took his gym pass seriously.

"Yes, you're right, but viruses are not like bacteria. They are really tough bastards. They don't have sex, they use other cells to reproduce, and they don't need oxygen like we do to make energy. Viruses are just a bunch of chemicals, like little machines." Yeah, right.

"This particular virus is very complex, and the whole zombie thing is so novel that we are lucky even to know it's a virus." There was no way I was going to get into details.

"You know, the jury is still out on whether these things are actually alive. I mean, bacteria are real cells. They require food, they have a real metabolism, they reproduce, and these guys are alive. I wish we were up against bacteria." I started to lose them. "We have antiviral drugs, but they are for specific viruses, and because viruses use the host cell to replicate these kinds of drugs, they are very difficult to make. I mean most antivirals don't kill the virus, they just prevent it from replicating." I now realized that I was just rambling and nothing I could say would make anything better, or our situation less precarious. By now, nobody was looking at me, so it was a good time to shut up and look at the stars.

The others drifted into a half dozen independent conversations. Liz came over with some sleeping pads and a couple of woolen blankets, and we moved to an isolated corner of the roof. We cuddled and talked about nothing for a bit. Actually I did all the talking. After an hour, I shut up and Liz drifted off into sleep. With the odor of oblivion wafting through the air and my mind racing, I couldn't sleep.

Chapter 10 ~ Lost Souls

May 25th

The last couple, Jim and Lucy, arrived at eight. Roy had hoped for six. They brought ominous, but not unexpected news. A large section of Bangor was indeed burning and the roads were clogged with desperate people, some of them armed. Lucy told us about a young couple they watched forcibly removed from their Jeep Cherokee. When the young guy fought back, he was pushed to his knees and executed, all in broad daylight, in front of hundreds of other people. The guys got in the Cherokee, fired it up, and started talking to the girl who was sitting by the side of the road crying hysterically. After a couple of minutes, she stood up and got in the Jeep.

"Three heavily armed men who knew what they were doing; we're talking automatic weapons here. Jesus H Christ! We had a shotgun and two pistols, loaded and ready to rock, and I didn't do a god-damn thing." As if to make his point, Jim held up a handgun, some kind of automatic monster, but I got the point. I knew exactly where he was coming from. It turns out that the explosion we heard last night was indeed from the airport; something about a commercial airliner trying to land. I didn't think at this late date there was any commercial planes flying. Wasn't SCATANA initiated over a week and a half ago? They had encountered maybe a dozen of the undead; just drove around them or in a couple of cases, over them. There was so much chaos, not necessarily caused by the zombies, but by real people, that you just did whatever you needed to do. They had arrived in a jeep that had been modified for off–roading, but were going to leave it behind. Why? You would think every little bit would help, but it was Roy's decision.

"We spent half the time cutting through people's backyards and across any open area we could find." This caused me serious concern. How were the Winnebago's going to make it?

"Some roads are clear and then just abruptly dead end with a wreck or a bunch of dead cars. People are starting to lose their shit big time, and you wonder what all the gunfire is really directed at. We are going to need to stay tight."

It took another twenty-seven minutes before we were off. Another review of the plans, recheck various lists, and we were on our way, heading for the coast, and the freedom of the seas. Our route involved staying on back roads as much as possible. This made it almost twice as long as it should have been. We were not to stop for anything or anyone. Roy and Hammer had given us a somber pep talk the night before, very heavy on unity, focus, and completing the mission. We could not help those in need, even children, if we hoped to get to the boats. The general gist was that we might see things that are going to tear us up inside, but we are going to complete the mission. People were dying by the tens of thousands in numbers, and ways we could not imagine. We cannot save them. We will be lucky to save ourselves. Just then, Van Halen's *Runnin with the Devil* exploded in my mind. Man, I really hope we are badass. We closed the meeting with a group prayer. Curiously enough, Roy chose the Serenity Prayer.

Getting out of the industrial park was no big deal. The place was empty and we didn't even close the gates behind us, but it only took five blocks to run into impossible traffic. Everyone was desperately heading out of Bangor. I don't know where they thought they were going. Whole families were stranded in their cars that had been pushed off the road. A lot of them just sat as if they were waiting for AAA. We were the only ones that seemed to have been prepared, by that, I mean heavily armed. We made a show of force and meant it. One of Roy's first orders was not to let anyone get inside our little convoy.

"They can tag along behind, but not between us. Use whatever force necessary to prevent this. We are covering our asses only."

Roy used the Hummer to force his way into traffic and we followed right behind, practically bumper to bumper. I heard a gunshot now and then, but not from my vehicle, I hoped it was from one of us, flexing our muscles.

We were taking a series of roads that ran somewhat parallel to the 1A to Ellsworth. At a place called Kidder Hill Road, we stopped. Roy barked over the radio something about state police and making a show of strength. Liz whispered that Roy had no special like or dislike for the police, but would use force in a heartbeat if necessary. After a minute, we started to move. I think the Saw, a SA80 badass looking machine gun in the turret on Winnie one, might have assisted our egress. I waved as we passed. I felt bad for those guys. My Dad was a Massachusetts State Trooper, so I partially understood where they were coming from. They might be a calming presence to a few, but the monsters were real and they were coming.

This was not chaos. This was anarchy. As we inched along, I saw hundreds, no, thousands of people walking on the side of the road carrying their life's possessions. A few were injured and everyone was desperate for a ride. As we passed, most of them stopped and stared at us with wide pleading eyes. It looked like one of those newsreels from World War Two showing refugees fleeing from the front. I swear at times, I was actually seeing all this in black and white. I was a bit surprised at the number of people just sitting there, shell-shocked. Every ten yards or so, we passed another vehicle on the side of the road, some abandoned. I saw women holding up infants and babies to us, pleading for the child's life. We never stopped. Part of my humanity died on that road.

The radio crackled that there was some kind of commotion up ahead. I couldn't see what was going on since Winnie two was last in line and I was dead in the back. All of a sudden, everybody on the road started running. People dropped whatever they were carrying and just took off in various directions. The radio hissed. It was Roy.

"We got zombies up ahead, could be a dozen or so. If they delay traffic, we will take them down," yelled Mary from the passenger seat.

From our already snail-like pace, we slowed considerably. I could sense they were close. The people outside were becoming more and more hyperactive. Terrance was driving and looked back at me, fear in his eyes. Something slammed into the side of our Winnie and Norm started blasting away. We didn't need orders. Here we go.

"Paul, do it!" someone yelled, and from our turret, he opened fire with his AK47. I heard the sound of other automatic fire and assumed this was Tim lighting up the SAW. Everything was noise, but I faintly heard a gut-moving crunching sound, metal on metal, an accident in slow motion. I guessed Roy was making his way through.

It was odd, but right then, I thought I was hearing bagpipes. Who would be playing bagpipes? It took me a couple of seconds before I realized it was not some crazed Scotsman, but car alarms and horns, hundreds of them.

We slowly passed one of those bloated SUV's like a Yukon or Escalade that had pulled off the road at an odd angle. The passenger's door was open and a female zombie was half in, attacking the driver. He was trying to fight back and I could clearly see blood and crescent shaped bite marks on both his arms. Another zombie lay dead next to the driver's door. There were two shrieking children, maybe six or seven, buckled up in the back seat. We didn't stop. About twenty yards down the road, I spotted this huge man in a U Maine lacrosse jersey running back to the SUV, shotgun at the ready. Just as he went out of view, I saw him tackled from behind by two zombies.

We eventually made a right turn and started making better time. I hoped this would mean less horror and chaos, but whom was I kidding? There were still lots of people running, walking, crawling. Individually or in small groups, the zombies would take down one person, start feeding even as the person struggled, look up, and go after another. It was like a pride of lions amidst a pack of newborn gazelles. I knew we were going to see some bad shit. I just didn't think it would happen so quickly. I could have sworn I saw one of them look at us and make a conscious decision to go for something else. Nobody talked. We were like spectators in the Coliseum watching the Christians get thrown to wild beasts. Safe in our little metal cocoon, it was all so fucking surreal.

Since I was the caboose, I had one of the best seats in the house. At first, the zombies didn't make any sense. I saw one run right past an unprotected screaming mother and child to attack a moving van. The occupants gunned him down in seconds, but this type of chaotic attack actually worked in the undead's favor, because you never knew when or where. The zombie 'front' quickly swarmed by us, but that is not to say they didn't leave plenty of representatives behind. As long as they don't mess with us, we won't mess with them. Where were they going? Maybe they have the same plan we do, grab a boat and head to the islands.

There were ten utterly terrified people inside Winnie Two. The AC was off to conserve fuel, most of the windows were covered, and it took only a couple of hours for the place to go rank. Leslie, a college student with long black hair, sat on the floor with a video camera filming. She was starting to piss me off since she didn't actually do anything but think and film shit. In theory, her job was to keep the interior clear and give us ammo. A quick glance from Liz was all I needed to know that the subject of the Camera Girl was taboo. M&M stayed to themselves and watched out the window. Norm and Jane were on opposite sides of the Winnie and totally gung ho. They had two large cross-shaped firing slots and could see quite a bit of what was going on, but only from their side, so they also kept this bizarre and increasing hilarious banter about what they saw.

Jane: 'Oh my God! You are joining the Army of the Undead dressed in that?'

Norm: 'In what?'

Jane: 'Like that pretty in pink girl, gross.'

Norm: 'You mean 'Legally Blonde'?'

Jane: 'What?'

Norm: 'You know... the movie, the musical?'

Jane: 'Musical? What the fuck are you talking about, Norm?'

Norm: 'Oh, come on. You know the blonde, Harvard... Holy Shit! That is one fat dude!'

Jane: 'How fat?'

This was about as deep as it got, and it would go on and on and on. And after an hour, it was like you are actually living in a sitcom, but with zombies.

I was back next to Liz and Derrick. Matt covered Terrence, who didn't say much, just listened to Mary in the passenger seat and drove.

After a couple of miles and a few direction changes, things seemed to become less chaotic, or maybe I was getting used to the view. We slowed down again. Slow is a relative term since I doubt we ever broke ten MPH. The crackle of the radio broke the silence.

"Let's pull over; I want to check this out."

Oh crap, it was Roy breaking his own rules, and we were going sightseeing. On both sides of the road were flat plowed farmland, and the guys in the turrets would have a clear view. I handed Paul up some binoculars.

"What's going on?"

"Have no clue. How are we looking?"

"Ah…lots of people by the side of the road. Some crap up ahead. Clear of zombies, for now."

Without thinking the situation through, I un-holstered the Ruger, made sure the safety was off, and went outside. I had reloaded it three times this morning just to be sure. I wasn't surprised to be the only one to leave the safety of the Winnie, or that they slammed the door shut the second I was clear. What the hell was I doing? No one asked me to go check things out and if they did, I would just get pissed at them. Yet, here I was in the middle of a zombie infested nowhere, taking a little walk.

To be one hundred percent honest, I was nervous, needed to move, wanted out of our little smelly metal box to get some fresh air. Also, I was curious. In the back of the Winnie, you can only see out the back window. It's covered in a heavy mesh, minus my shooting slots, but I can see just fine. Since I was in the back, everything that I saw had this look of something that had already happened. You quickly become totally disoriented and just hope the driver knows what the hell he is doing. But once outside. Fresh air. Beautiful day.

I joined Doc and Robert from Winnie one and could see now why Roy stopped. Ahead, the road was scattered with military equipment, a couple of Hummers, and about a dozen dead Army National guardsmen. There was also a couple of hundred dead zombies mostly concentrated around the immediate area, but also scattered in the field across the road to our right. The number of dead guardsmen was just a guess, since many were torn to shreds. The whole thing looked to be some kind of improvised roadblock. Off on one side there was a sandbag structure surrounding a truck with something that looked like a Gatling gun in back. From the looks of things, they were protecting some uninteresting dirt side road.

"Somebody made a stand, but why the hell would you put a roadblock way out here?" It was Robert.

"Good question. What do you think is up that road?"

"Doc, you are more than welcome to take a look, I don't think your ride will be waiting when, or if you come back, but knock yourself out." Robert was scanning with his binoculars.

"Yeah, thanks, Robert. Is it me, or is this a shit load of zombies?"

I bent over the headless corpse of a guardsman. They had done quite a job on him. His right arm was missing at the shoulder; it's a ball and socket type joint and could be ripped free, but that would take a precise twisting technique and incredible strength. Both legs were gone at the knees, shirt ripped open, abdomen and intestines exposed. I was always incredulous when watching a movie zombie rip open someone's belly with their bare hands, but apparently, they have found a way. As would be expected, there was a lot of blood and tissue scraps. Most of the blood was clotted, but the deeper pools still held liquid. The tissue smelled fresh and there was not much signs of scavenger activity.

"So, Doc, about when do you think this went down?" Roy seemed agitated.

"Maybe yesterday?"

"Guys, I think it was late last night or early this morning. It's past eleven now and the bodies, blood, everything looks real fresh, this scene is just going cold. But whatever happened, we have nothing to do with it and should be going." Taking in the sights was not part of the plan and would have no good outcome.

Robert came over and in an almost fatherly tone said, "John, you are right. We should be moving and whatever happened here really does not have anything to do with us, but you see those two guys over there? If not for them, we would be dead right now, so when Roy says stop, I stop." He slapped me on the back. "Besides, we are a bit lost. All the traffic and roadblocks have moved us on to plan J. How's everyone doing in number two?"

"So far so good. I think we are all a bit shell shocked, but about as ready as can be."

"Don't worry. Mary and Terrence are good people. Just make sure they follow us and stay close. Remember what I told you about shooting. Just go for the center chest and try to stay calm."

"Thanks, Robert."

I drifted away and over to Roy and Hammer. They were dressed like those guys you saw on CNN who provided non-military security to diplomats in war zones. All dressed in black; combat boots, gloves, baseball caps, flak jackets, cool sunglasses, and those smallish machine guns with scopes. Flak jackets? They definitely knew how to gown for this party. Roy was reading a map and talking to Hammer, who was intently scanning up road. I decided to give them some time. As I glanced around and absorbed the scene, the number of zombie corpses scattered across the plowed field surprised me. I didn't count, but it had to be at least fifty. It looked like they all came from one direction and the guardsmen were ready. I didn't like the fact that there were so many zombies already out here, there had to be more. Where were they?

Roy came sauntering over, carrying a shotgun and bandoleer loaded with shells. He handed it to me saying, "I hope you know how to use this. Should give Winnie two a little more fire power." He stepped back and I could swear he was about to say something else when he turned and yelled, "Hey, Robert, you and me need to pow-wow with Doc. Tim, how we looking?"

"No zombies so far, Roy." He lowered his binoculars and leaned down. "It's the people that bother me."

"Keep me posted. You still with us, Paul, or is Judgment Day boring for you?"

"Wouldn't miss this for the world, Boss."

"Very nicely put."

Roy walked over to Winnie One and I just stood there, arms outstretched, holding a cool shotgun and a full bandoleer. This could work. I draped the ammo over my shoulder and looked the shotgun over. Yeah, I could tell it was a shotgun, but in no way the kind I grew up with. There was no wood, just black matte plastic, a stock and pistol grip, way shorter than I remembered, and a cool looking scope. Maybe this was Roy's way of showing approval; that it was okay with him that I was with Elizabeth, and that if I had the balls to leave the Winnie, I might be able to handle something other than the Ruger. Or it could be that he knew Winnie Two was a bit light when it came to fire power. While Roy and Doc spoke with Terrence, Robert gave me a quick tutorial of the weapon.

"You ever shoot one of these?"

"A few times, but just skeet. Nothing like this one." I handed it to him.

"Same concept." He tried to look at me, but was distracted by the cars and people on the road.

"Robert?"

"Alright, it's only partially loaded." He started to examine it closely. "Maybe three rounds left." It only took him a minute to give the seal of approval.

"Okay, nine shots fully loaded, safety is here. You chamber rounds by pump action, like this, nice and smooth. Now, when you fire, hold it tight to the shoulder, as it will kick. If you don't hold it tight or try to play cowboy, you might be looking at bruised or broken ribs, maybe a dislocated shoulder."

We both kneeled down on one knee and he ejected some shells and quickly demonstrated how to load. I loaded exactly three shells. "You might want to practice this some. Look, the Winnies are tight, so watch the recoil and make damn sure the barrel is out the window when you pull the trigger. Got it?"

"Roger that, practice and keep my shit together."

He ignored my comment. "Outside, a one knee stance like this will give you a more stable platform and better accuracy. From what I see, you have a mix of ammo and none of it is for bird hunting." He stood and started back to his vehicle, stopped, and turned.

"Just remember to have that safety on at all times when not in use. Oh, and when things do get interesting, count your shots!"

You know how you are about to say something that you realize is stupid, and you want to stop but the brain has sent the signal, and you go ahead because maybe it would be funny? Yup.

"Hey, Robert, are things going to get interesting?" He looked at me with a totally blank face, glanced around, stared back, shook his head, turned, and went inside his Winnie.

When I stood and turned to go back to number two, I froze. For the first time, I was seeing our caravan all lined up and out in the open. It was a sight to behold. The vehicles fit that post-apocalyptic heavy metal vibe to a T. Most of the Winnies' modifications had taken place on the outside, with a quilt-work of metal diamond plate reinforcement and steel grills; looking very impressive, very dangerous. All we lacked were Mohawk haircuts and chain mail.

A crowd had started to gather on the opposite side of the road. They were quiet, almost polite. I tried not to look, but did. Men, women and children; confused, terrified, tired...lost. I cannot save these people. I turned my back, went into the Winnebago, and closed the door.

"Show's over." It was Mary, "Let's get back to our assigned positions." Terrence had kept her idling.

"I'm with you, Mary, let's get the fuck going!"

"You okay, John?"

"I'm alright, Liz." I mouthed the words, 'I love you,' and went to my position.

It took a few tense minutes and a blast from Paul's machine gun to get us all on the same page and moving. We passed the carnage of the roadblock in silence. It seemed like bodies and parts were everywhere. It was then I realized a lot of the 'zombies' were partially dressed and appeared to be wearing military uniforms. We started so slow that I could clearly see a guardsman, maybe ten feet away, on his back with his left arm missing and dark dried blood over half of his uniform (well not really a uniform since he had no pants). The blood had desiccated, leaving his tattered left sleeve sticking out at a crazy angle. I focused on his head wound. No dried blood. Everything looked relatively fresh. These were both terminal wounds that had occurred at different times. What the hell had gone on here? As we drove away, I got a better view. The distribution and orientation of the guards' bodies was one of defense. The barricade was not intended to stop us from going up the side road, just the opposite.

The carnival crawled along, maybe hitting the 10 MPH barrier every now and then. I didn't look anyone who was along the road in the eye, just searched for threats, whatever that means. After about forty-five minutes, we stopped.

"Folks," Mary turned from the passenger seat to face us, "it looks like our free spirited time on the Autobahn is over, a major traffic jam ahead, miles long." She went back to the radio and I couldn't really hear what was going on. In a five minute conversation, the only words that got to me was her raspy voice shouting, "We could be fucked!"

The highway was probably made in the fifties and now held the honor of being a 'Scenic Byway.' Two lanes, both clogged, everyone heading in the same direction. Where were these people going? Did they all have boats? Will our boats be there? We had a plan and now I don't even know where we are going. Mary spent her time talking on the radio and to Terrence. The rest of us were just quiet and glued to our posts.

"Hey, Bad Boy," it was Liz, "here's some water. Nice shotgun. I guess pilfering the dead must be in vogue these days?"

"Thanks, it's a wedding gift from your ex."

"In your dreams, sweetie."

The coast looked clear, so I checked the safety, ejected a few shells, and practiced loading. God, did I love this woman!

The guy in the car to the left of me was alone in a small red BMW convertible with the top up. He had a hunting rifle across his lap aimed at the driver's side window. Like all of us, he looked desperate to get moving and pounded his steering wheel, while talking/shouting to himself. He never looked right at our convoy, but I could tell he knew we were there. As I watched, he was suddenly startled by something off to his left and hastily tried to change directions of the rifle, but the car was too small. To do this, he would have to get out. I was pretty sure I knew what got his attention and was wondering what his decision would be when a loud thump rocked the Winnie.

Through the screen, I could see a bald obese man dressed in a pair of khaki farmer Johns, wobbling from side to side like one of those old Weeble toys. He was a big boy, six foot plus and easily three hundred. His right ear was missing, dried blood caked his entire right side and his skin was an oily, grayish white, just like the others. It seemed to me he was not concentrating on the people inside. The vehicle itself fascinated him. He would whack us, step back, look, then step forward and hit us again. He was quickly making his way to the back, too close for Paul to get him. So, now it's John Time!

"I'll get him," I casually yelled. The zombie kept pounding and moving closer and closer to my position. I was ready, sure of my stance and barrel position. Then...shit, the safety's on! Looking over to flip it off, I stuck the shotgun too far out and the big guy grabbed the barrel. I was totally caught off guard and he was way stronger than I would have guessed. Would have guessed? Would have guessed? The dude significantly moved the Winnebago every time he hit the damn thing. I prayed that as we struggled, he would move in front of the barrel and I could get off a shot, but he stayed to one side, moving it back and forth, trying to pull it from my hands. I felt someone next to me, and then a loud bang. It was Liz. She had two pistols, both dark and modern looking. She had blown the top of farm boy's head off. He fell against the Winnie, holding the barrel to the very end.

"Thanks, Liz." Still in a bit of a daze and now half deaf, "How did he know to grab the barrel?" I really wasn't asking her, just talking to myself.

"More than likely, it was the movement. That was incredible, guys." It was Leslie who had been filming the whole thing.

"Hey, John, next time you go for a little walk, will you take a camera with you?"

"Leslie, let me think about that. Ah...no. But you can join me and I will cover you, as best I can." Was she fucking crazy? Carry a camera? I think I will just stay away and let her do her own thing.

People, real people, were running in various directions. An older woman, somewhere past 70 and not real, came into view, probably attracted by the commotion with the big guy. She was not as fast as the others were, stumbling around dressed in a light blue nightgown with muddy, but I assume, matching slippers. It was difficult to tell where she was wounded, since there were large dark spots everywhere. I knew it was light blue, because she held both arms up like she was surrendering, and her underarms were not stained. I have no clue why her arms were up; maybe the position she was in when she died? Some bizarre form of rigor mortis? I eventually settled on the 'maybe she just liked them that way' theory. I had freed the barrel from the big, now really dead guy's hands, clicked the safety off, positioned myself, and waited a couple of seconds for her to get closer. I had never used a scope and it was cool, gave me a sense that I knew what I was doing. Maybe she was a real person. Maybe she was just hurt and wanted some help. The way we look, I wouldn't come close to our little cavalcade without surrendering. Then I focused on her face. It wasn't pain, anger, or confusion, but pure fury. I fired. A huge section of her left side just vanished in a spray of gore. I had aimed for the head. She didn't fall, but made a complete counterclockwise pirouette and just stood there. She lowered her arms and folded them across her chest. It was almost like she was thinking of what to do, or maybe scolding me. This gave me a chance to line up a better shot, calm down, control my breathing, and slowly pull the trigger. Her head just seemed to explode and she crumpled to the ground. Very simple and just like in the movies. Yes! My first official zombie kill. Of course, it probably had been somebody's grandma, but a kill was a kill.

More zombies were already moving towards us. Paul was firing away, although from the sounds of his stochastic bursts, he was obviously taking his time and conserving ammo. Shots were coming from other vehicles. Mary had the radio turned up and I could clearly hear Roy.

"I want fire to protect our convoy only! We have to conserve ammo," Mary yelled. It was a cold-hearted order, but the appropriate one. Jane, Liz, and Norm, were blasting away and the cabin started to fill with gun smoke. I didn't have any targets in my zone, just more and more cars and people.

Directly behind us was an old forest green station wagon, the kind with the fake wooden panels on the sides, a luggage rack on top, and a seat in the back so you can ride going backwards. As a kid, I used to love traveling like that. The car was crammed full of people, adults and children. They were screaming and crying. Two zombies were on the passenger side, both thin shirtless young males, naked with shaved heads. The only thing they had on was a bright yellow bracelet on each right wrist. They could have been brothers, maybe they were. One was furiously banging away at the rear passenger window, huge windmill strikes that made the whole car shudder. The other just stood there with this face of fury and confusion. His arms were just hanging limply at his side. Several open wounds on his back probably indicated bilateral disruption to the brachial plexus, surgery. The nerves to his arms had been damaged and he could no longer use them.

The wagon was boxed in and they were trapped, eventually, the undead would get what they wanted. I pulled out the Ruger and lined up a shot on the active one. I was afraid the shotgun would do more harm than good. My first round hit the zombie in the neck, which made him turn his attention to me, and freeze, perfect, since he was only fifteen feet away. My next one was through the right eye, although I was aiming for his forehead. Now I had two. The other one didn't know what to do. Its arms flopped about as he rapidly turned from me to the station wagon and back again. It was like the zombie's brain was caught in this loop and couldn't decide who to attack next.

"We have got to get out of here, now!"

It was Mary. She sounded pissed, and she was right. As time passed, not only did more of the undead show up, so did more vehicles. They were trying to pass and getting stuck on either side of us. Everyone gave us a wide berth.

Things were going downhill fast, and if we don't move soon, we would become trapped. Mary was on the radio but I couldn't make out what was being said over the gunfire and general commotion. The Winnie suddenly jerked backwards and slammed into the station wagon, and I was thrown against the rear window. The flapping zombie was crushed and disappeared from view. I made eye contact with the driver. He was a portly, middle-aged man. I assumed the woman in the passenger seat was his wife. He leaned forward and stared at me through the cracked windshield, his eyes full of anger, confusion, and fear. The driver side window had shattered from the impact. Then Terrance hit the gas and pushed them backwards till they hit the car behind them. Now steam was venting from their engine. It was never our intent to kill them, but we did.

We lurched forward and started to inch ahead. I just stared at the people in the now dead, unsafe, station wagon. I'm sorry. We started to gain some momentum and Bang! Another big bounce and the entire Winnie swished from side to side. Everything stored in the cupboards was liberated; equipment, food, ammo, and water were everywhere. I found the shotgun and struggled to my feet. We had managed to cross the road and were now traveling in the opposite direction, half on, half off the shoulder. Paul was the only one still shooting. The view out my window was horrible. Roy had amped up the level of havoc and cleared us a lane. Cars were turned sideways, some with smoke pouring from the engines. A few had been pinned so tightly they couldn't open their doors. People stood in the road just looking at us. Three guys had rifles with scopes, but didn't do anything. What were we becoming? I felt like shit, but this was just me trying to avoid the inevitable truth that we did what we had to do to stay alive, and it can only get worse.

We were the only group heading back. About two agonizingly slow miles up the road, we came to a stop. I moved from the back over behind Terrance. Hammer had left the Hummer and was working on some chains around a green metal tubular gate in the middle of a nicely maintained stonewall. A dirt road crossed a large open green field, disappearing in a grove of large trees about a quarter of a mile away. There were cows in the field. Where the hell are we going? Hammer threw open the gate and we were soon moving forward, down the dirt road. As soon as we passed the gate, the Winnie stopped and Mary turned.

"Hey, John, Roy wants you to secure the gate."

"What?"

"You need to close and secure the gate. We will cover you."

"What?"

Liz was already at the rear shooting slot and nodded her head. "John, close the damn gate."

This bites! Why me? No, really, this fucking sucks! So much for showing fucking initiative and leadership. All right, be cool. We're fully loaded and the safety is off!

"Paul, cover me! I have to close the gate!" I tried to sound confident, but my voice reverted to that of a thirteen year old.

"Ten-four!" He yelled back. "I got your twenty." I opened the door and cautiously stepped out. Got your twenty? What the hell did that mean?

It was bright outside and it took a second for my eyes to adjust. Yep, just like this morning, only better and hotter. Inside the Winnie, it was broiling, and the light breeze felt great. With my shotgun at the ready, I made my way toward the wide-open gate. People in their cars looked at me but no one made any effort to get out or even roll the windows down. I shoved the gate closed and tried not to look or think about them. I put my shotgun down, wrapped the chain through iron loops on the gate and end post, and I was trying to tie the ends into a knot when Paul fired. Oh, shit! I had no choice but to concentrate on tying the chain, putting all my faith in Paul, no choice since in opening the gate, Hammer cut the lock. I was almost there when he switched to full automatic. My faith was now shaken. My hands were not moving fast or as coordinated as I wanted them to. I needed to breathe and relax, but couldn't. Sweat dripped across my glasses. Faith failed completely when Liz started firing from the back of the Winnie. Her pistols made this sharp barking noise. I looked up to see a tall thin dude about twenty feet from me. His body was shaking as Paul ripped him apart. Behind the tall guy were three more zombies. I refocused and finished what I hoped was something that would require a fully functional brain to undo, and grabbed the shotgun. I could see two more making their way through the tangle of cars coming straight at me. One was moving so fast she actually did a hood slide, the kind I used to marvel at while watching the old *Starsky and Hutch* TV series. Paul had stopped firing and I guessed he was out of ammo. I could hear him yelling. Liz had stopped too. I was more than likely in her way, but now I was ready. The first was an older male screaming at the top of his lungs, and so concentrated on me that he ran straight into the gate and bounced to the ground. Keeping the butt tight to my shoulder, I fired and blew the top of his head off. Three. The second was the young woman in a blue tank top and jeans, the one who had done the great hood slide. I could tell from her pace that she clearly saw the gate and had other plans to get to me. The gate was maybe four feet high and she easily cleared it like someone running a steeplechase. I caught her just as she landed, the force of the blast sending her cart wheeling away from me and ending up as this twisted jerking mass lying in the grass. I walked up and put a round through her head at point blank range. Four. As I reloaded, I scanned the road and did not see more coming, but they would be. Okay, Roy, what's next?

"Hey, John!" It was Paul from the top of the Winnie.

"Roy wants you to stop screwing around and get back inside. We need to move." Screwing around? We were already moving when I jumped in.

"Nice work. We're going to move on beyond those trees and evaluate the situation." Mary had a map out and she was obviously trying to guess where in God's name we were.

As we moved forward, I reloaded and kept tabs on our rear. More zombies did arrive, but so did about half dozen desperate humans who had decided at the last second to risk all and try to follow us. They more than kept the incoming zombies busy. Two of the undead did see us and managed to cross over. Paul took care of them, and in half minute, we had created enough distance that the heavily packed road became more of a distraction than we were.

As I had half expected, the dirt road led to your classic New England farmhouse, complete with a large barn, chicken coops, barking dogs, and an old guy on the porch swing with a double barrel shotgun. Roy radioed for us to stay in our vehicles and he would deal with this. I could see him walk up to the porch, unarmed, and remove his well-seasoned Red Sox baseball cap. In the short time, I have known him, I don't think I have ever seen him without the cap. Huh, he's going bald. They talked for a while and made several gestures toward the barn. Ten minutes later, they shook hands and Roy walked back to the Hummer. The radio crackled.

"Okay, listen up. The old guy is Samuel, and his wife, Nancy. They seem like nice people. They don't have cable or TV, but they have been listening to the radio and got a good clue what is happening. He will let us stay in the barn for tonight at least. We will give them some food and leave them alone. I have asked them to join us, but we shall see. Obviously, we have some changes in our plans and we can discuss this as a group later. Winnie One, I want you in the barn, all the way in. You're leaking something. Winnie Two, you are going to get nice and cozy with the barn door. I want you to partially block the door, just give us enough room to get out of the barn. Make sure your door is on the barn side so you can get into her. Everybody understand?"

"Roger that." It was Mary. Cool, calm, and collected.

"The Hummer is staying outside, but out of sight. Let's keep noise and activity to a minimum! Something as simple as accidentally hitting the horn or grinding the gears and we're toast." Part of me was thinking 'no shit, Sherlock' and part going 'Okay, be quiet, remember be quiet.' Well, I guess this is home for now. I didn't really expect to make it to the boats in one day. No, that's not true. I fully expected to make it in one day, with all the back roads, it had to be thirty miles tops. I just anticipated the traffic to be something like crossing the Cape Cod bridges at the end of a summer holiday, slow, but you get there. I just did not add batshit crazy desperate panic to the equation. At least, we're out of sight and some decent distance from the road. With the distractions of the other vehicles and the gate secured against wanderers, we might have a reasonable hiding place for a little while.

"Winnie Two. Mary, tell John to get ready to start a sweep with me. Let Liz or Jane take the turret with the hunting rifle. Paul is going to check out Winnie One. Anybody think they can help him, just speak up. Hammer will set a defensive detail. Mary, grab whoever you need and get us something to eat, cold may have to do. I want Zack up in the loft with binoculars and a radio to keep an eye on things."

"Roger dodger, Roy," she turned to me.

"Okay, gang, you heard him. John, please let Paul know."

It was now clear that Robert, Doc, Roy and I, were the appointed ones when it came to EVAs. I felt better that there would be four of us and we had not spotted a zombie since I closed the gate. I knew Roy was drop dead serious and I wanted to stay close to Robert, but Doc? Well, we will see. I made sure the Ruger and shotgun were ready to go. Roy didn't even know me, but it made me feel special that I had been chosen to be on the first line of defense, like I was some badass Green Beret. I guessed now was not the right time to inform him that today was the first time I had fired a shotgun in at least two decades, and my shoulder hurt.

"Things look clear so far, so let's keep everything as low-key as possible; no banging shit and for God's sake, don't shoot unless you have to." Mary was definitely Winnie Two's leader and I liked her. She helped me feel comfortable. I opened the door and looked around. Wow, what a place. A two story classic white farm house, porch with swing and surrounded by ancient trees, very Norman P Rockwell! Two big old black Labs came over to say hi, tails waging. I was happy to see they were not on alert and seemed friendly. They would come in handy, as an extra alarm should anything unwanted come our way. Wait a minute, how do dogs deal with the undead? I never saw anything on YouTube or the topic come up in any of the Plague/Zombie blogs I followed. I knelt down and hugged the two large goofy dogs. Oh, my God, that felt good. Dogs! Would we also lose dogs? I stood and stared at them. The two just sat there and stared back with a totally blissed-out 'cool more people to play with' attitude. I remembered as a child, being just like these two beautiful dogs, and I thought I was getting some of that back while being around Liz. I don't imagine I will be feeling anything close to bliss for a long, long time.

I sauntered over to Robert, Doc, and Roy. I had to get rid of this black cloud. After hours of insane claustrophobic tension, it was good to have things ratchet down a notch or two. Roy looked around nervously.

"Okay, Jane, I want you to stay in the turret and make sure those binoculars never leave your eyes. We will do this in shifts, but for now, plan on staying a while. Can you give me an hour or two?"

"Ten-four!" I almost thought Jane was going to salute, but she just turned, giggled, and adjusted herself in the turret. Jane is cool.

"Nobody wanted this, but here we are. John, you're with me." What? He turned to Doc and Robert. "You guys go and check our rear. Let's see how fucked we are and if there's another way out of here."

As Roy and I walked around the barn, I noticed that the trees, which screened the farm from the road, actually formed an effective barrier. A small stream ran among them and over the years, had eroded a fairly deep ditch. Combined with various bushes, shrubs, and thorns, it made an impregnable fence between the fields and the farmhouse. Impregnable to cows, that is. The undead would be slowed down considerably and certainly make a lot of noise, but if they saw or heard us, they would get through. We crossed the yard to the road we came in on. A small bridge with a cowcatcher (just a series of parallel bars at the start of the bridge that discourage cows from crossing) spanned the creek. As far as I could tell, this was the only clear way in. We stayed out of sight, close to the trees. In the distance, I could hear car horns and alarms, and an occasional gunshot.

"Okay, John, when the gate falls, I want you right here. Yeah, I know, but it will fall and this bridge is the cork blocking the path of least resistance. Maybe a minute from now or never, okay? You did well at the gate, and I trust you will do the same here." He looked at the ground. The weight of it all was just so evident. Not just his wife and the apocalypse, it had to bug him that I was with his ex. In many ways, Roy wanted this to happen. Hey, maybe I thought survival would be cool too, no responsibilities other than protect the ones you love. Now, I think we both want our money back. "They will have help, but you got this one small corridor and you're on the wall. Kind of like the Alamo."

"No problem, Roy, I'll be here." As opposed to where else can I go? The Alamo? Did he really say the Alamo? Sometimes, I need to know when to shut up.

"You know, some guys surrendered at the Alamo, not that they was facing un-mortal Mexicans and shit." Now, why did I have to bust his balls? The day was total crap on all of us. I was treating Roy as if he was the only one with any culpability. It was like some kind of drive-by-shooting with only the guy who fired the gun having any guilt. Did I really say 'they was facing'?

He turned and stared at me. "You let me know how the whole surrendering thing works out, okay?"

"Probably about as well as it did for the Alamo guys," I said under my breath as we turned to the tree line. We walked/crept away in silence and cautiously entered the trees. Roy didn't say anything for a while and seemed to be deep in thought.

"Do you have an issue with what happened today?" It was more of a sigh than a question.

"Yeah, I do."

We crossed the stream in silence, scrambling up the steep sandy slope and gained the edge where the trees met the field. The wind shifted and you could hear moaning from the road, kind of like a distant dull roar. Roy got on one knee and spent a good bit of time just looking through his binoculars. I tried to be as still as the trees around me. The littlest thing might send a zombie our way. If one went, how many others would follow? Our one advantage was the sun. It was past zenith and it was reflecting off of all the metal and glass of the cars. It started to make the road glisten and shine. I thought of the yellow brick road, and then my mind instantly jumped to the Elton John song: "When are you gonna come down? When are you going to land?" The enormity of the day was sinking in. I heard Roy move.

"Stay out of sight. Tell me what you see."

He handed me the binoculars. I crawled closer to get a clear view, adjusted the focus, and scanned the road. Fuck! You could tell by the way that the things moved that they were not the living. They were just way too fast and chaotic, with no discernible purpose. From this distance and glare, it was hard to make out details, just lots of activity. I thought for a second of the old Pied Piper story. Maybe we could find a means of herding them down to the sea, and end all of this.

"What I see is a hopeless situation. There is nothing we could have done. I don't blame you, Roy. I don't blame anyone. I guess if there is blame to give, it's to God. The living has nothing to do with this." I handed him back the binoculars, knowing full well that the last statement was probably a lie.

We made our way back and found Doc and Robert crossing the large plowed field that was directly behind the barn.

Doc, a tall lanky middle-aged man with a crazy mustache and six shooters, yes, real gunslinger guns, on both hips waved all clear. I had seen him talking with Roy, Hammer, and some other guys yesterday. They were hunched over a bunch of maps and photos with a few taking notes, so I guess he was part of the original group.

"Roy, the field looks to be at least ten acres in size. Small, dense woods on two sides, pretty much east and west." He used his hands to draw an invisible map in the air. "We couldn't see through, but my guess is more fields. This farmhouse and barn are our southern boundary and a stonewall to the north. This service road we are standing on hugs the edge of these trees and then the stonewall. It leads to a closed gate that opens on to a gravel road."

"Thanks, Doc. Robert?"

"Roy, our scenic route is fucked, you know that. We both know that we have shit the Golden Fleece with finding this farm. We have to leave out the back and figure a way around this mess. So for the time being, it looks like we have a somewhat secure compound. We stay out of sight and sound, maybe we get a clear day or two." Robert muttered the last part under his breath.

"But better than a poke in the eye with a sharp stick." Roy sounded tired and I hoped this signaled the end of recon. We all needed rest, Roy in particular.

"Okay, back to the barn and another group meeting. Either way, we are here tonight. I want all of you thinking about the best way to get us to dawn." We trudged off to the barn. I half notice that only Robert and I maintained a constant state of alertness, arms at the ready, and looking for threats.

We entered to the sound of Paul yelling at the crew working on Winnie One. "Please find the damn oil plug! Maybe I could just put a damn piece of cloth in it. If I had one!" Paul was under Winnie One periodically banging on something and swearing to himself.

From out of the shadows, a huge figure emerged. "Paul, shut the fuck up." hissed Hammer. "We are ALL in God damn stealth mode!" He went over to Winnie two and looked around. "Okay, Winnie Two crew, over here, now." The group gathered around.

"The only way this place offers any kind of protection is if they don't notice us! That means no movement, no sound, and no light. We are behind enemy lines. I want all of you to keep repeating that! We are behind enemy lines, what will I do to give away our position?" His eyes were methodically moving from face to face so that everyone got the message. "With Winnie One out of service, we cannot afford a fight in daylight, let alone at two in the morning. This is the way it is, folks. Number two gets the shaft.

You go in shifts of two hours with three together at all times, and I mean together! Somebody in the turret, back window, and front seat. We don't know what these things do at night, so no fucking around with flashlights or casually firing up to get a smoke. The rest need to find someplace that's comfortable. If you snore, then you are SOL when it comes to sleeping tonight. Winnie One doing breakfast. Find whoever is holding on to the good night vision goggles and make sure they end up in the turret. Roy, Robert, and I, will take turns up in the loft with night vision. If you see or sense anything, you wake someone and send them to us. We'll decide what course of action to take. We eat now. If anyone has a problem, you bring it up with Roy, got it?" No one said a word. "Oh." and he vaguely pointed to some area inside the dark barn. "I have piled up some hay bales over in the corner. That's our head. I don't want anyone wondering outside wanting to do their business." He smiled. "Don't worry, there's a bucket." It was clearly now Hammer Time. As the group broke-up, I went over to Hammer.

"Hey, Hammer, can zombies smell?" It took him a couple of seconds.

"Everyone listen up." He hissed. "No Smoking."

He went over to a group from Winnie One and started to talk with Paul and give directions to the others. I went over and helped Mary and some other women getting dinner ready. I still did not have everyone's name down, and for the most part, I couldn't tell you who was in Winnie One. Nobody really talked or looked directly at each other. We were all on edge doing what had to be done and trying to get through this day. Dinner was going to be a simple affair; cold cuts, cheese, bread, salad stuff, and lemonade, basically, anything that was perishable, since refrigeration was an issue. Liz and I ate together, a bit away from the group and discussed the day's events.

"Is this a dream, Liz?"

"Jesus, John, don't scare me! You surprised me today."

"Huh, how?"

"Don't get upset, but you are not the macho fighter type. I was proud of you out there at the gate. You know, that's my man out there kicking some zombie butt."

"I guess you never noticed the stain in my crotch? Speaking of the gate, why me? Did I somehow piss Roy off?"

"No, John, you did not piss Roy off. He's an odd guy, the kind that only needs one look to know what he thinks of you. He put you out there, because he knew you could do the job. The fact that you did it and lived just elevated you to the next stage. I guess you're now a zombie fighter level two."

"Doesn't that mean I get a special sword or something?"

"I think with time, we'll find you already are in possession of a special sword."

"Oh, you nasty girl!" We laughed and held each other, oblivious to the world. I could not get to the islands soon enough.

"Liz, what about today? What really happened out there? Happened to us? All of us?"

"I don't know. I don't want to know." We looked into each other's eyes, not talking but both understanding that a line had been crossed. It was strange, because we both knew we did what we had to. We also understood there was a price to be paid for such actions. Later, we crawled to a corner and slept, spooning each other.

Chapter 11 ~ Murder by Numbers

May 26th

I woke well after midnight to a strange noise. Kind of like someone pouring sand on metal. It took me a minute to figure out it was rain, lots of rain. Oh no! We still have a ton of dirt road to cover. As quietly as possible, so as not to wake Liz, I made my way outside. I waved to Norm who was up in the turret in a poncho, looking absolutely miserable. Norm is a real nice guy, mid-sixties, in shape, baldhead, and a grey beard. He was laid back and competent with his nine millimeter. Roy was standing in the small gap between the Winnie and the barn, staring at the rain. I moved up next to him. He never looked me.

"This better stop soon or we might be screwed." It was around this time that I realized that my right shoulder was swollen and hurt like hell, the result of not paying attention while screwing around with the gate.

"Yeah, John, I am thinking the same thing. Mud could make getting out tomorrow a real bitch. If we were on the road, this would work to our advantage."

"You found a route?"

"We found a route."

"Thanks, Roy. Thank you for saving my life. I hope we live long enough to become friends."

"You're already my friend, John." Roy walked back into the barn.

And so it rained. It rained through a great breakfast. It rained through small arms training and tactics. It rained through an hour with Hammer on the proper use of a shotgun. It rained through an intimate conversation with Liz, where I almost proposed. It rained half way through lunch, and then stopped. It did give us a psychological break since all the commotion from the rain made it safer to talk and move around. The flip side is we would never see or hear them coming. Winnie One was out of service, so we couldn't leave today anyway. We had several AM/FM radios, but nobody wanted to hear what everybody already knew, except Roy and Hammer. They spent the most time trying to understand what was going on in the world. I occasionally wandered over, but never stayed long. You didn't need to listen, just go up to the barn loft and scan the road. The radio and the road just mirrored each other.

After lunch, Roy called Robert, Hammer, Doc, and me, to make a survey of the situation. We knew that our only realistic way out was by the back road. To nobody's surprise, the mud was nasty, the soil slick, and the grade just steep enough to make a run to the gate way more of an adventure than it should be.

"What about towing them up to the road?" Robert asked, as he checked out the route with our best binoculars. "It will take some time, but...shit, nobody move," then in a whisper, "two going by the back gate. Not looking our way." We stayed statue still until Robert gave the all clear. All I could see was some tiny dots.

As if nothing happened, Roy continued Roberts' train of thought. "One at a time is too much time. Towing's gonna make a lot of noise and be slow as shit. Good idea, but it is as it is, at least for today, we're here. I'll go talk with Samuel."

We went back to the barn. Liz and I spent most of the afternoon huddled together, exchanging small talk, nuzzling, and just enjoying that at least we had each other. I told her about Chile, volcanoes, flamingos, and about how much I wanted to take her there. Hammer spent the time with most of our group going over loading and general care of everyone's small arms, peppered with tactics, and his unique brand of philosophy, something of a cross between Attila the Hun and an angry Mister Rogers. He knew his stuff and loved to have an audience.

Like Liz mentioned, Matilda and Madeline (I refused to call them M&M as some others started to do) stayed by themselves; usually just talking, watching, or holding each other. What if they got separated? No one to talk with. Could I stand that kind of isolation? It reminded me of something Harlan Ellison wrote, *I*

Have No Mouth and I Must Scream. Right now, they had each other and two big, goofy, black Labradors.

Later on, I ran into Zack from Winnie One, and of course, we talked about zombies. About ten minutes into the conversation, without agreed upon rules, points, or anything, we started playing a quoting game. The game was based on Gorge Romero's first three zombie movies, *Night, Dawn* and *Day*. We both agreed that any remakes and Land/Diary/Survival were out of bounds, we both had only seen them once. Points were awarded on direct quotes from the movies. We eventually decided that you got one point for each letter in the quote, and the quote had to be in context with the current situation. For instance, Zack and I went up to check out the loft, still fleshing out the rules of the game. Out of the blue, I made some inane observation about zombie movement patterns, to which he quickly responded in the immortal words of Sheriff McClelland, "Yeah, they're dead. They're all messed up." I walked right into an easy one and Zack scored a quick thirty-one points. Matt seemed to have caught the Hollywood bug, and with Leslie, started filming our now boring yet tenuous existence.

We got down just as Roy called another meeting. I moved over to Liz and held her hand. Paul announced to the gang that we needed motor oil, and that without it Winnie was toast. We had brought along extra, but an earlier leak, just as we were leaving, had taken care of most of that reserve. Great, where the hell are we going to get motor oil? That's when Mary stepped forward and in a shaky voice, made an announcement.

"Lucy has a fever just over a one hundred and three." Everyone seemed to freeze. I was stunned and could hear myself breathing. One hundred and three? Shit, this has got to be the flu, but this isn't flu season. Oh please, God, let it be the flu. I looked at Zack who was just staring at the floor. I noticed out of the corner of my eye that Roy was looking at me. Our eyes locked and with a small nod, and the decision was made. I would do the exam.

"Mary, when did this start?" I said the words very slowly, in the hollow hope that maybe Lucy's sickness has been developing for the last few days, and only now with the rain and stress, had developed into a fever.

"John," she glanced around as if to generate support, "she told me she felt funny before lunch." Ah, fuck!

"Fever?"

"When I first took it an hour ago, it was around one hundred. Cramps all over and her throat's severely inflamed."

"Was she bit?"

"I asked her, and she said no."

I looked at Roy and as from far away, heard my voice say, "We have to quarantine her and keep her isolated. If this is the virus, we will know soon enough." Ah, shit, can I do this? Again, why me?

"How will we know?" asked Liz. Oh, thanks, Liz, for the one question that I did not want to hear.

"Well, we got rapid onset, high fever, sweats," I looked to Mary and she nodded her head yes. "Inflamed throat, severe headache, nausea, general pain all over?" Again to Mary and she said yes. "There are lots of diseases that can do this. If it is the virus, she will start slightly hemorrhaging both under the skin and then from every orifice in the body; mouth, nose, eyes, and everything down below. If this happens, the blood is highly contagious, including any vomit." John, shut the fuck up. Nice fucking question, Liz. A small group of us moved away to a corner.

"Is there any way to be sure?" My eyes were closed and I don't know who asked the question.

"Well, if we could perform an ELISA or an IFA test in this fucking barn, we might have a decent clue!" Wrong answer! "Sorry, guys."

I looked at Zack. "What's in the medical kit?"

"Just the usual stuff." Zack continued to stare at the floor as if examining something on his shoes.

"Saline? IV?"

"Yeah," said Hammer.

"Okay, get me a bag and a rig, also gloves, a mask, and Paul, I need your goggles." Liz gave me that 'why you?' look. I crouched down on my heels and folded my arms on my head. I started going over what needed to be done. Oh, God, please be just the flu, please. I got up and walked over to Zack.

"Dude, I can do this." His voice had a weird shaky quality.

"I know you can, Zack, but I think I know what to look for. Hey, maybe she is just sick and in a day or two, she will be better, the roads dried out, and our problems will be resolved. It will be back to the basics, just your everyday zombie apocalypse to worry about."

"I hope so." Zack then went through the medical kit and gave me gloves, facemask, and the thermometer.

"Zack, I want you to talk to the others, see if anyone else is feeling ill, anyone who has been hanging out with Lucy. Hey, man, just be discrete and low key about it, okay?"

"No problem. Be careful with Lucy. I am already way ahead in our game and I want a legitimate victory." Game? What the fuck.

Hammer pulled me aside and whispered, "If she starts hemorrhaging and you are sure, you come to me first." I just nodded and walked to the other side of the barn. Every eye was on me and I really had only a moderate clue as to what I was going to do.

Lucy was lying on a pile of hay. She seemed to be asleep, so Hammer, Norm, and some guy from Winnie One, quickly moved a dozen bales to make a wall and give her some privacy. Her eyes popped open as I came closer, and she looked terrified. Her eyes were wide and bloodshot, her clothes soaked with sweat. She was shivering and was giving off a slightly sour odor. This was one sick lady, and I really should not be near her. She was wrapped in several of those cheap Mexican blankets loved by hippies. In fact, I had a couple in the back of the Subaru. Lucy was probably around thirty; red hair, attractive, average build, and I don't think we had said two words to each other on our short adventure.

"Hi. I am John. I'm in Winnie Two."

"Lizzy's boyfriend?"

"Yeah." I kneeled next to her and tried to sound calm. "Lucy, it could be just the flu. We will get through this."

"You need to move. You need to get to the boats." Her voice was barely a whisper and the shivering made her sound like her mouth was full of water.

"We're stuck here anyway because of the rain, okay? I was just out there. The mud won't let the Winnies move; so you are not slowing us down and we are NOT going to leave you behind!" She nodded and gave me a little weak smile. She knew, so now I hoped she would help me.

"All right, I just want to check a couple of things and see what we can do to get you comfortable. I would first like to take your temperature. I also want to look under your arms into your arm pits." Okay, pay attention because everything is hot. I carefully placed the thermometer under her tongue and gently lifted her arm. Ah, shit! The lymph nodes were swollen to about the size of a chestnut, and starting to turn black. She had red rashes on her sides, something that looked like a heat or diaper rash. Her temperature was one hundred and four.

"How does your throat feel?"

"It hurts…it's on fire."

"Have you had anything to drink lately?"

She shook her head, no. Hammer came over with the saline and IV kit and put them next to me. He also had a broken wooden pole with a coat hanger duct taped around the top and stuck it in a bale near Lucy. "For the IV."

"Thanks, Hammer. Okay, Lucy, I'm going to put you on a drip and I will get you some water for your throat." I had actually worked as a phlebotomist during the summer back in grad school, have put in IV's, and helped out at the local clinic during the annual fall flu season, so I was comfortable around needles and knew how to do this.

I took my time and tried to be robotic. Lucy had stopped shivering, her arm was limp, and finding the vein was easy. What wasn't easy was the stick. Her skin was slippery and I popped the vein, she immediately began to hemorrhage under the skin. I tried again quickly before I lost the vein to the bruise or lost my cool. As I was finishing taping the needle in place, she reached out and grabbed my hand. Her grip was surprisingly strong. She looked at me and knew I was afraid. This gave her some comfort. Just then, she had a coughing fit. I jumped back, unsure if she had sprayed me and quickly started a detailed examination of my clothes. He coughing seemed to bring her around. When I looked up, she was watching me with watery blood-shot eyes and a sad smile.

"Do not let me come back." It was an order not a plea.

It took me a second, but I stammered, "Lucy, we don't know what we are dealing with here. It really could be the flu."

Tears were pouring down her cheek. "John, don't play cards, you would suck."

The rest of the group had left me alone with Lucy and congregated on the other side of the barn. I don't blame them. I used sterile technique to remove gloves and took the mask off.

I went to them and with a quiet voice said, "I would like to speak with Roy and Hammer in private please. No one goes near Lucy but me, okay?" I went inside Winnie Two, and the two quickly joined me.

"Guys, I am not a doctor. I did screw around with hemorrhagic fever when I was young and worked for the government. It's…this is all…happening too fast. She doesn't appear to have any trauma, so this is very rare. I've never seen anyone with an actual pulmonary infection, just the stuff on the internet. Yes or no? I think she has the virus."

No one said a word.

"We should wait for the bleeding and some other symptoms to start; this will be somewhat diagnostic, we have got to be absolutely sure." I grabbed someone's bottle of water and took a huge swig.

"Her underarm lymph nodes are swollen and turning black. That is not a sign of the flu, but most likely a sign of this virus. This is not your straight up run of the mill hemorrhagic fever." I sat down and put my head in my hands. "She's in a lot of pain and I have no idea how long this will last." The world was swirling around me. I have to do this.

"Think!"

"Roy, the odds are, and this is my best guess, she is infected."

Roy paced back and forth slamming his hand into his fist.

"She's at a hundred and four, dehydrated, we have no IV or saline, and this only started a couple of hours ago!" I stood up and needed to burn some unexpected energy.

"Listen, when this whole thing started, there was a lot of internet chatter about some strange zombies. The Asian bloggers were reporting a small percent of the infected showed no obvious signs of trauma. Some PhD in Easter Russia gave an estimate of five percent. The mode of infection was never determined, airborne? Body fluids? Unusual fevers were reported and I think everyone has seen 'the Seoul woman' video. A young beautiful naked woman slowly walking on a street in downtown Seoul, South Korea. It was so well filmed that it looks like an ad for some new perfume or something, that is until the camera pans to her front and you see the thin trails of dried blood coming from her eyes. Her inner thighs were coated with blood and feces. She just stumbles along, oblivious. You know something is wrong with her, Blind? Deaf? Both? I have watched it several dozen times and the only thing I am sure about the woman, is that she is a zombie. Boy, did I need to get some air.

"We all know how this is going to end. What we don't know is how long this is going to take." Everyone looked at me and no one said a word, so I proceeded. "If it progresses and we are sure...do we have any narcotics in the medical kit?"

"I'll look," said Hammer, and he left.

"Roy, what if she starts screaming in pain? Goes crazy? We have to have a plan. I am going to take her some water. She came in yesterday morning with someone, right?"

"Yeah, Jim."

"You might want to talk with him." I left to re-gown and get her some water. As I walked away, I heard Roy call Jim over to him. The fog descending over me was intense and settling in. I had a mission, and it was in all probability to kill a member of our team.

When I got back, she had just finished vomiting on herself. I didn't have anything to wipe her mouth, nothing. I helped her drink from a disposable cup, ever wary that if she did spit it up, none would go on me. The vomit smelled sour. There was nothing I could do, so I sat there holding her hand. After about ten minutes, I noticed a trickle of blood coming out her nose. She was in great pain and started whispering to someone who was not there. After ten more minutes, the decision was made.

"I will be right back." In her condition, I doubt she even knew I was there.

Someone, whom I guessed was Jim, was over by the Winnie with Roy. Hammer was to one side holding a small red pouch, waiting for me.

"Morphine, John, I will do it," he said in an uncharacteristically kind voice.

"Thank you, Hammer, and no, she's my patient now. I will do it. I have given injections before. Just put the bag down over there. She's real sick and I don't know if I am clean."

"Be careful, John. I look forward to getting to know you and finding out what you haven't done!"

I looked at Hammer and with a voice full of resignation said, "Kill someone."

Jim and Roy came over to us.

"Jim would like to say goodbye." He was maybe forty, tall, fit, and very quiet. I think Robert told me he was an expert sailor, something about soloing the Atlantic last year.

I stared at Roy and whispered, "Does he know?"

"Yes."

I stayed my distance and just nodded to him. "Okay, Jim, I really don't know what to say, but you know you can't touch her or even be close."

"Roy filled me in."

"I am sorry, Jim." What else could I say?

He walked around the bales and I followed, but kept a respectable distance. Roy got the group together and let them know what was happening.

Jim stood about six feet way and quietly called out her name. Lucy was lost. The fever, the pain; whatever had made her sick was rapidly killing her. After a couple of minutes, Jim told her he loved her and she needed some rest. He blew her a kiss, "I'll see you soon." After Jim left, I sat down next to her.

Now, amongst an ever-expanding list of issues, I only had one real problem. Having never used intravenous drugs, I didn't know the amount that would ensure an overdose. I have no clue what the LD50 is or how many milligrams per kilograms are needed. Since she was more than likely not a drug user and would have no tolerance to morphine, I decided to go with one hundred milligrams. It should be massive and more than enough, I hope.

Once injected into the IV port, she quickly fell asleep. I monitored her pulse and was really bothered that during all this, my hands didn't shake. Her whole body started to relax and the bleeding from her eyes and nose got worse. After five minutes, her pulse was thready and weak, her breathing shallow, and by ten, it was over. I pulled both blankets up and covered her head to reduce spray from the bullets impact. I then walked about thirty feet away, took careful aim. Ah, shit! What was I thinking? I can't fire; the noise could call attention to us. What the hell am I going to do now? I started to panic since I didn't know how long it would take for her to reanimate. Looking around the barn, I noticed a pile of pipes that were probably from an old irrigation system. I picked up a short one, about four feet long. It was heavy and seemed more than adequate to do what I need to do. I started to sweat. Hell, I already killed her and now I was just doing her a favor, but it was harder than giving the injection. From my angle, the rest of the group couldn't see me. Standing over Lucy's body was the loneliest moment of my life. The blow was swift and savage. Feeling the top of the skull cave in, I was relieved that it only took one hit. I am a murderer. I have just killed a real human being. Infected or not, she was human!

Roy, Zack, Robert, and Hammer came over and stood as a shield for Lucy's body and me. I looked at my clothes, no stains, but I wasn't sure. I very carefully peeled off my gloves and laid them near Lucy, next my facemask, and last, the goggles. I then put on a new pair of gloves and began to undress. I was completely naked when I walked back to Winnie Two. Roy and Hammer followed me.

"Are you alright?" It was Roy.

"I think so." The rest of the group walked in. No one said a word. I entered the Winnie, redressed, and went outside to get some air. I looked up at the sky. There was a quiet in me that some part of my brain seemed to recognize as peace, but if only I could hold it together just a few more days till we get to the boats. In a daze, I went to the backside of the barn, sat down, and cried. Liz came over. I motioned for her sit, but to stay away from me, and I slowly composed myself. We were just still and quiet for about ten minutes. How could I have been so cold and calculated? I knew I was in some form of shock, and nauseous.

Liz whispered, "Come on, John, let's go inside."

"Okay."

"She would have died a horrible death, you know that. What you did was a courageous thing. If I was bitten or caught the virus, I hope you would be as kind. John…"

"Let's not talk about this."

So we went inside. The mood was sad and somber, but with a distinct undertone of unity, relief. I didn't know what to do, so I looked for the closest shadow. What did they think of me now? Jim came up to me, tears streaming down his face. I was too stunned to be worried if he would hit or shoot me. I didn't know what their relationship was. I had never bothered looking for a ring. He gave me a big hug and held me tight. So much for my lame attempt at quarantine.

"Thank you," he whispered in my ear. He kissed me on the cheek and walked over to Winnie One, totally broken. The only thing going through my mind was a verse from Leonard Cohen, 'It's a cold and it's a broken hallelujah.' Yet again, I changed. I was now a completely different person from what I was forty-eight hours ago, for better or worse. This shit really needs to end soon.

Roy came up.

"Hell of a thing you did. I am going over to talk with Samuel about what happened and where we can find some motor oil. Why don't you go take the loft shift? This will give you some time alone."

"Thanks, Roy, tell everyone not to go near the body. We can't bury her, it's just too dangerous. Let me think about what's next."

He extended his hand and we shook.

Hammer approached me and put his rather large paw on my shoulder.

"Well, Hammer, I guess I can add another thing to that list."

"Yeah. Glad you're on our team."

I went up to the loft. Our luck was still with us, no zombies in the fields. Lots on the road and by the way they were acting, there were still people trapped in their cars. Later, Liz joined me. We embraced and I held her as close and as hard as I could.

I was coming out of my fog and starting to review the whole shitty day.

"Liz, this is not a good sign. From what I can gather, Lucy wasn't bitten and I doubt she came into intimate contact with someone who had the virus. This kind of virus doesn't really go airborne. Yeah, pulmonary cases have happened, but boy, is it rare. Maybe we're all infected? I wasn't going to tell you, but I spoke with a friend at the CDC a few days ago. There is a chance that the virus is not natural."

"Oh, God, John, you have got to be shitting me."

"Please keep it to yourself. I don't want people losing faith."

"Could we really have done this to ourselves? At their core, maybe humans really are mad?"

"Just look what we did to get here."

We hung out in the loft for the next several hours just holding each other and taking turns scanning the road and field. I wanted to savor the moment and forget what I had just done.

For dinner, it was the pinnacle of Western Culture gastronomic delights, canned Spam, a variety of crackers, cheese, and the last of our rapidly wilting salad mix. I grabbed what I wanted and moved off to myself quickly. Liz sat down next to me and looked at her can.

"Spam?"

Exactly at that moment, because there could be no other, Zack walked by and my mouth was full.

"Don't knock it. It's got its own key."

Oh, Son...Of... A...Bitch! I was going to use that one, a classic. He just looked at me, winked, and pulled out the little black book. Okay, I got to think of more from *Day of the Dead,* because he is killing me on *Dawn.* Dumb or not, this one little stupid incident really helped pull me back to whatever was passing as normal these days.

After dinner, Roy called everyone together.

"Okay, I talked with Samuel. He understands we are not leaving as soon as we wanted. He and Nancy appreciate how quiet and low key we've been. There is some kind of general store about five miles from here and he is positive they have the motor oil, if any is left. They also have a hunting section, so it could mean more ammo. We are going to take the Hummer. It's the only thing that can get through all this new mud. It's going to be me, Hammer, Allison, and John, first thing in the morning. We are in and out and back in an hour. Robert is in charge while we are gone. Doc, I want you in the loft. The rest of you divide the night shifts as you see fit. This has been a trying day for all of us. I know it's hard, but keep focused and try to get some rest. Thanks."

Roy walked over to me.

"Samuel would like to see you up at the house when you have the time. And, uh…about tomorrow, I want you on the team not for some bullshit psychobabble reason about keeping your head in the game. Hammer and Robert are the best, so one of them stays here. I have thrown some crap your way and you responded without whining. This side trip is a dangerous pain in the ass, but a necessary one, so I chose you. I don't know Allison all that well, but she comes highly recommended and could do with some Wild West time."

"Thanks, Roy. I'll whine more if that helps." He just shook his head and walked away. Allison? Who was Allison? Highly recommended by whom?

I grabbed my shotgun, told Liz where I was ordered and headed up to see Samuel and Nancy. I took my time walking the fifty or so yards to their house. When I got to the porch, I stood for a couple of minutes and concentrated on my breathing. So much had happened so fast that for the life of me, I could not recall what I was doing exactly one week ago. I knew I was on the computer, listening to the radio and TV, but did I call anyone? Send any emails? When was the last time I spoke with my mother, brothers, and sister? When was the last time I really thought about them?

Nancy opened the door. She had sad eyes, but a big smile.

"Hello, John. Thank you for coming to see us. I would have visited, but Samuel is adamant about staying out of sight."

I took my boots off and entered. The drapes were drawn and only two small candles were lit, but it was enough to show me that the living room was exactly as I would have envisioned it; hardwood floors, beautiful fireplace, framed paintings, family photos and practical, comfortable furniture. She led me to a chair and sat on the couch.

"Roy tells me you are a teacher, what discipline?"

"Anthropology, at the university in Bangor."

"Ah, Anthropology, my my. As a girl, I wanted to be an anthropologist, or an archaeologist, well same discipline, aren't they? I wanted to travel the world, excavate ancient civilizations, and stay with lost tribes. Be another Levi-Strauss, or Leaky, or Mead." Nancy had to be in her seventies, but she was not old.

"Yes, me too. How long have you lived here?"

"Forty eight years, it was Samuel's father's place and he inherited it when Bob passed. We raised three sons here." She suddenly stopped and looked at her hands. The past was not something you talked about these days, unless you were really ready.

Samuel came in cradling his double barrel, followed by the two Labs. He kissed Nancy on the forehead, gave me a nod, and sat down. For a couple of minutes, we just shared the intimacy of silence. I felt very comfortable around these nice salt of the earth people and sitting in this twilight was relaxing, but it didn't take me long before I felt like I had to say something.

"Well, our times are rough and desperate. If not me, then who? From a technical point of view, I think I know the virus better than anyone else in our group does. I know how to give an IV and although I did not want to, I knew I could." I could hear myself talk and I sounded like a bad actor from some cheap movie.

"I didn't know her. We were introduced just yesterday." I didn't have to justify my actions to anyone, but felt like a really naughty child in front of his parents.

We again sat there in silence, this time for a good five minutes, and then Samuel spoke.

"It's really one hundred percent fatal?"

"Yes." I meant to stop talking but the thought of another quiet spell disturbed me, so I babbled on. "It is a painful, horrible way to die and then to end up, well, you know. Humanity is in very deep trouble. Samuel, Nancy, I genuinely hope you decide to come with us. Nobody in our group has experience in farming or animal husbandry, or any of that shi...stuff. We don't know what we are going to find out there, but we know it's going to be bad and we need all the help we can get."

Samuel leaned closer and put his hand on my knee. "You showed a lot of guts and compassion today. John. If a tenth of the survivors have responded to this hell on Earth with your grit, we are going to make it. You, of all people, need to survive. We will pray that God watches over all of you."

What the hell did he just say? I looked over at both of them. Ah, fuck, they are not coming. I tried to sound upbeat.

"Thank you. Well, I am up early to go get that oil."

"Oh that reminds me. The guy who owns the store is named Joshua, and knowing Joshua as well as I do, he is still going to be there and he is going to want cash." We all just looked at each other for a second, and then started laughing.

Nancy turned to me.

"Samuel is right. He is about a million years old and as cantankerous as you know what. He is also going to be armed to the teeth, so you watch your step and mind your Ps and Qs. Let him know we sent you and that Samuel and I are doing bout as well as can be expected."

"I am sorry I'm not much company. Well, good night folks, I'll see tomorrow."

Nancy led me to the door and as I struggled to put my boots on, said, "You stay close to your special someone."

"What?"

"Don't give me what, John."

I smiled, "Yes, Ma'am, I'll take care of her." She gave me a hug and I waved goodbye.

I trudged back to the barn as the sun was setting and waved to Leslie who had watch in the turret. Camera in hand, she filmed my walk, giving it some narration that I couldn't quite make out.

When I entered, people were in various states of getting ready for bed. Liz and I had planned to sleep together, but tonight I blew her off and went to a far corner of the barn to be alone. What a day. It seemed like a week had been squeezed into a few hours, and already the death of Lucy was fading. I should be with my special someone, but that selfish part of me needed my solitude. I wanted to cultivate my armor, and get ready to put my rice-paper-thin badass on for tomorrow.

It had to be around three in the morning when I got a tap on my backside. It was Jim. He had two shovels, a short and a long handle one, and just said with his eyes, 'yes?' I nodded yes. We slowly worked our way to the other side of the barn. He had discovered a large canvas tarp we could wrap Lucy with. I put on gloves and removed the IV. We checked things out and found a nice piece of ground behind the barn where the cows would not be able to defecate. It helped that there was a full moon. We worked in silence, just a glance between us now and then. We were extremely cautious and even the people on watch did not hear us, or chose not to. Even with the now rain-softened earth, it took about two hours to dig a proper grave. We shared the last of a canteen of water when it was all done.

Light was just creeping over the eastern horizon when I thought I heard something. A second later, two dark forms came low around the corner of the barn, tails straight down. They came to see what's up, but didn't make a sound. I don't know what it is and I don't subscribe to this whole animal empathy thing, but they were totally silent. They didn't even wag their tails The two just sat looking at us with big, sad eyes.

We were very careful about contamination and I got us some gloves and masks from the medical kit. We used the tarp to lift and drag Lucy's body to her grave. It was hard being quiet. Suddenly, there was Zack. He didn't say a word, just joined in. Norm came out of the shadows and so did Liz. We all moved Lucy to her grave, which would soon be blanketed with summer wildflowers. With great care, we covered her up and prayed. I stayed the longest, sat in the grass, watched the sunrise, and just wondered. What if she did not have the virus?

Chapter 12 ~ Blood and Oil

May 27th

    I was already up and my mind was still fried from the last twenty-four hours, so I just hung out in the loft and whispered with Paul. He had been an executive at some British computer company in the European Real World. He was the company's colony representative. Paul was in his mid-thirties and loved working on cars. He mentioned that something about the look of a Shelby gave him an instant woody. 'Sucks, I will never get a chance to drive it.' Working on the car was his retreat from the pressure of a software start-up that was constantly on the edge of running out of money; one minute you're a multimillionaire, the next, broke. He seemed like a good guy, a good guy that had just lost a family of three. His wife and daughters went to visit a sister in West Barnstable on Cape Cod. The sister had cancer and stupid or not, the visit seemed like a good idea. When Atlanta went down, they tried to head north, but he never heard from them again. He didn't exactly tell me how he knew Roy, but when the call came and Bangor was next on the menu, like me, he just left.
    "You know if you want me to go on this shopping trip, I would gladly take your place."
    "Thanks, but it looks like the dance card has my name on it. Anyway, I would like to see more of what the area has to offer. Could be a nice place to settle down." I gave him a fake chuckle and started to crawl away from the open loft door.
    "Hey, Paul, how come you have a fake British accent?"
    "Because I grew-up outside of St Louis. Do you think you are going insane? Sometimes I do."

"Paul, I know I am going insane. Nobody can go through this and remain right in the head. I'll see you after the trip. Anything on your shopping list I should look for?"

"If you run into Slim Jims, I would not mind one or two."

"You got it, brother." He really did grow up in Missouri.

I went down to ground level and fired up three of my old Whisperlight stoves that I had nested together to boil a big pot of water for coffee. I made sure the shotgun and Ruger were fully loaded. The bandoleer was at its max and I had maybe a dozen in a small sack Hammer had left for me. I went outside, waved to Derrick in the turret of Winnie Two, and sneaked over to the bridge. Everything wet was smoldering and the air smelled like earth and spring. It smelled like redemption. This day has got to be better. I scanned the road. The coast was clear but they were still there running aimlessly from car to car. Three, maybe four days and people were still in their cars waiting for the end. The old rule of thumb was generally a factor of three. Three minutes without air, three days without water, and three weeks without food. Unless they brought water or collected some yesterday, there were people dying right this minute. Death by dehydration without palliative measures, just fear, would not be pleasant. Who was out there; Doctors? Farmers? Carpenters? People who had skills we so desperately were going to need.

I walked back to the barn and checked on the water. I had brought a couple of lightweight camping French presses with me, and others had the same thought, although theirs were much nicer and from William Sonoma. Nice, but in the long term, I'll take plastic over glass. We had enough varieties of ground coffee to last months, as well as an impressive assortment of instant, and at least two dozen different types of teas.

Liz was waiting and we just hugged and held each other for what seemed like a long time.

"Thank you for yesterday, I needed your support," I whispered. We all had not washed in days, but Elizabeth smelled wonderful to me. This day was definitely looking up.

"I knew you would not let us, let Jim down. They were engaged." Wow, I was actually feeling good enough to think, 'was that a hint?'

"Be real careful today. I thought we would be well south by now, safe."

"Hundreds of miles from here. How is everyone coping?"

"Yesterday freakedout a lot of us, okay all of us. People are getting antsy, causing some small talk about crowding into one Winnebago and making a run for it, using the Hummer to pull us through the mud. Obviously, not much is said to me, but Mary is head honcho of the W2, so she keeps all of us informed."

"To be expected, I'm just as scared as they are."

"Yes, John, but…You get to do something about it. Like this little trip, Roy should not be taking you! Not after yesterday, not after what you did at the gate!" Liz was getting angry and I had to diffuse the situation before others got involved.

"I'm ready. It's a good team and I am going. Would you like some coffee?" Liz thought for a moment and decided that coffee was a good idea. Soon, everyone but Jim, was up and having breakfast.

Roy came in and everyone turned.

"Hammer is out by the Hummer getting us ready. John, Doc, Robert, and Allison, come over here and let's review the route." We gathered around one of our hay bale tables.

"Okay, Hammer drives, and I ride shotgun. Allison is behind me and John is behind Hammer. We head out the back. John will get to the gate and make sure it is closed behind us." What is with gates and me? When did I become the gate guy?

"The mud should not be a problem. Turn left, after three miles we have another left, we will pass the right hand turn we take tomorrow, so it's a bit of a recon. About two miles down this second left, we get to the store. It's on our right. Samuel has informed us that the owner might still be there and a bit pissed off. His name is Joshua. We need to be polite and nice. The big problem is on the way back and not guiding a pack to the barn. Doc, I want you in the loft. Robert, you are in charge, do what you think is best."

"No problem. If there is gunfire, we are going to attract attention from the main road. With you guys gone and Winnie One out of action, we could be trapped. This has got to be as silent as possible."

"We will do our best, but we need that oil. Samuel says the road we are taking divides two of the larger farms in this area, only a couple of houses and not well used. We will see."

Like Lucy, Allison was in Winnie One and I didn't know her at all. She was about 5-6, long brown hair pulled back into a ponytail. She was in great shape, good looking, in her early forties (maybe), and I have no idea what her connection was with the group. At breakfast, Mary said she was from Massachusetts and was a professional Mountain bike racer, the kind without the motor. She carried an AK-47 and had duct taped the ammo clips together for a quick reload. I have seen this in the movies and Hammer didn't mention anything, so I guess it's cool, it looked cool. She also had two small side arms with odd-looking handles attached to a custom-made chest holster. Allison was generally quiet but gave off an air of competency. Her face always had a slight scowl and was one of the few in our group that looked like they belonged. Someone I instinctively felt I could rely on when the shit hit the fan.

I went over and gave Liz a hug and kiss, perhaps the best and most important kiss of my life. I just wanted to stay there holding her. I could close my eyes and maybe this would keep the demons at bay. I could hear her sigh as we rocked back and forth. I am a bit old, but for the first time in my life, I actually thought about starting a family. I love Elizabeth. She is the one anchor in this horrible world that holds me in place, keeps me in touch with reality, no matter how much I don't wish to be. I pulled away from her and looked into her deep blue eyes. We connected for a minute and then my Harlequin Romance moment was over. I then turned and walked out to talk with Hammer.

It took about ten minutes to sort our shit and get the hardtop off. Roy and Hammer were in their traditional black, I was in a faded green t-shirt that had a Darwin has a posse logo on front, and Allison wore a red t-shirt. At the time, it bothered me that she was the only one in red; maybe something to do with the Star Trek curse? Roy reminded us about the batteries, any kind of batteries, which were number three on the list behind motor oil, and ammunition. The Hummer handled the mud like a charm. With all the bitching about how large and unnecessary they were, thank you,

God, for the Hummer. The day was sunny and with all the rain, it was going to be humid.

We came around the side of the barn and stopped. Oh, yes! No zombies; just a nice open field and muddy road. The gate turned out to be a piece of cake, Samuel had given Roy the key. We turned left and headed west. After about a quarter mile, I saw one come running out of some woods onto a field next to us. I tapped Roy on the shoulder and pointed.

"Let him follow us. Too close to the barn."

By our next turn, we had seven. We saw our right hand turn for the next day and immediately picked up more. A pack of more than a dozen was now screaming in our direction ten to two hundred yard from us. We had a decision. Slow down and eliminate them, or try to lose them. Then I remembered Hammer was driving, so I cocked the shotgun and got ready. He then slowed down and let them get closer. Here we go. My first shot took down two. Allison put her AK on semi-automatic and with careful, patient, aiming, downed a quick three. Then, just as the pack started to group, something flew over my head. I just caught it from the corner of my eye. It looked like a rock, a baseball, or a..."Everyone down now!" Hammer roared and slammed on the gas.

Yep, Hammer Time. I was quickly hugging the seat and there was a not-so-loud boom. When I looked up, about six more were down. Oh that's nice, a grenade. That won't attract much attention. The last two I could see were seriously damaged and out of the game. From across the field to our left, and from the road behind us, more came.

"We need to get the fuck out of here and now." It was Roy.

"Go Hammer go, and I mean Go!"

Grenade? Was it just because he could? Maybe he had one handy? Seemed like a good idea? I am not going to live through this. THAT was fucking stupid! Now we are going a hundred miles an hour to a place we have never been before, a place that might be barricaded with someone inside who might just shoot first. Okay, Hammer, to you the grenade might make sense, but really fucking poor sense. So far, we could outdistance them, but we were only going a couple of miles. They would definitely have the ability to catch up.

The store was by itself on the right hand side of the road. It looked like a time rift back into the fifties. At least the signs in the windows were from that era, all very faded and wishing the 'Best of luck with your hunt!' My favorite one was of a good-looking young woodsy guy walking away with a shotgun over his shoulder, plaid jacket and denims rolled up at the bottom. He was turning to look at you and wave. The caption read, 'Bringing home the bacon.' It then went on to extol the virtues that only Remington ammunitions bring. I wondered; if he was really hunting pigs, why use a shotgun?

We pulled up front. Roy got out and went to the large glass door with a closed sign hanging in the middle of it. The door was in the center of an old one story, brick building. He knocked and called out, "Hello, anybody in there? Joshua? Joshua, you here?" several times. He tested the knob, locked. Roy looked around, "Everyone down." Boom. He carefully pushed the door in and called again. With his machine gun at the ready, he stepped inside. After about fifteen seconds, he ducked back out and yelled for me to get my ass in gear.

I jumped out and entered the store. With the lights off, the vast accumulation of window advertisements and dust, limited the natural light. It made for a certain dusk feel. I saw where Roy was and covered his back.

"John, head back to the sporting goods section and grab all the ammo you can find. We are good on weapons. It's the ammo we want." I started to move to the back of the store clearing all the aisles.

"Roy, I think Hammer or somebody with a clue should do that."

"Do you know what a bullet looks like?"

"Hey, look over there." My eyes had adjusted to the dim light. In the back corner, I could see a series of stuffed animal heads and assumed that this area was the one I was looking for, and it was. A series of rifles and shotguns were locked in a rack. Four handguns were in a glass case that served as the counter for this section. Underneath the counter were two swinging heavy wooden doors padlocked together.

"Roy!" I yelled.

"Yeah."

"I got to blow this padlock, so don't freak out."

"Go for it!" Out of the corner of my eye, I saw him exit the building carrying several cases of what I guessed were oil.

I cocked the shotgun, aimed at an angle I thought would take care of the lock and not ignite any ammo inside, and then fired. The shot more than worked. It blew the lock and hasp clear off. I just started to pile box after box into my knapsack. I didn't care what I was taking, but did pay attention to shotgun shells and took all of them. I was just about done when I heard gunshots. I put the backpack on quickly, cocked the shotgun, and headed for the door. Roy was gathering some stuff near the front. As I passed the main register, I noticed a large plastic pickle jug loaded with beef jerky, and you guessed it, Slim Jims. I grabbed the jug.

Hammer and Allison were blazing away. Hammer had moved and was standing in the passenger seat engaging about a dozen scattered in front of us. By far, Allison had the most difficult assignment. She was covering the road we had just driven and she was busy with the original group, now at least twenty with more behind them. I threw my stuff in the back and went to help her. I got to one knee and started picking off the ones she missed. The first was a girl in her teens, dressed in what probably was a softball uniform top. I caught her just below the chin and tore most of her head off. As she spun, I could read her shirt, Comet Cleaners. She was number nine and her last name was Matheson. I picked off two more but missed the next. Luckily, Allison didn't. I knew I was down to five shots; I simply didn't have time to reload. The last one I hit was in the abdomen. He went down in a hard tumble. He wasn't dead, but not really moving. It reminded me of the brother with the limp arms out on the road with the station wagon and the family we killed.

With all the commotion, I felt rather than heard the Hummer start. More shooting from the back gave me some clearance and a split second to pop in a couple of shells. My best guess would be around thirty on our ass, with seven or eight left in the first group. The second group was far enough behind to give us plenty of time to get away.

I stood. The head was too small a target for a shotgun. A good thorax shot, maybe get part of the spinal cord or the sacro-plexus nerves, and down they would go. It was as if you were changing them from fast zombie to traditional slow zombie. Aiming solely for the chest, I took down three fast. Only one got up and he was slow enough that a devastating head shot from Allison was nothing but an afterthought.

"Oh yeah! Now that's what I am talking about!" She was pumped and I gave her a fist-bump as I jumped in. She was sweating, breathing heavy. Her face was flushed and she had a most amazing smile, the kind I thought I would never see again. Roy made a good choice.

Roy hit the gas and off we went. I almost didn't feel the collision of the two zombies we had just mowed down. The road was straight and Roy made the best of it by putting the pedal to the metal. After about five minutes, he slowed down.

Roy came to a stop and jumped out with his binoculars. "I believe we have some decent distance. Damn, that was close. Hammer, do us all a favor and find us a way back."

Hammer was hunched over, intently studying a folded map and what looked like satellite photos on an iPad.

"Not as detailed as I would like. In order to avoid Deerfield, we have to do a loop, but it's big, easily twenty additional miles and we would have to pass through this small town. Connimicut, Never been there."

We could now faintly hear them in the distance. It was an odd sound, something like a bad marriage, between a moan and a roar.

Roy grabbed the binoculars and stood. After about a minute or two, he leaned down and spoke with Hammer. I looked back. We had stopped with a view of an open valley that ended in trees about a half mile away. There was smoke off in the distance, lots of it. The day was partly cloudy and windy, the clouds made dark moving shadows on the land. At first, I thought the dark mass moving towards us was a cloud shadow, and yet again, I was wrong. As Roy and Hammer were having their conversation, the mass got closer and eventually you could make out distinct individuals. Hard to count, but my best guess would be several fucking hundred. Boy, did we attract a crowd. They did not just stay on the road, but fanned out on either side. The ones on the road moved faster than those in the weeds did. From above, it must have looked like an arrowhead heading straight for the dot that was us, and they were getting closer. Beyond the obvious, two things were bugging me. One, why the hell do they group like this? What calls them together? And, two, where the fuck did all these people come from?

I decided to interrupt the guys. "Okay, we go. Now is a good time to go." I think the sound of my voice made them stop and look up.

Everything was thrown backwards as Roy pushed the Hummer to maximum. We had an open stretch of road and the horde began to vanish in the distance. Hammer studied the map and would occasionally yell some instructions to Roy. We slowed down to maybe forty as we came to a big tight curve, and suddenly, there they were. Three zombies were standing in the middle of the road, two men and a woman. There was no way we could avoid them without flipping, so we plowed right in. The first male hit the cattle guard and appeared to be sucked under the vehicle with a huge thump. The second was thrown onto the hood, rolled, and stuck to the windshield. This severely reduced Roy's vision and he hit the woman at such an odd angle that the zombie was able to grab the passenger's side view mirror. Roy slammed on the brakes in an attempt to knock the guy off the windshield. This slammed us all forward, but it worked. When he hit the gas, we all fell back and something slammed into the Hummer with a loud thud and the sound of wet cloth being torn.

Allison's gasp was one of surprise rather than pain. When I turned, it was hard to make out what was happening. The zombie's body had somehow been suspended across the passenger side at window level! The left arm was straight out in front of her, still holding the rear view mirror and she was parallel to the vehicle, just as if Superman was flying next to us! How could it be in that position? I focused on Allison and saw the answer, my brain froze, WTF? I took me more than a couple of long seconds to understand what had happened, and to comprehend the almost impossibility of what had happened.

Maybe it was the impact, or maybe she caught the tire. Who knows, but the rest of her leg was completely eviscerated from the right knee down; muscle, tibia, ankle, and foot, had been torn free. The sole exception was the fibula. The fibula is a long thin bone going from your knee to your ankle. The trauma had made it into a long thin needle. Her death grip on the mirror and the sudden stopping and starting motions of the Hummer had somehow tossed her onto the vehicle, and then things got really surreal. Somehow, the bone spike impaled Allison, entering behind the left jaw and exiting through the right cheek. She had turned herself around and was looking out the back when it happened. Allison never saw it coming. I didn't see pulses of blood and hoped this meant the carotid was not severed. I looked to Hammer as he blasted the zombie.

"No." When the zombie dropped, she almost took Allison out of the vehicle. The bone did slide out, but spun her head around, and here came the blood. I ripped off my t-shirt and tried to compress both wounds at once. Allison started choking and in between desperate breaths, she would spit out blood, all over me. She was quiet. I think shock was overriding pain.

"Allison! Try to lean forward and keep your airway open! Try not to swallow…" and then she vomited in my crotch. Hammer whacked me on the back and handed over a bunch of compresses. These helped slow the external bleeding, but not the holes inside her mouth. I held her head on my lap trying to keep the blood flowing out and not in. Hammer gave me more medical supplies and helped with the compresses.

"Listen, you can survive this!" I yelled. Richard Burton, the famous African explorer suffered a similar wound from a spear in the middle of nowhere Africa, with no medical assistance, and he made a complete recovery. "We have the supplies and people to deal with this."

"John!" It was Roy. "Side pocket of the grey bag, purple cap, grab one!"

I unzipped the compartment and inside was a collection of cylinders about the size of a cigar tube. The first one was black, an EpiPen, but the second was purple, Morphine Sulfate Injection 10 milligrams.

"Allison, morphine." I yelled. She slightly shook her head yes a couple of times and squeezed my knee. I pulled off the safety release, popped the cap, and in one swift motion, jabbed the needle into her outer thigh, right through her jeans. She never flinched or made a sound.

"It's intramuscular, so you should feel it in about five minutes or so. I know it sounds stupid, but just try to relax and not move." I slowly adjusted her head and shifted to get a better angle on the rear, not the best, but it would have to do. She was scrunched up on her left side with her head on my lap. Her blood had soaked my jeans and filled one of my hiking boots. I tried to make her as comfortable as possible. Hammer leaned in to get a closer look.

"Will she sleep?"

"I hope so."

In almost a whisper he asked, "Do we have the resources and people to handle this?"

"No. We'll get her on O2 back at the barn, but right now, we have to keep her warm. We need blankets," I whispered back.

"Let's hope she sleeps." He reached, took her rifle, and looked it over. "Use this first. It's on semi and is gonna buck, so don't try to go auto. Burn the ammo and back to the shotgun. Don't let them catch up. We can't lead them back to the barn, so it's an additional ten miles and we have to go through a village, might have a hundred or two at most." He handed me the AK47.

Only about a hundred or two, hell, what were we worried about? Did Hammer really call it a village?

We drove on, but at a reduced speed. We had enough distance, so we could now afford the luxury of caution. The bleeding was slowing down and her breathing became more regular. We passed half a dozen vehicles every mile or so. Most were empty and more than a few showed signs that the egress was forced. We did pass a couple that had zombies trapped inside. They just banged on the windows as we went by. Then we passed one that had dead bodies, real dead bodies, dead bodies that had not reanimated. These were people trapped in their cars, possibly dying of dehydration, lack of some medication, a heart attack, a stroke, or anything but a zombie bite. If we're not all infected, how the hell did Lucy get it? We stopped at an apparently abandoned RV. Hammer jumped out and casually went inside as if it was his. A few minutes later, he came out holding a couple of pillows, some thick homemade quilts and a six-pack of bottled water. We both carefully wrapped Allison as best we could. The pillows kept her head at the right height and freed me to move to a better defensive position.

After ten minutes, we crested a small hill that overlooked the town and it gave us a clear three hundred and sixty degree view. Nothing was sneaking up on us unnoticed. The town could be called a village. It was essentially just a Main Street with a church on either end. In between there were a dozen shops lining both sides of the road. Cars and trucks scattered about but nothing that looked impassable. Roy and Hammer spent some time just staring through the binoculars. I was on the 'everything but the town watch', and things were looking nice and quiet. Allison was visibly relaxed as the morphine took hold. It wouldn't peak for another forty-five minutes. This gave me time to reflect. Things started out okay, but now we are going to lose two members in two days. I am going to be intimately involved in the deaths of two people I don't really know, and that just seems wrong. I've never heard of someone contracting the virus other than through a scratch or a bite, except of course, the occasional pulmonary infection. I know it's cruel, but a small part of me wanted to see Allison live long enough to find out if she is infected.

"The town is not as infested as I thought and it looks like we should cruise through with ease. John, your assignment is simple. Keep our back clear. Just make sure you let Hammer know if things start to get out of hand. We got some traffic to avoid, so this won't be any kind of speed racer run." Roy motioned for me to lean closer.

"How does she look?"

"Roy, I haven't taken any vitals and I need to put in an IV. If you can give me just ten minutes, I will do that and let you know what I think, okay?"

He begrudgingly gave me the time. She was looking pale and used up, but not in pain. I couldn't tell how much blood she had lost but it was significant. My hands were sticky, I had problems getting the BP cuff on, and trying to auscultate was hopeless. Low blood pressure, high heart rate, a capillary refill time of almost six seconds; she was way into decompensatory shock. Anymore significant blood loss and she will fall into irreversible shock and death. I washed my hands with bottled water, getting the gloves on was far harder than doing the IV. The morphine was now in full force and Allison drifted.

"Guys, she is sleeping. She has very low blood pressure, a rapid heart and respiratory rate. All this is from the shock and blood loss. We'll keep her warm and hydrated. Her bleeding has slowed down considerably. Hammer, whoever put these kits together knew their shit."

"Thanks, John. They were made by my wife. She was a registered ER nurse." We did not make eye contact and I knew I had stumbled into a place I should not be. The look from Roy said it all, no more questions about Hammer and his family. I gave him a quick nod.

"Ladies and gentlemen, start your engines." Roy fired her up.

The road dropped down into the town, meaning we would have at least a mile with no coverage and be the only thing moving. Everyone who cared would know we were coming. Fortunately, the last half-mile or so was straight, and we could anticipate some of the obstacles. The first was a tractor-trailer on its side, blocking all the asphalt. No problem, we're in a Hummer! As we rounded the overturned cab, I saw the driver, now a zombie. He was covered in blood, probably in his fifties; mostly bald, beer belly, and a badly broken right leg. The trucker was stuck at the bottom of his cab with a useless leg, not realizing he would never get out the broken passenger window directly above him. There were more and more cars, as we got closer to the town. Some were scattered on the road and it was easy to either go around, or push them aside. As we got closer, the zombies got thicker.

"I got two, rear and coming fast!" I lined the AK up and they dropped like flies. I sighted the second group and pulled the trigger. I got off exactly one round. The AK-47 made a funny sound and stopped firing. I felt us slowing down but did not look back. Three more, then five behind them.

"I broke Allison's gun. We have eight on our ass! Let's move." I grabbed the shotgun, pumped, fired, and missed. How could I be firing at something so close with a shotgun, and miss? The second shot took down the lead. Okay, let's get real. I positioned myself on top of the booty we had just acquired from Joshua's and aimed for the chest. I got four in fewer than ten seconds, none got up. Hammer started to help and it was over before it started. Roy had slowed to get around a massive pile-up. The passageway was tight and if there were a few more like this, we could be toast. We weaved our way through and Main Street went by in a flash. Once we had cleared the town, things got easier, but for whatever reason, there were more cars and more isolated zombies.

Eventually, we reached a point where the coast looked clear. Allison was still on a morphine high which was a good thing, since there was not much more we could do for her. Her temperature had dropped to a hundred and one. Both blood pressure and heart rate were also looking better, but only slightly. Roy tried to contact the Winnies, but got no reply. Hammer used the time to top off the gas tank and do a quick inspection of the vehicle.

"John, sorry, but I feel awfully vulnerable just sitting here."

"No problem, Roy. This type of trauma is out of my league. Hey, Hammer, do we have oxygen back with the Winnies?"

"Yeah. Two, both full."

"Thanks, we'll need them. Well, Roy, let's get the hell out of Dodge." It was a good thing too, since, as we pulled away, a group of five came tearing ass from around a school bus about a hundred yards behind us. I didn't waste ammo and just watched them slowly fade away. I wish it could be that simple.

"Fuck me!" It was Hammer. For a couple of hundred yards, the road was straight and clear. Unfortunately, this ended in a massive pile-up of cars, trucks, ambulances, and just about every vehicle you could imagine. The road itself was completely blocked and the shoulders did not look all that promising, since on either side was a stonewall, not the old quaint New England type, but a modern one that was probably reinforced with steel and concrete. Done in a series of tiers, the wall was very beautiful. Unfortunately, it was really in our way. We moved on maybe fifty yards or so and came to a stop. Hammer was once again standing, scanning the scene, and swearing under his breath.

"Shit. We have to leave, Roy!"

"Roger that. John, is Allison secure?" I dropped the shotgun and went for the seatbelt. Everything was covered in blood, spent casings, and bandages, so this was going to take me a second.

"Just go, Roy." It took more than a second, but I did find the buckle. She didn't have to move much and when secured, I looked up to see what Roy might have in mind. Holy crap! We have to go back. Hammer turned around, kneeled up on the passenger seat, and started shooting over my shoulder. I grabbed the shotgun and sat on Allison's legs, everything you touched was tacky from the drying blood. Roy then did something really remarkable. There was a set of stone stairs normally used to get over the wall. The base was beveled to give it some sort of artistic flair. Roy used this as a way to get the driver's side wheels on the top corner of the second tier, and we rode up over the fist car and inched our way forward at this crazy angle for about forty yards, very Indiana Jones type stuff. I let Hammer take care of trouble and held Allison to keep her from being knocked about.

"Everyone hold on tight!" With a loud bang, we came off the wall. On crashing with the road, all of us were basically body slammed, but hey, we cleared the pileup. I immediately looked to see how Allison was doing and it was not good. She was awake, in pain, and bleeding profusely. This time there was some pulsing of blood. Her breathing was fast and sharp. She looked at me, scared.

"I need more compresses!" As Hammer worked the medical kit and I tried to stop the bleeding, we got hit. At least three from the driver's side and they came close to tipping us over, at least it felt that way to someone who has never done any real off-roading. The zombies seemed to get to the vehicle at the exact same time and this freaked me out. Roy hit the gas even though he would have to slalom a couple of wrecks ahead of us.

I went back to Allison. She was losing color and her eyes were closed. She was rapidly going into the later stages of hypovolemic shock. It would not be long now; she had lost just too much blood. Even in the real world, the only hope for this type of wound would be to have a magic teleport machine and get her to a Trauma One facility with a surgical team standing by. Her lips were moving and I bent down and got as close as possible without getting any drool on me.

She gurgled "... the people, shall not perish from the earth." With that, she opened her eyes. She was not afraid or sad, just serene...and a little bit confused. She reached out and we held hands.

"John?" Her voice sounded like she was talking through a wet sponge.

"I am right next to you, Allison." Her eyes were now open but not focusing on anything.

"Good luck." Her grip relaxed, her eyes glazed over, and she died.

"Okay, got the compresses." Hammer turned and it took only a brief glance. "Ah, goddamn it!"

Yes, you are right on that one, Hammer. I just stared at Allison, pulled the Ruger, piled all the bandages and gauze in one place on the side of her head, and fired. I turned and sure enough, there were two zombies running crazy fast right behind. I took careful aim and even with the bouncing of the Hummer and my slippery sticky hand, I dropped both with five shots. My first handgun zombie kill, and it was very satisfying. More were off in the distance, but too far away, for now.

I didn't know Allison. I knew nothing of substance about her, but I was sad she was dead. Weird, I didn't feel this way with Lucy. My mind started this crazy, almost jingle-like loop, turning the old spelling pneumonic into something else, 'I before we, except after z.' The world had been all about me. Yes, I had friends, students, and Liz was in the process of filling in a hole I didn't know I had, but it was always about me. The plague had forced a change in my priorities and opened my eyes. Did I really need all of this to open my eyes? I think I am going insane.

The rest of the trip was zigzagging around abandoned vehicles and avoiding the occasional group, never more than half a dozen or so. Twice, we slowed down for some small gangs who had cut us off, but all in all, it was clear sailing. Fortunately, there was no one around where we needed to open the gate and turn off for the barn. We got beside Winnie Two and killed the engine. Everyone came out to greet us. Paul asked about the oil, glanced at me, and stopped dead in his tracks. In fact, everyone stopped as soon as they saw me. Matilda and Madeline quickly spun and went back into the barn. Leslie even put her camera down. I looked around thinking something must be going on behind me. I then realized I was absolutely drenched in Allison's blood.

Hammer got out and in a restrained bark said, "We lost Allison. We have the oil. Let's get to work. Lizzy, would you take care of John." With that, he maneuvered most of them back into the barn. I got out and went to Liz. "When is this going to stop?" She asked.

In my shocked, fatigued, and slightly unbalanced state, my first thought was, 'I can tell you exactly when this will stop.' Fortunately, I went for the lesser of two evils.

"It's not going to." I then noticed I was holding a plastic jug with a smiling pickle on a big green faded sticker full of individually wrapped beef jerky sticks and Slim Jims. There were lots of bloody handprints on the plastic. In fact, the whole outside of the jug was a mess.

"Hey, Zack, here you go, brother, give this to Paul."

"Thanks." He didn't look me, just quickly grabbed the jug and walked away.

Roy pulled a few men over and was saying something about perimeter, or was it packing? I just kind of spaced out and looked at the ground. Okay, we traded a life for the group's best chance of living. We had to fix the Winnie and get the hell to the coast. After today's raid, one thing was clear; we did not have the firepower or provisions to hold this place.

I felt, rather than saw, Liz approach. "I'm very sorry, sweetie. Let's get you cleaned up. There is a water pump in the front yard, stay right here." She left to find a bucket. She sounded like I would sound when talking to someone you are not quite sure is all there. Samuel and Nancy were watching from the front porch. They came down the stairs and Nancy put her hand to her mouth when she got closer.

"There was a freak accident and it killed a team member named Allison, I'm fine, at least physically, I think. We did get the oil and some extra ammo, but no sign of Joshua." At least to me, it sounded like I was underwater, not on the same plane of reality as everyone else.

Elizabeth came over and handed me a face cloth and a bar of soap. "Strip." She then pumped a bucket of water. What are the odds that for a second day in a row, I would be standing naked, potentially infected, looking like shit, in front of strangers?

"John, this is going to be cold and we got zombies nearby. Let's remember to keep the theatrics in the mime range. We're talking Marcel Marceau here, now bend over."

What the hell was Liz talking about? Holy crap, that water is cold! I had leaned over so she could rinse my head first, and was looking down when Liz poured. The grass instantly turned red.

"Sorry."

When I did look up, Nancy was whispering into Samuel's ear. After a minute, he simply nodded and walked back to the house. Several more bucket loads and I was starting to get cold, like hypothermic cold, and looked about for a towel.

"Just one more. Samuel went to get you something and you need to use more soap."

By the time he made it back, Liz got me with four more dousings. Bitch! He handed me a neatly folded pile of clothes with a towel on top. It was a pair of Farmer John jeans and a faded John Deere t-shirt.

"You keep them." I looked at the Farmer Johns, the shirt, and then looked at Samuel, and we both started to laugh as I put them on.

"Thank you very much, Samuel."

As we headed back to the barn, several people were heading to the pump. I assumed it was to get water to clean the Hummer.

Liz stopped me, "Sorry about being naked and so cold, but getting you cleaned up was priority number one. John, look at the bright side. At the very least, we are sure you haven't been bitten." My silence must have said it all. "Was it bad?"

"Yes, very," he said.

We went inside and Hammer, of course, was the first to comment.

"Now all you need is the cap and some chewing tobacco, and son, you might be in." This made me smile.

He came over and lowered his voice, "John, we're going to bury her next to Lucy. You go rest."

"Thanks." Wow, Hammer was actually looking beat.

Liz and I went up to the loft and crashed out in a big pile of hay. Man, do I love the smell of hay. It smells like childhood. We held each other and I tried to sleep. I know it was not my fault and nothing I could do, but of all things, having your face impaled by a zombie's fibula? No, that would not have made my list of the top one million ways you could die. So I just laid there and reviewed the day, over and over. After a couple of hours and Liz soundly snoring, I crawled down to see what's up.

The barn was one of those old classic New England monsters, probably over a hundred years, maybe older. Two Coleman lanterns were lit but dimmed to a minimum, and it took a second for my eyes to adjust. It was a warm night, combined with the old barn smell of hay and manure, and the comforting light, I started to feel human. What night is it? Saturday or Sunday? Paul and Hammer were working on the leaking Winnebago. Hammer looked up.

"Good to get some personal time, eh?" He had a big shit-eating grin on his face. He thought I got laid! Well, fuck you, Hammer.

"Yeah, Hammer, I guess. So, how are things looking? Do we leave tomorrow?"

"So far, the leak is fixed and we have plenty of oil." Paul slid out and shut off his headlamp.

"Hi, John. Well, my big man, we are done! Don't look for fast speeds and the roads had better be kind. With that, I am going to crash. I'll see you two in a few hours."

"Hammer, I know it was a shitty day, but, why did you throw the hand grenade?" He didn't look at me. Just shrugged his shoulders and shook his head.

Roy was sitting in a folding chair talking with the lawyer guy, was his name Dom or Tom?

"Good evening, John, get some rest?"

"A bit." I crashed into a chair next to him and stayed quiet and half asleep till the sun came up. Roy and Tom spent the time drinking coffee and talking about various islands in the Caribbean. Tom was into scuba diving and had spent a good bit of time in an area I knew nothing about. I've never done a dive in crystal clear waters, this was good.

Chapter 13 ~ Run

May 28th

    I didn't sleep, but awake and sitting in that chair for a couple of hours was not smart. I hurt all over and my right shoulder was killing me. I downed a handful of aspirin and left the barn to get a bit of fresh air and look around the farm, as I didn't know when, if ever, I would be on one again. My God! Yet another fantastic Maine day; perfect for a hike up Mt. Katahdin or around Baxter. Would I ever go on a hike again? Would I ever see the fall foliage again? Why do I keep asking myself stupid questions?

    I noticed that the two nice, goofy, docile Labs were alert, frozen, and growling with the hairs on the back of their necks almost straight up. Still in a daze and not being the fastest kitten in the litter, I decided to go to the other side of the barn and see what was bothering them. I was too groggy from lack of sleep and just didn't think. As soon as I rounded the corner, I ran slap dead into a zombie. Right out of the Three Stooges, we smacked belly and face at the same time, which knocked him on his back and me suddenly very awake. It was a man in an expensive dark blue business suit somewhere in his fifties. I thought of several things at once: 1) holy shit a zombie, 2) I know exactly where my shotgun is and it's not in my arms, and 3) how come he has one bare foot?

    I started to trip but caught myself and my speed carried me around the corner of the barn. I turned to face him and reached for the Ruger, but in my rush, I couldn't get it out of the holster. I couldn't understand what the problem was. During the quick draw practices, things went well, it was easy. Now I could remove about an inch or so and then it was stuck, something was catching on something and I can't look down!

The zombie was up faster than I anticipated and I panicked. Okay, not like Jackie Chan fast, but he clearly had a sense of balance and purpose. I kept backing up, tugging at my side arm, backing up and frantically pulling at a weapon, which clearly did not want to leave its holster. He was closing the small distance between us fast, arms outstretched, drooling, and making that bizarre zombie growl/moan. His eyes were wide, bloodshot and dilated. We got so close I could smell his breath. Beyond being in need of some serious tooth brushing, it smelled similar to acetone, like nail polish. On this side of the barn was an attached old wooden shed with no door. I had checked it earlier and found it full of rusted farm stuff. I don't know why, but I backed into the shed and darkness just as the zombie got to me. I reached behind, grabbing the first thing I touched, and in one fluid motion, swung it over my head right into the top of the man's grey balding skull.

The zombie staggered back from the doorway into the full light of day. I think we both might have had the same expression, eyes wide and our mouths making a perfect O. In the middle of his head with the blade about three-quarters of a way in was an old rusted machete. The zombie took a second and fell on his back. I just stood there and stared. A machete. A fucking machete. I just killed a zombie with a fucking machete! Oh, my, God, what a cliché.

"Yeah, Oh yeah! That's what I am talking about. Tom Savini, eat your heart out!" I yelled. I hoped Tom was still alive, because he would just love this shit.

Roy and Samuel came running over and just stared. Roy folded his arms and looked at me for a good minute.

"What, your Ruger's not good enough? Man, Hammer is going to be pissed. A machete. Oh, John, you just raised the ante. This is going to be interesting."

I knew I was shaking and continued to stare at the dead undead guy. In the back of my mind, I wondered what the hell Roy was talking about. Samuel, laid back as usual, just gave me an approving nod.

I had to go sit down for a second, stepped over the body, and rushed to the tiny bathroom in my Winnie. I closed the door, sat, and stared into nothing. My God, that was close. My whole body was electric with adrenalin. It was then I realized that, yes, I had indeed pissed my pants. Son of a …Luckily, this was my Winnie and my clothes bag was inside. I opened the door and saw that Jane was in the turret talking with someone, so I sneaked over and grabbed some jeans. After emptying my pockets, changing and stowing the soiled ones, I sat down and it just came to me. I don't know exactly how many? A dozen? It had to be more than that. I was really a zombie killer. Yes, I was El Macho Machete, Zombie Killer! How cool was that? A middle-aged anthropologist was now El Macho Machete, Zombie Killer. It probably took me ten minutes to calm down and realize that insanity was not that bad. I also figured that a piece of leather had somehow gotten cut, stopping me from drawing the Ruger, which I fixed. I then got ready to meet my adoring public.

As soon as I opened the door, there stood Mary with arms tightly folded, tapping her feet, and obviously pissed off.

"Are you some kind of idiot? No, tell me, John, because I had a completely different opinion of you." She started to pace back and forth. "This is not a game. We need each other. The odds suck that we are going to get through this and you pull a stunt like that? You have been through a lot. We are all thankful, I am relieved you are with us, but you better screw your head on, boy." and she stomped away. I didn't have time to respond and was kind of stunned when Liz came storming in. The look on her face was anything but serene, oh shit.

"What the hell were you thinking? We need you. I need you. Don't you get it?" I thought she was about to punch me. "I am too pissed off to talk right now, but this conversation is definitely NOT OVER!" And she stormed off with this odd foot stomping movements that in a normal situation, I would have found amusing.

Well, so much for El Macho Machete. Everyone in the barn was staring at me and no one had an approving look on their face. Shit, I wasn't pulling any stunt. I was just keeping myself alive. What the hell? I decided that I had to seek refuge in the only bastion of machismo I could think of, a redneck or as we like to call them in this neck of the woods, a Swamp Yankee. I went to find Hammer.

He was over by the Hummer wiping grease off his hands, saw me coming, crossed his arms, and just stood there.

"A machete, huh?" I cannot emphasize how massive this guy is. He was not angry, but had this mischievous look in this eye.

"Yeah."

"Okay, okay." He slowly reached to his side and pulled out the biggest, nastiest knife I have ever seen. It was almost a foot long, curved, serrated. You knew it was so sharp you could shave with it. Definably something a Klingon would use.

"Well, then I'm going to get me one with this." He twirled it expertly in his hand. The knife just screamed pain.

I stared at him with my best poker face, nodding my head. Game on. I continued to nod and stare for half a minute.

"Yeah, well I got you beat, yes, sir. And I have it right here." I slowly reached into my jeans and pulled out my trusty basic Swiss Army knife. I knew there was more than likely, Spam on the dull blade from the night before, so I didn't open it. He just shook his head, laughed, and started to walk away.

"You know, Hammer, you could step it up and go for the office stapler option." This stopped him dead in his tracks and he turned back.

"Humm." He rubbed his chin. "That would require cunning, dexterity, quick hands, focus, and above all, dedication. You know, I like it."

"You do realize though that if you go the stapler route, and it is an impressive option, I would have to go for the next notch up, or down, depending on how you look at things." He walked back over to me.

"One whole notch up, eh? You, an academic with some luck with a shotgun is willing to cross that line?"

"Paper cuts."

"Ouch! I hate those things. Man, do they sting." He re-folded his arms. "Brother, you are now in the Crazy Zone. Okay, okay, I got it. You want paper cuts? Well then, I'm going for spit balls."

"Wow, back up there, cowboy. You can take an eye out with one of those." Hammer had this confident look about him, but I was not done.

"Well, Hammer, you leave me no choice. You have me in a corner and I have no option but to bring out my big guns, my trump cards...Taunts and insults."

"Taunts AND insults?"

"Well, they kind of overlap and you need to cover the bases here." We both lightly laughed. He slapped me on the back, and out of the corner of my eye, I saw Liz. I was SO in the doghouse.

"Come over here and let me show you what I am going to taunt them with," he said in the worst Tony Montoya impression ever. We walked over to the back of the Hummer and he opened the trunk.

I jumped back. "What the hell is that?" In the trunk was a large, like Terminator large, machine gun.

"This, my friend, is an M60." He lifted it out of the trunk and let out a sigh. Hammer was in love. This was The Rambo Machine Gun, fucking huge. There was no way I could hold this thing and fire away like in the movies, but still, way cool.

"When we get to the islands, I will introduce you to her. She is very special."

"Yes sir, Hammer. I definitely see her coming in handy for the whale hunting season." We both started to laugh and I noticed something beneath the belts of ammo.

"What's that?"

He pulled out a green tube about two feet long with brown waxy paper on the ends. "This is a M72 LAW rocket launcher"

"Cool, hunting zombies with a rocket." What? A rocket launcher?

"John, zombies are not our only problem. We got to be ready." He gently placed it in the back seat and started playing around with stuff in the trunk.

"Thanks for your time, Hammer. I needed the support."

"No problem, brother. A machete? You have got to be kidding me." He went back to moving stuff in the trunk, laughing.

I turned and started to the rear of the barn to get my stuff. Where do these guys get these things? They were definitely not at the place I got my gun, and I damn well know that Wal-Mart doesn't sell them, not even Super Wal-Mart! I made sure not to look at Liz, grabbed the gun, bandoleer, and headed for the door; at least someone had washed it.

"Hey, Tom Savini, Nice job and nine points for me." Zach must have been waiting above the door for at least fifteen minutes just to use that line.

"That's not a quote and I already used it." This guy was just killing me, and way ahead on points.

"Sorry, doesn't count unless we both hear it." He ignored me and had his little black book out, writing up his new score.

"Tell me the truth John, did you plan that?" Excellent, the spider has walked into the parlor or something like that.

"Your ignorance is exceeded only by your charm, Yes and thank you, Dr. Logan, and a massive thirty something for me."

Zack's face went blank for a long ten seconds. "Shit, fucking *Day*."

"You're right, but next time, call me Blades, now go check on the gate, Bud. And that's a quick," I counted with my fingers. "Nine back at you." I turned to go visit Samuel and Nancy.

"Was 'Blade' actually said in the movie? John?"

I looked over to the house and saw Samuel and Nancy on the porch swing, the two Labs at their feet and a pitcher of what must be lemonade on a table near them. They looked kind of odd, but happy and holding hands, slowly rocking back and forth. I started to walk over to them. God, I hope they come with us. And which now seems like a daily trend, the world took a turn for the nightmare.

"Oh fuck." It was Zach up in the loft.

"Gate's down! Gate is down!"

Oh No. No, no, no. Okay…calm down, you can do this, it's Alamo Time. I immediately ran to the bridge, ensured my shotgun was fully loaded and the Ruger ready. I cannot let the team down, please help me, I asked to myself. I could see some cars and zombies in the field, but still a couple of hundred yards away. I went to one knee firing position and waited. With the aspirin/adrenaline combination, I was feeling no pain. I stayed off just to the right hand side near some bushes with a clear shot and hoped the commotion behind me would keep the undead distracted until it was too late. Okay, calm down and count your shots.

Waiting, alone and scared, I concentrated on my breathing. As luck would have it, I picked probably the only spot on the road where it is really uncomfortable to kneel, as it had new gravel, I didn't move out of fear of losing what little concentration I had. Then, like a bolt out of the blue, it occurred to me; this was not the Alamo, this was Rorke's Drift and I was going to hold this line. I shifted my knee to a more accommodating spot.

It took some time for the first one to reach the bridge, maybe five minutes. A young man in his twenties, stained t-shirt, shorts, bare feet, and not at all disturbed by the sharp new gravel. So focused on the action behind me, he got to within fifteen feet when my movement stopped him dead in his tracks, so to speak. My shot blew most of the top of his head off, leaving only part of the face which turned in my direction. Pure anger filled his one eye and he fell.

I could now hear all sorts of activity behind me and just hoped reinforcements would come soon. Oh God, this one's a child. She was small, six, seven years old and staggered with straight legs like her knees didn't work. On purpose, I let her see me, let her get within maybe ten feet and then I blew her into the creek. My shot actually lifted her into the air and out of sight. Two spaced closely together were right after her. My brain could not process specific details just that it was more than one and they would arrive at roughly the same time. I was starting to be more comfortable with the shotgun. When you are cocked, and ready to fire with a clear target, you can let the undead get close, very close, and drop them with relative ease. Close was the name of the game.

The first was a woman in a badly coordinated sweat suit, think bright pink top, and bottoms in an orange color not seen in the natural world. I hit her mid stomach and must have caught part of the spine, because she went down and could only move using her forearms. Okay, not an immediate threat, so on to number two. Number two, was a paramedic with a t-shirt that read, Bucksport EMS. I took him down in one. The woman just flopped there and I ignored her as I reloaded. Where the hell is my support? I could hear a Winnie moving away, not in my direction. I stood, stretched, and got ready for the next batch.

I walked on to the bridge and had a clear view of the field and the road. A truck, with the gate still chained to it, lay on its side in the grass. At least half dozen zombies were crawling over it and banging on the window. That meant whoever drove it was alive and still inside. Two more were running in the truck's direction. While it offered a distraction and kept more of the undead off my ass, I couldn't help feeling frustrated that even though I was heavily armed, there was nothing I could do. If I decided to go all Rambo, I would most certainly die. There were more cars and more zombies. Two appeared stalled on the road and close to the bridge. The lead one had its passenger door open. The one behind was an old orange van with something about plumbing with a cross and fish symbol painted on its side. A zombie was most of the way through the driver side window, its feet kicking wildly back and forth. Just like on the highway, it was instant pandemonium, just add zombies.

Thank you, God, I silently said as I heard the Hummer come up beside me. My ass was covered.

"John! Good job! Maintain cover for maybe five minutes and we bug out!" It was Hammer. Gunshots from the Hummer. I quickly turned and saw Robert aiming out the passenger window. He glanced, gave me a wink and continued to fire. They pulled away.

I got the next one with a neck shot, It was a middle-aged woman in blue jeans and a 'World's Greatest Mom' t-shirt. Her scalp had been torn almost completely off and it hung behind her like some macabre mullet. You could see the glistening white of her skullcap. Blood had dripped everywhere except for the center of her forehead and face, almost as if someone had taken a wet cloth and neatly cleaned up the front of her. The next three were a blur. Three or four more bodies on the bridge and it would be hard to run at me without tripping. I reloaded and waited.

I got four more and was so focused that I jumped when I heard, "Get in the back, hotshot." It was Robert, who was holding the door open. I dove in next to him. It was cramped in back with gear and stuff but I managed to position myself to shoot out the back window. Hammer fired her up and we hauled ass out of there. The Winnies were already on their way.

I looked over at the house porch. "What about..." Nancy and Samuel were still on the swing, still holding hands, but their heads were tilted down at an odd angle. The swing wasn't moving and the two Labs didn't stir from all the commotion, everyone seemed to be asleep.

Roy turned to me. "They told me yesterday. Knew we were going and they couldn't stay undiscovered forever. They weren't leaving their home and wanted it to be on their terms."

"Yeah, they strongly hinted to me that they were not going to leave, but damn we needed them." I just stared at them and hoped that if it came to this, Elizabeth and I could go that way. It was sad, but romantic, and tears filled my eyes.

"We needed them?" It was Hammer and he sounded a bit incredulous.

"And how much farming have you done? Know how to grow a potato? Raised any cows? Yes, we needed them."

We rounded the barn and followed the road next to the tree break. When we reached the wall, I could finally see the Winnies ahead, almost at the gate. We got lucky. The Winnies were handling the road just fine, and so far, no zombies were following us.

The Winnies went through and as we reached the gate, a monster truck greeted us; one of those ultimate redneck vehicles that puts a normal truck chassis on humongous wheels. Roy pulled up next to it. The driver was a twenty something Swamp Yankee with a cigarette dangling out of his mouth and sipping on a Bud tallboy. Led Zeppelin's *Rock and Roll* blared from the cab.

"Hey, Man, nice rig. You guys with the Winnebagos?" He yelled.

Roy leaned out the window.

"Thanks, yeah, they're ours. You boys been out hunting?" It was then I noticed the gore that coved the wheels and the side of their beast.

"Hell yes! Season is open for dead people! We wanted to check on Samuel and Nancy. What's the story? Have you seen them?" He knew damn well we were coming from their place and I started to get nervous.

"Yes, but they are not with us now."

It must have been the way Roy said it or the look on his face, but the kid understood right away. He turned to his compatriot, said something, shut off the music, bowed his head, and started talking to himself. We all knew he was praying, and stayed silent. How come we didn't even think of praying for them or anyone else? After a minute, he looked up, took a big swig of beer.

"Where are you heading?"

"The harbor and we are getting the hell out of here. You?"

"Me and Bob are gonna see if we can reach a hundred by nightfall, only thirty seven so far."

"Good luck with your hunt and happy trails."

"You too, mister, God be with you." Then he tore off into the field.

I had to wonder how long they would last, about five days so far and that isn't bad. Shit, I need to realize that I am another human trying really hard to live. It doesn't matter how many books you have read, what clothes you wear, what church you go to, if any. Can we really be different from the person next to us? Redneck? God, what an asshole I have been.

It was all farmland out here so we had a somewhat clear view of everything. The big plus, something we discovered from the oil run, was that there were hardly any cars on this section of the road. We also had lots of fences, both stone and barbed wire, which kept everything compartmentalized. I started to feel good about our chances.

We caught up with the Winnies quickly. Roy was on the radio when all at once I realized why I was so damn uncomfortable. I didn't panic, but I started to sweat. I was still totally jacked with adrenaline and bravado and decided there was only one course of action. So I started to sing some *Little Feat*, loudly.

"I got a rocket in my pocket, I said rocket. Ya Fingers in the Socket. Fingers in the Socket, Fingers in the Socket."

Roy stopped the car, put the mike down, and in unison with Hammer, turned and looked at me. He had this kind of blank, but I know what is going on look.

"John. Is this your unique way of telling me you are sitting on the LAW?" It was Hammer.

"Yup."

"Well, try not to move too much and don't scratch your ass." They turned their attention back to the radio and we moved on.

Robert turned to me.

"You're sitting on a fucking rocket?"

"Yes, Robert." I had to milk this for all it's worth. I mean how often do you sit on a live rocket launcher? "Robert, I don't know how to break this but...I believe it is pointing towards you."

The look on his face said it all. Robert was not happy, not that I was all that thrilled. Do we really need a rocket? I don't know why, but my brain said, yes. Everything was falling down and falling down fast and hard. Hammer's comment earlier brought it home. I had always thought the zombies were THE singular problem with some minor irritants thrown in, like sanitation, food, clean water, health care, etc. I never considered other living people as an issue. I just didn't learn the lesson that's in every single Romero zombie film.

Naive John assumed we would all band together for the common cause. Yeah, just like we did on our first travel day, back on the crowded highway. How many did we, I, leave to die? It was a pain fueled Escher loop that you just had to live with. I thought we were good and honorable when we were actually desperate and scared. What limits could we endure? Yeah, my response has been somewhat cocky. I was a middle age nerd, now I'm a go-to gun slinger. I'm a scientist, not some Bruce Willis superhero, but I still kept my area of fire clear, shotgun fully loaded and ready to dance. What a life. At least I could shut part of it off and think of Elizabeth. At least I have that.

The Winnie moved aside and we were in front. It was nice actually to see the road, which was still remarkably clear. There were a few zombies tangled in the barbed wire that seemed to line every field, a few abandoned cars. Now philosophical John was wondering what went through their brains, spending eternity tangled up in barbed wire or stuck inside a Civic. Roy had the map. We all had studied this thing multiple times in the barn. We were real close. God, it should be easy till we reach the small town and the harbor. What the hell was it called?

Out first major turn was about a mile up, after that, the sea, the islands, a new life.

Everyone relaxed a bit and started small talk. Liz and I locked eyes and she gave me a wink, Norm looked like he was asleep, and Paul was belting out some tune from the eighties.

We were passing a small convenience store/gas station when Roy asked Hammer to stop, so we stopped.

"Have to get some supplies. Everyone stay frosty! This should take about ten. John, I want you out and cover forward. When we're done, get back to your position in Winnie Two."

"Roger that." At least I would not be sitting on a rocket. Stay frosty? What are we, Space Marines? I jumped out and scanned right. Thank you, God! Another field and yet more walls. Up road was clear of obstructions and a small dirt road ran left, beside the store, and into the rolling distance. Why the fuck were we stopping here? I heard glass breaking, which I really hoped was Roy clearing a door. Gas was okay! We could walk to the boats if we had to. We had ample oil, so what the hell did we need? I moved to the rear and glanced at Robert as he was leaving the Hummer. We locked eyes, nodded to each another and went off in different directions.

This was not good, but at least the coast was clear. Shit, if something comes around that corner, I am not going to be happy. I crept up to store window and looked inside. It was dark and took a few seconds for my eyes to adjust. There was Roy stuffing what looked like a pillowcase with cigarettes. With my shotgun at the ready, I stepped through the broken glass. In a somewhat restrained but desperate voice, I said, "Damn it, Roy, we have got to keep moving! Keep focused on the mission." I glanced to my immediate left. "Oh, hey, gummies!" Sorry, I love gummies and they were right in front of me. These were not the fancy Haribo kind but the cheap ones shaped like lobsters, at least they came in a bigger bag. I totally forgot Roy. Think about it, how many cigarettes are out there right now in hermetically sealed packages compared to gummies? It's got to be four or five to one, so I get some slack. I grabbed a fistful of bags and I was just leaving when I heard the first gunshot. I ran for Winnie Two. Liz had the door open and Paul was taking shots at something.

"Paul said it was only two. We will be okay."

"Oh." Maybe I can go back for more gummies.

Robert entered behind me and Terrance fired her up. I could hear Mary on the radio with Winnie One. Once I sat down, I noticed people looking at me, well, actually at my hands and slowly realized that I had several bags of gummies tightly clenched. I tossed a bag to Norm, Leslie, and opened mine.

"Okay, first of all, I want to explain the machete thing…" and I told them the story. "Guys, the last thing I want to do is fight the undead hand to hand."

"What about Nancy and Samuel?" Leslie had been quiet the whole trip so it caught me off guard. Robert looked at her and cleared his throat. "No." He then looked over to me.

"Good job at the gate, not funny about the rocket!" With the expected confused look from the group.

"Robert, I was the one sitting on it. Where do these guys get this stuff?"

Terrance spoke up.

"With a little luck and at this shitty speed, we'll make the boats in less than two hours." Finally! It had been just one delay after another with the odds against us, and going up on an hourly basis.

Robert went on to explain Roy and Hammer's military background. Both were Green Berets with lots of friends around the world and a mania for blowing things up. They had known each other their whole lives and they even grew up in the same small town, Belfast Maine. I am Irish, my family is from the south, and I believe in unification, so, of course, my saviors have to be from Belfast. Then he casually dropped that both had purple hearts, Roy had a Bronze Star, and Hammer a Silver. If Hammer had not been Hammer, he might have won the Medal of Honor.

Things kind of quieted down and we all just looked outside hoping to glimpse the Harbor at each turn in the road or break in the trees. It was slow going and the Hummer had to clear some cars now and then. Fortunately, all abandoned, all but one. It was a forest green Subaru Forester. A dog barrier divided the back third of the vehicle, you know, so they can't jump on your lap while you're cruising at seventy. In the back was a girl. She looked, I don't know… twelve? Alive, really alive! We stopped and someone not in Winnie Two quickly checked it out. Thank you, I was getting a break, and maybe we can change and start to save the world instead of kicking the shit out of it. After about five minutes of chatter over the radio, the Subie was suddenly lit up. Combined, Tim, Paul, and whatever the Hummer was throwing, evaporated the back of vehicle.

"What the hell did we just do?" All my view gave me was a desperate girl stuck in cage, a cage for dogs, and a cage that we had just ripped to shreds.

"What. John, you didn't see her hand? Part of her palm was gone. Give it up, she was toast."

So, we did see zombies here and there, but not in the amount we encountered on my last road trip. Liz and I sat together in the back and I dozed for a bit. I dreamt of going swimming, and realized when I woke up that in a day, I actually could.

We finally hit a clear section of the road and we were making good time when suddenly there was a loud bang. The whole Winnebago shuddered and veered left. "Hold on! We've lost a tire!" Terrance yelled. Crap, yet again, fell everywhere and I was concerned we might tip over. With a huge lurch, I knew we had bought the side of the road. Finally, he brought the behemoth to a screeching halt.

Mary, in the front passenger seat immediately called the others, "This is Winnie Two. We got a flat and will need assistance." She was calm. "Which one, Terrance? What side?"

"Ah, left...left side. I, I think it's the left front." He sounded dazed and shaken up.

Mary relayed the information to the others and I looked around. The place was a mess with equipment and supplies scattered everywhere. Robert was sitting up behind the passenger seat looking dazed. Elizabeth was helping Leslie, blood pouring down her face. Everyone else was groaning and getting up. I got one of our medical kits and threw it back to Liz.

"Is it bad, Liz?"

"She has a nice cut on her scalp but should be okay." To Leslie's credit, she was not crying or making a scene, just stoically letting Liz do what she needed to do, and of course, trying to film it all.

"Hey, John, I think I dislocated my shoulder, maybe Doc can help." I'm not sure who it was, but Mary heard him and was quickly on the radio informing everyone of our injuries. Oh, it's Norm. I wonder if he knows that Doc is just a nickname?

I looked up at the turret. Instead of seeing Paul's long skinny white legs dangling from the lounge chair, I saw blue sky.

"Shit." I quickly set up the mini ladder and scrambled up to the roof. I hoped he had hung on and was waiting for someone to pull him up, but no such luck. I did see Winnie One turning around and heading in our direction. I looked back down the road. Paul sat off to one side holding his right arm, head down, about 50 yards behind us. His AK-47 lay on the road maybe twenty feet behind him, and his right leg was in an anatomically impossible position. He was wearing shorts and the bone was visible.

"Paul!" I screamed. "Get up, man, get up now!" He looked over to where his rifle lay and started moving in that direction. It was obvious he was badly hurt.

"NO! Move to me! Paul, to me! Screw the weapon! To me! Move to me!" He didn't acknowledge me or turn in my direction, he just slid along the asphalt at an agonizingly slow pace, using his broken legs and left arm. I turned and shouted down to the rest that Paul was behind us on the road and injured.

"Terrance, you have to back up. Somebody get me the hunting rifle." I knew that my Ruger would be useless at this range with my non-existing handgun skills. I heard commotion below and a door open. I looked back to Paul who was still trying to crawl to his rifle. Mary was yelling for him to stop and turn around. The side of the road we were on was mercifully next to a large open field, clear of the undead. The other side was a classic northern mixed hardwood forest, and I just knew.

With a metal on metal growl, the Winnie shook as Terrance tried to get her in reverse. Between the revving sound of the engine and Mary's pleading, I didn't hear them, but out of the corner of my eye, I caught motion. Turning, I pulled the Ruger and aimed. Three of them had just emerged from the edge of the trees, all adults, hard to tell sex. They stopped for a second, fixated on our little parade.

Yes, that's it! Keep focused on us, the nice big shiny slipstream of death.

"Mary, get your ass inside, now!" I yelled and fired a few rounds. I knew there was almost zero chance of a lethal hit. I just wanted to keep their attention. It might have worked had not another stumbled out further down the road much closer to Paul. She saw us first, maybe seventy-five yards away and then Paul, fifteen yards at best. Her scream at our fallen comrade brought the first group immediately to a standstill, in unison they turned. I kept firing and was almost immediately supported by the rest of the Winnie. Two went down and one got up instantly. The zombie furthest away just hurled herself towards Paul. I could now hear the sound of a machine gun behind me. I swear the passing rounds made my shirt flutter. This had to be Tim and his SAW from Winnie One. He had mounted the SAW on the turret in some kind of three-hundred and sixty degree rotating thing. Whereas in Two, we have to hump and shift seats to change directions, he just spins. Works for me, and he is throwing some serious shit downfield.

Paul didn't even look up, just kept crawling to his weapon with a single minded purpose and determination. A thin, shiny, dark streak of blood trailed behind him. The first reached him, jumped on his legs, and without delay, tore a chunk out of his calf. Paul let out a high-pitched scream as the second one dove on his back and buried her face in his neck. Winnie One passed us, just as the third one reached Paul. Tim opened up with all he had. He was not aiming for the zombies anymore. He knew what he had to do and it was all over in a matter of seconds. We had lost another one. I really liked Paul. He was smart and friendly, a nice guy. I felt guilty because all I could focus on was that I know jack about cars and we just lost our best mechanic.

Even with all the crap going on, Terrance did manage to get us up onto the road and killed the engine. I got ready to jump into the belly of Winnie Two and I paused. It was quiet for about a couple of hundredths seconds and it hit me. You know it's more than déjà vu, I know this moment, and I am going to be really fucked, really soon.

"John, they want you. I'll take the penthouse." It was Jane. She was carrying the hunting rifle and a small knapsack that I knew contained extra ammo, binoculars, and a radio. I took one last look at Paul but all I could see was a pile of dead smoking bodies, goodbye Paul. I went below.

"Okay, let's keep our shit together. We have to change that tire and Robert has a plan. Just give us a minute." I don't think I ever heard Mary swear before. It also didn't help that there was considerable fear in her voice. There was another minute of chatter on the radio. I just took up my position in the back. So far, no more visitors, but with the racket we just made, I'll give us five to ten. Robert turned and spoke up, but he didn't look at me.

"Listen up! We are going to stay put. Winnie One will pull up next to us giving just enough room to change the tire. Roy will block in front. That gives us a U shape perimeter and we have to cover the open back side and protect the people changing the tire." He just glanced my way. This was okay with me. I was pissed off and ready for revenge.

"I am going to need two volunteers to do the tire change, preferably people who have done this before."

Elizabeth's hand went immediately up. "My dad had one for years, no sweat." No, I did not like this at all. I had my shotgun, probably in the lead with zombie kills, and had more than a little attitude. I did not want Liz out there, and there was shit I could do about it. I just glared. She knew I was unhappy and did her best not to lock eyes.

"Well, I am sitting above it, so I might as well go." It was obvious Terrance was still dazed from the blowout. Great, Terrance might be in shock.

Robert looked over to me, and for the first time, I saw concern in his eyes.

"Watch it, John."

"Oh, I am more than ready to kick some zombie ass." I said this faster than I should, and it did little to alleviate Robert's concern. I took a second to calm down. "I know, Robert, I am focused and ready."

"Use a knee stance and remember your count."

"Yes, Dad." I took some deep breaths, made sure the gun and bandoleer were fully loaded.

"We got incoming from behind." Jane yelled in a voice that gave me absolutely zero encouragement. "Looks like at least a dozen, more behind them." She fired. I looked at Liz and cocked the gun.

WTF? A dozen? "Rodeo Time!" I opened the door.

Stepping outside, I quickly noticed that Roy was still trying to move into position. Several people were firing from the back to cover my ass. Let's see; nice tight kill zone? Check. Everything loaded? Check. Breathing controlled? Check. Let's dance! The first one was pretty damn close and I was glad to have cocked the weapon in the Winnie, not something I would normally recommend. He was my age, in blue jeans and a black polo shirt. Something must have been wrong with one of his legs, because he dragged it slightly behind him. This guy would be easy. I aimed and pulled the trigger. You know, a shotgun blast in a closed space is really fucking loud! I moved forward and got to one knee. The second one was another piece of cake and he dropped right where I wanted him to. My plan was to stack them up, making a zombie barricade between the Winnies. After the first few, I couldn't hear a thing. It was all smoke and gore. The Winnies were doing their job and I could see some dropping on the road. By the time I reached five, my plan started to look like it would work. I caught a short break; used the time to reload and turn around. Oh shit, Liz and Terrance were still inside!

The next one came suddenly around corner and my little barricade saved my ass. She was a tall, young, redhead, who ran so fast I couldn't get into a decent firing position. My shot caught her in the lower abdomen and she dropped in front of me and flopped about like a giant fish. I used my boot heel to pin her neck and blew the top of her head off. Macho? No. Just a really stupid thing to do and I got lucky and sprayed gore all over the Winnies and not in my face. After her was the deal sealer, manna from heaven. The guy was at least three hundred fifty pounds and maybe seven feet, bald, with blood covering his mouth and dripping onto a giant tattoo of Jesus on the cross that adorned his immense bare-chest. Ladies and gentlemen, this was truly a zombie's zombie. This guy did not mindlessly run at me, but instead, kind of sauntered carrying with him a certain air of doom.

I have never been hunting, so until recently, I didn't have a true appreciation of mass and velocity. 27 pellet #4 buck at close range is indeed an irresistible force, and does things to flesh and bone that are just plain wrong. He went down immediately and was the cork I needed.

A tapping on my shoulder told me the tire team was finally out. When I turned, I could see they were saying something to me. I always thought that reading lips is one of the coolest things in the world. Of course, I can't. I just pointed to the tire, turned, and fired. The undead now had to crawl over their fallen compañeros, and combined with the support from the death machines around me, more than adequately slowed them down. Time to reload and check on the tire change. The way they were gesticulating at each other did not encourage me. God, this is going to take a lot longer than I thought! John, stay where you are and just do your job. Being temporarily deaf has some advantages. You are in your own little world and it's easy to focus. I mean we could be overwhelmed at the front, over Roy, and I would not know. By now, I could take my time and get some practice using the Ruger.

Where the hell were these zombies coming from? We're in the middle of frigin nowhere. Well, for Maine this would technically be called semi-rural, still, Where The Fuck Are They Coming From? The loud racket we had/were made/making was certainly ringing the dinner bell, but come on, somebody throw me a bone here. Now their numbers would seriously start to work against them, as they jockeyed for position to get at this confused dude with a shotgun. This gave Jane and the others more time to line up shots, and the carnage continued.

It took a solid fifteen minutes to change the tire; I was told later that was a very good time, considering our situation. While this was happening, things were going so slow on their end and I felt time going backwards. I just could not watch. It's just a damn tire. I thought they had done this before.

I didn't see it happen, but I just knew. I turned and Elizabeth was on the ground leaning up against Winnie One. She was white, breathing fast with sweat covering her face. Her left arm was tucked into her right armpit. In her right hand, her sidearm. Why was she just lying there? No. Not Liz, we are so close. Not my Liz! My brain could not really register it. She must have caught her hand while changing the tire, just a cut. Terrance helped her into the Winnie. Mary was in the door yelling something to me and waving her hands. I knew it was my time to leave. As I stepped up and in, Mary grabbed my arm and pulled me a little. We looked into each other's eyes. Rodeo…Over.

She was placed in the back. Later, Terrance told me that a young zombie girl, maybe around ten or so, had crawled under from the front where the shielding was not as low as the sides. She caught Liz unaware and bit off her little left finger and part of her hand. I went to her side.

"Let me amputate!" I could not hear myself, so I made a chopping motion. Maybe if we cut off her hand, we can isolate the infection. She just looked at me with sad eyes and caressed my cheek. Jane bandaged her hand and gave her some morphine for the pain. I knew that Robert was radioing the news.

After about fifteen minutes, my hearing was returning. My mind raced as I thought of a way, any way. No, no. Not My Elizabeth! More and more of my hearing was coming back. I know that people were talking to me, but I was in a fog. Liz and I just looked at each other. God, she is beautiful. I was trying to absorb every nanosecond I had with her. In this new savage world, you don't want to know the future, but I knew ours. My fate was set and I did everything to break time into little sections, trying to squeeze the moment, make time stop. I ignored everyone. My world was Elizabeth, a world I would never really know. After a while, she gave me a gentle kiss on the cheek and said in a soft brave voice, "Time."

We stopped when the coast was clear. There was a beautiful rolling field on our left and the two of us exited the Winnie. No one said a word. Liz turned, stood a minute, and walked outside. She waved to Roy. The day was spectacular, sky clear, warm, but with a mild breeze that let you just smell the sea. We walked out about twenty-five yards. I was behind her. She turned and handed me her pistol. A couple of days ago, while cuddling in the loft, she told me it's a sin to kill yourself and I made the promise. Her eyes said she had made peace, but what about me. She turned her back to me.

I can't…

"I love you, John."

Do this.

"I love you, Elizabeth."

I raised the gun and pulled the trigger. Immediately, I turned, dropped the pistol, and mechanically walked back to my vehicle.

I just sat there watching the countryside go by. Numb. One fucking flat tire and she was gone. "Elizabeth," I said in a whisper. I felt hollow inside, as if I was full of dead dried leaves. I didn't want to cry or get emotional in any way. I wasn't trying to hide anything, it just wasn't there. Buddha once wrote, *"Suffering, if it does not diminish love, will transport you to the furthest shore."* Fuck him. Was this what life was going to be like? No more sleeping in late, no more comfortable lazy Sunday afternoons, no more birthdays, Christmas, Valentine's Day, or the Fourth of July? Could we really live this way? Could I really live this way? Some primordial part of my brain told me to live, if not for me, then for Elizabeth, keep fighting. In the end, only three things matter; how well did you live? How true did you love? How deeply did you learn to let go? I now knew that I would never live well again, never truly love again, and it would be a damn long time before I would let go.

No one said a word, or if they did, I didn't hear them. Roy continued to push abandoned cars out of the way. Somebody occasionally shot a zombie and we slowly crept toward our goal, toward the sea.

We were passing through a small town about a half mile from the harbor. I knew focusing on anything was better than where my mind was at, but I just couldn't make it click. Looking out the window, I saw a few zombies off in the distance and a whole lot more scattered on the ground. Good, fuck them. Sections of the road were starting to get relatively clear. We were only slowing down when having to change lanes to get around any blockage. I closed my eyes, focus, okay, harbor next, what do I need to do? I tried to envision a checklist that I assumed Roy and Hammer had worked out. You would have guessed with all our free time the last few days, we would have had this part down cold, nope. I presume we would divide into covering fire, and loaders, but exactly where were the boats? What if the harbor was already overrun? How many trips to get all supplies on the boats? What if the boats were not there? What about other survivors? Why were there suddenly so many dead zombies around? I was trying to focus on the last question when the world exploded.

I was suddenly thrown across the Winnie and slammed into the far wall. What the hell? Glass, insulation, aluminum, and various crap were scattered everywhere. Everything slowed down. I could hear the rush of wind and the scratching of aluminum on aluminum. Smoke filled the cabin and there was screaming and lots of commotion. I just lay crumpled on my side trying to make sense of where I was and what had happened. Maybe this all was a dream. Maybe this is the way my mind has chosen to forget and escape. This could be kind of fun, if you knew it was just a dream. I looked around and I would swear I could hear a Beethoven sonata in the background. Oh, thank God! This is just a dream. This is all some weird response to shock. I tasted something salty in my mouth. Can you taste in a dream? I started to think really hard.

"I'm hit," cried Norm, but he seemed very distant like hearing someone in another room, another place. I looked and the force of the explosion had somehow blown Jane out of the turret and inside our Winnie. She was holding her throat, blood squirting through her fingers. An explosion? Jane's a bad ass. Of all of us, she was going to make it! Boy, that looks so real. Wow. I have got to tell her about this when I wake up. Robert was looking back and yelling, but with all the noise and music, I could not hear what he was saying. His hand movements just didn't make any sense. My right eye blurred as something hot dripped down my face. When I reached up, I felt some warm viscous fluid. I looked at my hands and they were covered in a dark red sticky substance. Nothing hurt, so this must be part of the dream. Things started to speed up and bang. As if pulled from a deep well, I was suddenly back and this was not a dream.

"GO! GO! It's an ambush!" I heard Robert roar. Sound was everywhere. I could smell smoke and something sweet. In disbelief, I looked around. The Winnie was an absolute disaster zone with supplies scattered everywhere. I turned at the sound of gurgling.

"Oh shit!" The right side of Jane's throat had been sliced open. I leaped over to her and helped put pressure on the wound. "I need the medical kit, now" Back in the real world now, why could this not be just a dream and stop? The carotid was severed and everything I did was just a formality. "Stay with me, Jane. Don't let go, we can deal with this." In pulses, the blood flowed like a river. "Jane. Come on, bitch, fight it! Jane. Jane. Stay with me." I was now yelling at the top of my lungs. She rapidly turned pale and was dead before I could get a proper compress. In her eyes, I could see her go. There was someone there, someone real, cool, smart, sexy, and then nothing. Jane was gone. Norm had been hit with most of his right calf muscle torn away and you could see bone. I found the med kit, threw it to Mary and yelled something about a tourniquet. Norm had passed out from the shock and pain. Leslie was in shock, but still filming. I was envious that she could withdraw and observe all this shit as if in a theater. Oh no. Madeline cradled her sister's head in her lap. Matilda was seriously wounded in the abdomen. A section had been ripped open and she was holding in some loops of small intestine. Her eyes were open. She didn't move or moan, but just stared at the blood spattered ceiling.

I pulled myself up forward and grabbed the back of the passenger's seat.

"Robert, did you see what happened?" I yelled.

"I think we got hit with an RPG." He bellowed above the racket.

"What!" several of yelled at once.

"Bandits." replied Robert.

"Jane's dead," I said this to no one in particular. Leaning close to Robert, I whispered, "Norm needs his leg amputated and Matilda needs abdominal surgery."

Roy's Hummer went screaming back the way we had come, Hammer was holding the rocket launcher. "Now what?" I yelled, again asking to no one in particular.

"Don't worry about Roy. He thought this might happen and he's got some big toys," yelled, Terrance.

"Yeah, I know about his toys, but…"

"We got our turn coming up and I don't see Winnie One." Terrance was in a panic, but hey, he insisted on driving.

"We are going on!" Robert yelled.

"Terrance, Doc planned the route. He knows where to go. We stay on course," I said to calm Terrance, and me too.

As we made the turn to our final stretch of the road, I felt the shudder, and smoke poured from the engine. It was as if the Winnie had developed the hiccups. We slowly staggered forward, and then she stopped. "That's it, we're toast." Terrance announced in a remarkably calm voice.

"John, are you in the game?" Robert asked in a dead serious voice.

"Yes, Robert, I am in." I just never thought of this as a game. I looked around and chambered the shotgun. The place was a fucking disaster area. I got some compresses and went over to M&M. Whatever had hit Matilda, had ripped her belly from side to side. I opened a bottle of water, soaked the bandages and carefully removed her hands. Almost dead center was about a five-inch incision where the abdominal muscles and peritoneum had been severed. Protruding from this gap were several stands of pinkish grey fat sausages that was part of her small intestine. M&M both looked at me with eyes pleading for hope, but I had none to give and Matilda was going to die. After gently placing the compresses on the wound, I turned to Robert. "Robert, would you get me the Saran Wrap from the floor over there." Mary joined me and let out a little gasp. "John?"

"Mary, let's get her some morphine. It's in the right side pocket with the autoinjectors." I leaned in close so the sisters could not see my face and whispered, "Mary, we have to get some defenses going. You take care of Norm and Matilda. Just manage their pain. Don't waste the antibiotics." I sealed the wound with the plastic and taped everything in place. Robert was now outside, shooting at something. I went to join him.

"Terrance, get your hands off the steering wheel and your fucking ass in gear and help Mary." I yelled.

When I stepped outside, the circus was definitely in town. At least ten were coming with more following. Here we go! Robert in action is a sight to behold. He dropped six of them in about ten seconds. He seemed to anticipate their movement. It was as if the zombies walked into his shots. I got up next to him and nailed the closest three.

"We need Winnie One back! Norm and Matilda will have to be prone. With supplies, I don't think we will all fit." I dropped two more.

"We're real close, maybe half a mile to the harbor." He dropped four and looked over to me. Ah, damn, here it comes. "Let's work our way back and get a better view. Some of us might have to hoof it."

Shit! Why is it always me? I'm not a soldier, I'm a fucking anthropologist!

"Yeah, I kind of figured that." Robert, may you die in a grease fire.

Winnie One pulled up next to us.

"So, Robert, what are our odds?"

"Not really fucking good," he hissed as he scanned the road around us.

"Is that the line out of Vegas? You think those guys…" Kaboom! A huge explosion from the direction we just came. The shock wave knocked me on my ass and blew out store windows.

"Robert?"

"Stay in the game! Let's take the group in front of us while they're still confused." We calmly walked up to a group of five zombies about twenty-five yards from us who were mesmerized by the smoke and fireball, and blew them away.

I jumped when Tim opened up with the SAW. Derrick joined us with his Glock and for the next fifteen minutes, it was just rinse and repeat while they loaded up the Winnie. Almost all of the undead came down the road from the north, where the blast had been. They were mostly clustered in groups of three or four. Overall, they were never a real threat, I wonder how many were coming after us, and are now sidetracked by whatever the hell went boom. Those that came out of the various alleyways, side streets, and from the south, were never more than two, Tim usually did the job before I even saw them.

Once the supplies were loaded, I gave Mary a hug and waved goodbye to the rest. Norm was asleep and absolutely white. Matilda was covered in blankets and her head was again in her sister's lap. Zack had placed IVs in both of them. Leslie just kept filming. I'm starting to think there is something really wrong with that girl.

There was not any discussion or explanation; just this group-wide assumption that Robert and John would walk to the boat. They slowly limped away and for the first hundred yards or so, we kept up. Everyone who could hold a gun was shooting at anything that moved. The Winnie was like the Death Star and we were two TIE fighters. This could work! Then the confident giddy feeling started to wane in direct proportion to the increasing distance between the Death Star and us. Robert looked me.

"Let's get the hell out of here!"

"Roger that!"

We started trotting, firing, and just being alive. The Winnie gave us some cover but rapidly got ahead. I have no clue why they were not staying with us. I was getting out of breath and my shoulder was killing me. To drop to one knee meant stopping, so I didn't and my accuracy dramatically plunged. It might be the adrenalin hitting me yet again or exhaustion or maybe this is really it, time to shine elsewhere, but suddenly, everything seemed to project a weird light. It was like twilight during the middle of a sunny day. Time slowed down and I was in this dream world. Calm and concentrated, but aloof. I should be terrified, but I wasn't. My shoulder no longer hurt. I didn't want to die, but if I did that would be okay. I don't know how many I re-killed, but I started to put them down with ease. We were very lucky that, they tend to scream when attacking, because it alerts you as to where you are going to shoot. I had no clue where we were going, since the Winnie got out of view. I just followed Robert and assumed we were heading to the now visible ocean in front of us. I kept expecting a mob around every corner, but there wasn't. There was one guy who looked just like my high school math teacher; I can't quite describe it, but he didn't run like the rest. It looked for a second that he was running from the zombies, but I still blew him away. While I was in this strange high, it was easy just to shoot at anything that moves without really checking your targets, and I wonder maybe, just maybe...

God, had my attitude changed. Maybe this is what a runner's high is like. I really wanted to kill zombies. I was calm and called out my targets. I was in the zone, totally in the moment. I even somehow knew how many rounds I had. Robert knew I would let them get closer than he would, but I never missed, always counted and never passed up an opportunity to reload. We got lucky in that, more than five at a time never swarmed us, and we constantly communicated.

"I got two southeast by the gas pumps."

"They're yours. One from north, mine."

"Five, Six, Seven, Shit! Reloading." I yelled.

"Let them get closer if it will save you a shot."

"I get the plan, Robert, Alleyway West. I made the meeting. I read the memo. Don't worry, I think I am down to slugs after this set."

We just walked, stayed together, and killed everything that moved. That included a stray Germen Sheppard who almost ran into Robert. At one point, I actually laughed when I nailed some dude in the abdomen. The shot must have severed the spinal cord because he went down hard and the legs stopped moving. The guy did not try to crawl to me, or even look my way, he just lay there and pounded the asphalt as if he was pissed off that he missed his chance. Then, there it was, not a mirage, but there was the harbor. All that separated us from the dock and an incredibly unlikely stroll was a large half-filled parking lot. No fence, just a guardrail and from what I could see, almost no zombies. My God, we made it.

"Robert, what the hell did we just do?"

"We stayed breathing, John. That's all we did."

"Ah...I think and I could be wrong, but since they make sounds, I believe zombies also breathe." I kept anxiously glancing back and forth.

"Ah, John...Just shut the fuck up. You know, Professor, ever since I met you, I have been using more and more profanity. Why is that?"

"Fuck if I know."

When we casually strolled into the marina, I had only a tenuous contact with reality and thought we were studs. No one would be able to comprehend how we could have possibly survived and that included Robert and me, but something was wrong. People weren't loading boats, but hiding around the Winnies in a defensive position. Doc gave us the news. They had been ambushed. Some sort of militia hit them a minute of two after arriving. Mostly small arms fire.

"We were a bit suspicious when there were only dead zombies in the harbor parking lot, way too quiet. Once we got out of the Winnie, they opened up. No hands up, no call for surrender, nothing. We got lucky. I don't think they had it planned all that well, everyone in one building. Well, Hammer always said you never take a handgun to an automatic weapons party."

"Same guys from up the road?" I asked.

"More than likely, they could be back. Norm died before the attack, Matilda during. Where the hell is Roy and Hammer?"

"No one knows. What about the boats?"

"You mean boat, single boat."

Robert looked about. "Well, even a blind pig finds an apple every now and then, she's mine." What are fucking odds that of the few boats left, one would be Robert's? It helped that he was anchored the furthest out.

"Let's clean out the Winnie and get what we can on the dock. Make a defensive position. I'll go get her." With that, Robert took off in a sprint, now all energized at getting his lady back.

Tim and Derrick gently led Madeline to the dock. Mary, Doc, Zack, Matt and I, made a semi-circular perimeter around the Winnie. Tim stayed in the turret. Not all the noise we were making went unrewarded. For the first few minutes, they dribbled in by ones and twos. Getting on towards the ten-minute mark, the numbers started dramatically to increase to groups of five to ten. Between the various cars, the Winnie and the harbor Master's shack, we had a halfway decent defensive perimeter with some nice kill zones. Mary and I had somehow ended up at the end of the line next to the water. As long as the scattered cars kept them somewhat separated, we would be able to handle the next few minutes.

Once again, I tried to remain calm and focus on my breathing. My best guess was that I had about ten rounds remaining and really hoped my additional ammo had been transferred from Winnie Two. All I could do was burn what I have, drop the shotgun and go with the Ruger. Without taking my eyes off the incoming zombies, I reached down and made damn sure the safety was off and I would actually be able to remove my side arm when the moment came, and it was coming. An exceedingly loud bang from my right made me jump and waste the next shot.

It was Mary and her zany, metal polished, custom grip, three fifty seven magnum. I mean come on, that monster was almost a quarter her size. Mary had backed up against a light post and used two hands to fire the cannon. One thing for sure, that old gal knew how to tap that behemoth. She quickly found her zone and went to work. I was at a great angle to observe Mary going down town. I think she was saying something, at least her mouth was moving. She would tense up and flex her back against the pole just before she fired. Like me, she let them get a bit close and like me, she never missed. She dropped six in about thirty seconds, ejected empty, picked out a speed loader from a vest pocket, loaded, and dropped six in the next thirty. Holy shit! I thought I was badass. I wanted to get closer to hear what she was saying, because, come on, and think about it. The stuff coming out of her mouth has got to be a comedy goldmine for the Mary's roast we would have on the island.

"Time to go!" Couldn't tell who yelled in my ear but he/she needed some serious intimate oral hygiene time. I waited until I caught a little break and then turned around. Everyone was falling back to the dock, and some were already on board. At best, I had three rounds left, which should get me to the boat, and allow me to save my shotgun.

"Mary, Let's go!" Given the situation, I assumed the call to retreat would be welcome and she would turn and run. My assumptions were based on the reactions that a normal terrified human being faced, with a rapidly approaching zombie horde might have. I had Mary. I know she had reloaded because in haste, I saw her drop the empty speed loader. She took this really long second to respond to me.

"I know." She then lined up the next two.

"Mary, now is a really great time." I heard/felt rounds going by me. It was support from the boat, and then Mary's cannon roared.

"Mary, please. I need you. Now!"

"Oh, all right." With that, she popped off two more, turned towards the boat, and marched away. She didn't look at me or say a word, or seem to particularly care that we had a serious zombie problem. I was trying to stay calm and quickly walk backwards, oh, and kill anything that got close. I ran dry just as I made it to the dock. Once on board, I threw the shotgun into the cockpit and pulled out the Ruger. The shooting had started to wind down. Once again, it was their numbers and our fortuitous environment that saved our asses. Once the zombies started dropping on the narrow dock, the blood and gore made the old wood, even with the anti-slip patches, slick and the bodies became a hassle to get over. Combined with at least a dozen armed people guarding a meter wide path, nobody was getting close to us. I moved over to where Robert was at the helm.

"Can I breathe now?"

"Yeah, John, you can breathe." So I leaned over the side and vomited.

"Hold on. Stop firing!" Robert bellowed. "Jesus H Christ. Save the ammunition."

"We're safe. Let's not shoot one another. Listen up, this boat was not made for this many people. The good news is that the weather looks clear and calm. We should be able to find some place nice and safe to spend the night. The bad news is that we have to keep this boat balanced, so think of yourself as ballast. We need even weight on either side. Let's go." So we went about getting ourselves squared away. I got lucky and scored a topside port seat with a great view of the shore.

"Everyone, quiet up!" It was actually nice to hear someone shout again. Robert continued, "Okay, here's the plan. Right now, for tonight at least, we have one boat, this boat. We are going to stay right where we are and wait for Roy and Hammer. Mary if you can hear me, you are in charge of the supplies."

"Ten four, Captain," yelled a muffled voice from somewhere below.

"Doc and Jim, keep your eyes on the shore and let's see what happens. Everybody else, get some rest and drink some damn water."

Essentially, that was it. We, or what was left of us, had made it to a boat to temporary safety. A strange combination of feelings that kept me up that night. I felt ashamed for making it, a real case of the 'why me?' I killed Liz; the one person, the one thing that could have made me whole and all I feel is a guilty relief? No applause for the badass academic warrior? At one point, in this totally sane mental loop I'm experiencing, I almost laughed out loud. It dawned on me that this must be what it is like to be a character in a horror/adventure video game. We have just completed a quest and are now waiting for the new quest to load. Then, it is off to another voyage of adventure and excitement and death.

Robert and I fired flares every fifteen minutes, but no sign of Roy and Hammer. No talk, which was good. He was particularly agitated that his computer didn't work and I had just murdered the love of my life. We were maybe a hundred yards from shore. A bit too close for me when you consider there are living people out there who, for whatever twisted fucking reason, want to shoot at you, but I wanted those guys back. They were my, our, leaders. So far, no one was shooting at us, or for that matter, shooting at all. As for what is now passing for usual, the zombies did not let us down. From every imaginable point on shore they came. If we had not made it to the boats, we would have been overwhelmed. With all the noise, we've been making, I suppose some of them might have been following us the better part of the day. The firefight at the dock did little to conceal our actions. They just spent their time gathering forces, milling about and glaring at us. A few made a mad dash for the boat, and as soon as the water got above their head, they just went under, and we never saw them again. I kept glancing over the side expecting to see just below the surface, the outstretched fingertips of hundreds of the undead reaching up for us. As if, I needed help with not sleeping. Once it got dark, we fired up the spotlight. Robert spent about thirty minutes hooking it up and I don't know what 70K candlepower means, but in my terms, really really bright. Holy crap. Just a solid wall of zombies as far as the beam could project. Once the light from the flare died down and you looked at the beam of light on the grey horde, it almost looked alive, like it was one creature.

I lay down on the side that was hurting least, my back. My mind was in meltdown. What happened today? Where the hell are Roy and Hammer? They killed the dogs? Where is Elizabeth? Samuel and Nancy killed the dogs, Roy and Hammer are gone and

I killed Liz. Liz is dead. After a while, I began to notice the gentle rocking of the *Providence*. In about ten minutes, the rhythm dragged me to sleep.

Like one who, on a lonely road,
Doth walk in fear and dread,
And having once turn'd round, walks on,
And turns no more his head,
Because he knows a frightful fiend
Doth close behind him tred.
Samuel Taylor Coleridge *The Rime of the Ancyent Maninere*

Chapter 14 ~ In the Navy

June 12th

I was jolted awake by a loud knock. It took me a minute to realize where I was and this was clearly not the *Providence*. I was on ship. How the hell did I get on a ship? The door opened and a sailor entered the room. He had a lot of stuff on his sleeves, so I am guessing he had some rank.

"Sorry to wake you, sir. You have a meeting scheduled for thirteen hundred hours and I thought you might want to shower and get something to eat first. It's eleven thirty now. I will help orient you around."

"Well, give me a second to come back to reality. Can we eat first?"

"No problem, sir."

"How long have I been out?"

"About eighteen hours, sir."

"What?"

"You were visited by medics and everything seemed okay. Sometimes, you just need to get rest on your own schedule."

"Name's John, yours?"

"Oh, I apologize, Luke, pleased to meet you, John." I sat up, we shook hands, and I very slowly got to my feet.

"Give me a second. I don't think I have ever slept that long."

"No problem. Welcome aboard the *Harry Truman*."

I felt like I had been out for days, as if I was drugged. Everything seemed out of focus, but not in a good stoned sort of way. Wow, that was way too much to recall. Did I just ask him to eat after he told me we were going to eat? God, I need to get a grip. Man, did the shower help.

Luke came back and led me through a maze of grey corridors, which ended in a large room packed with sailors and marines, eating what I guessed was dinner, might have been lunch.

Cool! Fried chicken, green beans, mashed potatoes, and a real salad, oh yeah! All of a sudden, I was really hungry. In a haze, but I still noticed that the cooks were giving me larger portions than the guys in front. I went to the dispenser and got milk, real milk? I poured some and just stood there looking at it. It was cool and white with beads of condensation already making its way down the outside of the glass, absolutely beautiful. How long would we have milk? I just stood there, looking and looking.

It took me a while, but I began to notice that the loud racket of the room had died down. As I turned to find a seat, I saw that everyone was looking at me. Had they not seen a survivor before? Was I not supposed to eat here? I felt like a party crasher who had just been busted. I moved to a table at the far end of the room that had a couple of empty seats. The guys at the table stood as I approached. They were all marines and I instantly thought I had done something to piss them off.

"Is this seat empty?"

"It would be an honor if you dined with us, sir." It came from a large black man and almost sounded like an order rather than an invitation. I later learned that his name was Roland, from Seattle, and one of the nicest guys in the world, just don't get him angry.

"Okay, thanks. Name's John, I just came on board yesterday. I think I am some kind of consultant."

They all looked at me as if I had two heads. I glanced around the room and almost everyone was still staring. My mind was foggy from sleeping, but what the hell was going on here? Then I saw the suspended flat screen monitors scattered around the dining hall, and I froze. Each monitor had a rather distorted image of me, I was almost sure it was one of the last video entries I made at the lighthouse. Shit! They had seen the video! My video! I just lowered my head and started to eat my salad. It was obvious that I had been caught off guard.

Everyone was quiet and then Roland spoke up.

"Sir, the top brass thought we could learn something, and understand the mainland situation better through your experience. We thought you knew."

"Ah…sergeant? It's okay. Robert and I handed over the tapes without reservation, and if any good can come from them…well…if it's helpful." I could only look at my plate of food. I was tired and just so dead inside. Too much has happened and way too fast to adequately process. El Macho Machete was gone forever. John was back to being John, so I guess I might as well eat.

"Sir, name's Marvin, I don't mean to be disrespectful but…that was really you? No special effects? CGI?"

I swallowed a mouthful of chicken and tried not to choke. "Yes, no, and I hope not." I went back to eating.

"John," said Roland again. "That was some serious shit you and Robert went through. We'll get our turn and we will not let you down." The rest of the table yelled, 'Oorah!'

"Thanks, we did our best, but only two out of twenty-two, two out of twenty…" I went back to eating and everyone gave me some space. After I finished and I was feeling comfortable and full, it just hit me. Somehow, I understood that I was in for the long haul. I mean, why not? I could just fade into the Vineyard, but I was going all the way. I only have one choice. I'm sorry, Liz, but I'm going back to the mainland.

"Hey, Roland, since I am an official consultant and supposed to be an expert on zombies, is there any chance I can tag along when you go?"

"You heard something?"

"No, no, but I don't see anyone raising chickens or milking cows, not to mention the whole agriculture thing. I'm serious. I want to go back and see how this is all playing out. Maybe I can find some way they react, respond to different stimuli that might give us an additional edge."

Roland just looked at me for about sixty uncomfortable seconds. The rest of the table was quiet.

"I'll see what I can do."

Luke showed up and asked me if I was ready for the conference. When I stood, Roland was still looking at me.

"Thanks, guys. I'm not playing around, Roland." I was just in the act of turning.

"John, have you ever seen your movie?"

"No."

"I would not recommend it. You'll hear from me."

Once again, a maze of corridors, but we went up and up. Our sojourn ended up in front of a highly polished mahogany door. Okay, must be special people inside, not like the short bus but with some similarities. Before we could knock, the door opened for us. In front of me was an impeccably dressed and an absolutely massive seaman, who politely ushered me into the room and to my seat. I did not sit down. Oh, what the hell am I doing here?

We were arranged around a large oval cherry table. As far as rank went, I had no clue, so I just assumed the guys with the most bling, win. Where the hell was Robert? The gentleman at the far end spoke up, "I am Admiral Spencer. I am in command of the North Atlantic fleet. Please sit down and we will get this started." So I sat, cool, I got a laptop. He continued.

"Dr. Patrick, thank you for being here. You have been filled in on the basics of our mission. We will continue an aggressive search for survivors. We also are in the mop-up stages on Martha's Vineyard and have already moved on to Block Island. We have read your account of the events from the last several weeks, and yes, I have seen the video. It was my order that the fleet also have access to it. You have been through a ton of shit, pardon my vulgarity, but it seems appropriate. My staff and I need to understand the undead as well as you. We need you to help us carve a path to renewal, and gaining back what we have lost."

A little internal voice told me to shut up and then I heard myself talking. "Excuse me, Admiral. What we have lost is hard to comprehend. It's not just the people. It's the infrastructure and the knowledge. We are no longer a technology/industrial society. We are scavengers. We cannot reproduce the material and ingenuity that went into this magnificent vessel. At best, we are going to have to work to get back to being an agrarian society. I'm talking about the middle ages, but with really smart peasants." Where the fuck is Robert?

There was an officer sitting next to me on my right. He immediately made some sort of snorting sound when I had finished talking. It was low enough that I could hear it and probably no one else. He, in his late twenties or early thirties, with a thin face and a pug-like nose, was obviously of some high rank, but I had no clue as to what it was. We looked at each other for a second and I instantly knew I was not going to be invited to his next birthday party.

"Then what do you suggest we do?" Everyone at the table except the Admiral and the freak next to me had their pads and pens out ready to take notes. I was about to suggest inventing a time machine so we can all go back to an age when life just kind-of-sucked.

"Sir, this is going to last far longer than anyone has anticipated. There is no wait it out strategy. These things will be here for a long time, maybe years."

"Why do you say that? A zombie can only go so far and it breaks down, it decays. Everything I have been told is that decomposition should run its course in a matter of months, so how do you come up with years?" I don't know who spoke, but he was not happy.

"Sir, the infection spread is exponential, not linear, and with what I am assuming is a classified R-zero, very quickly."

"But for years?"

"Sir, for one, they breathe."

"What!" It was the freak speaking up. "You have been close enough to them to know they are breathing?" It was really not a question, but an exercise in condemnation that I am sure he hoped would eventually lead to humiliation. Besides, they have to know all this already.

I turned and looked at him. His nametag read H. Owens. "Well, Owens…"

"It's Captain Owens," he said in a slow cold voice, emphasizing the word captain. This guy really didn't like me and we had never met!

"That's great, I'm sure your mom is proud," I said this fast in the hopes of avoiding a reprimand and quickly segued to the important part. "I did not have to get close. You see, it is impossible to make the sounds the zombies make, or really any vocal sound, without air passing across the vocal cords, usually during phonation." I turned to look at freak. "That is to say during exhalation."

Once again, I quickly continued. "They also have a functioning circulatory system. I have seen no signs of livor mortis, plus I've touched them. They are warm, so no algor mortis." This really caught the room's attention and several people started talking at once. Freak just pushed his chair back and crossed his arms and legs waiting for me to hang myself. He had this smug look on his face and I started to dislike him as much as he seemed to dislike me.

"Okay, gentlemen, let Dr. Patrick finish what he was saying, Doctor?"

"Well, to simply state it, if you don't have a functioning circulatory system, you don't have bio-available oxygen. No oxygen, no cellular respiration. No cellular respiration, no production of Adenosine Triphosphate, also more commonly known as ATP. No ATP, no energy to move muscles. No ATP and you get muscular contracture, something I like to call rigor mortis. Rigor mortis is clearly not an issue with our current population of undead. If the other two are true, and they are, the zombies have a partially functioning digestive system."

My 'friend' was a bit louder and just a fraction ahead of the rest. "But you can't be sure. Maybe there is another way of generating this energy. Something we have never seen. Speaking of seeing, have you ever seen a zombie take a shit? You make a lot of assumptions."

"That could be true, and no, I have not observed a zombie defecating. Staying with this line of thinking, I did get close enough to smell their breath. It smelled fruity and like acetone or nail polish. Something we see in ketoacidosis. This is usually the result of low insulin levels, but maybe, just maybe, these guys can fluctuate and use both glucose and fat depending upon energy needs."

"Dr. Patrick, your area of anthropology seems to cover a lot of things."

"Admiral, I have an affinity for remote places and am trained as a wilderness EMT. Type 1 diabetes is unfortunately a common illness."

"Wonderful." He glanced at the freak next to me. "Any other good news?" I could tell from the Admiral's voice that this whole meeting was not going down the way he had planned.

Oh nuts, I really didn't want to dump all my suspicions at once. I thought that maybe we could go over each point, kind of like breaking down bullet points in a particularly bad PowerPoint presentation. Ah well, okay, piece de resistance - I took a deep breath.

"They hydrate. I've seen them drink. With everything I watched on the TV and internet, I thought this was our ace in the hole. We weather the storm surge and then, with time, back to sea level. They may be around a lot longer than anticipated."

"How long?" This came from somebody near the admiral who was not in a strictly military uniform, public health, maybe.

"My guess is months, maybe more. We should be seeing a sharp drop in the population from those that have already suffered major injuries, but after that, I have no clue. This is of course all predicated on the belief that the infection is transmitted solely through intimate contact with the infected." If looks could kill, I was already dead. The admiral and the two sitting next to him were shooting laser beams at me. I guess with power comes 'the look', and this one was clearly telling me to move on to another topic.

"There is another thing that bothers me. Those with major trauma and I'm talking cases of substantial soft tissue damage, don't seem to be bleeding out. This means that coagulation at the trauma site is occurring at a rapid and highly efficacious rate."

"They don't bleed?"

"It's clear they bleed, because all wounds show signs of hemorrhaging. I just don't know why more of them are not dead from loss of blood."

Another voice spoke up from the far end of a very quiet room. "What does this all mean?"

"What this means?" I thought by now that was obvious. "It means that, biologically speaking, they are alive."

This time, the room remained silent as everyone contemplated the true meaning of what I just said. This concept had to have been expected or at least suspected. I don't know about reproduction, but these things do fill most, if not all the criteria for being classified as living organisms.

"Admiral, all this had to have been known soon after the Plague started. I mean, the whole world was working on it."

"Yes, they were working on it, but even when the situation became critical, nobody, and I mean nobody, played as a team. We had agencies within our own government who were not talking to each other, let alone sharing information. So we start again. We have some ships that have been retrofitted for this purpose and we move forward from here." The Admiral was clearly indicating that this line of investigation was ended.

"Dr. Patrick, your observations and assumptions are in line with the information I have been getting from a variety of sources. I just wanted to hear it from someone outside the government. The biology and physiology of our opponents is a top priority and something you will be involved in. For now, I want a detailed report of everything you have observed, theorized, and guessed about our situation. No detail is too insignificant."

"I will get right on it, sir." Well, at least I had something official to do.

Admiral Spencer looked to a sailor standing by the door, nodded his head, and the sailor left.

"Okay, gentlemen, we are going to take ten." Everyone got up and stretched. I just looked at the table and the patterns the wood made. It was beautiful. How could there not have been worldwide cooperation? Everything was crashing and burning and we would not talk to each other? Maybe Liz was right. Maybe deep down inside, humans were mad.

When I looked up, the side tables were loaded with coffee, tea, soda, fruit, sandwiches, and all sorts of assorted goodies. It brought me back to the milk in the cafeteria. Didn't they know this was all going away? Then the Admiral was at my side.

"Doctor Patrick, do you have a second?" His voice was polite but it was not a question.

"Of course, Admiral." We moved to the corner of the room by a window that overlooked the flight deck. I still could not get over the size of this ship.

"I don't know what is going on between you and Owens, but you are going to stop it right now."

"Yes, sir, I understand. I also don't know what is going on either, but you will have no more problems from me." I looked at the admiral as he walked away. You know, I liked the guy. He had the weight of the world on his shoulders, or at least the weight of tens of thousands of lives, but he kept his shit together and focused on what was relevant and important. It reminded me of Captain Picard from Star Trek, Next Generation. I decided to forgo the treats and waited to find out what I should do next.

When I sat down, the Freak looked at me with this, 'I won asshole, don't fuck with me' attitude. I guess he thought the Admiral was chewing me out. I looked away and tried to focus on the work ahead. I have no clue how to put together this report. Eventually, everyone sat down, papers were shuffled and the meeting started.

"Captain Owens."

"Yes sir."

"Thank you for your contribution, but you are no longer needed, dismissed." He stood, saluted and walked out. My eyes never left the table.

I waited for my name to be called next, but only heard, "Okay, let's get back to the situation at hand." So we went around the room with everyone giving their opinion on where we were and what we should do. It was kind of like the old bull sessions I used to have at Phi Sigma Kappa back in college. The discussion was not specific to the zombies, but a general review of the overall situation. I decided to keep a low profile and let the upperclassmen do the talking.

From what was said, I started to put together a clearer picture of the last couple of weeks. It seems that the President and most of the political establishment had survived and were now safely ensconced on several Caribbean islands. A number of military instillations around the world still survived, but most were under siege. There still were many civilian holdouts, but their numbers were steadily declining. There had been another 'radiological incident' somewhere in the Midwest. Another? Long term food and fuel issues were not discussed. After about an hour of general conversation, we eventually centered on what could be accomplished with the land we already had. Land? We had a couple of desert islands! Even Gilligan would not be happy. Someone mentioned the ease with which we could take Cape Cod. Block Island seemed to be a given, but none of it really made any sense. I kept quiet, trying to absorb the inanity that was going on around me. I noticed the admiral did the same. It's not that the points being presented weren't valid; it's just that everyone was looking at the pretty leaves and missing the raging forest fire. After about another hour, I started to get fidgety and looked around, I noticed the Admiral was staring at me. Shit, apparently it was my turn. I guess, since I was an outsider it would not matter much if I crashed and burned, and looked like a fool, so I took a deep breath and with no real idea what I was going to say, I dove in.

"Gentlemen." Holy cow, they actually stopped talking and looked at me; brain, this better be good. "I have been to Block Island, been to the Vineyard and Nantucket. I was born on Cape Cod and all these places are great for a nice family vacation. Wonderful beaches, fantastic restaurants, but they are not what we need."

A rather portly gentleman with a baldhead, ribbons and stuff all over his chest and a kind voice spoke up. "What do you suggest we need? Ah…"

"John, sir, we need everything; security, sustainable food, clean water, reliable power, you name it."

It was now the admiral's turn, although from the sound of his voice, he already knew the answer. "And just where do we find this, Doctor?"

"Well, as far as the east coast is concerned, Long Island would be a good start." Everyone just stared at me. At first, I think they thought that this was some kind of joke and the punch line was next. After thirty seconds, it dawned on the group that I was not kidding.

"If you think about it…it's got some good farmland and a nuclear reactor in…"

"East Shorham, Dr. Patrick. It also has a population of around eight million people or should I say zombies, which is approximately the same as Ireland."

"Yes, but the vast majority is in the southern part of the island, in Brooklyn and Queens. Between these two boroughs, we have a population of what, maybe six plus million. We eliminate the bridges and tunnels and isolate the island. Do everything possible to encourage the zombies on the northern portion of the island to visit New York City. I don't know how, some kind of super noise maker or something. Then when everybody thinks we've done enough, obliterate the southern portion of the island. We are still talking about a large undead population, numbers like two million or three, but it can be done."

"How?" Now it was just the admiral and me talking. I could sense the other's heads darting back and forth as if watching a tennis match.

"With almighty force."

"All of it?"

"Is there a choice?" Here it comes.

"So, Dr. Patrick, how do you propose we deal with these five to six million zombies on the southern end of Long Island?"

"We need some time to get everyone south. We have to isolate, so we don't allow Manhattan, New Jersey, and Connecticut to come to our party. Once you decide the dance card is full, you nuke them." This produced the expected result; a bit of shock and a whole lot of outrage. More than one declared I was out of my mind. It took only a simple clearing of his throat and Admiral Spencer calmed the room down.

He just stared at me and in a calm steady voice asked, "Are you insane?"

Well, I guess the game did have rules. "Perhaps, but from my imperfect knowledge base, it seems time is critical and options are rather limited."

He looked around the room. "I am openly having a conversation with an individual who says he is perhaps insane! Gentlemen, I need more alternatives than nuking New York and I need them now."

"Admiral, I don't want to nuke the city, just the two boroughs. I don't think we should get crazy or anything." The room became so silent you could hear a pin drop. Oh boy, do I need Robert.

"I apologize, that was uncalled for. Once the island is isolated, we are talking about a finite number of zombies. Unfortunately, this will be a very large number. Basically, we find out where we can safely segregate the southern portion of the island, the area that gets nuked, with a fence or something. We clear everything north of the fence. This will take time and cost lives. We need to find out who knows something about farming, raising animals, plumbing, electrical, carpentry, public works immediately and get Shorham up and running. Admiral, at the very least, it gives us something to do."

He stared at the table for a while and then started to look around the room. So far, nobody had raised any objections. The admiral turned to a forty-something incredibly fit red haired man on his right.

"Danny, Cape Cod and Block Island are all yours. Good luck."

"Thank you, sir."

Most of the others were given various assignments; stocks, weapons inventory, fuel and a variety of other things. The Admiral was going to lead a sub-team to review the isolation of the island and the use of all options in eliminating the zombies. Needless to say, I was given nothing to do, but the Admiral did ask me to stay after the others had left.

"John, you don't really have a plethora of inhibition, do you?"

"I apologize again. I'm not familiar with military protocol. I know that without some form of command, we stand a zero chance of survival."

"Speaking of survival, Captain Walker has informed me that you wanted to do some demographic research, something to do with the chances of having a maintainable population, something about a genetic bottleneck?"

"Yes, I was surprised at the low number of survivors, I just expected a lot more. I ..."

"I want you to put this research on hold. John. No good can come out of this. You and I know that the results will more than likely not be positive, and the last thing we need is to bring the seed of doubt to this mission. We have been at sea for two months, and like you, have lost everything. The fleet knows this, but most of them just don't realize it yet."

"Yeah, I know what you mean. I don't know if I truly realize my loss. Admiral, let me know what I can do, what I should do."

"John, in private, you can call me Chris. Your Long Island strategy has merit and has been previously discussed. The Cape and Block Island are just training missions, feasibility studies for the big mission. You are correct when you mention the need to focus, and the need for hope."

"Well, hope springs eternal."

"What?"

"It's Alexander Pope, sir, from the eighteenth century. *'Hope springs eternal in the human breast. Man never is, but always to be blest. The soul, uneasy and confined from home, Rests and expatiates in a life to come'.* You know, I never really understood exactly what the hell he was trying to say. Maybe now, I think I do."

We moved two chairs from the table and sat across from each other. "John, there are a couple of other things I want you to do. First, I want you to be quiet about your involvement with the Long Island plan with Robert and the crew, even if we do not implement it. I want anything that we do to be seen as something the military conceived. Yet another brilliant, innovated, fool proof plan. I can't have the crew thinking we have been sitting here with our heads up our asses until some civilian comes along with a bunch of bright ideas."

"No problem, Chris."

"Second, and this will put you back in familiar territory, I want you to put together a short, let's say two hour review of what zombies are: biology, tactics, virology, sociology, and any other 'ology' you can think of. Dr. Patrick, you are going to be my zombie expert and I am sending you on a lecture tour of the North Fleet. Give what you gave us and as much more as possible, A through Z. These boys are the ones who are going to be fighting them. Don't worry, because you'll have plenty of assistance."

"No problem."

"Dinner's in a couple of hours. Would you care to join me?"

"Thanks, that would be great." Well, I guess this means I have a title. Now I'm a consultant, or something.

"I'll send someone by. Do you know the way back?"

"In a roundabout sort of, no, not really." He laughed.

"I'll find you an escort." Damn! The witty comeback was there right on the tip of my tongue, but he's an Admiral! This was the major leagues and I had to play by their rules, so I just stood, shook his hand, and told him I looked forward to dinner.

Robert was waiting for me in my new suite.

"So, Dr. Patrick, how did it go?"

"Well, I think I can safely say that I may have exceeded expectations and assured anyone with even a modicum of lingering doubt that I have mental issues." I stretched out on the bunk.

"And you needed several hours to do this? How were you communicating, in Braille?"

"It is comforting to know that I will always have the succor of your warm bosom in times of need." We both laughed, he sat on the bed and left the door open so it wouldn't feel as claustrophobic as it actually was.

"Like you guessed, Robert, it's a land grab. Makes sense. You have to feed a crap load of people, you can raid all you want, but you are going to run out and the power all these ships must require is a phenomenal amount of energy. Of course, some are nuclear, but the rest." I shrugged.

"Well, you also have to take into account that just within the North Fleet, you are talking a hell of a lot of people who have watched the world die, all the while being cooped up on these vessels. At least, you and I had an outlet, of sorts." I knew he didn't mean it that way, but it stung.

"John, they need to do something. Long Island? Cape Cod?"

"Both. You ever see a nuclear explosion?"

"No."

"Me neither, should be interesting, I hope they brought lots of ammo. Oh, this stuff is secret and I'm not supposed to tell you." Do I smell Dewers?

"So we're going with the bomb. Well, if done right, it's quick, efficient, and let's everyone know you aren't fucking around."

We spent the next couple of hours or so talking shit. We yakked about everything under the sun except the one thing we both wanted to talk about. The *Providence* was now on its way to the Vineyard, and Robert would be soon to follow. He knew where I was going.

"We may make it to the islands, after all. You never know. We're civilians so we can stay out of this mess. We did our part." He leaned close and in his best fatherly voice, almost whispering, "John, the dance has ended."

"It's okay, Robert. I don't make this decision lightly. You have many skills the world will need in the long run, since you're an engineer. Me, I have some insight that might be needed in the short term."

"So what? Now you're a Zombie Fighter? Okay, badass professor, are you going to offer your services to the highest bidder?" He was starting to get pissed.

"Robert, if you had a time machine that would send you to only one place and time, pre-dawn, Tuesday June 6th 1944, you are a member of the 2nd Ranger battalion, in a landing craft heading for Pointe du Hoc and you have three days to choose, would you go? Even though you know your chances are dubious at best?"

"How old?"

"22?"

"Yes, I would. You do know zombies are not Nazis?"

"I don't see much of a difference. Robert, I have to see what's going on!" I knew what he was getting at, so I might as well break the ice.

"The pain won't go away. It will become something inside me, might plug the spot in my soul that I lost in that field." Okay done, on to another topic. "Besides, it's gonna be one hell of a show."

I didn't want to reminisce, but I really wanted to move on. "It would have been fun to have made it to the islands; the ladies in bikinis, boat drinks, and hunting whales with Hammer and machine guns."

"No, a rocket launcher."

"Yes! A fucking rocket launcher!" I started to laugh so hard that for a second time in less than a month, I pissed my pants, but fortunately just a little. I didn't see the guy standing at the door till my eyes started to clear up.

"Dinner time! You want to come?"

"No. Did you know we're some kind of celebrities?"

"Why are we celebrities?"

"We'll talk when you come back."

"Oh, that old video thing?"

"Fuck you, John."

I was freaked out about the prospect of losing Robert, but fortunately, dinner was more laid back than anticipated. Everyone was in their everyday uniforms and the atmosphere relaxed. There were half a dozen of us. I was the only non-navy, non-officer in an itchy jumpsuit. Dinner was real salad on real china, water with ice and a lemon wedge, some kind of mouth watering Asian pork dish with rice, an iced lemon thingy and real coffee. While we ate, the conversation centered on logistics, but in a casual broad sense. Several of the other guys at the table were obviously captains or something, and spent most of the time talking about the food supply. I enjoyed the meal and listened. The general gist was that the fleet goes through a whole crap load of food every day, well no shit, Sherlock! No one talked about fuel.

After dinner, someone asked me if my first kill was hard.

"I suppose it shouldn't be, but for me it was easy. It was an old woman in a nightgown. I had a shotgun and was protected, and there was no way she could get to me. It took me two shots." Has anyone in this room killed a zombie?

"Since then?" This question came from the guy I was sitting next to who looked an awful lot like Jack Nicolson from A Few Good Men. He had the whole stern-motif thing going. He didn't talk much during dinner, I never saw him smile, and had the distinct impression he didn't like me. Maybe there is this section of the military that is naturally disposed to dislike me.

"Well, since then, it has been a question of survival. I don't think, just act, and so far, it has worked."

Maybe it was the sound of my voice or the party really was breaking up, but within ten minutes, I was back at my room and in bed.

June 13 - 14th

I spent the next two days, with the help of a couple of IT guys, putting together a ninety-minute presentation on everything I knew about zombies. It took my mind off the here and now. I kind of got into it; peppered the talk with clips and stills from American, British, and Italian films, try to separate zombie fiction from the zombie reality. I thought of a couple amusing anecdotes, mostly made up, and tales from my past, also made up. By the end, I was excited. I had something to do and of course it doesn't hurt the ego to be back in professor mode! It took two days to get the damn thing ready because IT was adamant I use some of the Bangor video in the talk. I was just as stubborn and said no. They thought it was too obviously relevant not to use and I thought it was way too personal to use. It was funny because they thought I was interfering with their project. The resolution eventually came all the way from the top. Attendees would watch the video as part of preparation for the lecture. Fine by me.

I did get one of the most thorough physical exams I have ever had, and never want to do it again. I should be happy, I now weighed one-seventy one! It also gave me a chance to see the optometrist and score new glasses.

Robert was mostly off doing something, but I have no clue what, but I think bowling and beer was somehow tied in. I got to know the ship a whole lot better and continued to be astonished. It was so damn huge and complex, but really well thought out. You initially think, 'Okay, it's big' and then you start to wander around and begin to realize what BIG really means. It would suck to fight zombies in a place like this. Strange to think that after the ISS, this might very well be the high water mark in human technology for a long time to come, which stinks, because I really wanted a flying car.

Dinner with Robert the first night was nothing short of bizarre. As soon as we sat down, people started coming over to ask questions, take pictures from their phones and for the first time in my life, someone actually asked for my autograph! It was as if what they saw wasn't real and we were actors.

Dinner the second night was with the admiral. Robert went off with Marine friends to watch *Guadalcanal Diary* and *The Sands of Iwo Jim*a. I had nothing new to report but I brought my laptop along and got ready to premier my 'why zombies are not your friends' extravaganza. As hoped, it was an intimate affair; only the admiral, another admiral, and three women, who were not in uniform. Introductions went around. I have no clue what the second admiral did, but it seems all three ladies had some affiliation with the CDC or the NIH.

"Admiral Spencer, I don't mean to buck protocol but there are two admirals and four doctors, sorry, two real doctors and two PhD doctors." I looked at Robin, at least I think her first name was Robin, and she shook her head yes. "So, I'm going to go with first names and if I forget yours, I'll just nod in your general direction." Man was I glad my wardrobe had been upgraded into some rugged yet sophisticated khaki look.

"Thanks, John, you never do aim to disappoint."

With that, we drifted into various conversations, ate, and enjoyed a nice normal dinner like we had all met in a book club and Chris invited us over to his house for supper. It turns out that Robin was the other 'didn't go to medical school' doctor, a term we both despised. She was about my age with short brown hair, athletic, and had a huge platinum diamond ring on her left hand. She was a forensic entomologist, really into insects and things decomposing.

"So, Robin, how come the bugs aren't batting for our team?"

"Nice segue, John. I think you brought it up two days ago. They are alive. I thought with the hot weather the last few weeks, we would see some blow, and flesh fly activity, lots of maggots and fly larva on those with severe trauma nope. Field reports are steady around six percent."

"What about the really little bugs, biotic decomposition?" She was at the meeting? There is no way I could have missed her.

"Some wound samples show slight activity, but beyond that, they have a functioning immune system. We still don't know exactly what we mean by that. The only significant abiotic contribution would be with those who were physically or physiologically restrained, like some of the ones you shot. They do attract insect activity, but end up dehydrating out in a few days, depending on the situation."

"What are you seeing dehydration wise in the general population?"

"We have some isolated populations in good shape, without water, and limited food. It can take over four weeks but a lot in our study are still with us. You saw it yourself. They are not mindless and they have a strong drive to survive. Oh, and you need to modify your presentation a bit. You are right, there are unusual coagulation factors going on, but with a significant, read massive, fibrin reaction. These suckers clot like nobody's business. Don't worry, I do look forward to dessert and seeing it all live." She gave me a good-natured chuckle.

I wasn't really surprised. The presentation went well and lots of good questions meant I would be up late tonight.

June 15th

My fourth full day on the *Truman* and I was off on my tour. I was scheduled for three lectures a day for the next four days, then off to other ships. The first one is always the worst. You think of everything that can possibly go wrong, but last night had me confident this would be a walk in the park. The room sat around a hundred and fifty and was packed with what looked to be mostly officer types, men and women, but mostly men. Wait a minute, it's only men. So I was introduced and the show began. I rambled on, showed some videos, talked physiology, reviewed my tactics and presented my WAGS as to why they act the way they do. I answered a bunch of questions, nothing I hadn't been asked before, so this was going to be a breeze. For the rest of the day, it was, although something was definitely going on, no more women.

After dinner, I went back to my room, made some notes, played with the presentation, finished Solzhenitsyn and started on *Mason and Dixson*. Robert was off playing video games.

June 16th

The next day after my second lecture, Roland, the big Marine from the cafeteria, came down to say hi.

"Good job, Professor." We shook hands. "You kept it nice and simple."

"Thanks, Roland. So you and your guys ready to kick some zombie butt?" I liked Roland. He gave off this natural calm vibe and reminded me of Robert.

"I hope so. Your talk didn't exactly fill me with confidence." We both sat down in some chairs near the podium.

"Up until a month ago, I was a middle aged, rapidly thickening professor, thinking I finally had life by the balls. I am not a warrior, just a very, very lucky SOB."

"Luck? Warrior? One is just goddamn chance and the other…well there ain't no warriors on this boat. These kids don't know shit. I think what's holding most of us together is the chance for payback. To do something! At least blow up some shit."

I have been so wrapped up in myself that I thought these guys were living the life of Reilly sitting safe in the middle of the ocean while I had to deal with the shit. At least I had something to do; my mind was constantly occupied and by seeing everything first hand, I knew everyone I loved was gone. I needed to keep reminding myself that this went down differently for everyone, and in a sense, I was one of the lucky ones.

"What's the buzz? When are we going?" He didn't really know me, so I expected the usual 'when the orders come down' or something like that. Instead, what he said floored me.

"I expect within the week. Lots of meetings, I don't think I'm going to get much sleep. Don't worry, man. I'll keep you up to date."

"Within the week? That soon?"

"Yeah. They started a series of noisemakers a few days ago. They have cameras and sensors and are monitored, so when the bus is full, they shut it off and start the next one in the relay, wait a while and turn it back on. Keep everyone heading south."

"Will it work?"

"Oh, it will work, it's an island, but at what price? It's alright, because we need to get active. Lots of guys excited about going home. Home, I'll never go home."

"Where's home, Roland?"

"Seattle." You're goddamn right, you ain't ever going home, you and me both. I let a couple of seconds go by.

"I still want to go. I would like to see how they respond. Sciency stuff."

"Sciency? Fuck you, John. B.A. Psychology, third generation Fisk University."

"Why aren't you..."

"Long story. I will see what I can do." We drifted off to some small talk about possible zombie psychology and whoa, Roland got it. I was relieved to see he wasn't one of the Rambo types. He knew this was not going to be easy.

"So professor, what's with this herd mentality? Is it like some kind of migration like you see in Africa?"

"I don't think it's a herd instinct, more akin to flocking birds. Boy, they know when there's a party...might be something in the way they vocalize when excited. I heard a swarm back in Maine that had to be three-quarters of a mile away. Every zombie I have seen does this roar shit every time they get motivated. I need to see this, Roland." Motivated? What the hell did I mean by that?

"We'll talk. Have fun with your next dog and pony show."

My next lecture, number six, was not for three hours and by now, I had the presentation down, so to kill some time, I wandered around yet again. Since I wasn't in the military, I didn't salute. I had it down to this curt nod. The higher the rank I thought you were, the more pronounced the nod. Everyone seemed to have something to do, so nobody paid much attention to me. It helped that my badge got me through the few places on the ship where they bothered to check them. I got to some outside stairs and saw something I thought I would never see: an honest-to-god real nuclear submarine that was not docked and charged admission. She was surfaced and a little bit back of the *Truman*, so I started to move to get a better view. The submariners have been trained for long periods of crowded isolation. They may be the sanest people in our whole group.

I don't know what caused me to stop, maybe it was all the guys with automatic weapons, but I did and started watching several other sailors fussing over a long silvery grey cylinder.

"May I help you, sir?"

I spun around to face two marines. "Sorry, I was curious."

"You have to keep moving, sir, or should I say Machete Man!" The taller of the two broke into a huge smile. "We knew you were on board. You went through some badass shit, dude!"

"You said it, brother," said the smaller guy and they fist bumped. Where the hell have I heard that accent before?

"Guys, uh." And I tipped my head to the other group. "That's a nuke? Right?"

"Yes sir. Payback gonna be a real bitch." It was the shorter guy again. "That, sir, is a B61 thermonuclear weapon; variable yield, may be used for both tactical and strategic purposes, designed for air, ground, and laydown detonation. That is one bad day waiting to happen."

"So we are going to nuke ourselves?"

"Don't know about that, but everything topside is locked down. Seems like we are about to lay down some serious shit on New York. Bridges and tunnels go bye-bye tonight."

"Thanks, guys." We shook hands again and I took off to find either my room or the lecture hall, whichever came first. Holy crap! So the bridges and tunnels are getting hit tonight. Give them a couple of days for assessment, then in maybe four days, depending on weather, we nuke.

I ran into this little lounge-esque area with some padded chairs and sat down. And so it starts. Let's see; I have been across the Verrazano-Narrows, Throgs Neck and the Queensboro, but never the Brooklyn. How many bridges in all? Maybe half a dozen, no clue about how many tunnels. You know, if I was a pilot, this might be some big fun to blow some serious shit up, unless of course I grew up in this area, then the mission might suck. Then we nuke. Then we invade. Man, do I hope someone has really thought this through. Me? I get to stand on the sidelines and watch it all go down.

At my next talk, the room was full, all young males. My best guess is that virtually everyone was of the same rank, one bar, lieutenants. The talk had already been taped, so now it was going to be beamed live. I was never told exactly where this was being beamed to, but beamed it was. The Q&A time was also unusual.

Instead of the questions being all over the map, these guys were focused on the practical applications of my knowledge and experience to the battlefield. Do they always attack in a straight line? Do they stay focused once prey has been identified? What attracts them more, sound or movement? What about odor? Can they open doors? If so, what type? Tool use? How do they recognize each other? Do they sleep? Any signs of leadership or hierarchy? Can you make them form a horde? What is their roar like and is it always the same? Do you think they have any memory or skill sets from their former life? Well, so much for being an expert. My standard reply quickly became, "I don't know."

"Guys, and whoever else is watching, all I can really tell you can be summed up in four words; shit will go down. The archetype of these zombies is that there is no archetype. They are as unique as each of us. They also happen to be bat shit insane and just a bit dead-like. Oh, and one other piece of prudent advice: bring lots and lots of bullets."

After the talk, I was informed that with all the changes going on, my road show was a no go for tomorrow and I was on hold. Basically, I was told to hang out. So, that was my lecture/consultant/zombie expert career with the navy. I now had nothing to do. Everyone was so focused on the invasion of Long Island and I was expected just to stay available and out of the way. And there was Robert.

"I guess this is it. Time for me to go. Buckaroo, you have made some strides." He seemed in good spirits.

"I don't know, Robert. Things are starting to get surreal."

"Just wait, the real crazy is right around the bend. John, are you sure? Is it Elizabeth?" He stopped me in my tracks with that one. What the hell did he mean, Elizabeth?

"Yes, it is. Don't imagine it's me doing a Freudian Todestrieb thing, Robert. I want to see how they react to massive firepower. I don't know why, but I think something interesting will happen Anyway, I will be anything but near the front."

"Bullshit! You will come see me when this particular bout of insanity is in remission?"

"Only during visiting hours. Robert. I am coming back from this one, no problem. I mean holy cow, I have the whole Marine

Corps behind me. There ain't no way no zombie is getting close to me. I have to see this, because it could be important."

"Or you want it to be important. Bullshit, anything comes out of this! John, pull back. It's no longer your war, our war. John, No Rodeo." Now of all times Robert is getting almost emotional, shit.

Very slowly, I said, "It is an indulgence on my part. If I am lucky, I will get to choose the place and time." I gave him a hug. "Right now, I think I can find my way around a bunch of guys with big guns." Okay, so now I am ready to cry, you bastard.

"God speed, John Patrick. You go, watch and tell me the tales of what you saw." And with that, Robert and I embraced again and parted. Good bye, Robert.

Chapter 15 ~ A Bright Light

June 17-19th

For the next three days, I ate, read, watched movies, and slept. I did see Roland in the cafeteria just as he was leaving. He simply winked, gave me a smile and a thumbs up. The marines were getting active and they were always doing something (exercises, drills, football, soccer) on the now rarely used flight deck. I had to be alert because it was getting easier and easier to believe that Maine happened a long time ago. Since I finished one Pynchon, and discovered that you can actually be bored during an apocalypse, I would start another, and again venture into the world of *Gravities Rainbow*.

One breakfast, I sat with some guys who worked IT or something. They told me there had just been a disaster during a rescue attempt. They were working on another project in central ops and they overheard the whole thing. It seems the navy has stepped up recon on 'The City' and surrounding area since the decision to go ahead with the Long Island plan. So far, over thirty successful missions and three hundred plus rescued, but all from outlying areas. Nothing was coming out of the dense urban zones. I did have access to this information. The survivors all came from small fortified groups. They were ordinary people who were in the right place at the right time, did the right thing and were lucky. None was 'Doomsday Preppers' or any kind of survivalist. I also learned that the ISS was still manned by three Russians who decided to keep going as long as they could; didn't hurt that the last cargo mission was after the plague had started and carried a special shipment of Stolichnaya. Good for them.

Then the story got interesting. Against all odds, a group of twenty-one was alive in one of those high-rises right off of Central

Park. They had secured the top three floors by throwing anything they could find into the various fire escapes. It blocked them in. They were safe, but the clock was ticking. I don't know what happened to the first chopper, maybe wind. Well, it hit something and went down. The pilot and co-pilot were hurt but alive. The two paramedics in the back were dead. They said thousands of the undead surrounded the chopper. They couldn't break through the helicopter's windshield and by now there were too many of them to gain any leverage. We knew exactly where they were, west, 105th street between Central Park West and Manhattan Ave., but they might as well be on the moon. Second rescue chopper made it in and picked up seven, the third eight. A fourth, the last chopper went in and was overrun. The IT dude said everyone was on and they were just lifting off when the chopper was taken.

"The audio was insane, man. Seconds, it took only seconds and those guys were screwed. From the video feed, it looked like a sea of zombies rushing in. All the pilot could utter was something like, 'what the...'" He just looked down and shook his head.

"How did the zombies get in? What about the pilots on the ground?"

"No clue how they got in. A couple of AH-64 Apaches were sent. Those guys were not going to be left behind, not trapped like that. Besides, it won't be particularly good places to hang out come tomorrow."

"You'll get no beef from me on that one." I thought about the people that I had seen trapped in their cars, defenseless. How long would it take me before dehydration, exhaustion and fear had me opening the door? Not the way I wanted to go. "What about tomorrow?"

"Tomorrow? Don't you know? Tomorrow, everything changes."

The next day was going to be special, the kind of special that makes history, for good or bad. The United States military, under orders from whoever is in control of the government, was going to drop nuclear bombs on United States soil. Not just any soil; the boroughs of Brooklyn and Queens were to be hit with three bombs, airburst for maximum damage; I wasn't told what the yield was going to be. It was decided to do the detonations during the day. A night explosion would have been visually spectacular, but there was concern about the moral and psychological implications. I found out later that some people in powers wanted to do the operation without telling the general population. Just have some planes take off, big boom, it's over. In the small city that is the *Harry Truman*, the odds of pulling off such a maneuver in secret were exactly zero. An interesting thing happened, once it became general knowledge. The event turned into something to be treated with the utmost respect and reverence. This was not a joke. Chapel services were going twenty-four seven and even though invasion preparations set everyone at a frantic pace, the general demeanor was one of curious politeness. No one smiled or laughed but this unthinkable event was forcing everyone to live in the moment. From the cooks all the way to the pilots (as a 'consultant' I could eat almost anywhere I wanted) there was a palpable sense of focus. They continued to drop all sorts of noisemakers on a large swath of southern Long Island, to bring in as many for the kill as possible. We lost a Blackhawk and crew today while on a meteorological mission.

The navy was prepared to wait until the weather, particularly the winds, was perfect. They got everything they wanted on day one. For maybe the first time since The War of 1812, the US was making a major military decision based on things happening in Canada. A large weather front was predicted to head our way bringing lots of rain and a strong southern wind. After that, the best weather models indicated a long stretch of stable dry weather. Here we go.

June 20th

It was one of those mornings when you wake up, I mean you really wake up and are ready to go. It didn't feel like Easter or your birthday or that something special was going on. It just felt odd. I skipped breakfast and made my way to a small balcony on the port side of the ship. A dozen civilians and a couple of navy guys soon joined me. This is where I was told to go, so I went and would have a great view. They gave us dark tinted goggles and a general rundown about the size of the blast, which was big and the amount of energy the blast gave off, which was huge, the massive damage it would do and why. At this point in the game, I think most of us were aware of the zombie problem. Then we chitchatted and waited. They told us there was not much danger from the EMP due to low yield and low altitude of detonation. The ship's intercom kept a running update on distance to target for the first jet, first bomb.

    Suddenly, some stuff was said in rapid fire and a countdown started. When it reached zero, a new sun grew on the horizon. Even with the goggles and more than twenty-five miles away, it was impossibly bright and incredibly beautiful. Goodbye Queens, goodbye to the Coney Island I would never visit. It took about twenty minutes before you could clearly see this twisty ribbon of black extending way up in the troposphere. It looked like this sick finger pointing to heaven. An hour or so later, a great part of Brooklyn and Flushing Meadows were gone. I was more of a fan of Wimbledon and the French Open but it would have been fun to have gone to the US Open. Sorry, but I don't think most people in the US know they play tennis in Australia. Two hours after that, the last one was dropped and the show was over. During the whole time, I just hogged a section of railing and stared mutely at the horizon. To be honest, I really didn't give a damn about Queens and Brooklyn. I had never been there and I didn't know anyone from there. I just couldn't shake this sense that we had just crossed some messed-up Rubicon and I had no clue if it was a good or bad thing.

    In less than an hour after the first blast, there were already all kinds of data and computer generated damage projections and radiation issues. It would be the same for the second and third, and by the third blast, it was clear that southern Long Island had gotten the living shit kicked out of it. Sunset that night was just shades of grey and black with a slight stench of something like rubbish burning. Zombies aside, it will be a very long time before you can visit Manhattan as a normal human being. Once the sunset, the live videos were starting to give a glimpse of the true extent of the destruction. The two boroughs were gone. There were thousands upon thousands of fires, just like the WWII videos of fire bombings in Europe and Japan. Across the East River, more of The City was on fire as well as areas of New Jersey and Connecticut.

June 21st

I woke up, thinking that now the easy part was over and in a couple of days, the bloody part starts. I lay for hours assessing the various scenarios. By the end of tomorrow, we should know how much of the plan worked. For the past week, there have been dozens of near shore exercises. You go in close, make a lot of noise, and mow down any zombie that comes near. The tactic was sound and very successful, thousands and thousands of zombies were eliminated without the loss of a single human life. It had been used on the Vineyard and Nantucket essentially to clear the islands before you set foot on dry land. This also meant that thousands and thousands of zombies were washed into the ocean just to bloat and float somewhere else. Now there was a push to do the same with Long Island. The problem was one of size. Long Island is not small. It is over one hundred miles long and twenty some odd wide in many places. A shitload of zombies are also left on the island. Plan estimates were around two to three million. However, this was yet another WAG, since for reasons that have yet to be explained, we have a hard time seeing them when they are not moving, especially at night. There are a whole lot of people eating a whole lot of food everyday, 24/7, and the fleet was running out. They simply could not wait a month.

I had breakfast with several guys who were involved with the Nantucket clearing and the first words out of their mouths floored me. Part of the fleet was being sent to join another battle group that was to do something with Newport News. WTF? Later on, they explained to me the military's strict inventory control policy, a fancy way of saying organized looting. Everything, and they meant everything, went into an inventory system. For example, it wasn't just a car, it was a 2009 Lexus LS460 in excellent condition, and then it would go on, GPS coordinates, the type of engine, tires, mileage, even the VIN number. The two most important boxes; does it run? How much gas?

"You have to watch these guys running around with their iPads tapping in every little thing. If you ask me, it's more than inventory going into those computers. There's also non-military with them, so watch out." Hey, I'm non-military, and I have a beard!

The primary areas of interest were supermarkets, Sam's Club, and Wal-Mart. Clean water, found in (wells, fresh water ponds, and natural springs. Energy, such as gasoline, propane, firewood, solar and wind and so called contraband, such as alcohol and tobacco, and drugs, pharmaceuticals and otherwise. Personal looting was not tolerated and if caught, you got hard labor on chain gangs doing all the things public works used to do, but by hand. Your portfolio and paper money now meant nothing. Contraband was king and cigarettes were the new gold standard. One of the guys mentioned he saw a sailor trade a gold watch for a carton. Long Island was a huge treasure chest just waiting to be opened. There was a lot of jockeying going on to be among the first to land, the first to kick zombie ass one-on-one and the first to secure certain items. I couldn't blame them, because I was once a pirate.

June 22 - 25th

I spent the next few days doing my zombie song and dance to groups of soldiers, one after another. It made the days go by, keeping me busy, and in touch as to what was going on. The excitement got to the point where the enthusiasm had me, and not to go ashore in the first couple of waves was almost insulting. Hell, I'm a consultant. I had to see what was going to happen. It's my job. I did have dinner with the Admiral on several occasions and thought about bringing it up, but I guess that I already knew the answer.

It's not to say the Admiral and I didn't have nice, interesting, and bizarre dinners. Chris was a good guy in a tough spot. He was big into backcountry camping so we connected and it built from there. We joked about various movies and novels and the points of interest, now lost to us. How can there not be a Brooklyn Bridge? How can there not be a New York? There came a moment I had to ask, "Admiral, do you think we can do this? Not just Long Island but…"

"John, you might actually get this. My philosophy, like color television, is all there in black and white. He laughed, turned, and looked out at the sea. "Who the hell knows."

Chapter 16 ~ The Battle for Long Island

June 26th

It was on the sixth morning post-nuking that my time came. Five a.m., there was a knock on the door. When I answered, a very large marine stepped into my room.

"Pardon me, sir. Please put these on." He handed me a pile of clothes.

"I'll be back in ten." He placed some boots on the floor.

"Excuse me, but back in ten for what?"

"To make sure you find the chopper."

"And where am I going?"

"You're going to Long Island, buddy. You're going to war."

So I changed and went to war.

I had been in a helicopter before but nothing like this. It was a Sea Knight, the kind with two rotors! Way cool. The guy next to me showed me how to use the headphones.

"Where we going?"

"Someplace called Gardiners Island. It's out on the north end of Long Island. We took it two days ago and now it's our advanced base for the operation. We thought it was going to be a nice soft way of getting us close and safe. Five square miles, privately owned, and just a hop, skip and a jump to the Hamptons. It turned out about every third person in the area thought the same thing. Last body count was somewhere north of thirteen thousand."

"Thirteen thousand in five square miles?"

"That's what I heard."

"Two days? Who got that job?"

"The marines. The navy proper is still getting all the pussy stuff and by two days, I mean boots on the ground days. We spent a week getting them close to the shore and picking them off. We eventually got them to crowd some areas and we could use bigger stuff. Then the boys went in. If you ask me, they should have waited a day or two. What's the rush? The bonfires are still burning in some places. I hear it looks fucking medieval."

"Yeah, I read the initial reports. Didn't like the way some of them seemed to hide in the woods. We still go in twelve hours?"

"As far as I know."

The report was essentially a hastily assembled timeline of events from the shore operations, landing on Gardiners to the cessation of hostilities. Basically, it's what I expected. I just never expected to be going there. No one was really ready for the single minded ferocity of the few that were left. Casualties were from stupid mistakes and just a general underestimation of the enemy. We would learn, but we better be quick. What jumped out at me were a few references to some wooded areas that had been cleared, suddenly sprouting a couple of dozen zombies. One report questioned whether some of the attacks were coordinated. The couple of general reports I had access to from the Nantucket and Vineyard campaigns didn't mention anything unusual like this.

We landed, and holy shit, I was back in the USA. The place was total controlled chaos. Stuff and people were everywhere. The only thing I could think of was that all this was part of a vast movie set. I kept looking for some camera guy on this big boom filming the whole thing. I didn't have much time to gawk and was quickly hustled to the front of a really big tent filled with soldiers.

Roland was standing in front of a large wall map talking tactics and getting everyone oriented on the mission; my mission. I'm going back. I felt like a five year old who has been whining about a real bike for the past year and finally gets one on his birthday only to realize he now has to learn to ride it. With my khakis and beard, it was impossible to blend in, so I concentrated on the map and was trying to make sense of arrows, triangles, dots, and all kinds of stuff; essentially what we are supposed to do, when I heard my name called.

"Dr. Patrick, do you have anything to add?" I really didn't but I knew he wanted me to say something. I guess I needed to validate my presence. So I stood and looked out at a sea of heavily armed green and started rambling.

Okay, let's see. "I guess the only point I want to keep reminding everyone of is that we are facing an enemy that has no ideology, no country, no family, no cowardice, and definitely no fear. I have no idea why they do what they do, but they are very good at it. We need to be better." Some slight murmurs of approval. "Never assume you are dealing with some dumb fucks out looking for brains." Good, more approval.

"Remember, a head shot will end it for them, but, and this is really important, if you sever the spinal cord they will go down, be a much reduced threat and the center of mass a hell of a lot easier a target." I stopped. Even though the majority of these guys were officers, all I saw was mostly kids all ramped up and ready to kick some zombie ass. Yes, all of them were far better fighters than I would ever be, but none was really aware of what was waiting for them on shore. I just hoped to hell I was.

"Firepower is the answer. Stick together and if you have a side arm, remember to use it. Always remember there are a shitload of zombies out there - count your shots." I guessed a little levity wouldn't hurt, so I continued. "Having faced the undead and actually pissed my pants in the process, I guess the only important thing to remember is, don't panic." I didn't expect many to get the Doug Adams reference, but when no one did, I started to feel out of touch and old. I was turning to sit down when a hand in the back went up.

"Sir, are the bites really one hundred percent fatal?" Why do people always keep asking me this question? What part of yes is so complicated?

"All the recent data suggests, yes, but there are a few very credible reports of rapid amputation for certain types of bites in stopping transmission. I've read over a dozen cases and they all involved fingers or hands, one case of a toe, don't ask me. And when I say rapid amputation, I mean heart beats."

Once again from the back, "Do they have to break the skin to get you infected?"

Okay, now that is a good question. "Hu...that's a good point. Actually, I don't know. I assume the infectious agent is transmitted directly from the saliva into the victim via the breaking of the skin from the bite, but um…I did have a chance to see if it could be passed other ways, that uh, that didn't work out."

Now, from someone near the front, "Sir, what happened?"

"Allison died before the virus could take effect and I didn't have time to wait and…" I realized that I was talking to myself. "Well, I guess what I am trying to say is, stay as far away from them as possible." With that, I made a beeline for my chair.

Someone else spoke but I didn't listen and eventually they were dismissed. I hung around for about an hour talking with various people, and by the time I did leave, the tent things had started to happen at an incredibly fast rate. It was like this weird dream where all of a sudden everyone knows where they are going and what they need to do, but you. I stood around and felt left out, but very impressed by the show. A couple of jets flew and I had this American Patriotic moment; filled with pride, I knew we could do this, let's kick some ass!

Eventually, someone directed me to an area where a few medics were organizing a field hospital. I tried to find out what I could do, but as it turns out, absolutely nothing. So I just hung out and tried to blend in.

"Dr. Patrick?" I turned and looked into the chest of a very vast Marine.

"Yes." He must have been fifteen. How can you grow that big and be so young?

"Sergeant Roland sent me to get you, sir. You doing okay? Any Questions? Fitting in?"

That would be, yes, lots, and what? "What's up?"

"Well, I'm here to take you to the Big Dance, sir, the name's Calvin."

"Well, Calvin, name's John. You know, when they said twelve hours, I thought that meant I would get my marching orders in twelve hours." He laughed, we shook, but I was serious.

"So, Calvin, have you seen one in the flesh?"

"No. Just some poorly made documentaries, TV news, internet, and of course, your video. But I am looking forward to making my acquaintance."

WTF? My video? Has everyone seen me kill someone I love?

"Follow me. Oh, the Sergeant sent you a gift." He handed me my shotgun. Once again, I was snapped back, "Well, alright." I had my Mossberg back. At least I think it's mine. Hell's bells, I AM back in the game.

"He said you would know what to do with it."

"Yes, I do, Calvin."

"Just follow me."

The two of us walked down a clean, straight row of large olive colored tents full of guys packing/unpacking, talking on cell phones and radios, or looking at computers. Everyone seemed to be in motion. We got to yet another large tent and entered. Calvin looked around and walked over to a guy sitting in a corner, talked to him a bit and motioned me over.

"Dr. Patrick, this is Corporal Calati. He's a medic and your sidekick on this safari. If you listen to him and do what he says when he says, you probably won't get eaten and you might not get shot."

"Thanks! I'll remember that. Be careful man!" We shook hands and the big guy walked away.

"So you're the dude from the video." The guy in the corner was yet another kid; had to be early twenties at best, about my height and one huge nose. No really, it has to be mentioned that his nose was indeed significant. He was also a medic.

"Yeah, I'm John."

"Bartholomew. Call me BC." He stood up and held out his hand.

"Good to meet you, BC. What are we going to do?"

"To be honest, I don't really know. I was ordered to provide you suitable orientation, protection, direction and explanation, the kind of shit a PR guy would normally do. Like, we need a PR guy right now." BC turned to put his pack on. Wait, I've heard that accent before.

"I'll give you some technical details on what's happening and get you around so you can observe."

"Observe, well that's a job I might be qualified for. BC, aren't you supposed to be doing some medic stuff?"

"Well, as far as I know, the enemy is not bombing us, setting off IEDs or in general, firing back, and if you do get injured by a close encounter, well, not much I can do. There are plenty of us around for the twisted ankles and skinned knees. You and I get to watch the show." He motioned to a green and black backpack on the floor.

"That's yours; sleeping bag, sleeping pad, water bottle, small stove, food, socks, that kind of stuff. I'm told you are familiar with roughing it."

"Yup."

"Oh, the bag next to it is a change of clothes. Time to lose the Banana Republic look. I hope you like black."

"Sounds like a plan. Any chance I can score a little more ammo, just in case we have a close encounter." Yes, I am fully aware I am in the middle of a massive military camp, but nine shots do not cut it for me, at least it feels like nine. If I stay anal, I will stay alive.

"Follow me and all will be revealed." We exited the tent and headed for the shore.

"Where are you from?" I asked.

"Rhode Island, East Providence." Yes, I did know that accent.

"No shit! I grew up in Warwick."

"Holy Crap! Mobsters and lobsters."

"Where the debris meets the sea!" We turned to each other and did the whole upper forearm embrace, very gladiator-like.

"You know The Hill?" He asked. Holy crap, how could I have not known the accent?

"Know The Hill? Are you busting my balls? Come on, The Blue Grotto, Cassarino's. I love Angelo's, chicken parm, stewed calamari, shopping for that crazy ravioli; lobster ravioli! Damn, going to be a while before that comes back, if ever."

"Yeah, I could go for a nice sausage manicotti right now. What school?"

"Hendricken, you?"

"Are you fucking kidding me? I went to LaSalle! Hendricken, no shit. I went to RIC, B.S. in Biology."

"URI, B.A. in Anthropology. Nice to see we are putting those degrees to good use."

"How many have you killed? Or whatever you call putting them down. I'm just asking, you know."

"That's okay, putting them down, actually a good way of looking at it. I don't know how many, maybe thirty to forty, somewhere around there. So BC, how is all this going to go down?"

"All the activity you've been hearing about the last few days have been probes and feints, trying to gauge what kind of shit we're getting into. Get the natives nice and restless."

"And?"

"And the shit is deep. Those fuckers are everywhere. Intel indicates that where you see one, expect a thousand in ten to fifteen minutes. We're just blasting everything that moves." He pulled out a couple of 1:100 K topo maps. A thousand in ten minutes? One hundred a minute? Not a bad plan if you give it enough time.

"The press starts to grind and we push them into a radioactive hell. We start with Montauk, Napeague and Amagansett. If all goes well, this group will move on to the Hamptons by the end of day one. Another force is assigned Greenport. Another to Sag Harbor. You, my Rhode Island brother, are going to the islands."

I looked at the map. What we were going to do was invade the north end of the island, take out the major population centers and move south. Shelter Island was on the tip of Long Island and no bridges, just ferry service. It looked to be about a dozen square miles in size. The location and amount of roads indicated a fairly large population and from what we saw on Gardiners, the numbers will easily be in the thousands, if not tens of thousands. I know there had been lots of planning and surveillance, but my guess is that we were really going to stir up a hornet's nest. The only real question is how many bugs. I guess the idea was to get some defendable areas and learn large-scale zombie land warfare, with air and sea support, on the fly. The guys that drew the short straw were going to Sag Harbor. Everyone else had limited fronts since most sides were protected by water. Sag Harbor was going to be wide open, a real Wild West Show with only the bay covering your ass. And, as BC explained in detail, it must have been ordained by God that the mission went to the 1st Marine Division, 5th and 7th regiments. Add it to their history; Vera Cruz, Guadalcanal, the fucking Chosin Reservoir, Tet Offensive, and now The Battle For Long Island.

"BC, how many are on Shelter?"

"Last I heard, it was ten thousand and we are not getting time to draw most of them to the beach."

"Ten thousand? How many are we attacking with?"

"We will be in company C, going to start here, Ram Island." He stuck a big stubby finger onto a scary small spot. I had to multiply what I was seeing since I was used to the standard USGS 1:24 K and far superior to what was guiding us. I was about to make an inane comment, when he pulled out a large flat computer tablet, turned it on, and opened something akin to Google Earth, but way better.

"Holy shit, BC."

"Cool, ain't it? We land about here and go between these houses. The gates and walls will not be an issue, turn right, and cruise the road to here. We're gonna set up a defensive position here and defend this spot. Oh, and right here, is where we will watch the action and it's also a bar, what are the odds? You know what I mean?"

"How many soldiers are in a company?" The computer tour gave some relief since the island was small and protected by a nice narrow and highly defendable road that connected to the main island.

"Ours should have around a hundred and fifty. Captain Wallace is in charge, but you and I will hang with Sergeant Roland. I hear you guys know each other."

"Yes, I do, great guy. I look forward to working with him."

BC continued to play with the computer. "Invade Long Island? Who was the genius that thought that one up?"

"Fuck, if I know."

It only took thirty minutes for things to inch downhill. The current rumor was that Intel gave us shit and some satellite data was saying close to twenty-five thousand. I heard the pre-plague population of the island was under three thousand, and we were going here, why? Just isolate and bypass the place. Only twenty-five thousand on the nearest island of any size, which is right next door to the third, maybe fourth, largest population center in the world, right. Even if the estimates are close, that's a shitload of bad guys on a very small piece of land! There was no way this was going to end nicely.

I learned from another medic that the reason the estimates are so messed up is that zombie body temperature goes almost to ambient when they don't move or are resting, thirty minutes to three hours depending on the environment and the condition of the zombie.

"Inactive, we're talking BPM tenish, respiration fiveish, and hypotension that will blow your mind."

"Devon, where did you get this information?"

"We got away teams, research vessels, some bases doing stuff. We were prepped on this a week ago."

"News to me." Why didn't anyone tell me? "What away teams?"

"A retired special forces guy, you know the ones doing the private contract work? Well, his wife was an MD and worked for the CDC. She died studying zombies so he decided to die studying zombies. He got backing from the military, gathered a bunch of team members and went to the wasteland to study monsters. Dr. Bill didn't do that bad first time out. Got choppered into some kind of research facility in the middle of Connecticut, they were on their own and forty miles to the coast, only lost six. The powers that be, liked what they saw and they sent Dr. Bill and his Morrigan Explorers to check out Cape Cod, lost no one. Most of the stuff I told you today is from his work."

"Sounds like my kind of guy. What's he doing now?"

"We don't know. He and his men went to do a transverse of the island, from LI Sound to the Atlantic. We haven't heard from them in four days."

June 27th

I awoke totally psyched! This was going to be a very interesting day. We were taken to the island on a LCAC, essentially a hovercraft on a colossal amount of steroids, and came ashore in the second wave at a place named Rams Head, which was just a collection of nice expensive beach houses. The first wave had met with expected resistance, maybe a thousand, and quickly started moving inland and to our objective, a sandbar with a road across called Lower Beach, which separated Ram Island from Little Ram Island and the rest of Shelter Island.

The marines were everywhere. Some of these guys had been sitting on their asses for over two months and were ready to move. The distant pop, pop, pop, was getting further away by the minute. A nice Colonial style house was commandeered as the temp HQ. Dead zombies were already being piled up for incineration. Unloading next to us were special units, whose job according to BC was quarantine every secured house and business. These must be the guys I was told about.

"Yo! This is old news. Let's catch up with the first wave." He slapped me on the back and like that, BC was off at a quick trot down the road, west I think. I was under the obviously false impression that we would be moving around in groups larger than two! I knew my shotgun was fully loaded and I had plenty of ammo, but no side arm. The road curved to our left with woods on the left and beachfront houses on the right. It was July and the foliage was in bloom, which meant that the woods were green and dense and we would have zero notice if attacked from the trees.

"Hey, BC!" I bent over and grabbed my knees as I struggled to catch my breath. "We have too much camouflage on our flank, so let's slow down and stick close to the cleared houses!"

Two Humvees screamed by, both mounted with large automatic weapons. Third Wave?

"No problemo." He slightly bowed. "Age before beauty, you know what I mean?"

Yes, BC, I fucking know what you mean. We kept up a very light jog and soon started to come across encounters that had happened maybe fifteen minutes ago with no clean-up crew disturbances. The bodies laid in various contorted positions; lots of bodies, like hundreds. After looking around, I noticed they weren't as randomly sprinkled about as I had initially anticipated. The amount of bodies, sometimes three dozen or more, in relatively small compact groups was not all that unexpected. The same flocking behavior I saw in Maine. When we reached Lower Beach, the fighting was over. The military had set up a defensive position across a sandbar leading to the next objective. This means that everything behind me was, in theory, zombie-free.

The sandbar really looked like a sandbar; a narrow strip of, well, sand. I didn't think I would be near one so soon. Down its center is a two-lane road, connecting point A to point B. Including the beach, the line was roughly fifty yards across and chock full of motivated Marines. It wouldn't take long before they were tested.

BC and I made our way to the Rams Head Inn where we ran into some medic friends we had crashed with last night. We learned that, so far, the bite count is zero and the only KIA was some private from Alaska who had been hit by friendly fire. The front line was perhaps one hundred yards away and for the first ten minutes, we could occasionally hear a shot or two. Then all at once, it started to increase. BC noticed it at the same time I did. He decided we should hang around for the time being. Within minutes, the area started getting crowded and it sounded like things were really picking up. The pop, pop, pop, was now replaced by full-on automatic fire. Within five minutes, the fire was so constant that it almost made this wall of sound, punctuated by a couple of low booms every now and then. Like a moth to a flame, I left the aid station and climbed up on the roof of a truck to get a better look.

The view was not great, but I did have a funky angle on our northern flank, just at the very end where the Marines met the sea, their natural environment. A moderate wind was blowing from the east, which kept my view clear of smoke. There had to be at least a couple thousand zombies already down. They were everywhere, like a moving carpet, and big explosions rocked further inland. The wind shifted again and I got a view of the zombie-controlled shoreline. More and more of the undead were going straight into and under the water. They went in tight groups like ice calving from a glacier. It didn't appear to be an intentional effort to flank the marines, there were just way too many zombies, and not nearly enough places at the dinner table.

"Let's get closer." It was BC. I jumped down and we made our way about twenty-five yards nearer to the front. I got lucky again and found an abandoned Ford F150 pushed off to the side of the road, which I climbed to get a better view of the slaughter. Being the gentleman he is, BC pointed out that I had some binoculars in my vest. There was now a visible death zone with areas literally knee deep in gore. Somewhere in the distance, Warren Zevon nods with approval. However, the zombies kept on coming. They would just run right into this no-zombie-land-of-lead-and-fire and have their bodies dismembered by a few rounds of fifty cal, at least in the movies it's a fifty cal. The undead eventually had to jump over and wade through an ever-increasing field of offal. I could also look down the road to where it meets Little Rams Head and more open space. As I watched, an impossible horde converged at what was now becoming a bottleneck, as every zombie on the island wanted to get to us, and I had a nice view of the show, and what a show.

After five more minutes of rapid-fire carnage, the amount of bodies and body parts did indeed start forming a formidable obstacle that the undead were finding more and more difficult to climb over. They eventually had to enter the water and actually try to outflank us. This slowed them down and the depth of the water limited where they could attack. So far, things were going about as well as anyone could expect. We had secured an easily defendable position, had enough ammo, and enough men. No problem, but they kept coming, more and more. No problem, Rams Island Drive would be more than adequate. The view over to Little Rams Head was a disquieting site. Oh, thank God. I have used the term disquieting in a real thinking process at least once in my life. I had no real clue on the crowd numbers, but based on my extensive knowledge of college football stadium capacities, i.e.: Alfond Stadium at UMaine holds ten thousand, my guess was that about ten thousand now lay in the bottleneck. Thousands more were coming. The horde was compressed together into a solid writhing mass that constantly bled fresh zombies onto the defenders. However, the wall was getting higher and it started taking on the characteristics of a forming wave. With enough numbers, it would overwhelm our defenses. I heard a couple of booms coming from somewhere out in the bay and a second later, Little Rams Head disappeared in fire. The concussions from the blast knocked me off the roof and I was viscerally reminded how hollow most of our organs are. It took me ten minutes to realize I wasn't concussed and another ten to get back onto the roof, this time on my ass. When the smoke cleared, there were no more zombies, none. None wandering in to join the party, I couldn't even see injured party goers. That's it? Did we kill them all?

And that was all. Over the course of the next two and a half hours, I saw only eighteen incidents where the zombie came out of the mountains of bodies to attack. About half appeared successful. None seemed to be coming from deeper in the island.

BC found us a place to crash in the Inn. Every part ached from the fall, so I ate an early dinner, made notes in my tablet, and crashed. Sometime later, the rain started. I just assumed it's another summer shower, but the heavens opened and poured, and poured, and then rained some more. This was the tail end of the Canadian front that was hoped would help reduce radiation levels. I assumed the sporadic booms were not thunder.

June 28th

It was around five a.m. and I had been dozing, thinking about the Vineyard and a house on the beach and a real life, when my brain registered that either the raining had stopped, or I had gone deaf. So I sat up, waking BC.

"I guess it's over," I said to no one in particular, got up, and went to the bathroom. There was enough light to see myself in the mirror. God, have I aged. The little sprinkling of grey was now in full riot. There were wrinkles around my eyes. Oh well, the weight loss more than made up for the aging. Thinking about the Vineyard started the squirrels running. Thinking about the past, thinking about Liz.

BC and I got breakfast with the other medics. Just as the last doughnut morsel entered my mouth, I saw Roland. He stopped by to tell us we were moving out. This was just the distraction I needed.

"Good morning, John."

"Good morning, Roland. I am now a firm believer in the power of whining. Thank you for getting me here."

"No problem, my friend, so now it's mop up time. Intel indicates that all the carnival activity brought most of the zombies on the mainland to us." Little Rams Head was taken in the night and we were moving into Shelter Island proper. The bad news was that the marines at Sag Harbor had been hit hard by unending waves of the undead. Casualties were high, as one medic told me, not in the hundreds.

The journey in was in the back of the same F-150 I had stood on yesterday. Little Rams Head was a vision directly from the mind of Hieronymus Bosch. The landscape was blackened and torn apart. The dead were everywhere. The bodies stacked easily six feet deep. BC told me they used the island's only snowplow to carve the road. High up in the skeletons of trees, dozens of corpses were impaled. All of the two dozen or so houses were just shells. There was no color other than black, brown, grey, and red. I could not see a single spot of green.

Things got better as we moved onto the main island. By better, I mean it went from absolute carnage to just utter destruction. We were going to the southeast part of the island, the part with the Mashomack nature preserve. At our speed, this was going to take a while. Then it started to rain, again, which was fine with me, since I could see jack from my position.

The rain stopped and the sun popped out right when we got to our destination; better, but now, damp and humid. The trip had been a breeze. We stopped a few times, some shots, but none from my truck. Everyone started to smoke from the wet khaki rapidly evaporating. We assembled near a barn on some estate that was once worth a gazillion dollars. We crossed an old stonewall into the next large field. This one was neat, as in not used for agriculture, probably horses. The grass, covered with thick dew, seemed to be razor-sharp trimmed and an amazing shade of deep forest green, a definite kick-ass place for a game of ultimate. You could hear gunfire all around us and see smoke in every direction. It was really hard to tell if we were in front or somewhere near the middle. Once everyone was over the wall, we were given ten minutes to piss, get some water, and reorganize. I was pleased to see that the order to keep all structures as intact as possible was being respected, since what we had just crossed could easily be two hundred years old. Then again, why the fuck should I care. I used the time to sit down, get my butt wet, prop my back up against the cool stones, and relax a bit. It felt good to be armed again and part of a team. I closed my eyes...

"What the fuck?" Someone yelled. Pop, pop, pop, pop, "SHHIT!"

I leapt up and clicked the safety off. In the field to the south, was supposed to be another well armed group; one of similar size, firepower and intent, but something had gone wrong and from our south, a massive block of undead emerged from the trees and slammed into our right flank. With all the chaos, I decided to stand my ground. There were far too many living in the way to use a shotgun effectively. Most of the other soldiers had fanned out into the field and were immediately heavily engaged. After an intense few minutes, the fighting started to die down as we regained control of our field. During the skirmish, I stayed out of the way and realized how stupid it was to bring a shotgun to a machine gun fight. Then I glanced over the wall into the field next to us, east. East was supposed to be free of zombies and our safe zone.

The dead aren't particularly smart, but they are annoyingly persistent, and yet again, here they come. I had no choice but to hope the wall would be adequate protection.

"One. Two. Three. Shit, four!" I was yelling to myself at the top of my lungs, "Five, fuck, six. Seven. Eight. Reload!" I fired my last round and quickly moved to the rear, reloaded, and right back at the wall. I was now in front of maybe twenty zombies and I just unloaded on them; ten seconds of the real 'Hand of God' type carnage, clearing a small section directly in front of me and my partner, an apple tree. On my third reload, things were gradually slowing down and it took me going Bruce Campbell for maybe twenty seconds to run dry. I was now also getting some significant support from others who had noticed our less than favorable predicament.

Our little group was now engaged on two fronts. Stonewalls, which we thought were protection, were actually pinning us in. Back at the wall, I took my time and tried to drop them as far away from me as possible, something to help prevent a full on speed run at me. Boy, did I ever need my Ruger. Fifth reload and I am officially running out of ammo, and nobody else is using a shotgun. Back at the wall, this time I am between two soldiers. I now wait and only take down the ones right on top of us. Why the hell aren't we doing something? We can't stay here forever.

Right then, someone tapped me on the shoulder and yelled something in my ear. I think it was something like, we were moving west and I was to stay by the wall and defend our flank as we moved. Not a bad idea, and one I was more than willing to support, but I was almost out of ammo! Everyone moved quickly and with some semblance of order. I only went for those going over the wall. By the time we came to the inevitable next wall crossing, I was out and the only thing I had to fight with was now a club. We made it over and someone else took my place. With all haste, I made for whatever passed as the rear, which as it turns out was the other side of yet another field next to yet another relatively well preserved, Colonial Period, probably Native American made, field stonewall. There was much more firepower about, but it still looked like we were fighting on two fronts, south and east. More explosions off to the south, big ones, ground shakers. No one around me looks bitten or hurt, just out of breath and scared. I know I am, and all I have to defend myself with is a club. This sucks.

As I caught my breath, BC came by. "That was fucking crazy, man! Oh, my God, did you see that shit? Did you see it, man! That was incredible! You know what I mean?" He dropped a bag onto my lap. "You might need these."

"Thanks, they have been known help. BC, I'm not bitten or anything, so don't worry." Nine rounds never went in so fast.

"Why don't you look military?" The guy next to me asked.

"I'm not." The world to the south of us erupted. "Shit. Here we go again."

I turned south. Don't they ever stop? I guess not, what else were they going to do? They started to break through the forward lines. First, just a few, then bigger gaps, then the gaps turned outward on each other. Nobody in front of me was going to make it, and then all of a sudden, I was the front.

"Get over the wall!" I screamed.

Like the mid-forty year old guy that I am, I pulled a classic flounder move and partially destroyed the wall getting over. Here they come.

"Hold the line. Get organized!" Someone yelled, Yeah, no shit.

The mass was not nearly as thick as the last time, but I still had to wait till they got close, defend the wall.

"Fire!" A very high-pitched voice yelled. At least three dozen zombies in almost ballet-like unison fell in front of me. Wow, that was effective.

"Conserve ammo! Watch your target!" The line was coming together. I got a little girl as she flew over the wall. I never actually saw her. She just popped up in front of my barrel. The next was some guy in a plaid jacket who looked totally confused, as if he had just showed up and was wondering what the hell was going on. They kept coming. Reload number two, déjà vu, yet again! By now, I was in the zone and just focused on those who were an immediate threat to me. I made every shot count. They kept attacking, but never made it over. Half-way through my rounds, I was able to reload calmly. Just about then, the front started to wane and a couple more humongous explosions to the south. After five minutes, it was over.

I got through another one, another attack, holy crap. We are on a fucking island! Where did they all come from? Man, I was tired. I just sat, looking at the ground, or should I say mud, and I concentrated on the droplets of sweat that rained from my forehead. I knew I was in a daze and probably in some form of shock. What the hell just happened? They weren't really organized but… I could hear a thunderous roar off somewhere to my left. It was a combination of weapons fire and zombies. It went on for what seemed like five or more minutes, and then slowly faded to the occasional automatic fire. I started to calm down and realized that someone was yelling at me. It was Roland.

"Hi, Roland."

"John, are you okay? Where have you been? Have you been bit?"

Oh, shit. It had never crossed my mind! I was quickly standing, ripping off clothing and examining every inch of my body. Oh, thank God, no bites or scratches, just sweat and mud. "I'm okay, I'm okay," I said to no one in particular.

Roland moved on and I started to re-dress. I looked down our ragged line. Now we are all Prime Time zombie fighters. Maybe a dozen guys down from me on my right was a medic talking to some dude. As I watch, I noticed that the guy he was talking to, more like yelling, just stared up into the sky. Other soldiers were looking his way, and nobody was saying a word. The guy stood up in front of the medic and said something, I could tell he was a marine and I thought I could see one bar on his collar, so I guess he was a lieutenant. He then walked out in front of the line, stood rock solid straight, turned to us and saluted. There was a large amount of blood on his shirt. After he saluted, he calmly walked through the line to about fifty yards behind us and looked to the sky. He then pulled his side arm, placed it under his chin, and fired. No hesitation. Holy crap. My God, could I do that? Could I be that strong? Another soldier stood, much further down the line, stepped forward, and saluted, walked to the body of the lieutenant, crossed himself and took his own life. There was then some commotion on my left, and this guy stood. I think he was a sailor. He had his helmet off and I thought there was no way he was of legal military age. Tears streamed down his face, a face that was pure determination. The medic and someone else was trying to talk to him. He just stepped forward and saluted. He came close to me as he walked to the two bodies lying in the grass. His breathing was fast and hard and his hands were shaking, and he did his duty. I knew that, the next time I encountered Captain Walker, I had to revise the estimate I gave him way back on the Kauffman. It just went way up.

Everyone was quiet. We were all thinking the same thing. Roland, the medic, and another guy, started down the line in my direction again, telling each soldier to get their weapon ready. When they came to me, I realized the third guy was a Chaplin.

"How are you doing, John?"

"I'm okay, Roland, going to need more ammo. Where is BC?" Just then, two jets streaked low overhead and a second later, the ground shook with an absolutely massive explosion somewhere south of us.

"Doing his job, I imagine. I'm sure he is here somewhere. Hang in there. You will get your ammo."

"Roland, when you get a second, we have to talk, it might be important." He looked me right in the eyes and I shook my head. He then turned to the two others.

"You guys continue on. I'll catch up in a second." We then walked over to the tree line to get out of voice range.

"You're not going to want to hear this right now, but the initial contact was what we all expected. Ah, you know, coming at us singly or in small groups. But these waves that hit us later, don't make any sense unless they waited to attack en masse. You saw what happened at the sandbar. Maybe it's just chance, but I don't like it! This changes everything." I was definitely not calm and I was well on the way to getting pretty darn scared. Things had started out well and kicking undead ass was the order of business, but something was not right. It seemed too easy. I was fully aware I knew shit about the military and how they operate. I was dazzled by the fact that we had more armament than God did, but deep down inside, some part of me realized that this was not going to work. Maybe I should just stop all the thinking and enjoy all the shooting and blowing shit up.

"I was under the impression they did not think, or plan, or fucking talk to each other!"

"As far as I know, they don't, but remember that guy I told you about at the lighthouse? Roland, zombies do some crazy shit from time to time. I still think it's some kind of flock mentality. They are grouping on purpose, but why?" I stood and stretched my back.

"Roland, cut me some slack. This is an island, where are they coming from?"

He took a long look at me and with a blank face, and said, "Long Island, we've been breached. All the bombing cut loose a lot of flotsam and jetsam, add all those bodies, and I am not really surprised no one thought of this."

"Roland, we need to pull back now!'

"Why?"

"We're being probed."

A fresh company passed through us, advanced across the field, and through the next tree line of ancient maples.

We both went back and sat down. Roland didn't say a word. From the sound of it, our comrades in front of us were catching some serious shit. Everyone with a weapon was going full bore, and I am not talking just bullets. There were all sorts of thuds, bangs, and booms. Just then, a couple of helicopters screamed low overhead.

"Okay, John, explain…"

Suddenly, the tree line seemed to come alive with scattered groups of olive green figures emerging from the dust and smoke. Something was terribly wrong. There was another huge explosion beyond the trees. All around me, the men sprang into action as orders were yelled up and down the line. Here we go again! Just then, a hand grabbed me from behind and yelled something into my ear about moving back. When I turned around, it was another medic, who looked surprised, confused, and about sixteen. I seem to be attracting medics.

"What's going on?"

"I don't know. We have orders to fall back!" His pupils were massive and darting between the field and me. I think I actually acquired the ability to read lips, because I could hear absolutely nothing over all the shooting, but understood everything he said.

"All of us?"

"No, it's just us, you and me. Let's go." I turned around and looked up my right flank. Coming at us in a perfect angular formation was a low grey curtain of doom. It was like some giant wedge methodically absorbing everyone in its path. Everyone; the guy who gave me ammo, the Chaplin, Roland, and BC.

"FUCK ME! That's a left echelon." Screamed the now frozen-in-place medic. I turned to run and slammed right into him. Thank God, we didn't fall, but we sure as shit ran. We passed more troops traveling in the opposite direction, but we still ran. We passed another defensive position and the medic made it clear that I was his charge, so we just kept moving to the rear, now more at a trot than a dead out run. I needed to catch my breath. That was way too damn close.

We entered into the next field, as two Blackhawk helicopters were getting ready to take off. At first, I thought, great, my ride's here, then stopped, and watched as several stretchers were loaded. Everything about the scene made sense, the evacuation of the wounded, except for the inordinate amount of security and how heavily strapped down the wounded were.

The medic ushered me over to a tent where a dozen computer screens were presenting the action up front and live! One in particular got my attention. It was coming from what I guessed was a helicopter, and in some kind of thermal black and white, showed a two story house besieged by this vast swarm of zombies. The point of view kept rotating and zooming in and out. What I assumed was piles of dead, surrounded the house forming a crude blockade. Every few seconds, some kind of automatic weapon would open up and cut a huge cone shaped swath through them. It looked like a slo-mo version of someone trying to stop the incoming tide using a shovel. They just filled the gap. A series of flashes, and large, almost uniform holes developed in the mass, with hundreds of bodies lying about.

"You Dr. Patrick?" The medic was gone and in his place was an officer about my age, my height, except his hair had never been longer than maybe a quarter of an inch off his scalp since birth, and he had been going to the gym every single goddamn day of his life.

"Yes." Oops, I should have said sir. Oh well, too late.

"What the hell are you doing here?"

"I'm observing." I really should have said sir.

"Yeah? Under whose orders?" I wasn't thinking military and he caught me off guard on that one.

"Orders?"

"That's what I thought. Your ass is out of here. Now."

And that was it. I was fired from the marines and my battle for Long Island was over. It took me three days to get back to the *Truman*, and two hours to be called to see the Admiral.

July 1st

I was led to the Admiral's office by two large MPs. I wonder, are there any small MPs? They didn't say a word and gave off this air that I was in deep trouble. They knocked and we entered.

"What the hell were you thinking? Who gave you permission to go to the mainland?" I have never seen the Admiral this pissed. I knew from the start that I was asking for trouble, and payback was going to be a bitch.

"No one did, sir. I thought I could give some help, some additional insight into the actions of the undead. I did not say I had permission. I just went along. There is no one to blame but me."

"No one bothered to ask? No one looked for orders? You just went along?"

"Yes sir. I wanted to see how the zombies would respond to large scale coordinated opposition, if there would there be any unusual reaction, or some kind of group response."

"Was there?"

"Yes sir! Some of the attacks seemed coordinated, but this could be just a fluke of the environment or random chance. You know a bunch of them showing up at the same place at the same time going in the same direction. Sir, the last attack I saw was in formation. There was no way that was random! We also need to look at their vocalization. It's almost like a crude but efficient alert system. I will put together a report on my observations. I have notes and the field reports will be a big help, if I can get access to them."

He looked at me long and hard. He wanted to yell, but I had just thrown him a nice bone. "You will get access and I want that report ASAP. Okay, I want you to sign this." He slid a piece of paper across his desk.

"May I ask what I am signing?"

"No." and he meant it.

"Okay, Chris." So I signed away. Of course, I knew what I was getting into.

"Dr. John Ross Patrick, welcome to the US Navy." His voice had a certain ring of victory and that kind of pissed me off.

"Great, do I have to wear bellbottoms?"

That surprised him and his face started to turn red. I knew I was pushing all the wrong buttons, and odds are, that I would never fight zombies again, so I had to press on.

"I'm just asking because I don't look good in bellbottoms, but I do like the small white caps."

"Get the hell out of my office." I didn't need to clarify his order, and quickly left, without saluting.

Once outside and the doors were closed, I was again escorted through the maze. After a couple of minutes, the two MPs stopped, looked at me, and burst out laughing.

"You probably don't want to do that again," the bigger of the two said.

"I don't think he will give me the opportunity. So what's next?"

"You are off to the *Cassandra*, a frigate that has been turned into some kind of research vessel. All of your gear has already been sent over. A chopper should be ready within the hour, sir." This wasn't a casual, "Hi civilian, I am being polite" sir; this was a formal, "You outrank me" sir.

"What?"

"You gear has been …"

"No, what's with the sir thing?"

"Our commanding officer informed us that once you signed on, you became an officer."

"I'm a officer? Can he do that? What's my rank?"

"Yes, and I don't know. Let's get moving. You have a chopper to catch, Sir."

Chapter 17 ~ Cassandra

July 1st (continued)

I thought I would be jaded because nothing could beat my last ride, but you know a four hundred foot plus, long ship is a big boat. Wow, I thought of it in feet rather than meters. It's like one hundred and twenty something meters. Anyway, it's really big. You first see it as a tiny blob, then a small grayish blackish blob, and then a real ship. Then it becomes, we're landing on that? Eventually, the scene evolves into, oh, it's a really big ship.

So, this was to be my new home. A crew of about one-fifty, with me still wondering what the hell was I supposed to do here. But hey, there are no more zombies. Let some other son of a bitch deal with that crap.

I stepped off the chopper and waited to be instructed where to go. I was the sole passenger. The rest of the craft was crammed full of supplies. There was also only one pilot, and I am damn sure with all the skirting of land we had to do, the regulations required a co-pilot. So I wandered, stayed out of the way, and looked around. My hair was now in a short ponytail, I had a decently trimmed beard, in blue jeans and khaki, and should have stuck out, but nobody seemed to notice me. Not of a lot of activity on deck, but it was obvious that far more stuff was now stored here than under normal conditions. I was still hanging around when the chopper left, taking four guys in suits with it. Okay, I already exist in a bad horror movie, but what's with the guys in the suits?

"Dr. Patrick?"

"Hi, I'm Dr. Fitzgerald. Welcome aboard the *Cassandra*." We shook hands. Dr. Fitzgerald was about five-five and a petite one-twenty something. We looked to be about the same age.

"Thanks. It's John by the way. Good to be here, I think?" She gave me a sideways look.

"Kathy. This way." She led me inside. She was wearing a white lab coat over pink scrubs.

"So, what do we, me, do here?"

"Me do here? Great. You're on my team. Gross examination, tissue sample procurement, anatomy, and physiology observations. Some up front and intimate quality time with some real live zombies! Ever been near one?"

"It depends on how you define near."

"Fantastic." After a couple of corridors, we came to a door.

"Your name will be up soon. The ship's not all that big and you should have no real trouble orienting yourself. If you get lost, just ask somebody. You will know the restricted areas."

"Big signs?"

"No, armed guards. Don't ask me." She opened the door. "Welcome to your new home. You have a few of hours till we get to work. I'll come get you in two. Enjoy your adventure exploring the magical *Cassandra*."

That's just what I needed, more adventure. She was right about finding my way around quickly. It seemed like half the ship was off limits, I just glanced at the guards. After some hellos' and poking about, I went back to my cabin. It was small, but would have been tiny if there were two, as the bunk beds indicated was standard. The bunk was made, so I crashed out and tried to doze. What the hell did she mean get to work?

I was just about to doze off when there was a knock on the door. "It's open!"

In walks Kathy and she looks pissed. "Thanks, asshole! You could have filled me in on who you are. You know, I had no idea why they were dumping somebody like you on me, I can use the help but…"

"Sorry. Really, Kathy, I had no idea the whole video thing would give me this weird rep."

"Okay, let's go. Enjoy you civvies, because the rest of your life will be in scrubs."

"Pink?" Rest of my life?

"Asshole."

My new best friend started to calm down and gave me the ten-cent tour, and helped fill in some blanks, important things like, where we eat. We eventually got to a section of makeshift labs that needed card key access. By makeshift, I mean everything didn't quite fit, a lot of new welding, the ship was obviously not made to do certified laboratory stuff.

"You'll get yours when you get your ID badge. You will always travel in groups of two in these areas. Let's go over some of the basics for a Biological Safety Level Four lab."

"What? This is a BSL- 4 lab?"

"Yes, and a couple of BSL-4 glove boxes."

"Kathy, are they certified? I mean Real BSL- 4?"

"Quit being such a jerk, John. Have you even been in one?"

"Yes. Fort Detrick, USAMRIID, not big fun, but it does get the heart going. Isn't this a bit of overkill? I have spent plenty of time around them, and so far, have not been infected. Heck, guys are doing kung fu fighting with them even as we speak, and they are not in bio-suits."

"If I were you, I would be very happy we have what we have and what we have is our orders. Okay? And while we are on the subject, you need to remember that while your smug ass has been out adventuring and becoming some kind of master zombie killer, we have been sitting here rotting on these ships! All of us have people out there! Our lives! I have a fiancé. I had a fiancé." She was pissed and upset, but way too tough to shed a tear or break down. "So stop being such a self centered asshole."

What the hell am I doing here? A fucking BSL- 4 lab and me? Not one iota of this can come to good. Is the universe trying to truly screw me over? Think back to all the mess-ups in your life. Is God trying to screw with me? I am not a marine, I am not a virologist, and I am definitely not someone to play with this virus. Why does everyone think I am an asshole?

What took me a month of SOP study, gowning practice, emergency response rehearsal, and trial runs in a dry lab almost twenty-five years ago, we reviewed in two hours, brave new world. The main lab consisted of what was essentially a very clean and shinny autopsy room; various scales, instruments, a large metal multi draw box like those huge toolsets you see in garages, a chair and small metal desk with a handgun in a holster on top. On the far wall was a large red button, on which someone had written Panic Button in red marker.

"Kathy, is that the panic button?"

She ignored me and we watched a team gown and go through their work. My job was indeed tissue recovery. They basically dissected the zombie and recovered samples from a printed out plastic list. The samples went to another lab, a restricted one. The team was two guys, Gus and Peter, both sailors. I got to talk with them when they came out to de-gown.

"So, you're machete, dude."

"I'm machete dude." The guys were in their early twenties at best and had been surgery techs before being transferred. One was from Arizona and the other Delaware. I'm not sure who was from where.

"You guys went through some sick shit."

"You're telling me. How many do you have to do on an average day?"

"Well, that depends," said Peter or Gus. "We keep a limited amount on board. I'm told no more than four. We get our morning marching orders at the O-seven hundred briefing, usually about two a day. With you here, there are now two teams and Dr. Kathy will have to get to work. Beyond the couple of hours suited up and some paper work, it's a breeze."

For me, the breeze started with a meeting. Since I had just arrived and nobody wanted to know how to play with the free-range undead, I had absolutely nothing to contribute. Everyone was in lab coats and different color scrubs. Essentially, it was just a review of the samples retrieved that day with special attention to their accurate location, no data presentation, nothing to analyze. We were organ harvesters, great. I was introduced and of course, the video was mentioned as well as my short stint with troops on Long Island. The group was impressed enough that it was fairly easy to surmise that none of them had spent any time around a free-range zombie. That's fine with me I believe El Macho Machete has officially retired. After dinner, I went with a new group, another list of names I didn't remember, to watch a movie; *Apocalypse Now*.

July 2rd

I was in the cafeteria by five-thirty in my light blue scrubs, and my way too white lab coat, no name. I wanted to go over some of the information Kathy had sent to my cabin. The place was big and could probably sit a hundred. It was a quarter full. People were scattered in small groups, talking. Everyone was in either scrubs of different colors or military uniform. Breakfast wasn't bad; powdered OJ, instant coffee, instant creamer. I have no idea, but I thinks it's scrambled eggs and no, that is not bacon, yes, bacon! One of the scientifically proven essential food groups. I loaded my plate. There was one other highlight; fresh baked bread and butter. I half expected some kind of rationing, but it was serve yourself. So I loaded my plate and found a nice quiet spot to eat and read. After fifteen minutes, I saw Kathy coming across the room with her tray.

"They've canceled the morning meeting and we have a sample list to turn in by ten." She sat down quickly and dropped her tray and iPad hard on the table. "Time to earn your keep."

"Just be gentle with me, it's my first time you know." It wasn't worth looking up. I now had a clue what I was expected to do. Some of it could be very interesting. I thought back to the lighthouse and Robert, and the dead boy. I guess sometimes, you do get what you ask for.

"Asshole." So with that classic interlude, our professional relationship started.

"I see you like bacon."

"Well, Kathy, you know what they say; bacon is red, violets are blue, poetry is hard, Bacon!"

Number one, actually number BH4-7P1417, for the day was a thin young woman, maybe mid twenties, her head and complete body had been recently shaved and washed as part of the quarantine procedure. All in all, it was impossible to tell what in the real world she had once looked like. Sagging small breasts and female genitalia was our only way to determine sex accurately, as for race, it was anyone's guess. A good portion of the left side of her face was gone, as well as all the fingers on the right hand. She had that grey greasy skin that all the zombies exhibit, some kind of oily sweat that made the skin shiny. Her musculature seemed particularly well toned. Maybe that's what happens when you have spent the last few weeks running down your prey, one after another. She was supine and naked. Her ankles, calves, thighs, abdomen, chest, arms, jaw, and forehead, were secured to the stainless steel autopsy table by thick leather straps. I would have to remove some of the straps as part of the procedure. Kathy would walk me through it and be the back up. The zombie's eyes darted back and forth, alternating her gaze from Kathy to me, full of infinite fury and not even an inkling of fear. Her blinking stayed at a constant one per every three seconds, and it never seemed to change. Kathy took some photos and I noted on the chart that she was sixty five inches tall, and weighed one-hundred and twenty-two pounds.

"What's up with this?" I pointed out an approximate three inch by three inch square section of skin that had been incised from the zombie's upper right arm, just over the deltoid.

"That's odd." Kathy moved over to a large green plastic binder. There were no computers in the room. "Let's see, records indicate she came from the Oyster Bay area, uh, we have had her for two days. Nothing out of the ordinary listed. Okay, let's get rolling. You can do this, right?"

"I don't think there is a right anymore. Kathy, why are we really doing this? What's the point?" She just looked at me and shrugged.

The guys who processed the zombies just cleaned them up, shaved them, strapped em down, and moved them into place. The problem for me was that I had to have access to the chest and abdomen, which meant removing two of the straps. This would result in a dangerous, bucking zombie. Kathy showed me the way. To solve this problem, we used meat hooks, yes, real meat hooks, and yes, the kind right out of *Texas Chainsaw*. I had to insert them into the back and make sure I had successfully hooked several ribs and lumbar vertebrae. Once tension was applied, the creature would literally be pinned to the table. Even so, she moved quite a bit and I wore a steel mesh glove on my left hand to avoid cutting myself. Kathy's job was just to watch, take notes, supervise me, and shoot the zombie if things started to go south. Once done with the immobilization, I proceeded to make the standard Y chest incision and carefully pulled back the skin. The zombie never even flinched or showed any signs of pain. The skin pulled back far more effortlessly than on a standard human cadaver, and the tissue layers separated from the muscle with remarkable ease. It was like peeling a banana. As expected, the muscles were well developed. She was flexing even as I cut. The surprising thing was that there was very little bleeding. There would be some initial, sometimes intense, blood flow with each cut, but this quickly turned into slight seepage and rapidly stopped. That medic was not kidding. They really do clot like nobody's business. I used retractors to hold some of the tissue back.

"Kathy, the pupils didn't even dilate?"

"That's normal."

Now I had to be more careful than ever as I proceeded to cut the ribs. The bones were softer than I expected, but a bad snip combined with the tension they were under and... I stopped half way. Sweat and heavy breathing had fogged my mask. I quickly felt claustrophobic and trapped in my biohazard suit. This sucks. All you do is sweat, get slimy and you're stuck in this fucking piece of...

"Sorry, I just need to calm down. I don't like this any more than you do. What is her pulse like?"

"Steady at thirty-five BPM. John, just take your time and watch your breathing."

Once my mask had cleared, I continued to snip each rib until all twenty-two were cut and the skeletal breast removed. I could see the lungs, a pinkish grey, slowly fill with air and exhale. The heart was beating. How could this thing be alive?

"How does the EKG look?"

"Steady so far."

"You know, Kathy, this had to have been done a thousand times before, with people much better qualified than me or you. All we are doing is reinventing the wheel. Why does it feel like we are being set up?"

She looked at me. "Desperation."

"Then you know this is bullshit. We only do tissue samples. This gross anatomy crap is just not going to get us anywhere."

When I looked back at the zombie, she had stopped shifting around. I think she realized she was stuck and just waited for the opportunity. Her eyes never left me. But we continued. I took tissue samples from the lung, liver, and various other organs. Why did we do nothing with the cardiovascular system? Why vivisect and not dissect? In general, everything looked okay, all things considered. The brain was next. I had to move the headband over her eyes so I could cut away the scalp and pull the skin and hair over her face, exposing the glistening white skullcap. This tissue is highly vascularized and she should be bleeding like a stuffed pig, but wasn't. I cut away the calvaria and the meninges to expose the brain. There it was again, while the rest of the zombie's soft tissue exhibited some degree of decomposition, the brain seemed fairly fresh. What about the rest of the central nervous system. The zombie was still with us, struggling to blow her scalp off her mouth and get more air into her one functioning lung. Without thinking, I grabbed a surgical spatula, slid it behind her cerebrum, cerebellum, and severed her medulla, and she just switched off and died, again.

"John, I suppose you had a good reason for that." There was more than a hint of anger in her voice.

"Not really." I collected the neural sample, reviewed the sample bags and made sure everything was in order. "We've got what we needed. Let's get out of here."

By the book, it should take us twenty minutes to do a post shower de-gown. Kathy showed me short cuts to bring it down to around five.

"Are you hungry?" I felt my stomach growl.

"Not really; it's fish and beans tonight."

"Fish and beans? Oh well, I cannot pass up this culinary experience. I never really liked fish, but I think now is the point in time to force an acquired taste. I think fish is going to be on the menu for quite some time to come. What time do we meet?"

"Eighteen-thirty. Enjoy!" At least she was not mad at me. Kathy got half way down the hall when she spun. "Hey, you're from New England, right? I heard the Bourne and Sagamore bridges were blown and Cape Cod is isolated."

"Thanks. Well, we will have some great beach parties next summer." I continued in search of food. Holy cow. The Sagamore and the Bourne are gone. Just thinking about them brought back the memory of all those childhood trips to the Cape, crossing the bridge sitting in the back seat, my father driving and all was well. It didn't matter what direction or what bridge. What was important, was the good window seats. I have, had, two brothers and a sister so it was good behavior and a roll of the dice as to who got it. You see, the good seat is the one with the view of the canal through the girders of the bridge. Time goes to a funny place when you are crossing the bridge, sitting in the good window seats. Oh well, I still have the beaches.

I took off for the cafeteria. I still didn't really know anybody but Kathy, and generally kept to myself, hanging out on deck whenever time and weather made it possible. Lots of great hiding places among the crates on deck, plenty of spots to read or zone. You know, it is kind of strange that no one has asked me to shave.

The place was maybe a quarter full and it was five o'clock, or seventeen hundred if you cared. Holy crap, did it stink! Someone clearly had a culinary brain fart. What normally would have been a decent meal of fresh fish, red beans, canned onions and tomatoes, and various spices, had been miraculously turned into a pile of inedible steaming shit, with fish bones. On the plus side, someone had made bread! Gradually, I began to notice how each day a tiny chunk of the old world was removed. Today, it was butter. If there is anyone left in twenty years, the concept of toilet paper is gonna blow their minds.

I had an hour to kill before the meeting, the third in two days. About half a dozen of us 'scientists' will sit around a big table and pretend we are doing something of value. I went back to my bunk and lay down, tried to rest. All in all, things were not bad. I was still surviving the apocalypse and eating on a regular basis, well sometimes. Stuff was moving along on the Island, or on the L&I, as it has become known. The military quickly adapted to a million fucking zombies all attacking at once. The key was patience, using their flocking mentality to set them up in areas of your choosing, and taking them out en masse. This meant less destruction to the infrastructure. The barrier route has been worked out and some test construction underway. Block Island has been liberated and soon the Cape. I don't know why I keep thinking of it as a totally military thing. It's actually all of us, a human thing. I'm just glad humanity lucked out and ended with a bunch of well disciplined, armed young people to do what needed to be done.

July 3rd-5th

Day three, four, and five, was more of the same. Each day, we would get a report at the morning meeting with stats about the subject, tissue checklist, special requests, and any important info the other teams wanted to pass along. Size of sample was specified and whole organs were sometimes requested. We are currently spending a lot of time with lungs. The group found it amusing that one of the people making the requests sent them in German. We would be asked for something like, 'Zahlen Sie Aufmerksamkeit, um einen großen Teil des rechten vorhergehenden Kostgängers zurückzugewinnen vorhergehend vorsprung' or something like 'Pay attention to recover a large portion of the right anterior lobe boarder' and nobody passing along the orders seemed to notice. Luckily, the computer could translate. Each team got one zombie a day. Kathy and I got the morning shift, and if we started at seven, we would be finished by lunch. A couple of techs would clean up after us and take care of the corpse. In a couple of hours, the lab was ready and the second team went in, and then the third. After two weeks, we would rotate one shift forward. I thought it strange, considering what the future holds, that we were told this project had a two month life span and we should expect no real breaks till then.

Kathy and I usually had dinner together and talked about life before everything went south. I haven't heard of an official name for the end of the world. Talking about the past was one huge minefield and often prefaced with before all this happened or simply, in the past. I learned the she was not a huge fan of the military, but they allowed her to do research into areas she loved. Like me, she liked the outdoors. She also had a son who just graduated from the University of Colorado in Boulder with a degree in mechanical engineering. I told her about teaching and my anthropology research. We spent a lot of time telling stories of the places we had traveled and the strange things we had seen. I never talked about the sad twists and turns that had brought me to *Cassandra*, and she never mentioned the video or asked me any stupid zombie questions.

Kathy did drop a couple of hints that she was aware of some of the details of my immediate past, but it was understood that for now, this area was off limits. Another item that had an unspoken taboo was the future. Nobody, and I mean nobody, talked of things to come. We didn't even ask what tomorrow's dinner would be. You stay in the day, in the moment, and let the future take care of itself. With just a couple simple rules, you could remain in the safe zone, and maybe, hold on to a minute piece of sanity.

After a day or two, I actually began to like Kathy. She really wasn't that much of a bitch and I guess she was starting to find out that I wasn't that big of an asshole. We both knew what we were doing didn't make much sense, and I suspected, she knew some stuff she was not letting me in on, but that was okay. At least, I had a friend.

When I was done for the day, I would find a hiding place on deck and watch the sea and the sunset over Connecticut. There were still a number of fires burning, which paradoxically made the sunsets all the more beautiful. I wondered how Robert was doing on the Vineyard, always promising myself I would give him a call tomorrow. I miss you, Elizabeth. I keep waiting for the dam to burst, but I don't think I am consciously repressing it. It's just these storm clouds on the horizon that never get any closer. God, do I need a good therapist.

We never celebrated the 4th of July.

One day, dinner was pizza, and Maureen, the very Irish, very redhead lab manager, informed me that most of my free time would be devoted to being trained as an EMT. Everybody not up to date and qualified would be taking the course. Some specialists from the army were going to chopper in for the task. Sounded like one of the first really good, e.g. head out of ass, ideas I have heard of in a while. Things might be looking up.

Chapter 18 ~ The Tone of the Thunder

July 6th

The next day, someone pounding at my door waked me. My clock read four twenty-six a.m., it was one of the techs.

"There has been an incident in the lab. You are to get down there now!"

"Huh? Okay." And do what? There was no need to dress, since I was sleeping in some scrubs.

There was no claxon or alarm sounding, but people were rushing about. I was still half-asleep thinking about my dream, the roller coaster at Rocky Point Park and the remote possibility of bacon with breakfast, when I literally ran into Kathy.

"Good, it's you. We have to get down there and gowned up now. Something went wrong in the second lab."

What second lab? "Okay, but we both know gowning is BS. What second lab?"

"John, listen to me. They gave you a commission because you're some kind of hero to some people, but you don't know how this thing works. If you don't follow orders, you won't be let in and you may not get let out. Get it? Now, let's just see what the hell is going on." And with that, she headed down the hallway.

I followed her. "What second lab, Kathy? I'm not joking. What the hell is going on here?"

She spoke as we went. "I found out earlier this week. There is some kind of other lab facility on this ship, somewhere in the restricted area."

"Hey, hey, wait a second." She stopped.

"What the hell is going on here? I was under the impression that the restricted area was basically for the zombies and maybe some medical shit. Now you're telling me it's a real research facility?"

"If you took a second to think about it, a shit load of this vessel is off limits. Yes, they keep the zombies there, but there is this whole other world we are not supposed to interact with. Who do you think we send the tissue samples to? Who do you think gives us our orders in the first place? Get your goddamn head out of your ass and stay close to me." And off she went again.

Crap, I had not considered the restricted area all that much. I just made assumption after assumption. That's where they keep the zombies, the samples go to another ship, and I didn't care where the orders came from.

We started to make our way deeper into the belly of the ship when we ran into a couple of armed marines. They seemed to be expecting us.

"Fitzgerald, Patrick, right? Okay, this way." Without waiting for a response, they turned and headed for a closed door.

Using a key card, one of the marines opened the restricted door. Nothing really changed; no change in air pressure, same color scheme, just deeper in the ship where I did not wish to be. Everyone was armed and seemed agitated. We passed one room where the door was cracked open. Inside, someone was crying hysterically and some kind of violent commotion was going on. We stopped at another door and just as the guards swiped his key card, I heard muffled sounds that had to be gunfire. Kathy and I looked at each other. The marines opened the door with weapons at the ready. Several people in scrubs and lab coats came streaming out, and all had side arms.

Someone screamed as they rushed by our escorts. "Con Three! Con Three!" Okay…Con Three…I have no clue what this means. I could look past the open door and see a long well lit passageway, which could easily run the rest of the ship. All the doors were open, giving it this weird tunnel effect. At the far end, were some figures going back and forth across the hallway. Just glimpses. Most of them appeared white. Lab coats? A few were dull green. Then much closer to us another figure stepped into the corridor. This one was naked, tall, skinny, bald and grey: a fucking zombie!

"Oh shit," one of the marines yelled, which caused the creature to turn in our direction. His eyes were impossibly wide and he leaned towards us as he let out an annoying, yet terrifying sort of roar, and immediately sprinted in our direction. The marines struggled to close the door, but as it got to maybe twenty-five feet from us, it skidded to a stop, looked to its right, and ran in that direction. More sounds of gunfire. Just as the door was secured, the klaxons sounded. Kathy was trying to say something to me, but we were too close to a horn. She pulled me over to a corner and yelled in my ear.

"We have to get out of here and find some weapons."

Now, why didn't I think of that? Leave the area of the ship infested with the undead and arm ourselves, brilliant. All of our taxpayer sponsored fine tuned training was really paying off. You go, girl. I had almost thought of a decent riposte when it dawned on me that we were all alone, and still unarmed. How come I am armed to the teeth when I am not around the military, and have jack to defend myself with when I am? So off we went, running. I wanted to go topside, but I followed Kathy. She kept running back and to what seemed to me, deeper into the ship. We passed people going in all different directions. She eventually stopped at a door. It was her room.

"Hey, Kathy, I am starting to warm to you too, but we got other things to do." I thought she wouldn't hear me over the klaxons.

"Asshole, you just don't stop, do you?"

"What? Oh, I was just trying to add some levity to this fucked up situation! What is going on?"

She entered and grabbed a holstered pistol and belt which was hanging on the wall and started to put it on.

"Excuse me. I don't really want to play swinging dicks right now, but exactly how many zombies have you killed? I mean in the wild so to speak," and extended my hand.

She took a second, muttered something to herself and handed me the belt.

"Nice! A nine millimeter M9 Beretta." Two extra clips. This was like one of Hammer's sidearms and he had shown me how to use it. Well, I should say he reviewed the basics in Hammer time, which was about forty-five seconds. I struggled to extend the belt and put it on. "This should not be a big deal. We keep, what, four or five on ship at one time? No problem, the marines should have this cleaned up by now." I pulled the pistol out and started to look it over, loaded, check, safety off, check…

"There's more than that." The voice didn't sound at all like confident Kathy.

I stopped and looked over at her. She was now sitting on her bed with her head down.

"What did you say?"

"Listen, I really didn't know what they were doing. It was all very secret. You ever noticed that we did not even eat with them, watch a movie with them? The researchers from the restricted area? I have only been in a couple of meetings and nothing specific was discussed. It wasn't until maybe a week ago that I started putting some of it together." She wasn't looking at me, just intently staring at the floor. "They weren't necessarily looking for a cure. It was some kind of reverse engineering project, trying to figure out how this all started."

"Oh no. No, no, no! Do not tell me we were going down that road." Now I sat down.

"There's at least one other ship involved, the *Appomattox*. The more technical work was being done there. I only know this because someone died there last week, a friend of mine I went to grad school with, her, she…"

"Kathy back up. Just how many are on *Cassandra*? How many zombies do we have?" I tried to sound calm, almost brotherly. Just then, the klaxons stopped and I could hear more gunfire. Somewhere below us, I heard a high-pitched scream.

"I don't know the exact number, maybe thirty."

"Thirty!" Screw the brotherly approach. "Jesus H Christ On-A-Pogo-Stick. What the hell are we doing with thirty of those fuckers on board?" I jumped up and shut the door to her room. More gunfire.

"The project was entering a new phase. Our work was to be terminated at the end of next week. We were done. The entire ship was going to be turned over to them. We were going to a new facility at Barnstable on the Cape."

"Them? There it is again. It's the goddamn suits, right? I see one of Them, and I am shooting, just assuming it's a zombie." I was now pacing back and forth. "Okay, we have to get topside. I do not want to be playing Cowboys and Indians in these tight metal corridors." The klaxons started again but the closed door muted the sound.

"What's the fastest way to the deck?"

Kathy finally looked up. "To the left is a set of stairs, they will bring us up near the cafeteria. We have lots of choices from there." Her voice sounded weak and confused.

"How many floors up?" I had the pistol out, holding it in two hands in the down position the way Robert would. Oh, Robert, man, do I wish you were covering my ass right now.

"Two."

"Okay." Now I was back to the calm brotherly voice, albeit an absolutely terrified, calm brotherly voice. "You are going to open the door when I tell you. Stay behind the door. If we got one right outside, I want them coming for me. When we leave, you keep behind me and close. You're my eyes in the back of my head. If you see one, let me know, and get out of my way, I really don't want to shoot you. It's going to be okay, Kathy. Get ready with the door."

Kathy got up and moved into position. She looked terrified and she was starting to lose color. Just don't go into shock, please God, don't go into shock. I, on the other hand, felt great. Maybe it was the combination of adrenaline and being really pissed off, but I finally had something to do, at least something I knew how to do. I took a second to compose myself, slightly bouncing on the balls of my feet. Once again, it was time to fight zombies. Once again, it was Rodeo Time.

"Kathy, on three." She nodded.

In a surprisingly calm voice, I said, "One... two... three." She opened the door.

"Stay where you are," I whispered. Actually, I doubt she heard me over the annoying alarm, but she stayed behind the door. I now had the gun up, still in two hands, made my way over, and glanced into the hall. I looked to the right quickly, the way we had come originally and the direction the zombies should be in, I hoped. The corridors aren't brightly lit and I saw a bright flash. Because of the klaxons, I couldn't tell if it was someone firing a gun or taking a picture, so I erred on the side of caution and assumed it was the former. The left was also clear. I stepped back in, looked at Kathy, and nodded.

"Stay real close," I yelled in her ear.

Once back into the corridor, we went left and after about twenty feet, we found the stairs. They were the grated kind and you could see above and below you. A good thing too, since right below us stood a zombie. He was naked and bald and looked in great shape. He wasn't looking at us, but down the corridor that ran parallel to ours, one floor below. He just stood there kind of shaking and shuffling back and forth, as if he was waiting for someone who was late. Due to the obnoxious alarms, he didn't hear us or look up. Oh, great. The grating was too small to shoot him and I really didn't want to try to sneak away and leave someone else to deal with him. We backed up. Someone was running down the passageway toward us. It was a young sailor with blood streaming down the side of his head. I tried to stop him, but he pushed me aside and ran into the stairway heading up. He got to the landing in between alarm bursts and was making enough noise that I knew my moral dilemma was now solved. So up went the kid, up went the zombie, up went John. The zombie flashed past us and met the kid a second before I met both of them. In the ensuing struggle, I noticed that the kid's right ear was completely gone, like someone took a razor and just sliced it off, leaving a bloody hole. The zombie caught him from behind, jumping on his back, wrapping his arms and legs around the sailor, and sank his teeth into the back of the neck. With an almost super human jerk, the zombie ripped a huge chunk of the kid's trapezius muscle. How the fuck, do they do that? Do they sharpen their teeth or something? I just walked up, placed the gun against the zombie's temple, determined the shot would not hit the kid, and pulled the trigger. Blood sprayed over the side of the stairway and the creature rolled down the stairs.

The kid didn't look back, and on all fours continued going up. Upon making the next landing, he sat in a corner and curled himself up into a ball. When I got to him, he was breathing heavily, rocking back and forth and whispering to himself, absolutely drenched in blood.

"What are we going to do?" It was Kathy.

"We have to get topside. Let's go." I started up again.

"We're going to leave him?"

"Yes, let's go, now!" In the frantic attempt to process all the shit that was going down, my brain finally registered that the alarms had stopped, again.

"Kathy, now." I moved up to the next landing, which I assumed was the one we wanted and opened the door. You know when you don't hear the shot and a bullet flies by you, it makes a funny sound, kind of a soft whoosh, and all I could think of was, 'God, that's moving really fast.' Nobody was shooting at me, yet, but directing the fire down the passageway the door opened up onto. In an ordinary situation like this, I would more than likely close the door, but I really wanted to see what someone was shooting at, as if I couldn't guess.

"Don't shoot! Don't shoot!" I yelled and cautiously looked through the doorway.

People don't randomly fire weapons in small tight metal tubes unless there is a really good reason to. The guy with the handgun just to my right had an excellent reason, zombies. I meant to get to one knee to give me a stable platform in which to shoot, but slipped and ended up on my butt. All I could tell was: A, it was more than one zombie, B. there was three in total, C. all young fit bald males and D. the second in line was carrying/dragging somebody small in a white lab coat. Oh, and they were naked, the zombies that is. My first shot hit the lead creature at the same time as the marines. Our bullets made two small holes, cheek and forehead. As he fell, he turned around and the whole back of his head was gone, like someone with a grotesque giant ice cream scoop had carved everything out like a Jack-O-Lantern. The second one was sprayed in the face by the gore, but this didn't slow him down. Eyes focused on the marine, he quickly stepped over his fallen brethren and abruptly stopped. Whoever, he was dragging had grabbed on to the dead zombie with its legs and free arm. He/she was covered in blood and had such a high-pitched scream that I couldn't initially tell the sex. It was a she. The creature temporarily forgot about us and just kept violently tugging at his captive. The marine only needed that second. There was a third, but he was further down the corridor and moving slowly. His left leg had been shattered above the knee and he hopped along using the wall for support.

"I got him!" I yelled. My first shot missed and just like in the movies, I could hear the bullet ricochet down the passageway. My second was right on target. I was so concentrated on my shot that I forgot about the second one's victim. He had fallen back on her and she struggled to get out, still screaming. I stood up and he came over. Kathy was behind me. I looked into his eyes. He was a young black man, maybe twenty and absolutely terrified. The woman, more like a girl, had now freed herself and just stood there, shaking and crying. Her lab coat and scrubs were drenched in blood. The sleeve from the arm she was being pulled with had hiked up to her shoulder, and yet again, like something out of a cartoon, someone had taken a great ragged semicircular bite out of her forearm. I could clearly see the white bone of her ulna. I looked at the marine who had Dawson on his name tag.

"Cafeteria?" He just pointed to the door behind him and continued to stare at the dead zombies.

"Kathy, take him, I'll meet you there." She didn't even glance at me, just slid by, grabbed Dawson by the arm, and went down the hall.

When I heard the door close, I walked back to the stairway and down a flight. The kid was still curled up in the corner, softly talking to himself. I didn't say a word and he never looked up. Back in the corridor, she was still standing in the middle of the carnage. She had stopped crying, but was violently shivering. Thank God, her eyes were closed.

The door opened into the large room that was the main part of the cafeteria. I have to admit I was not paying attention. The sense of well being and control was absolutely gone. I kind of felt very small and lost. I now know I have killed at least four real human beings, and with one major life changing exception, I don't have a whole lot of regret. The last few days had tricked me into believing that this great adventure was over and I was back to a routine, back to a normal life. As I stepped inside, I noticed the half dozen or so guns pointed directly at me, which greatly assisted in bringing me back to reality.

"Secure that fucking door!" someone yelled.

There were several dozen people in the room, most in uniform, but a few in lab coats or scrubs, and no one in a suit. People had concentrated in the center, and more than half were armed. Several of the exits were blocked by the kind of table that folds up, seats and all, to make moving them around and washing the floor easier. I walked over to the main group. Since I was the only one on board with a beard, I stood a bit out and people just stared at me. I had had been getting this kind of attention ever since that damn video was shown. Now the look was not just out of curiosity, it was out of desperation. Kathy was sitting down next to Dawson. When I sat, they didn't look up or say a word. There was no way they hadn't heard the shots.

There was more shooting from somewhere below us. Once again, something was bugging me. Something Kathy had said. It was right at the tip of my tongue. If I could just have a minute to breathe, I would get it.

I looked up even before I heard the sharp sounds of pots and pans crashing and someone yelling, 'Noooo!' There was only one light on deep in the kitchen area, and because of the steam, tables, and the plastic sneeze guards, I couldn't get a clear view. I really didn't need one. What the duce? I just got here! How the hell are these things getting around so fast?

The first one that came running into the room was the now standard young somewhat grey-skinned naked bald male. He made a beeline to a couple of medics bent over treating someone that I couldn't see. The zombie was not particular and just made a superman dive right into the guys. The whole game was changed with the second zombie. He, maybe she, was a marine, in that crazy digital green and black camouflage clothing and still carrying a sidearm. Its head was hanging to one side, due to the fact that most of the flesh on the same side of his neck was gone. This must have affected its vision or something, because he was not nearly as fast as the first and kept bumping into tables, but at a very rapid rate. Needless to say, in a room full of terrified armed people, most of whom had been jolted awake in the middle of the night and had no real clue as to what was going on, a classic cluster fuck was ready to commence. I grabbed Kathy and pushed her to the floor. The zombies were now secondary. As if a light just turned green, everyone fired at once. This was bad and rapidly segued into really bad, as some asshole opened up with a machine gun. When I looked up, this guy who was dressed like a cook, you know, white pants, white t-shirt, white apron, white guy, was standing in front of me. He had dropped his pistol and just stared straight ahead. It took me a second before I noticed he had this little hole dead center of his chest that was starting to seep blood. The red patch got bigger and bigger and began to look like one of those Rorschach inkblots, but he still just stood there, not saying a word. Lots of people were now hugging the ground and the gunfire was dying down. I was trying to get Kathy's attention when I heard the thump of the cook finally falling down.

"Kathy. Have you been hit? Are you okay?"

"I think so, no, you?"

"Maybe. Let's get out of the middle and find a corner or something, but stay down." So I started crawling to the back of the cafeteria where I knew the doors were barricaded. Almost everyone else was on the floor and staying in place. We did pass a guy who had been shot in the hand, but the wound didn't look all that serious. From the sounds, it appeared that there was some kind of activity near the kitchen, lots of yelling and an occasional gunshot, but beyond that, everyone was really kind of quiet. We made it over to some folded tables blocking a door. It felt good to have a wall behind me.

"Where does this door lead?"

"Not sure. Give me a second." She was breathing hard and still looked pale. I cautiously stood up, both to get oriented and to scan for threats. Gun smoke made the room hazy and gave it a sort of dream-like quality. The area where the two medics were working was now a gore fest. Blood covering the wall and the bodies tangled in a heap, this was obviously, where some nimrod had cut loose with the automatic weapon. After a minute or so, people started to stand and look around. Some guys, real people, were in the kitchen area moving tables and stuff around. I felt Kathy standing next to me, when she tugged on my arm.

"Hey, are you hurt?" The sound of her voice was strange, comforting, as if she really cared.

"No, I'm alright." I lowered my voice, "Is there some kind of abandon ship plan? You know, like if the ship was sinking or we became infested with zombies?" Some people from the center group carried over an older guy who was bleeding from somewhere on his face.

"I don't know. We have an evacuation policy that the Captain would…" Kathy continued to talk but I stopped listening. The guy with the messed up face was laid down about five feet from me and someone was cleaning his wound with a wet towel. As soon as most of the blood was wiped away, I knew all I needed to know. A chunk of flesh about the size of a hockey puck had been ripped off just below his left eye. This was no gunshot wound. I still had both hands on the pistol, just staring at this guy who was complaining of being cold. I tried to rethink what I saw come out of the kitchen; there was Superman who attacked the medics and the floppy head marine. I didn't see how he could have done this, so was there a third?

"…I am sure someone has radioed for help. We just have to hang tight and let rescue come to us." I think she was about to ask if I had been listening to her when she followed my gaze to the guy on the floor.

"Is he going to be all right?"

"No, he's dead. Well, eventually." All at once, the ship shuddered, like a mini earthquake, not hard enough to knock you down, but sufficient to get our attention.

"Some kind of explosion." A slightly older woman, heavyset, about my height, and definitely not military, was standing next to me, in matching powder blue pajamas and slippers.

"Somewhere aft, too small for a grenade, don't think it was the engine room, could be the lab. Hmm, yes it could be. But it definitely wasn't the engine room." She wasn't exactly talking to me or Kathy. I guess it was more to herself. I moved over to her.

"Hey, are you okay?" Now that I really took a good look at her, I decided that she was older than I was, and based on the roots, if she hadn't been coloring her hair, it would be completely white. She was clutching a purse tightly to her chest. On her right side, midway between her shoulder and breast, was a bloody handprint. When she looked at me, it was with the strangest face I have ever seen; all kind of scrunched up. She didn't have makeup on or anything, but the first image that came to my mind was a scared clown. I turned to go back to Kathy.

"We should have techs on the way by now. The lyophilizers failed, you know. I have no idea where we were in the recipe. It must have been toward the end. Yes, it had to have been in secondary drying. It's okay, the seals will hold, they should hold you know." Her voice sounded thin and distant, as if she knew she was talking, but at the same time thinking of something else.

I stopped. What did she just say? Did I really hear that? Now I was scared. In a slow, obviously concerned voice, I said, "Kathy, what the hell is she talking about?" Kathy didn't look at me but continued to stare at the woman. This was starting to be too much to absorb at once. I went over to a table and sat down. Lyophilization? Why would anyone want to freeze dry anything? Oh no. Like the proverbial light bulb, it all started to make sense. Please let this be a dream.

"Kathy, you mentioned something about reverse engineering. How far along were they?" She was now staring at me. Was she afraid of me? "What was the talk about progress?" I was trying to calm down a bit.

"Apparently, things were moving faster than was originally anticipated. In the last meeting, somebody actually used the word gangbuster to describe his project's rapid development. That's why our part was ending." She hadn't moved to sit down, and actually, might be moving slowly away from me.

"All that rush for the lung samples. How could we have been so stupid?"

"Wait a second, John, we..."

"We what? Kathy, I know what lyophilization is."

Lyophilization is the fancy term used in biotech for freeze-drying. It's a common practice in the pharmaceutical industry to stabilize a product. The process is fine-tuned to the particular compound you are making; The Eutectic point has to be known, how long are your freeze cycles, how fast, at what temperature and what pressure. Each compound has a unique lyophilization procedure and is often called a recipe. Lyophilization is also used to stabilize biologicals, like viruses. Only the military could put something like this together on the fly, part of me was very impressed.

"Okay, Kathy, straight up, could someone be weaponizing the virus? Is that what they are fucking freeze-drying? The tissue sample we take would be stored in liquid nitrogen, right? You don't need to freeze dry them. So what the fuck are we freeze drying?"

"It could be. I've heard nothing about a vaccine. All the work I know of deals with the structure and various characteristics of the virus. So, yes, maybe small batches for research, but what kind of research, I have no clue."

"How small? Are we talking grams or kilos?"

"I don't know. My guess is the units they are using are not industrial sized. Maybe research size. Grams? Could be more."

"Our military at its most efficient. Your tax dollars at work. They are freeze-drying the virus and they're doing it on this ship! My ship! Jesus Christ!" I put my head in my hands while my mind raced. Okay, slow down, slow down and breathe. I am starting to think that T.S. Elliot was right all along, this really is the way the world will end. Can we really be that stupid? That arrogant? Who would have thought this was a good idea? The fucking world was dying! Were we just trying to ensure the job was done right?

Stop it, John. Think! I opened my eyes and found myself staring at the gun in my hand. I had been gripping it so hard for so long that my hands where white. I was tired, hungry, and way past depressed. I felt cheated, as if someone had interrupted my vacation. I was retired from the zombie fighting game. John had officially called it a day. I had compressed a lifetime of gunplay into a couple of months! I had done my duty and now I just wanted to crawl back into bed and drift off to a sound sleep. I was still staring at the gun.

"Too easy. Not my way. Not today." It was only after I said it that I realized I was talking out loud.

"John, what?"

I stood and looked at Kathy, and in an instant, I knew my future. I am going to die on a ship in Long Island Sound. I will never be forty-seven. I will never again eat barbecued ribs. I will never have sex. I will never finish *Gravities Rainbow,* again. I will never see the Grand Canyon, or the pyramids, or for that matter, dry land again. I am going to die on a ship in Long Island Sound. However, I am not going out with a fucking whimper. I went over to the woman.

"Ma'am, hey, lady, look at me." I grabbed her shoulders. "You need to talk to me right now, okay?"

"I don't know. Who are you?"

"That doesn't matter. I have some quick questions and you have to answer me. It's important." I was trying to keep my voice low so as not to attract attention. I was also trying to sound calm and nice, but I knew I was not doing that good of a job. I took my hands off her and saw her eyes dart to the gun. "Ma'am. Where are the freeze driers located?"

"Do I know you? I don't know you, so leave me alone." She started to walk away. With my one free hand, I grabbed her shoulder again, but this time I was not gentle. Again, in a low voice without the slightest hint of politeness or pleasantry, I spoke.

"Listen, you old bitch. If there is a hell, my ticket was punched long ago, so do not think I will have any qualms about putting you down like a sick dog. So, ma'am, where the fuck are the freeze driers?" My gun was now firmly jutting into her ribs. From the corner of my eye, I saw Kathy back away.

She looked down at the gun, and then into my eyes. She knew, and more importantly, I knew I would do it. Shit, I should do it just on principle.

"There are two of them, but they are in the same lab. Deck four, lab six. It will have a biohazard sign painted on the door, a green biohazard sign. You will see the air lock and have to gown to get in."

"Where is it stockpiled? On this ship or another, and if so, which ship?"

"I don't know."

"Give me your card key. Are there any codes or locks that I need to know about?" She started fumbling with her purse and pulled out a lanyard with her ID and a small cream-colored tag about the size of a credit card.

"No. This will get you in." Then her eyes went wide with understanding. "You're not going down there. What about the zombies?" It was around this time that I noticed she was wearing a small gold cross.

"Fuck you. Pray to your God, because you're going to need it." I let go of the hag and turned to Kathy.

"John, you have to understand that I had no idea. I thought they were…"

"Kathy, if I can trust anybody right now, it's going to be you. Maybe she is just some crazy old bag woman who happens to have survived the zombie apocalypse and just ended up on this navy vessel in the middle of some classified research, if there is such a thing as classified research. I have to check this lab out."

"Why? Let's just get to a safe place, maybe stay here, and wait for rescue." As if on cue, a loud scream came from the other side of the door nearest us, followed by gunfire and someone banging on the door; some indeterminate sounds of commotion and the banging stopped.

"John, are you insane? So you find the lab, big deal."

"Yes, to your first question, and I need to know if the ship has been compromised. We both agreed these labs were slapped together and would never pass spec in the real world. If this shit has been developed to the point of freeze drying and the machine's compromised, then the ship is more than likely compromised, we're compromised."

"But, John…"

"Kathy, if this is true… they will sink the ship." Something in her face changed. Just a subtle relaxation of some facial muscles and I knew she understood. There is a good chance that no rescue would be possible. We are not going home. The hag sat down and I noticed that Dawson had taken her place.

"I'll go with you."

"Okay, what's your first name?"

"Peter."

"Alright, Peter, let's saddle up. Grab anything with a trigger and lots of ammo. We…"

"I'm going too." It was Kathy. She no longer looked pale.

"Okay, find something that goes bang." Why am I being such an ass to Kathy? She really is my only friend on board.

I'm bouncing on the balls of my feet again. Where did this come from? I really want some breakfast. Somewhere way back in the recesses of my messed up head, a cowbell was being rung.

The door is going to open inward. I need an angle. Peter is going to open it. He looks ready. Kathy is behind me. Okay, John, here we go, again. More gunfire from somewhere.

Spotcheck Billy got down on his hands and knees. He said 'Hey mama hey, let me check your oil all right?' Why the fuck is my brain playing a song called *Fat Man in the Bathtub*?

I nod and he pulls the handle.

The zombie is right outside the door with his back to me, maybe twelve feet away. They are fast, but now, I am faster. I don't shoot, but with exaggerated steps cover the distance in a heartbeat. By the time it turns, my muzzle is a foot away from its face and I pop a cap right between the eyes. The eyes of a tall, athletic, bald, naked zombie. What the heck is going on here?

'Come back Monday, come back Tuesday and then I might.'

The corridor is clear and I step over the corpse and start to walk in what I believe to be the direction of the labs, which I know are several decks lower. I hear sounds behind me, which I really hope are Kathy and Peter, but I don't turn to check.

'I said Juanita, my sweet Juanita, what are you up to?'

I am now singing to myself. What the hell is it with this *Little Feat* song? *Little Feat.* I saw them with Tom in Albany around nineteen eighty-seven, just after they had reunited. Lowell George died, what? Late seventies? Albany's gone, Tom's gone.

Stairs leading down were just off to my right. Thank God, the door was open. When I stepped onto the landing, I heard more gunfire, this time above. The coast was clear, so I started down.

"John, wait up." It was Kathy. Kathy is a petite woman and looked a bit comical carrying a large pistol. I was glad to see she was using a two handed technique like me, but the comedic value of the image she presented was instantly lost when I realized it was pointed at my thigh.

"Kathy! Let's keep this bad boy aimed in the right direction." She blushed, muttered something and pointed her gun at the floor.

Great, I again have someone behind me with a loaded gun and possibly no clue as how to use it.

"Hey, Kathy, let me take care of the bad guys. You shoot only if necessary, okay?"

"John, why are you eternally the asshole?" Boy, that's a good question. Peter joined us. Just then, there was another explosion somewhere in the bowels of the ship. I went down the steps expecting a zombie at each landing I came to, but my luck was holding. At level four, I entered the corridor and realized it was a lot, and I was no longer singing about a fat man in a bathtub.

"Kathy?"

"Aft. Straight ahead." I was back in the corridor from earlier this morning, but without the guards. Oh, shit, I take that back. About twenty yards down the hall from me lay two zombies, obviously dead, and a marine. He was sitting next to the corpses and he looked up at me as I approached. Drenched in blood and holding his right arm, we made eye contact. He looked remarkably calm and didn't say a word. At least three fingers were missing from the bloody stump that used to be his hand. Next to him was a sidearm with the slide-bar extended, out of ammunition. Behind me Peter muttered, "holy shit," but didn't approach. Our eyes locked again. He gave me a faint smile and nodded, yes. I mouthed the word, okay and started to pass him, stopped, quickly turned, and blew the top of his head off. His eyes were closed and his face had an almost serene appearance.

"Fuck me!" It was Peter. "Are you fucking insane, John?"

"Peter, he was dead, man." And will people stop asking me that stupid question, because the answer is yes.

"Yeah? You a doctor? You gonna shoot me if I get bit?"

"It depends on the situation. If you don't do it yourself, then yes." I started down the corridor. It took me about a three steps to realize no one was following. When I turned, I saw two things at once: Kathy and Peter staring at me dumbfounded, and some kind of frenetic commotion going on behind them, rapidly moving in their direction.

"Fuck! Behind you!" I yelled and dropped to one knee, pointing my weapon straight at them. With the two of them in the way, it was hard to tell exactly what was approaching us, but the jerky movements and dull roar significantly narrowed the options.

Kathy fired first. She was shooting so fast that I knew she was not really aiming, just unloading a whole lot of lead down the corridor. In a second, Peter was joining her. Ah shit! I jumped up and ran to them. The two zombies had been hit multiple times each. Unfortunately, their central nervous system had not and the first zombie crashed into us. Kathy had been reloading, Peter blasting away, and me just thinking, fuck.

The first one ran right into Kathy. He didn't tackle her, but instead, literally ran into her. It was if its brain was not processing distance correctly. They both fell to the floor. What saved her life, was that the zombie continued to try moving beyond her to a prey that he was already on top of. They both were squirming, trying to get away from each other. The creature was almost free when I stepped on the back of its neck and ended its misery. This left Kathy in a very awkward position, since the now dead zombie's groin was right in her face. John being John, I immediately started thinking of a variety of witty observations. I came up with three real zingers in about a nanosecond, and was on the verge of a fourth that I knew was destined for some kind of hall of fame, when the second zombie slammed into me. This one had no issues with depth perception.

I hit the ground hard with most of our weight landing directly on my right elbow. The shock made my entire body go electric with pain, and my arm went numb. I dropped my pistol. What kind of sick fuck would call this your funny bone? It's your fucking unprotected ulnar nerve and it fucking hurts when you hit it just right, and I just nailed that son of a bitch! I got lucky, again, because I fell in such a way that my knees were bent and I was able to push the creature slightly away, preventing him from immediately taking a bite out of me. Out of the corner of my left eye, I saw the barrel of Peter's gun. This gave me the second I needed to turn my head and close my mouth and eyes. I could not close my ears and the sound of the blast rendered me temporarily deaf. I gave myself a couple of seconds just to lie there and let some feeling return to my arm. Zombie body temperature is significantly cooler than human, but still slightly warm to the touch, and the heat from the big dead marine on top of me was somewhat comforting.

Marine. There, I thought of it again. The consistency of appearance, age, physical conditioning, hell, I knew something incredibly fucked up was going on. The zombies who had patches of skin removed. Someone was cutting out tattoos, trying to hide who these guys really were. Why would we do this?

I still couldn't hear anything, but several hands were pulling me to my feet. I looked around and made sure the coast was clear. How many rounds did I have? A full clip is fifteen, so I should have around ten, maybe. Kathy and Peter looked okay, just shook up. I shook myself free and stumbled down the corridor past the card swipe door. With each step, my hearing returned and by the time I reached the labs, I was only half-deaf.

The third door on my left had the green biohazard symbol, why green, and not black or orange? This kind of bothered me. Like green makes it kinder? Less deadly?

"All right, this is it." I knew I was talking far louder than necessary. To the right of the door was a small grey box with a slot on one side. Okay, bingo. Or …should I say …Fuck me. The door was slightly ajar, and the light above it green. Could things get any worse?

Why would I even think such a question? I am living in an absolute FUBAR reality and things here can always go downhill. And they did. Just beyond the biohazard door was a short well-lit standard hallway that led directly to another door, also half closed. Off the corridor, there were four other doors. Now the Angel of God must be watching over us because the right two doors actually looked closed. The first room was small and obviously some kind of storeroom. My hearing was still coming around when I noticed some kind of loud banging. When I turned, I noticed Peter and Kathy had their weapons trained on the second open door.

"Cover me. I'll take him." Once again, way louder than necessary.

I didn't wait for a response and sidestepped into the doorway. The room was large, maybe forty by forty, all tightly draped in some kind of plastic. Against the far wall stood two lyophilizers, slightly larger than a refrigerator with thick Plexiglas doors. In the middle of the room, splayed out like some sick play on Da Vinci's Vitruvian Man, was an extra large faceless zombie. The lab itself was a disaster area. Several tables had been overturned and the floor was littered with lab crap. Along the right wall was a series of 'elephant trunks' for localized ventilation, hanging limply over where tables used to be. In the far corner, next to one of the freeze driers, was a fully gowned researcher. I entered and went to the back of the lab. The noise we had been hearing was the researcher banging his head against the side of a Plexiglas box. I reached out and gently touched him on the shoulder.

"It's okay, man, it's over." This time, I intended to be loud. He turned to look at me. At first, his eyes expressed surprise; I don't know if it was because we were not zombies or because we were not gowned. He started to say something, but his hood made him sound muddled.

"You can take your hood off." I mimicked, unzipping it from the back and made the universal okay sign.

He was an older man, maybe sixties? And just looked at me with sad eyes, shook his head no and pointed at the floor.

The floor. The linoleum was new with this special anti-slip texture grey, which wraps up the walls a couple of feet. Let's see; there are test tubes of various sizes, paper, a variety of equipment (scales, pipet guns, a small pump, etc…), several stainless steel trays covered in a light yellow powder. Lots of light yellow powder. Ah, crap. I turned back to the researcher. He now faced me full on. His right arm was shredded. There was so much blood it was impossible to tell exactly where he was injured, or how the injury happened. He leaned back in the corner formed by the lyo and the wall. He started to say something, stopped, and just continued shaking his head. Man, it is getting hot in here.

"Stay out of this lab!" I yelled, too late. The two were right behind me.

"Oh no." It was Kathy.

"What?" Peter.

"Everyone stop moving and stand still! Kathy…"

"I see it. Peter back out into the hallway, very slowly. Let's try not to kick up anymore of this yellow crap. John, what's his story?" She nodded toward the researcher.

"He's history." Sweat was starting to be an issue with my glasses and I had to clean them every minute or so. Once I did get a good look around, I noticed a pair of gowned legs sticking out behind an overturned table.

"Hey, Kathy, there's someone down behind that table to your right. Not moving, for now. I'm not sure what to …"

I swear to God, I saw it before I heard it; and then it was like seeing cartoon panels from a comic book, no captions, and everything drawn as exaggerated. Frame one, Peter flying backwards through the doorway. Frame two, Peter in the midst of being perfectly tackled by a zombie with the exact physique of a young Mike Tyson. The next frame is the tackle continued, but now, Peter has been lifted several feet off the floor. Frame four is the inevitable crashing to the already littered and highly contagious lab floor. The Iron Mike zombie had hit Peter so hard that even after tripping, the momentum carried them to the far side of the room and into the lyos. The angle of the light was such that I could easily see the huge plume of dust they raised. Dust? Dust is harmless. This isn't dust. What the hell do I do now? Peter was firing, but it was not stopping the mini Hulk. I couldn't go for a head shot, so I quickly put two in his back. Iron Mike turned and looked at me. Peter's blood made the zombies face shiny and glistening. His eyes were so wide they seemed to glow. His face seemed paralyzed with this peculiar expression; a cross between 'I hate you and will eat your liver' and 'don't I know you from somewhere?' Its face never changed, even when Peter blew the back of its skull off.

"Kathy, why is it so hot in here?" I didn't want to focus on Peter.

"Ventilation is off." I hope I don't sound nearly as scared as her. She glanced over the table for a quick look, took a second to steady herself and then leaned back and fired a single round. I was just staring at her, watching her become absolutely still for a couple of seconds, and then as if a light switched on inside, she suddenly looked up and carefully walked over to a large grey metal box mounted on the wall.

"John, the negative pressure is not working, only positive."

"You mean everything is blowing out of this lab?"

"Yes." We just looked at each other.

"Kathy, what are the odds the…" The force of the body slam threw me to the ground. Holy crap, it's Peter.

"You will not shoot me!" Both his hands were clamped on my right wrist, which he started banging on the floor. The only thing I could do is try to roll him off of me.

"Peter!" Then a very audible, click.

Our scuffle was over. He froze, Kathy had her gun about a foot from the side of his head, and I struggled to get away. Now with two guns trained on him, one being held by someone who is going to kill him, Peter gave up and started crying.

All right, there are four of us, two who are literally dead men walking. Who am I kidding? I looked at Peter, and he was coated in the yellow dust. I looked at my arms, coated in yellow dust. I looked at Kathy, and the lab, and I knew: total contamination.

"We have to close this lab." I went over and looked at the Tyson zombie. He was a compact mass of muscle. Damn it! There it was again. He had cutouts on both shoulders. This sucks. I will never get to find out exactly what the fuck was going on, but this boy is military.

"Peter, let's go." I turned and walked to the research dude.

"John!" Kathy screamed, and in a flash, Peter was gone. Contaminated Peter was gone. I looked at the researcher and started talking with my hands, New England style.

"Let's go. We have to go now!" I could see he was looking at me and knew what was going on, but he didn't move. After a half minute or so, he held up his left, good arm, and gestured that he was staying. He also indicated he wanted my pistol. I looked around. Kathy was by the door covering us. I had to get out of here ASAP and hit a decontamination shower. Right, so if I give him the gun, I am weaponless in a ship full of zombies and now contaminated people. If I shoot him, I get to keep the gun.

So I turned and shot him in the forehead. I then joined Kathy by the door.

"Let's close this in the best way we can. Without air balance, it won't seal," Kathy yelled. We did get the door latched, but the amount of air being forced through the seals made a loud whistling noise. After the second door, we were in the clear, not really. I rushed both of us under a showerhead and pulled the steel rod down. Ah, man, that's cold! Yes, I knew this was all just a game to convince myself and Kathy that the five minutes or so we spent in an intensely dirty lab did not contaminate us. Hey, maybe it's not what I think it is. It hasn't been milled, so maybe it's not the right size to get deep into the lungs to the alveoli. Maybe it needs an activator and that is done on another ship; hence this good-for-nothing, shitty so-called BSL-4 crap setup. Yeah, and I'm just whistling past the graveyard. We're toast.

After a few minutes, the water stopped and we were completely drenched. Kathy had on pink scrubs and for the first time, I noticed she wasn't wearing a bra. Okay, one, the now soaking wet light colored shirt made this patently obvious, and two, I'm a fucking male with a death sentence, so get off my back.

"What now?" Kathy was shivering.

"Find out what's going on, with the ship I mean. Topside?" I replaced my clip.

"Sure, why not?" We didn't talk about it. For now, it was understood.

We made our way up several landings without incident, although we did hear an intense round of gunfire deep in the innards of the ship. When we got to the deck, people were scattered into small groups, usually around someone with a firearm. We went over to the nearest group.

"We're alright. We're not bitten." Maybe this was the wrong thing to say when the leader of this small group is a huge Aryan looking dude, whose left hand was a bloody bandaged mess. Either he had been bitten or lost round one to the garbage disposal.

"Who are you?" Instead of even trying to be unobtrusive, he was staring at Kathy's breasts. Yes, all men are dogs.

"We're with research. What's going on?" Kathy tried to sound officer-like.

"What's going on? What's going on is we're being overrun by zombies."

"Thanks for the news flash, but are there any orders?" I was way past tired of playing Captain Obvious. "I mean, what's next?" The group was made up of four navy personnel and the big marine. One of the navy guys looked sick, really sick.

"Survive. Where you coming from?"

"The forward labs." Just then, there was gunfire aft of us, but close enough to get everyone nervous. Crates and various pieces of equipment blocked our view and this did wonders for our anxiety. Kathy and I backed up against a humongous wooden crate. Its contents registered as a series of numbers and capital letters that I was not meant to decipher. Kathy moved close to me, she was shivering.

I leaned forward and whispered in her ear, "Let's move around here in the sun and out of the wind." It was kind of a mini hallway between the giant crate and the ship, maybe twelve feet long. It did put us with our backs to the sea, but we would only need one person to stand guard.

"Try to dry out the best you can." I moved to the middle, hunkered down in a little patch of morning sunlight, and waited. I had a nice narrow kill lane, and what, thirty rounds? A good ten minutes went by with nothing happening, and by nothing, I mean no one and nothing went by and no gunfire. Kathy and I didn't talk, we just waited. And waited.

At about the forty-five minute mark, just as my breathing was falling into the rhythm of Kathy's snoring, all hell broke loose. I was thrown forward into the shipping crate. It was if the *Cassandra* had suddenly turned sideways. Lots of gunfire aft of us, smoke, the shuddering of the ship felt like bones snapping deep down inside. Kathy's awake. What the hell do we do now? I got up and crept to the end of our hallway, hoping to get a look back and see what the fuck was happening.

"John!" Kathy cried.

I turned and wow. Kathy was standing by the ship's railing, pointing outward. I don't know how far, but like rock throwing close to the ship was a marine Harrier Jump Jet. It was simply hanging there, as if someone had it suspended by an invisible string. Between the shit storm happening behind us and the wind, we never heard it approach. The light was at a perfect angle and I could clearly see the pilot. He was just casually sitting there, glancing around and taking in the sights. You know, to see this huge majestic bird of war just hovering in the air would, for most people, make their year. For me, if the Harrier plays its cards right, it might make my hour. He gently moved off aft. Of course, he was trying to figure what the hell was going on, which meant…

"Kathy, what's with that recon?" I shouted.

"I don't know." More stochastic automatic fire from somewhere aft.

"You look pale."

"I don't feel all that great. You know how you can sometimes feel something coming on?"

"Yeah, me too." My lungs have been getting progressively hotter and raw for the last twenty minutes. No fluid or real cough, so far. This was not the time and place to think about it.

I must have zombie radar or something, because I turned and raised my pistol just as the creature came around the corner. This was no bald athletic male, but an anorexic female in dark pink scrubs and a lab coat. Her face and long blonde hair were covered in blood and one whole side was chewed up. Her speed and outreached arms made her too close to shoot. So while she lunged, I parried and tripped her. She ended up on her knees, about three feet from the end of the barrel of Kathy's pistol. The creature looked up and they both seemed to freeze. The picture they presented was almost religious. There is the penitent, down on her knees, there was Kathy looming over her, ready to pass judgment, and there was the Great Atlantic, the Glory of God. Then she blew the back of its head off.

"Thanks. Can you still see the jet?" I turned back to cover the opening.

"No, but a Blackhawk just flew by."

"Landing?"

"No, just low, slow, and tight." The wind died down and I could tell she was looking at me.

"John, you know how we usually travel in a nice tight flotilla with lots of friends around?"

"Yeah."

"Well, from my vantage point, we are now sailing solo."

 "Kathy, I think we're screwed."

"We knew that an hour ago, but I know what you mean, and I think you're right."

Well, someone had to say it, and at least I now know we are on the same page.

"I am going to die on a ship in Long Island Sound. I guess it could be worse," I whispered to myself.

"What?"

"Nothing. Let's get out of here. Forward?" I glanced around the corner and the coast was clear. Whatever had been going on had subsided.

"Why not." So, yet again, I slink forward doing my best impression of someone who knows what they were doing.

"How about up here?" Kathy pointed to a ladder that we could use to climb on top of a really big crate. Easily twelve feet high, it would keep us safe from attack, well, at least from a zombie attack. The ladder was attached to the ship and had a safety cage around it. You had to climb outside the cage and make an interesting giant step to get to the top of the crate, a series of maneuvers I assumed would slow down even the most determined and ambidextrous zombie. I helped Kathy over and for the first time, looked around.

"Ah crap." The back of the boat was on fire. At least something was burning and putting off a lot of black smoke. The wind kept the worst away from us. A traditional *Cassandra* zombie came running down the hall we had just climbed up from, never looking up at us. He just made this determined beeline sprint up the ship. After what, I have no clue, but that was one angry zombie late for something. I think the monkey house has been officially overthrown and I was starting to sweat and felt like shit. I knew I was starting a temperature and really needed to sit down.

"Hey look," Kathy yelled. On the other side of the ship was another group on top of another gigantic crate, four in all. They were something like thirty yards from us and there was really no reason to try to communicate, so we both gave this really weak, playground-esque, half wave to each other. Do they also know the game's over? Would I, if I hadn't seen the lab? I didn't know how many zombies are now onboard, but my best guess is that it just doesn't matter anymore. An injured sailor came down the main corridor; staggering and holding his left arm. He passed directly below me.

"Hey! Up Here, Look out!" He didn't even glance up, but just kept trudging along. At the next intersection, he half turned as if surprised by something and was gone in a grey flash. I started to cough.

Kathy and I found a semi comfortable place on some coiled rope, and sat back to back. From my position, I had a magnificent view of the Connecticut shoreline and the fires still burning inland. I suppose they will be all summer and well into the fall, maybe till the snowfalls. We held hands. Even on a hot day out in the sun, her warmth was comforting. It was nice not to be alone. I think we were both relatively calm, no shaking, no sweating, no nervous rambling, just quiet. You could smell the sea and all seemed good. God, what a beautiful day! Who knows, maybe we're not infected. Maybe rescue is on the way, maybe.

I could hear the roar of jets off in the distance, screaming our way. It was over, oh well. It is as it is, and in a surprisingly slow calm voice, I asked, "You know, Kathy, what I really like about the ocean?"

"No, John, what do you really like about the ocean?" I could tell from the inflection in her voice that she was ready for a bad punch line.

"Well, now that you ask. It's so…

Martha's Vineyard

Robert was sitting on the small porch of a grey-shingled cottage, reading, when the car pulled up. He kind of knew why they were here, but still thought it was funny that they arrived in a lime green Kia. The navy had allocated him a one hundred year old cottage within sight of the sea. He was still considered something of a hero for his actions with John and the zombies, one of the stars of the now famous video and now a consultant, for what I don't know. Ah, there was Captain Walker with someone who looked official. Well, here we go.

"Hi, Robert."

"Captain, good to see you."

They walked up to the porch and stood a second, both seemed a bit nervous. Robert took a deep breath and looked out to the sea. All things come to an end, he thought.

"Robert, he is gone. The *Cassandra* became contaminated. They had no choice."

Robert continued to stare at the ocean. There was no shock or grief. He knew this was going to happen eventually, and so did John.

"John was on a ship? Contaminated? Contaminated with what?"

"I don't know."

He turned and looked at Captain Walker.

"David, I thought he was on the mainland goofing off with the marines?"

"The Admiral pulled him for research over a week ago. He volunteered. Word is they figured something out about the virus, but I don't know what that really means. It must mean something. I don't have to tell you that I liked him. A strange guy and a bit batshit crazy, but he got the job done. Was he police or military in the real world before the university stuff?"

"No…he was an Anthropologist. And yup, he was bat-shit crazy."

The other gentleman just stood there cradling a little box in his hand and sweating. He looked to Captain Walker who nodded.

"Sir, on behalf of a grateful nation, we would like to present John Ross Patrick the Navy Distinguished Service Medal for services…"

"Son, you can stop right there. John would not give a damn about a piece of metal and you know what I am going to do with it. So just hand it over and have a good day."

He reluctantly handed the small box over and stepped back. David had that shit eating grin and extended his hand.

"I'll be back in a couple of weeks. Maybe you can take me sailing. Until then, you take care, Robert."

"You too, Captain. Ah, with the world dying and all, what's with this medal shit?"

"Sometimes, the questions are complicated, and the answers are simple."

"Thanks, Captain. So what are you, Plato now?"

"No. It's Dr. Seuss."

He started to turn, but stopped. It was as if he wanted to say something, but at the last minute, changed the subject. "So, Robert, what are you reading?"

"*Moby Dick*, ever read it?"

"No."

"Don't worry, most people haven't, unless forced to."

"Are you being forced?"

"You might say so."

"Have a good day, Robert."

"Good luck, David."

"Thanks, we're going to need it."

Later that day, Robert went down to the shore. The sun was about to set and the water was exceptionally calm. He could see the *Providence* moored about a quarter mile up the beach. Everything was so peaceful. He took out his knife and opened the box, carefully cutting off the dark blue ribbon with the gold strip and putting it in his pocket. The medal was heavier than he anticipated. With the water like a pane of glass, he was sure he could get four. He focused and calmly let it fly. Seven skips! John would be pleased. Goodbye, John.

Robert turned and slowly walked back to his cabin. He looked forward to finishing *Moby Dick* and finding out what was to happen to the *Pequod* and her crew. He had a feeling that things were not going to go all that well.

THE END

Definitions/Abbreviations

Abiotic decomposition - degradation of a substance by a chemical or physical process.

Aft/Stern - The rear part of the ship.

AK47 - A selective fire (semi or full) assault rifle. 7.62x39mm cartridge. Effective range ~ 400yd semi-automatic, ~ 300yd automatic. Standard magazine capacity is 30 rounds.

Algor mortis -. Cooling of a dead body to ambient temperature. Time duration is dependent on environment and manor of death.

Alveoli - The smallest endpoint in the lungs. Where gas exchange takes place (oxygen and carbon dioxide).

Ambient Temperature - The temperature of the environment.

Archetype - An original model or type after which all similar things are patterned. The prototype.

ASAP - As soon as possible.

Atacama Desert - Desert covering the north of Chile and southern Peru. The oldest and driest desert on earth.

ATP - Adenosine triphosphate. ATP transports chemical energy within cells for metabolism.

Auscultation - The act of listening for sounds made by internal organs, like the heart and lungs. Usually with the aid of a stethoscope.

Biological Anthropology - A branch of anthropology that studies the development of the homonid line (also known as physical anthropology).

Biotic decomposition - The metabolic breakdown of material into simpler components by living organisms, usually microorganisms.

Bow - The forward part of a ship.

BPM - Heartbeats per minute.

BS - Bull Shit.

BSL - Biological Safety Level. Level four is the highest rated labs and used for the most virulent pathogens.

BXP - Milkor 9mm BXP sub-machine gun. 9x19mm parabellum. Effective range 75 yd.

Cassandra - From Greek mythology. She is the daughter of King Priam and Queen Hecuba of Troy. Apollo gave the gift of prophecy but when she declined his advances, he cursed her so no one would believe her predictions.

Cavlvaria - Skullcap. Top dome of the skull.

Cerebellum - A structure of the brain in the bottom back of the cranial cavity.

Cerebrum - Large rounded structure of the brain. Divided into two hemispheres. Controls higher mental function (thought, reason, emotion and memories).

CDC - Center for Disease Control and Prevention.

CGI - Computer-generated imagery.

COG - Continuity of Government. Condition levels vary but similar to DEFCON for the military.

Demographics - The quantifiable statistics of a given population (e.g., age, sex, marital status, etc…).

Desalinization - A process that removes salt and other minerals from seawater to make potable water.

EAS - Emergency Alert System. National warning system in the U.S.

Echelon - A formation in which its units are arranged diagonally.

ELISA - Enzyme-linked ImmunoSorbent Assey.

EMP - Electromagnetic pulse. A burst of electromagnetic radiation released on nuclear warhead detonation damaging unshielded electrical/electronic systems.

EMS - Emergency Medical Services.

EpiPen - An epinephrine autoinjector. Typically used to treat acute allergic reactions.

ER - Emergency room.

Eutectic Point - Formed at the lowest possible temperature of solidification for any mixture of specified constitutes.

EVA - Extra Vehicular Activity.

Exponential Growth - Increases at an expanding rate.

FEMA - Federal Emergency Management Agency.

Fibrin - A fibrous protein that forms a mesh assisting in clot formation at the site of a wound.

Fibula - A long thin bone extending from the knee to the ankle lying lateral (on the outside) to the Tibia (shinbone).

Flotsam - Floating wreckage of a ship or its cargo,

Forensic entomology - The use of insects and arthropods that inhabit decomposing remains to aid in legal investigations.

FUBAR - Fucked/fouled up beyond all repair.

Glock17 - A 9mm semi-automatic pistol. 19 rounds (extended). Effective range - 55yd.

Homonid - The taxonomic family that includes chimpanzees, gorillas, humans and orangutans.

Hypotension - Low blood pressure.

IFA - Immunofluorescent antibody analysis.

ISS - International Space Station.

IV - Inter-Venous.

Jetsam - Part of a ship or cargo that is thrown (jettisoned) overboard and either sinks or washes ashore.

Jump Kit - Advanced medical bag used by EMT and Paramedics.

K - The International System of Units abbreviation for one thousand.

Ketoacidosis - A metabolic condition when the body has inadequate levels of insulin and breaks down fat for energy (instead of glucose).

LCAC - Landing Craft Air Cushion.

LD50 - Dose required to kill half the members of a tested population after a specific test duration.

Linear Growth - Increases at the same rate.

Livor mortis - Settling of blood to lower portions of the body after death. Results in purplish red discoloration of the skin, similar to a bruise.

M82A - Barrett M82A1 is a semi-automatic anti-material rifle. 50 BMG or .416 Barrett cartridge. Effective range 1,900+ yd.

Medulla - Lowest portion of the brain and continuous with the spinal cord.

Meninges - Three layers of membrane that envelops the central nervous system.

Morbidity Rate - The incidence or prevalence of a disease in a population over a given period of time.

Morrigan - Goddess of battle, strife and sovereignty in Celtic mythology.

Mortality Rate - The number of deaths in a population in relation to the population size over a given period of time.

NAS - National Academy of Sciences.

National Response Network (NRF) - Guiding principles on all domestic levels to provide a unified national response in times of national emergency.

National Strategy for Homeland Security - Outlines strategic considerations as well as cooperation between federal and state governments, private enterprises and ordinary citizens in times of national significance.

Nucleotide - Organic molecules that act as a subunit of nucleic acids, the building blocks of DNA and RNA.

Oorah - A Marine battle cry.

Peritoneum - A membrane that forms the lining of the abdominal cavity.

Pod - A social group of whales, like Orcas.

Port - When facing the bow, the left side of the ship

Prion - An infectious protein in a misfolded form. Affects brain and other neural tissue.

R-zero - The average number of individuals each infected individual will infect in a population that has no immunity to the disease.

R&R - Rest and relaxation.

RIC - Rhode Island College.

Rigor mortis - Chemical changes in muscles after death that causes them to stiffen.

RNA - Ribonucleic Acid.

Rorke's Drift - Battle in the Anglo-Zulu War. In 1879 a small group of British and colonial troops successfully defended a mission station against overwhelming odds.

Ruger-SR9 - A 9mm semi-automatic pistol. 17 rounds.

RV - Recreational Vehicle.

SAW - Squad/Section Automatic Weapon.

SCATANA - Security Control of Air Traffic and Air Navigation Aids.

SI - Sports Illustrated.

SOL - Shit Out of Luck.
SOP - Standard Operating Procedure.
Starboard - Facing the bow, the right side of the ship.
Stolichnaya - A popular Soviet era vodka brand.
Storm surge - Low pressure weather events, like hurricanes, cause high winds that push water inland causing flooding.
Supine - On your back.
Troposphere - The lowest major atmospheric layer, extending from the Earth's surface to the bottom of the Stratosphere (5 - 8 miles).
Todestrieb - Freudian psychoanalytic theory. It is the death drive to self-destruction and the return to the inanimate state.
Ulna - One of two bones that make up the forearm, the other being the radius. The ulna is the bone on the little finger side of your arm.
USAMRIID - US Army Medical Research Institute of Infectious Diseases.
URI - University of Rhode Island.
Vivisection - Surgery conducted for experimental purposes on a living organism.
WAGS - Wild ass guesses.
WHO - World Health Organization. Part of the United Nations.
Wilderness EMT - Emergency medical technician trained to provide care in remote areas.

Printed in Poland
by Amazon Fulfillment
Poland Sp. z o.o., Wrocław